The Taste of Innocence

Stephanie Laurens

piatkus

PIATKUS

First published in the United States in 2007 by HarperCollins Publishers, USA,
This paperback edition published in 2007 by Piatkus Books
First published in Great Britain in 2007 by Portrait
This paperback edition published in 2007 by Piatkus

5 7 9 10 8 6 4

Copyright © Savdek Management Proprietory Ltd.

The moral right of the author has been asserted.

A CIP catalogue record for this book
is available from the British Library.

ISBN 978-0-7499-3863-5

Data manipulation by Phoenix Photosetting, Chatham, Kent
www.phoenixphotosetting.co.uk

Printed and bound by CPI Group (UK) Ltd, Croydon, CR0 4YY

Papers used by Piatkus are from well-managed forests
and other responsible sources.

MIX
Paper from
responsible sources
FSC® C104740

Piatkus
An imprint of
Little, Brown Book Group
100 Victoria Embankment
London EC4Y 0DY

An Hachette UK Company
www.hachette.co.uk

www.piatkus.co.uk

The Taste of Innocence

1

He had to marry, so he would.

But on his terms.

The latter words resonated through Charlie Morwellan's mind, repeating to the thud of his horse's hooves as he cantered steadily north. The winter air was crisp and clear. About him the lush green foothills of the western face of the Quantocks rippled and rolled. He'd been born to this country, at Morwellan Park, his home, now a mile behind him, yet he paid the arcadian views scant heed, his mind relentlessly focused on other vistas.

He was lord and master of the fields about him, filling the valley between the Quantocks to the east and the western end of the Brendon Hills. His lands stretched south well beyond the Park itself to where they abutted those managed by his brother-in-law, Gabriel Cynster. The northern boundary lay ahead, following a rise; as his dappled gray gelding, Storm, crested it, Charlie drew rein and paused, looking ahead yet not really seeing.

Cold air caressed his cheeks. Jaw set, expression impassive, he let the reasons behind his present direction run through his mind—one last time.

He'd inherited the earldom of Meredith on his father's death three years previously. Both before and since, he'd ducked and dodged the inevitable attempts to trap him into matrimony. Although the prospect of a wealthy, now over thirty-year-old, as-yet-unwed earl kept the matchmakers perennially salivating, after a decade in the ton he was awake to all their tricks; time and again he slipped free of their nets, taking a cynical male delight in so doing.

Yet for Lord Charles Morwellan, eighth Earl of Meredith, matrimony itself was inescapable.

That, however, wasn't the spur that had finally pricked him into action.

Nearly two years ago his closest friends, Gerrard Debbington and Dillon Caxton, had both married. Neither had been looking for a wife, neither had needed to marry, yet fate had set her snares and each had happily walked to the altar; he'd stood beside them there and known they'd been right to seize the moment.

Both Gerrard and Dillon were now fathers.

Storm shifted, restless; absentmindedly Charlie patted his neck.

Connected via their links to the powerful Cynster clan, he, Gerrard, and Dillon, and their wives, Jacqueline and Priscilla, had met as they always did after Christmas at Somersham Place, principal residence of the Dukes of St. Ives and ancestral home of the Cynsters. The large family and its multifarious connections met biannually there, at the so-called Summer Celebration in August and again over the festive season, the connections joining the family after spending Christmas itself with their own families.

He'd always enjoyed the boisterous warmth of those gatherings, yet this time . . . it hadn't been Gerrard's and Dillon's children per se that had fed his restlessness but rather what they represented. Of the three of them, friends for over a decade, *he* was the one with a recognized duty to wed and produce an heir. While theoretically he could leave his brother Jeremy, now twenty-three, to father the next generation of Morwellans, when it came to family duty he'd long ago accepted that he was constitutionally incapable of ducking. Letting one of the major responsibilities attached to the position of earl devolve onto Jeremy's shoulders was not something his conscience or his nature, his sense of self, would allow.

Which was why he was heading for Conningham Manor.

Continuing to tempt fate, courting the risk of that dangerous deity stepping in and organizing his life, and his wife, for him, as she had with Gerrard and Dillon, would be beyond foolish; ergo it was time for him to choose his bride. Now, before the start of the coming season, so he could exercise his prerogative, choose the lady who would suit *him* best, and have the deed done, final and complete, before society even got wind of it.

Before fate had any further chance to throw love across his path.

He needed to act now to retain complete and absolute control over his own destiny, something he considered a necessity, not an option.

Storm pranced, infected with Charlie's underlying impatience. Subduing the powerful gelding, Charlie focused on the landscape ahead. A mile away, comfortably nestled in a dip, the slate roofs of Conningham Manor rose above the naked branches of its orchard. Weak morning sunlight glinted off diamond-paned windows; a chill breeze caught the smoke drifting from the tall Elizabethan chimney pots and whisked it away. There'd been Conninghams at the Manor for nearly as long as there'd been Morwellans at the Park.

Charlie stared at the Manor for a minute more, then stirred, eased Storm's reins, and cantered down the rise.

"*Regardless*, Sarah, Clary and I *firmly* believe that you have to marry first."

Seated facing the bow window in the back parlor of Conningham Manor, the undisputed domain of the daughters of the house, Sarah Conningham glanced at her sixteen-year-old sister Gloria, who stared pugnaciously at her from her perch on the window seat.

"*Before* us." The clarification came in determined tones from seventeen-year-old Clara—Clary—seated beside Gloria and likewise focused on Sarah and their relentless pursuit to urge her into matrimony.

Stifling a sigh, Sarah looked down at the ribbon trim she was unpicking from the neckline of her new spencer, and with unimpaired calm set about reiterating her well-trod arguments. "You know that's not true. I've told you so, Twitters has told you so, and Mama has told you so. Whether I marry or not will have no effect whatever on your come-outs." Freeing the last stitch, she tugged the ribbon away, then shook out the spencer. "Clary will have her first season next year, and you, Gloria, will follow the year after."

"Yes *but*, that's not the point." Clary fixed Sarah with a frown. "It's the . . . the *way* of things."

When Sarah cocked a questioning brow at her, Clary blushed and rushed on, "It's the unfulfilled expectations. Mama and Papa will be taking you to London in a few weeks for your *fourth* season. It's obvious they still hope you'll attract the notice of a suitable gentleman. Both Maria and Angela accepted offers in their second season, after all."

Maria and Angela were their older sisters, twenty-eight and twenty-six years old, both married and living with their husbands and children on said husbands' distant estates. Unlike Sarah, both Maria and Angela had been perfectly content to marry gentlemen of their station with whom they were merely comfortable, given those men were blessed with fortunes and estates of appropriate degree.

Both marriages were conventional; neither Maria nor Angela had ever considered any other prospect, let alone dreamed of it.

As far as Sarah knew, neither had Clary or Gloria. At least, not yet.

She suppressed another sigh. "I assure you I will happily accept should an offer eventuate from a gentleman I can countenance being married to. However, as that happy occurrence seems increasingly unlikely"—she gave passing thanks that neither Clary nor Gloria had any notion of the number of offers she'd received and declined over the past three years—"I assure you I'm resigned to a spinster's life."

That was a massive overstatement, but . . . Sarah flicked a glance at the fourth occupant of the room, her erstwhile governess, Miss Twitterton, fondly known as Twitters, seated in an armchair to one side of the wide window. Twitters's gray head was bent over a piece of darning; she gave no sign of following the familar discussion.

If she couldn't imagine being happy with a life like Maria's or Angela's, Sarah could equally not imagine being content with a life like Twitters's.

Gloria made a rude sound. Clary looked disgusted. The pair exchanged glances, then embarked on a verbal catalogue of what they considered the most pertinent criteria for defining a "suitable gentleman," one to whom Sarah would countenance being wed.

Folding her new spencer with the garish scarlet ribbon now removed, Sarah smiled distantly and let them ramble. She was sincerely fond of her younger sisters, yet the gap between her twenty-three years and their ages was, in terms of the present discussion, a significant gulf.

They naively considered marriage a simple matter easily decided on a list of definable attributes, while she had seen enough to appreciate how unsatisfactory such an approach often was. Most marriages in their circle were indeed contracted on the basis of such criteria—and the vast majority, underpinned by nothing stronger than mild affection, degenerated into hollow relationships in which both partners turned elsewhere for comfort.

For love.

Such as love, in such circumstances, could be. Somehow less, somehow tawdry.

For herself, she'd approached the question of marriage with an open mind, and open eyes. No one had ever deemed her rebellious, yet she'd never been one to blindly follow others' dictates, especially on topics of personal importance. So she'd looked, and studied.

She now believed that when it came to marriage there was something better than the conventional norm. Something finer; an ideal, a commitment that compelled one to grasp it, a state glorious enough to fill the heart with yearning and need, and ultimately with satisfaction, a construct in which love existed *within* the bonds of matrimony rather than outside them.

And she'd seen it. Not in her parents' marriage, for that was a conventional if successful union, one without passion but based instead on affection, duty, and common cause. But to the south lay Morwellan Park, and beyond that Casleigh, the home of Lord Martin and Lady Celia Cynster, and now also home to their elder son, Gabriel, and his wife, Lady Alathea née Morwellan.

Sarah had known Alathea, Gabriel, and his parents for all of her life. Alathea and Gabriel had married for love; Alathea had waited until she was twenty-nine before Gabriel had come to his senses and claimed her as his bride. As for Martin and Celia, they had eloped long ago in a statement of passion impossible to mistake.

Sarah met both couples frequently. Her conviction that a love match, for want of a better title, was a goal worthy of her aspiration derived from what she'd observed between Gabriel and Alathea and, once her wits had been sharpened and her eyes had grown accustomed, from the older and somehow deeper and stronger interaction between Martin and Celia.

She freely admitted she didn't know what love was, had no concept of what the emotion would feel like within a marriage. Yet she'd seen evidence of its existence in the quality of a smile, in the subtle meeting of eyes, the gentle touch of a hand. A caress outwardly innocent yet laden with meaning.

When it was there, love colored such moments. When it wasn't . . .

But how did one define that love?

And did it mysteriously appear, or did one need to work for it? How did it come about?

She had no answers, not even a glimmer, hence her unwed state. Despite her sisters' trenchant beliefs, there was no reason she needed to marry. And if the emotion that infused the Cynsters' marriages was not part of an offer made to her, then she doubted any man, no matter how wealthy, how handsome or charming, could tempt her to surrender her hand.

To her, marriage without love held no attraction. She had no need of a union devoid of that finer glory, devoid of passion, yearning, need, and satisfaction. She had no reason to accept a lesser union.

"You will promise to look, won't you?"

Sarah glanced up to find Gloria leaning forward, brown brows beetling at her.

"*Properly,* I mean."

"*And* that you'll seriously consider and *encourage* any likely gentleman," Clary added.

Sarah blinked, then laughed and sat up to lay aside her spencer. "No, I will not. You two are far too impertinent—I'm sure Twitters agrees."

She glanced at Twitters to find the governess, whose ears were uncommonly sharp, peering myopically out of the window in the direction of the front drive.

"Now who is that, I wonder?" Twitters squinted past Clary, who swiveled to look out, as did Gloria. "No doubt some gentleman come to call on your papa."

Sarah looked past Gloria. Blessed with excellent eyesight, she instantly recognized the horseman trotting up the drive, but surprise and a frisson of unnerving reaction—something she felt whenever she first saw him—stilled her tongue.

"It's Charlie Morwellan," Gloria said. "I wonder what he's doing here."

Clary shrugged. "Probably to see Papa about the hunting."

"But he's never here for the hunting," Gloria pointed out. "These days he spends almost all his time in London. Augusta said she hardly ever sees him."

"Maybe he's staying in the country this year," Clary said. "I heard Lady Castleton tell Mama that he's going to be hunted without quarter this season from the absolute instant he returns to town."

Sarah had heard the same thing, but she knew Charlie well enough to predict that he would be no easy quarry. She watched as he drew rein at the edge of the forecourt and swung lithely down from the back of his gray hunter.

The breeze ruffled his elegantly cropped golden locks. His morning coat of brown Bath superfine was the apogee of some London tailor's art, stretching over Charlie's broad shoulders before tapering to hug his lean waist and narrow hips. His linen was pristine and precise; his waistcoat, glimpsed as he moved, was a subtle medley of browns and black. Buckskin breeches molded to long powerful legs before disappearing into glossy black Hessians, completing a picture that might have been titled *Fashionable Peer in the Country*.

Irritation stirring, Sarah drank in the vision; his appearance—and its ridiculous effect on her—really wasn't fair. He knew she existed, but beyond that . . . From this distance, she couldn't see his features clearly, yet her besotted memory filled in the details—the classic lines of brow, nose, and chin; the aristocratic angles and planes; the patriarchal cast of high cheekbones; the large, heavy-lidded, lushly lashed blue eyes; and the distracting, frankly sensual mouth and mobile lips that allowed his expression to change from delightfully charming to ruthlessly dominating in the blink of an eye.

She'd studied that face—and him—for years. She'd never known him to appear other than he was, a wealthy aristocrat descended from Norman lords with a streak of Viking thrown in. Despite his aura of ineffable control, of being born to rule without question, a hint of the unpredictable warrior remained, lurking beneath his smooth surface.

A stable boy came running. Charlie handed over his reins, spoke to the lad, then turned for the front door. As he passed out of their sight around the central wing, Clary and Gloria uttered identical sighs and turned back to face the room.

"He's really top of the trees, isn't he?"

Sarah doubted Clary required an answer.

"Gertrude Riordan said that in town he drives the most *fabulous* pair of matched grays." Gloria bounced, eyes alight. "I wonder if he drove them home? He would have, don't you think?"

While her sisters discussed various means of ascertaining whether Charlie's vaunted matched pair were at Morwellan Park, Sarah watched the stable boy lead Charlie's hunter off to the stables rather than walk the horse in the forecourt. Whatever Charlie's reasons for calling, he expected to be there for some little while.

Her sisters' voices filled her ears; recollections of their earlier comments whirled kaleidoscopically—to settle, abruptly, into an unexpected pattern. Leading to a startling thought.

Another frisson, different, more intense, slithered down Sarah's spine.

"Well, m'boy—" Lord Conningham broke off and laughingly grimaced at Charlie. "Daresay I shouldn't call you that anymore, but it's hard to forget how long I've known you."

Seated in the chair before the desk in his lordship's study, Charlie smiled and waved the comment aside. Lord Conningham was a bluff, good-natured man, one with whom Charlie felt entirely comfortable.

"For myself and her ladyship," Lord Conningham continued, "I can say without reservation that we're both honored and delighted by your offer. However, as a man with five daughters, two already wed, I have to tell you that their decisions are their own. It's Sarah herself whose approval you'll have to win, but on that score I know of nothing whatever that stands between you and your goal."

After a fractional hesitation, Charlie clarified, "She has no interest in any other gentleman?"

"No." Lord Conningham grinned. "And I would know if she had. Sarah's never been one to play her cards close to her chest. If any gentleman had captured her attention, her ladyship and I would know of it."

The door opened; Lord Conningham looked up. "Ah, there you are, m'dear. I hardly need to introduce you to Charlie. He has something to tell us."

With a smile, Charlie rose to greet Lady Conningham, a sensible, well-bred female he could with nothing more than the mildest of qualms imagine as his mother-in-law.

Ten minutes later, her wits in a whirl, Sarah left her bedchamber and hurried to the main stairs. A footman had brought a summons to join her mother in the front hall. She'd detoured via her dressing table, dallying just long enough to reassure herself that her gown of fine periwinkle-blue wool wasn't rumpled, that the lace edging the neckline hadn't crinkled, that her brown-blond hair was neat in its knot at the back of her head and not too many strands had escaped.

Quite a few had, but she didn't have time to let her hair down and redo the knot. Besides, she only needed to be neat enough to pass muster in case Charlie saw her in passing; it was too early for him to be staying for luncheon and there was no reason to imagine that her mother's summons was in any way connected with his visit . . . other than the ridiculous suspicion that had flared in her mind and set her heart racing. Reaching the head of the stairs, she started down, her stomach a hard knot, her nerves jangling.

All for nothing, she chided herself. It was a nonsensical supposition.

Her slippers pattered on the treads; her mother appeared from the corridor beside the stairs. Sarah's gaze flew to her face, willing her mother to speak and explain and ease her nerves.

Instead, her mother's countenance, already wreathed in a glorious smile, brightened even more. "Good. You've tidied." Her mother scanned her comprehensively, from her forehead to her toes, then beamed and took her arm.

Entirely at sea, her questions in her eyes, Sarah let her mother draw her a few yards down the corridor to an alcove nestled under the stairs.

Releasing her arm, her mother clasped her hand and squeezed her fingers. "Well, my dear, the long and short of this is that Charlie Morwellan wishes to offer for your hand."

Sarah blinked; for one instant, her mind literally reeled.

Her mother smiled, not unsympathetically. "Indeed, it's a surprise, quite out of the blue, but heaven knows you've dealt with offers enough—you know the ropes. As always the decision is yours, and your father and I will stand by you regardless of what that decision might be." Her mother paused. "However, in this case both your father and I would ask that you consider very carefully. An offer from any earl would command extra attention, but an offer from the eighth Earl of Meredith warrants even deeper consideration."

Sarah looked into her mother's dark eyes. Quite aside from her pleasure over Charlie's offer, in advising her in this, her mother was very serious.

"My dear, you already have sufficient comprehension of Charlie's wealth. You know his home, his standing—you know *of* him, although I accept that you do not know him, himself, well. But you do know his family."

Taking both her hands, her mother lightly squeezed, her excitement returning. "With no other gentleman have you had, nor will you have, such a close prior connection, such a known foundation on which you might build. It's an unlooked-for, entirely unexpected opportunity, yes, but a very good one."

Her mother searched her eyes, trying to read her reaction. Sarah knew all she would see was confusion.

"Well." Her mother's lips set just a little; her tone became more brisk. "You must hear him out. Listen carefully to what he has to say, then you must make your decision."

Releasing her hands, her mother stepped back, reached up and tweaked Sarah's neckline, then nodded. "Very well. Go in—he's waiting in the drawing room. As I said, your father and I will accept whatever decision you make. But please, do think very carefully about Charlie."

Sarah nodded, feeling numb. She could barely breathe. Turning from her mother, she walked, slowly, toward the drawing room door.

Charlie heard a light footstep beyond the door. He turned from the window as the doorknob turned, watched as the door opened and the lady he'd chosen to be his wife entered.

She was of average height, subtly but sensuously curved; her slenderness made her appear taller than she was. Her face was heart-shaped, framed by the soft fullness of her lustrous hair, an eye-catching shade of gilded light brown. Her features were delicate, her complexion flawless—including, to his mind, the row of tiny freckles across the bridge of her nose. A wide brow, that straight nose, arched brown brows, and long lashes combined with rose-tinted lips and a sweetly curved chin to complete a picture of restful loveliness.

Her gaze was unusually direct; he waited for her to move, knowing that when she did it would be with innate grace.

Her hand on the doorknob, she paused, scanning the room.

His eyes narrowed slightly. Even across the distance he sensed her uncertainty, yet when her gaze found him she hesitated for only a second before, without looking away, she closed the door and came toward him.

Calmly, serenely, but with her hands clasped, fingers twined.

She couldn't have expected this; he'd given her no indication that marrying her had ever entered his head. The last time they'd met socially, at the Hunt Ball last November, he'd waltzed with her once, remained by her side for fifteen minutes or so, exchanging the usual pleasantries, and that had been all.

Deliberately on his part. He'd known—for years if he stopped to consider it—that she . . . regarded him differently. That it would be very easy, with just a smile and a few words, for him to awaken an infatuation in her, a fascination with him. Not that she'd ever been so gauche as to give the slightest sign, yet he was too attuned to women, certainly, it seemed, to her, not to know what quivered just beneath her cool, clear surface, the sensible serenity she showed to the world. He'd made a decision, not once but many times over the years, that it wouldn't do to stir that pool, to ripple her surface. She was, after all, sweet Sarah, a neighbor's daughter he'd known all her life.

So he'd been careful not to do what his instincts had so frequently prompted. He'd studiously treated her as just another young lady of his local acquaintance.

Yet when he'd finally decided to select a wife, one face had leapt to his mind. He hadn't even had to think—he'd simply known that she was his choice.

And then, of course, he had thought, and visited all the arguments, the numerous criteria a man like him needed to evaluate in selecting a wife. The exercise had only confirmed that Sarah Conningham was the perfect candidate.

She halted before him, confidently facing him with less than two feet between them. Confusion shadowed her eyes, a delicate blue the color of a pale cornflower, as she searched his face.

"Charlie." She inclined her head. To his surprise, her voice was even, steady if a trifle breathless. "Mama said you wished to speak with me."

Head high so she could continue to meet his gaze—the top of her head barely reached his chin—she waited.

He felt his lips curve, entirely spontaneously. No fuss, no fluster, and no "Lord Charles," either. They'd never stood on formality, not in any circumstances, and for that he was grateful.

Despite her outward calm, he sensed the brittle, expectant tension that held her, that kept her breathing shallow. Respect stirred, unexpected but definite, yet was he really surprised that she had more backbone than the norm?

No; that, in part, was why he was there.

The urge to reach out and run his fingertips across her collarbone—just to see how smooth the fine alabaster skin was—struck unexpectedly; he toyed with the notion for a heartbeat, but rejected it. Such an action wasn't appropriate given the nature of what he had to say, the tone he wished to maintain.

"As I daresay your mother mentioned, I've asked your father's permission to address you. I would like to ask you to do me the honor of becoming my wife."

He could have dressed up the bare words in any amount of platitudes, but to what end? They knew each other well, perhaps not in a private sense, but his sisters and hers were close; he doubted there was much in his general life of which she was unaware.

And there was nothing in her response to suggest he'd gauged that wrongly, even though, after the briefest of moments, she frowned.

"Why?"

It was his turn to feel confused.

Her lips tightened and she clarified, "Why me?"

Why now? Why after all these years have you finally deigned to do more than smile at me? Sarah kept the words from her tongue, but looking up into Charlie's impassive face, she felt an almost overpowering urge to sink her hands into her hair, pull loose the neatly arranged tresses, and run her fingers through them while she paced. And thought. And tried to understand.

She couldn't remember a time when she hadn't had to, every time she first set eyes on him, pause, just for a second, to let her senses breathe. To let them catch their breath after it had been stolen away simply by his presence. Once the moment passed, as it always did, then all she had to do was battle to ensure she did nothing foolish, nothing to give away her secret obsession—infatuation—with him.

It was nonsense and brought her nothing but aggravation, but no amount of lecturing over its inanity had ever done an ounce of good. She'd decided it was simply the way she reacted to him, Viking-Norman Adonis that he was. She'd reluctantly concluded that her reaction wasn't her fault. Or his. It just *was;* she'd been born this way, and she simply had to deal with it.

And now here he was, without so much as a proper smile in warning, asking for her hand.

Wanting to *marry her.*

It didn't seem possible. She pinched her thumb, just to make sure, but he remained before her, solid and real, the heat of him, the strength of him wrapping about her in pure masculine temptation, even if now he was frowning, too.

His lips firmed, losing the intoxicating curve that had softened them. "Because I believe we'll deal exceptionally well together." He hesitated, then went on, "I could give you chapter and verse about our stations, our families, our backgrounds, but you already know every aspect as well as I. And"—his gaze sharpened—"as I'm sure you understand, I need a countess."

He paused, then his lips quirked. "Will you be mine?"

Nicely ambiguous. Sarah stared into his gray-blue eyes, a paler shade of blue than her own, and heard again in her mind her mother's words: *Think very carefully about Charlie.*

She searched his eyes, and accepted that she'd have to, that this time her answer wasn't so clear. She'd lost count of the times she'd faced a gentleman like this and framed an answer to that question, couched though it had been in many different ways. Never before had she even had to think of the crux of her reply, only the words in which to deliver it.

This time, facing Charlie . . .

Still holding his gaze, she compressed her lips fleetingly, drew in a breath and let it out with, "If you want my honest answer, then that honest answer is that I can't answer you, not yet."

His dark gold lashes, impossibly thick, screened his eyes for an instant; when he again met her gaze his frown was back. "What do you mean? When will you be able to answer?"

Aggression reached her, reined but definitely there. Unsurprised—she knew his charm was nothing more than a veneer, that under that glossy surface he was stubborn, even ruthless—she studied his eyes, and unexpectedly found answers to two of the many questions crowding her mind. He did indeed want her—specifically *her*—as his wife. And he wanted her soon.

Quite what she was to make of that last, she wasn't sure. Nor did she know how much trust she could place in the former.

She was aware that he expected her to back away from his veiled challenge, to temporize, to in one way or another back down. She smiled tightly and lifted her chin. "In answer to your first question, you know perfectly well that I had no warning of your offer. I had no idea you were even thinking of such a thing. Your proposal has come entirely out of the blue, and the simple fact is I don't know you well enough"—she held up a hand—"regardless of our long acquaintance—and don't pretend you don't know what I mean—to be able to answer you yay or nay."

She paused, waiting to see if he would argue. When he simply waited, lips even thinner, his gaze razor sharp and locked on her eyes, she continued, "As for your second question, I'll be able to answer you once I know you well enough to know which answer to give."

His eyes bored into hers for a long moment, then he stated, "You want me to woo you."

His tone was resigned; she'd gained that much at least.

"Not precisely. It's more that I need to spend time with you so I can get to know you better." She paused, her eyes on his. "And so you can get to know me."

That last surprised him; he held her gaze, then his lips quirked and he inclined his head.

"Agreed." His voice had lowered. Now he was talking to her, with her, no longer on any formal plane but on an increasingly personal one; his tone had deepened, becoming more private. More intimate.

She quelled a tiny shiver; at that lower note his voice reverberated through her. She'd wanted to increase the space between them for several minutes, but there was something in the way he looked at her, the way his gaze held her, that made her hesitate, as if to edge back would be tantamount to admitting weakness.

Like fleeing from a predator. An invitation to . . . Her mouth was dry.

He'd tilted his head, studying her face. "So how long do you think getting to know each other better—well enough—will take?"

There was not a glint so much as a carefully veiled idea lurking in the depths of his eyes that made her inwardly frown. She was tempted to state that she had no intention of being swayed by his undoubted, unquestioned, utterly obvious sexual expertise, but that, like fleeing, might be seriously unwise. He'd all too likely interpret such a comment as an outright challenge.

And that was, she was certain, one challenge she couldn't meet.

She hadn't, not for one moment, been able to—felt able to—shift her gaze from his. "A month or two should be sufficient."

His face hardened. "A week."

She narrowed her eyes. "That's impossible. Four weeks."

He narrowed his back. "Two."

The word held a ring of finality she wished she could challenge— wished she thought she *could* challenge. Lips set, she nodded. Curtly. "Very well. Two weeks—and then I'll answer you yay or nay."

His eyes held hers. Although he didn't move, she felt as if he leaned closer.

"I have a caveat." His gaze, at last, shifted from her eyes, drifting mesmerically lower. His voice deepened, becoming even more hypnotic. "In return for my agreeing to a two-week courtship, you will agree that once you answer and accept my offer"—his gaze rose to her eyes—"we'll be married by special license no more than a week later."

She licked her dry lips, started to form the word "why."

He stepped nearer. "Do you agree?"

Trapped—in his gaze, by his nearness—she managed, just, to draw in a breath. "Very well. *If* I agree to marry you, then we can be married by special license."

He smiled—and she suddenly decided that no matter how he took it, fleeing was an excellent idea. She tensed to step back.

Just as his arm swept around her, and tightened.

His eyes held hers as he drew her, gently but inexorably, into his arms. "Our two-week courtship . . . remember?"

She leaned back, keeping her eyes on his, her hands on his upper arms. His strength surrounded her. She felt giddy. "What of it?"

His lips curved in a wholly masculine smile. "It starts now."

Then he bent his head and covered her lips with his.

2

S he'd been kissed a number of times. None of them had been like this.

Never before had her senses spun, never before had her thoughts suspended. Simply stopped.

Stopped to allow sensation to burgeon, to well and grow and fill her mind.

She didn't question the wisdom of it, couldn't think enough to do so. Couldn't free her mind from the sinfully tempting touch of his lips on hers, from the artfully applied evocative pressure, from the warmth that seemed to steal into her bones—just from a simple, not-so-innocent kiss.

A kiss with which he fully intended to steal away her wits.

She realized, understood, yet was too intrigued, too enthralled, to deny him.

Charlie knew it. Knew she was fascinated, that she was perfectly willing to have him show her more.

Precisely as he wished, as he wanted.

Enough; this was supposed to be just a kiss, nothing more. Yet to his surprise it took an exercise of will before he could bring himself to give up the subtle pleasure. Before he could force himself to break the kiss, to draw back from the rose-tinted lips that had proved more luscious, more tempting, than he'd thought.

Fresh, delicate; as he lifted his head and drew in a breath, he wondered if that was the taste of innocence. And if it was that unfamiliar elixir or her underlying skittish flightiness that was setting unanticipated spurs to his desire.

Regardless, as he studied her eyes as she blinked rather dazedly up at him, he couldn't suppress an inward smugness. She felt warm, soft, and desirable in his arms, but he gently set her back, and let his lips curve in an easy, charming—reasonably innocent—gesture. "I'll see you tonight I believe—at Lady Finsbury's." His smile deepened. "And we can continue to get to know each other better."

Her eyes narrowed fractionally.

Raising a hand, with the back of one finger he lightly stroked her cheek, then stepped back, bowed, and left her.

Before he was tempted to do anything more.

Sarah Conningham had definitely been the right choice.

Sarah next set eyes on her would-be betrothed when he stepped into Lady Finsbury's drawing room that evening. Tall, strikingly handsome, exuding restrained rakish elegance in his walnut-brown coat, gold-striped waistcoat, and pristine ivory linen, he bowed over her ladyship's hand with ineffable grace. Smiling charmingly, he complimented her—Sarah could tell by her pleased expression—then moved into the room.

When he'd left her that afternoon, she'd gathered her still reeling wits and gone to her father's study. Her parents had been waiting there; without roundaboutness she'd explained her and Charlie's agreement. Despite it not being quite what they'd hoped, her parents had been nonetheless delighted. While she hadn't said yes, she equally hadn't said no; after the briefest consideration, their faces had brightened. They clearly had every confidence that her getting to know Charlie better would result in a positive outcome.

Their optimism wasn't surprising. As she watched him move smoothly through the guests, all locals and therefore well known to them both, greeting one here, stopping to exchange a word there, all the time head-

ing inexorably in her direction, she had to admit it was difficult to conjure any conventional shortcoming that might turn her against him.

But assessing conventional aspects wasn't why she'd insisted on a
period of courtship. She needed to confirm that the one critical aspect
she deemed absolutely essential to her future happiness with Charlie
existed in him, that it was a part of what he was offering her, whether
consciously or otherwise. She owed it to herself, to her dreams, to her
future—and to all the gentlemen whose offers she'd dismissed—to assure herself it was there, somewhere within the scope of his intentions.
At the very least, she needed to find evidence it *could* exist, that he
could give her that one vital thing, that it would be there, acknowledged or not, an integral part of their marriage.

A love match or no match; that was her aim—her view of her future if said future involved marriage.

Their interlude that morning had only strengthened her resolve,
only clarified her direction. If it was marriage he was set on, then love
was her price.

While ostensibly listening to the other ladies and gentlemen in the
group she'd joined by the window, from the corner of her eye she
watched Charlie approach. He skirted a group of younger girls, only
to have one in a sweetpea-pink gown gaily turn and waylay him.

Sarah caught her breath, then remembered that Clary knew nothing
of Charlie's offer or their agreement; she'd asked her parents to keep
their situation in the strictest confidence. She had only two weeks to
learn what she sought, to assure herself that Charlie and what he offered were what she wanted; having Clary and Gloria "helping" would
be a nightmare.

With a laugh, Charlie parted from Clary; half a minute later he
stood before Sarah, taking her hand, bowing over it, meeting her eyes.

Making her nerves unfurl, reach, stretch, then tense; an anticipa-
tory shiver ran down her spine.

"Good evening, Charlie." They stood among longtime acquaintances; she didn't think to "my lord" him. Holding his blue-gray gaze,
she lowered her voice. "I dare say Lady Finsbury's wondering at her
good fortune."

The curve of his lips deepened; he gently squeezed her fingers, then
released them. "I do occasionally attend such events. Tonight, her ladyship's held a certain lure."

Her. She inclined her head and waited with feigned patience while he greeted the others, exchanging quips and sporting news with the gentlemen.

One thing between them had already changed; the odd breathlessness that had previously attacked her whenever she set eyes on him hadn't afflicted her tonight. She'd been studying him, assessing; perhaps that was why. Why the effect of his presence hadn't struck until he'd been much nearer—close enough for their eyes to meet, for him to touch her hand.

Then it had struck with a vengeance, stronger, more powerful, a trifle unnerving, but by the time he turned back to her, she had her nerves well in hand.

By shifting a fraction, taking her attention with him, he subtly separated them from the group.

Before he could speak, she did, her gaze going past his shoulder. "Tell me, do your family know of your . . . direction?"

He followed her gaze to his mother, Serena, his sister Augusta, and his brother Jeremy, who had just entered and were greeting their hostess. "No." Turning back, he met her eyes. "My decision is my own. Awakening their interest will only make 'getting to know each other better' more difficult." His lips quirked. "That said, they're far from blind—they'll guess soon enough. I assume your sisters don't know?"

"If they did, Clary would be hanging on your arm."

"In that case, let's pray for continued obliviousness." He glanced around, over the heads. "It appears it's time for the first dance—shall we?"

Charlie offered his arm as the introductory chords of a cotillion welled; he would have preferred a waltz, but he wasn't about to stand aside and watch some other gentleman dance first with Sarah. With a nod of acceptance, she placed her hand on his sleeve. As he steered her through the guests in the direction of the dining room, tonight cleared to accommodate the dancing, he was once again conscious of matters not progressing quite as he'd expected, of being just a trifle off balance, of having to adjust.

To her. *She* was the source of the tilt in his world, the point from which the ripples in his plans originated.

That afternoon he'd been distracted by having to deal with her demand for a period of courtship; only once he'd left her and was riding home had it struck him how far from his original script they'd strayed. He'd fully expected to be an affianced man by that point; he'd expected her to accept him without question.

Instead . . . he'd encountered something he hadn't anticipated, something strong enough to not change his direction but replot his course. Even as he turned her and they took their positions in the set, arms raised, fingers twined, he was conscious of a certain strength in her, a fluid supple quality, true, yet something he'd be unwise to ignore. However . . .

The music swelled and they moved into the figures, dipping, swaying, circling, coming together, then gliding apart; with his attention locked on her, on her face, on her graceful figure, he was aware to his bones just how entrancing she was, just how much her svelte curves lured him—even if they concealed steel. Or was it because of that?

She twirled; gazes locking, they moved in concert, then opposition, only to glide together again, side by side, arms brushing. Senses reaching, touching.

Meeting, meshing. Held, commanded, by her cornflower-blue eyes, he felt the intangible caress of the sensual tendrils nascent desire sent weaving between them, twining and twirling as the music steered them through the intricate steps. As he retook her hand and their fingers interlinked, he all but felt the net draw close, and tighten. Drawing them nearer as the dance did the same, as he circled her, their eyes linked, and the beat escalated and his pulse responded—and he saw desire rise and swirl through her eyes.

Abruptly he looked away, then drew in a deep breath. Rapidly reasserted his will and reassembled his wits.

He was more attracted to her than he'd anticipated; that was undeniable. Her unexpected resistance to accepting his suit had focused his attention in a way he hadn't forseen.

It was, he told himself, the scent of the chase, spurred on by that alluring taste of innocence—something he was keen to savor again. Once he'd gained her agreement, her hand, and her, no doubt his burgeoning fascination would fade.

But that time was not yet.

The dance concluded. He raised her from her curtsy; the movement left them closer than they had been to that point.

Closer than they had been since the moment in her parents' drawing room when he'd kissed her.

Her eyes, wide, were raised to his. He looked into them, and the impulse to kiss her flared again, stronger, more compelling. For one finite instant there was no other in the room, only them. Her gaze lowered to his lips; hers parted.

They stood in the center of a dance floor surrounded by a horde of others who would be fascinated by any hint of a connection between them.

He hauled in a breath, mentally gritted his teeth, and forced himself to step back—enough to break the spell. She blinked, then dropped her gaze and eased back.

His fingers tightened about hers. Lifting his head, he scanned the room, but there was no chance of slipping away, of finding some quiet spot in which to pursue their aims, if not mutual, then at least parallel. She wanted to get to know him better; he wanted to kiss her again, to taste her more definitely.

But Finsbury Hall was relatively small, and it was raining outside.

Lips compressing, he looked at her, and found his inner frown reflected in her eyes. "This venue is a trifle restrictive for our purpose. If I call on you tomorrow, will you be free?"

She thought before she nodded. "Yes."

"Good." Setting her hand on his sleeve, he turned her toward the drawing room. "We can spend the day together, and then we'll see."

He called in the morning to take her driving—behind his matched, utterly peerless grays. To Sarah's intense relief, Clary and Gloria had gone for a walk with Twitters and weren't there to see—not the horses, Charlie, or how he whisked her from the house, handed her into his curricle, then leapt up, took the reins and drove off, whipping up his horses as if he and she were escaping. . . .

Well wrapped in her forest-green pelisse, she settled beside him and reflected that perhaps they were leaving behind the restrictions of their families and the familiar but sometimes suffocating bounds of local society. At the end of the Manor drive, he turned his horses north. She glanced at him, glad she'd decided against a hat; he, of course, looked predictably impressive in his many-caped greatcoat, his long-fingered hands wielding whip and reins with absentminded dexterity. "Where are we going?"

"Watchet." Briefly he met her eyes. "I have business interests there, on the docks and in the warehouses behind them. I need to speak with my agent, but that won't take long. After that, I thought we could stroll, have lunch at the inn, and maybe"—he glanced at her again—"go for a sail if the weather stays fine and the winds oblige."

She widened her eyes even though he'd looked to his horses. "You enjoy sailing?"

"I own a small boat, single-masted. I can sail it alone—I usually do—but it will carry three comfortably. It's tied up at Watchet pier."

She imagined him sailing alone on the waves, sails billowing in the winds that whipped over Bridgwater Bay. Watchet was one of the ports scattered along the southern shore. "I haven't been sailing for years—not since I was a child. I quite enjoyed it." She glanced at him. "I know the basics."

His lips curved. "Good. You can crew."

He slowed his pair as they approached Crowcombe. They rattled through the village; as the last house fell behind, he whipped up his horses and they rocketed on into open countryside. Once they were bowling freely along, she asked, "What do you do in London? How do you pass your time—not the balls and parties, the evenings, those I can imagine—but the days? Alathea once told me that you and Gabriel shared similar interests."

Eyes on his horses as he deftly steered them along the country road, he nodded. "Around the time of their marriage, I caught a glimpse into the world of finance—it seemed challenging, exciting, and Gabriel was willing to teach me. I more or less fell into it. These days . . ."

Somewhat to his surprise, Charlie found it easy to describe his liking for the intricacies of high finance, to outline his absorption with investments and innovations and the development of projects that ultimately led to major improvements for all. Perhaps it was because Sarah wasn't asking simply to be polite; she sincerely wanted to know—and her occasional questions demonstrated that her understanding was up to the task.

"Infrastructure is currently my principal area of interest, certainly in the sense of looking ahead, in terms of speculative investments. Most of the funds I manage—my own as well as the family's—are in safe and solid stocks and bonds, but that type of investment requires little time or acumen to oversee. It's the new ventures that excite me. Dealing in that arena is more demanding, making success more rewarding, in both monetary terms as well as satisfaction."

"Because there isn't any danger in the safe and secure—the other has more risk, so it's therefore more challenging?"

He glanced at her. She met his eyes, her brows arching in question. He nodded and looked back to his horses, just a touch unnerved that she'd seen that quite so clearly.

Still, if she were to be his bride, such understanding would only help.

They rattled through Williton. A little way on, he drew rein on a wide bend in the road, and they looked down on the port of Watchet.

It was a bustling small town, the houses forming embracing arms around the docks and wharves that were the focus of town life. The docks ran out into deep water; the wharves ran along the shoreline, connecting them. Immediately behind stood rows of warehouses, all old but clearly in use.

Beyond the western end of the town, between the last houses and the cliffs that rose to border the sea, a shelf of land was in the process of being cleared and leveled.

"You said you had interests in the warehouses here." Sarah glanced at him. "In which set of investments do they fall—the safe, sure, and unexciting or the risky and challenging?"

He grinned. "A bit of both. With the industries and mills in Taunton expanding, and those in Wellington, too, the future growth of Watchet as a port is assured. The next nearest is Minehead." He nodded to the west. "Not only farther away, but with the cliffs to manage." He looked back at the port below, at the rigging of the ships at anchor, at the steel-green waves of the bay and the Bristol Channel farther out. "Watchet will grow. The only questions are by how much, and how soon. The risk comes in balancing how much to invest against the time needed to make an acceptable return."

The grays stamped, impatient to get on. The road leading down was well graded with no overly steep sections, perfect for the heavy wagons that trundled down to the docks, disbursed their loads of cloth or fleeces, then took on the wines and wood off-loaded from the ships.

Charlie checked that no large dray was on the upward slope, then flicked the reins and sent the grays down.

He drove into the town and turned in under the arch of the Bell Inn. They left the horses in the reverent care of the head ostler, who knew Charlie well. Her hand on Charlie's arm, Sarah walked beside him into the High Street.

What followed was a minor education into the business of Watchet port. Charlie's man on the ground was part shipping agent, part landlord's agent; he matched the available warehouse space with the cargoes coming in and out of the town, passing through the docks.

Sarah sat in a chair alongside Charlie's and listened as Mr. Jones reviewed the dispositions of goods in the warehouses Charlie owned. All were close to full, earning Charlie's approbation.

"Now." Jones leaned forward to lay a sheet of figures before Charlie. "These are the projections you wanted on the volumes needed to make a go of any new warehouse. They're well within range of what we're likely to see coming through within a year."

Charlie picked up the sheet, rapidly scanned the figures, then peppered Jones with questions.

Sarah listened intently; Charlie had explained enough for her to follow his tack—enough for her to appreciate the risk and the potential reward.

When ten minutes later they left Jones, she smiled and gave him her hand, aware of the speculation her presence by Charlie's side had sparked.

From Jones's office, they walked west along the main wharf, feeling the tug of the salt breeze and with the raucous cries of gulls ringing in their ears. At the end of the wharf, Charlie took her elbow and turned her up a cobbled street; after passing between two old and weathered warehouses, it gave onto the large flat section of rocky land beyond which the sea cliffs rose.

There were pegs in the ground with ropes strung between. Charlie led her on a little way, then they halted and looked seaward. All the town and the warehouses lay to their right. Ahead, they could see the newest and most westerly dock stretching out into the choppy waters of the bay.

"I'm thinking of building a new warehouse here." Charlie looked at her. "What do you think?"

Lifting her hands to tuck back the hair the wind had whipped about her face, she looked at the nearest warehouse, thought of the figures Jones had let fall. "If it were me, I'd be thinking of two—or at least one twice the size of that one. I'm not very good at estimating spaces, but it seemed that the anticipated increase in goods through Watchet would easily fill another two, if not three."

Charlie grinned. "If not four or more. You're right." He looked at the dock, then scanned the area in which they stood. "I was thinking of two—very little risk there. The projected volumes will fill them easily. No need to be greedy—two will do. But building one twice the size . . ." He paused, then added, "That might well be an excellent notion."

Sarah inwardly preened. "Who owns the land?"

Retaking her arm, Charlie turned back to the town. "I do. I bought it years ago."

She raised her brows. "A speculative investment?"

"One that's about to pay handsomely."

They walked back to the inn, taking their time, casting their eyes over the various ships tied up at the docks, at the cargoes being unloaded. The central wharf was a bustling hive of activity; Charlie helped her over various ropes and between piles of crates until they could turn the corner for the inn.

Once within its portals they were greeted by the owner; he knew them both, but Charlie—his lordship, the earl—clearly commanded extra special attention. They were shown to a table in a private nook by a window from which they could see the harbor.

The meal was excellent. Sarah had expected their conversation to falter, but Charlie quizzed her on local affairs and the time sped by. It was only as they were leaving the inn that it occurred to her that he'd been using her to refresh his memory; much of what he'd asked he wouldn't have seen over the last ten years—the years he'd spent mostly in London.

Pausing on the inn's porch, they studied the sea. The wind had dropped to a gentle offshore breeze, and the waves were no longer choppy. The sun had found a break in the clouds and shone down, gilding the scene, easing the earlier chill.

Charlie glanced at her. "Are you game?"

She met his eyes, and smiled. "Where's your boat?"

He steered her down the wharf, heading east beyond the commercial docks to where narrower piers afforded berths to smaller, private craft. Charlie's boat was moored toward the end of one pier. One look at its bright paintwork, at its neat and shining trim, was enough to assure her that it was in excellent condition.

The glow in Charlie's eyes as she helped him cast off, then hoist the sail, informed her that sailing was a passion; his expertise as he tacked, taking them swiftly from the pier out into the open harbor, told her it was one in which he often indulged. Or had. It seemed unlikely that he'd managed all that much sailing over recent years.

She sat back and watched him manage the tiller. Watched the wind of their passage ruffle his golden locks; she didn't want to think what her own coiffure must look like.

"Do you miss this when you're in London?"

His eyes, very gray now that they were on the water, swung to her face. "Yes." The wind snatched the word away. He shifted closer, leaning as he tacked; she moved nearer the better to hear.

"I've always loved the feeling of running before the wind, when the sail fills and the hull lifts, then slices through the water. You can feel the power, you can harness it, but it's not something you can control. It always feels like a blessing, whenever I'm out here on a day like this." He met her eyes. "As if the gods are smiling."

She smiled back, restraining her whipping hair as they reached the end of their eastward leg and he shifted to tack. And then they were racing away again, faster, farther. She leaned back and laughed, looking up at the clouds that careened overhead, then gasping as a larger wave struck and they jolted, then flew anew.

The gods continued to smile for the next hour.

Again and again, she found herself gazing at Charlie, a silly smile on her lips as she drank in the sight of him, his hair whipped wild, gray eyes narrowed against the spray, shoulders flexing, arms powerfully bracing as he managed the tiller; never before had she seen the Viking side of him more transparently on display. Time and again she'd catch herself mooning and look away, only to have her eyes drift back to their obsession.

At first she thought her awareness was one-sided, then she realized that whenever she moved to assist with the sail, his gaze traveled over her, lingering on her breasts, her hips, her legs as she stretched and shifted. That gaze felt strangely hard, possessive; she told herself it was her imagination running wild with thoughts of Vikings and plunder, yet she couldn't stop a reactive shiver every time he glanced at her that way. Couldn't stop her nerves from tightening in expectation each time he gave an order.

Luckily, he knew nothing of that, so she felt free to let her nerves and senses indulge as they might, while she pondered the implications.

They fell into an easy partnership; she did, indeed, remember enough to act as crew, ducking low when the boom passed overhead, deftly taking in slack in the appropriate ropes.

By the time Charlie turned the bow for the pier, she felt wrung out yet exhilarated. Although they'd spoken little, she'd learned more than she'd expected; the day had revealed aspects of him she hadn't known were there.

The boat was gliding toward the pier on a slack sail when, leaning back against the side and looking up at the town, she noticed a gentleman with another man on the shelf of land where Charlie was proposing to build his new warehouse. Shading her eyes, she peered. "Someone's looking over your land."

Charlie followed her gaze. He frowned. "Who is he—the gentleman? Do you know?"

She stared, taking in the neat attire, the fair hair. She shook her head. "He's not anyone local. That's Skilling, the land agent, with him."

Charlie was forced to shift his attention to the rapidly nearing pier. "I bought the land through Skilling, so he knows it's mine."

"Perhaps the other gentleman is looking to build warehouses, too?"

Charlie shot a narrow-eyed glance at the mysterious newcomer. He and Skilling were now leaving the vacant land, heading not to the wharves but into the town. "Perhaps."

As he guided the boat into her mooring, he made a mental note to ask Skilling who the gentleman was. A nonlocal gentleman—if Sarah didn't know him at least by sight he was definitely not local—who happened to have an interest in land and/or warehouses in Watchet was someone he needed to identify, to know about.

Unfortunately, he didn't have time to speak with Skilling now; the sun was already slanting low. He needed to get Sarah home before the light faded.

He leapt up to the pier and lashed the craft securely. Sarah finished furling the sail, then reached up and gave him her hands. He lifted her easily, balancing her until she steadied, her soft curves pressing fleetingly against him.

Desire leapt.

He felt it surge and sweep through him, urging him to lock her against him, bend his head and take her lips—and plunder. The power of the impulse rocked him; its hunger shocked him.

Unaware, she laughed up at him; he forced a smile at the musical sound. He looked into her eyes, alight with simple joy—and cursed the fact that kissing her witless in full view of the multitudes bustling about the docks was something he really couldn't do.

Gritting his teeth, ruthlessly ignoring his baser self, the increasingly compulsive need to kiss her again, he set her back from him.

"Come." His voice had lowered. Drawing in a breath, he took her hand. "We'd better head back to the manor."

The next day was Sunday. As he usually did when in the country, Charlie attended morning service at the church at Combe Florey with those of his family residing at Morwellan Park—on this occasion his mother, brother, and youngest sister, Augusta.

His other three sisters—Alathea, the eldest, and Mary and Alice—were married and living elsewhere. Although Alathea, married to Gabriel Cynster and mostly resident at Casleigh to the south, lived close, she and the Cynsters attended services at the church near Casleigh.

A fact for which Charlie was grateful; Alathea's eyes were uncommonly sharp, especially when it came to him. Throughout his minority she'd guarded his interests zealously; it was largely due to her that there'd been an estate for him to inherit. For that, he could never thank her enough, yet while he understood that she had a vested interest in his life—in the well-being of the earldom and therefore him as the earl—her acuity made him wary.

He didn't, at this point, wish undue attention focused on himself and Sarah.

Sitting in the ornately carved Morwellan pew, in the front to the left of the aisle, he listened to the sermon with barely half an ear. From the corner of his eye he could see Sarah's bright head as she sat in the Conningham pew, the other front pew, across the aisle.

She'd smiled at him when he'd followed his mother down the nave to take his seat. He'd smiled easily back, all too conscious that the gesture was a mask; inwardly he hadn't felt like smiling at all.

Gaining time alone was proving difficult, time alone in which he could further his aim. *Her* aim was progressing reasonably well, but *his* aim required greater privacy than he'd yet been able to arrange.

Yesterday he'd hoped that when they'd returned to the manor, he would have a moment when he walked her to the door—one moment he could grasp to kiss her again. But her sisters had come running from the house; they'd all but mobbed his curricle, even though there'd been only two of them. From what he'd gathered, they'd been harboring designs on his grays. They'd smothered him with questions, many ridiculous, but he hadn't missed the sharp glances they'd thrown Sarah and him.

Clary and Gloria were now wondering. A dangerous situation. When it came to those two, he shared Sarah's reservations.

The service finally ended; he rose and escorted his mother up the aisle with the rest of the congregation falling in behind, the Conninghams foremost among them.

Instinct prodded him to turn and smile at Sarah, almost directly behind him with only her parents between—but Clary and Gloria were immediately behind her. Lips compressing, he told himself to wait; they'd be able to chat once they gained the church lawn.

But the Combe Florey church was well attended, the congregation thick with the local gentry; he and his mother were in instant demand. As he was so rarely in the country these days, there were many who wanted a word with him.

Tamping down his unruly impatience—Sarah and her family were coming to lunch at the Park—he forced himself to do the socially correct thing and chat with Sir Walter Criscombe about the foxes, and with Henry Wallace about the state of the road.

Yet even while discussing the qualities of macadam, he was acutely conscious that Sarah was close. She stood a yard behind him; straining his ears, he caught snippets of her conversation with Mrs. Duncliffe, the vicar's wife.

The tenor of that conversation—about the orphanage at Crowcombe—recalled the impression he'd received at the Finsburys';

while watching Sarah dance, then standing by her side chatting to others, he'd noticed that she was respected, and often deferred to, by their peers, by the unmarried gentlemen and young ladies of their wider social circle, that her quiet assurance was admired by many.

From Mrs. Duncliffe's tone, it seemed that the older generation, too, accorded Sarah a status beyond her years. She was twenty-three, yet it seemed she'd carved a place for herself in the local community somewhat at odds with those tender years and her as-yet-unmarried state.

Precisely the right sort of status on which, as his countess, she could build. He hadn't given a thought to such aspects when fixing on her as his wife, but he knew such nebulous qualities mattered.

Finally, Henry Wallace was satisfied. They parted. Expectation surging, Charlie turned to Sarah—only to discover her father gathering his family preparatory to herding them to their waiting carriage.

Smiling, Lord Conningham nodded his way. "We'll see you shortly, Charlie."

His jaw set, but he forced a smile in reply. He caught Sarah's eye, caught the understanding quirk of her lips; he half bowed, then, his expression impassive, turned to gather his own family and head for Morwellan Park.

S arah relaxed into a comfortable armchair in the drawing room at the Park, and rendered mute thanks that neither Clary nor Gloria, nor Augusta nor Jeremy, had yet tumbled to Charlie's intention. She'd wondered if this luncheon would prove hideously awkward, but the meal had passed as over the years so many similar Sunday luncheons had, in pleasant and easy comfort.

The invitation had arrived yesterday while she'd been in Watchet with Charlie, but such short notice wasn't unusual; the Morwellans and the Conninghams had been sharing Sunday luncheons every few months for as long as she could recall. Her mother and Charlie's were contemporaries, and their childrens' ages overlapped; naturally the families, both long-standing in the area and with estates abutting, had drawn close.

Observing her parents and Charlie's mother, Serena, grouped about the fireplace and discussing some tonnish scandal, Sarah felt sure Serena, at least, knew. Or had guessed. There'd been a hint of encouragement, of a certain unvoiced hope in the way Serena had squeezed her hand when she'd arrived, in the warmth of the older woman's smile. Serena approved of Charlie's choice and would welcome Sarah as her daughter-in-law; all that had been conveyed without words. However, although comforting, the point was still moot. She had yet to learn what she needed to know.

She'd learned more about Charlie, but not the vital point. On that, she'd made very little headway.

"Sarah!" From the French door, Clary called, "We're going to walk around the lake. Do you want to come?"

She smiled, shook her head, and waved off her sisters and Augusta, one year older than Clary and shortly to embark on her first season. Jeremy had buttonholed Charlie at the other end of the room; the instant he saw the three girls step outside, Jeremy grinned, said something to Charlie, then turned and slipped out of another door, escaping while he could.

The door closed silently; Sarah's gaze had already shifted to Charlie. He glanced at their parents, engrossed in their discussion, then came down the long room to her side.

Halting, he held out a hand. His blue-gray eyes trapped hers. "Come. Let's go for a walk, too."

Sarah considered his face, his eyes; she was perfectly certain he didn't intend to join their sisters. Anticipation leaping, she put her hand in his and allowed him to pull her to her feet. "Where to?" she asked, as if only vaguely interested.

He gestured to the French doors. "Let's start with the terrace."

Without looking back—she had no need to catch any hopeful glances their parents might throw their way—she let him lead her out onto the flagstones. He waited while she hitched her shawl about her shoulders, then offered his arm. She took it, and they strolled side by side along the terrace.

Their sisters were three small figures dwindling in size as they followed the path that bordered the ornamental lake.

"Pray they don't see us and turn back."

She glanced up; Charlie, eyes narrowed, was watching the other three. Smiling, she looked ahead. "They're discussing Augusta's come-out. It would require something significantly startling to distract them from that."

He humphed. "True." He glanced at her as they continued along the terrace. "You don't appear as afflicted as the norm when it comes to feminine mania for the Season."

She shrugged. "I enjoyed my seasons well enough, but after the first blush, the balls are just balls, the parties just more glittering examples of the parties we have here. If one had a reason for being there, I suspect it might be different, but behind the glamor I found it rather empty—devoid of purpose, if you like."

He raised his brows, but made no reply.

They reached the end of the terrace; instead of turning back, he led her around the corner where the terrace continued down the south side of the house.

He glanced up at the façade beside them. "You must know this house nearly as well as I."

"I doubt anyone knows this house as well as you. Perhaps Jeremy . . ." She shook her head. "No, not even he. You grew up here; it's your home, and you always knew you would inherit it. It's Jeremy's home, but it isn't his in the same way. I'd wager you know every corner of every attic." Head tilted, she caught his eye.

He grinned. "You're right. I used to poke into every distant corner—and yes, I always knew it would be mine."

Halting before another set of French doors, he opened one, then stood back and waved her in.

"The library. I haven't been in here for years." Stepping over the threshold, she looked around. "You've redecorated."

He nodded. "This was Alathea's domain until she married, then it became mine. For some reason my father rarely came here."

She slowly pirouetted, absorbing the changes—the masculine atmosphere imparted by deeply padded armchairs covered in dark brown leather, the heavy forest-green velvet curtains framing the windows, the lack of delicate vases and lamps, the ornaments she'd grown accustomed to seeing scattered about the room during Alathea's tenure. But the sense of luxury, of pervasive wealth, was still there, carried in the rich hues in the portrait of some ancestor hanging above the fireplace, in the clean lines of the crystal decanter on the tantalus, in the large urn by the door with its transparent antiquity.

"The desk's the same." She studied the massive, wonderfully carved piece that sat across one end of the room. Its surface was lovingly polished, but the stacked papers, pens and pencils upon it bore mute witness that the space was in use.

Charlie had closed the French doors on the chill air outside. At the other end of the room a fire leapt and crackled beneath the old, carved stone mantelpiece, shedding warmth and light onto the Aubusson carpet—a new one in shades of deep greens and browns. Firelight flickered over myriad leather-bound tomes crowding the shelves lining the inner and end walls, striking glints from the gold-embossed titles.

Sarah drank it all in, then turned to where Charlie had halted before the middle of the three sets of French doors facing the terrace, the south lawn, and, in the distance, an arm of the lake. He was looking out. She moved to join him.

Turning his head, he caught her eyes, held her gaze for a moment, then asked, his voice deep, quiet, "Wouldn't you like to be mistress of all this?"

He meant the house, the grounds, the estate. His home. But she wanted to be mistress of so much more.

She searched his eyes, their regard unwavering. Inwardly she quivered in reaction to his tone, and to his question. The answer rang clearly in her mind, but how to voice it?

"Yes." Lifting her head, she stiffened her resistance against the temptation being this close to him posed. "*But* . . . that's not enough."

He frowned. "What—"

"What I want . . ." She blinked, suddenly seeing a way to explain. "Consider—when you invest, you require both the risky and challenging as well as the safe and secure to feel satisfied, to feel fulfilled. When it comes to marriage, I want the same." She held his gaze. "Not just the conventional, the mundane—the safe and sure—but . . ."

She ran out of words, had no words, not ones that would do the concept justice. In the end, she simply said, "I want the excitement, the thrills, to take the risk and grasp the satisfaction. I want to experience the glory."

Thanks to years of maintaining an unreadable expression while engaged in business dealings, Charlie kept all trace of surprise from his face. She was an innocent twenty-three, untouched; he knew that to his bones. Yet unless his ears had failed him, she'd just stipulated that were she to marry him, in order for her to be satisfied, their marriage would need to be a passionate one.

And, by extension, if that point was influencing her decision, then presumably part of her "getting to know him better" involved assessing whether a liaison between them would spark such passion, resulting in the glory she sought.

He hadn't been expecting such a tack, but he certainly wasn't about to argue. He let his lips curve. "I see no impediment in that."

She frowned. "You don't?"

He assumed the question derived from lack of self-confidence, from lack of conviction that she—her fair self—could fire his passions in that way.

Given his reputation, all of it entirely deserved, that wasn't, perhaps, such a nonsensical uncertainty.

It was, however, as he was perfectly—indeed painfully—aware, entirely groundless.

He reached for her, careful not to seize, not to give her nerves reason to leap too much; sliding his hands around her waist, he encouraged her nearer.

She came, hesitantly. What he sensed in her . . . his instincts saw her as wild, skittish, untamed—unused to a man's hand. Untouched in the truest sense. And he wanted her, desired her with a passion remarkable in its sharpness, unique in its strength.

Ruthlessly he held it down, concealed it, suppressed it. He held her gaze. "Whatever you want in that regard, I'm willing to give you."

She searched his eyes. Moistened her lips. "I—"

"But of course you want to ascertain the prospect before you agree." He had to fight to keep his gaze from fixing on her sheening lips.

Her eyes widened; relief slid through them. "Yes."

Smiling, he lowered his head. "As I said before, I see no impediment in that. None at all." He breathed the last words over her lips.

Her lids fluttered, then fell. He brushed her lips with his, lightly, tantalizingly, then swooped and took them in a long, easy, unthreatening kiss, a caress specifically designed to ease her trepidations, to calm any maidenly fears. To gently, so gently she wouldn't notice it, sweep her away.

He tempted, lured, and she came, hesitant but willing, following his lead as fraction by tiniest fraction he deepened the caress. Her lips were as pliant, as delicate as he remembered; he held his breath as with the tip of his tongue he traced the lower, then gently probed . . . her lips parted on a sigh and she let him in.

Let him slide his tongue into the warm haven of her mouth, find hers and stroke.

Tantalized, fascinated, enthralled.

Her, yes, but him, too; despite his experience he wasn't immune to the moment. Wasn't above feeling a shiver of excitement as she oh-so-tentatively returned the caress.

Sarah's head was spinning, her wits waltzing to a luxurious, decadent beat, one built on pleasure. It swelled and burgeoned and grew more demanding as the kiss lengthened, deepened, as he and his seductive magic slid under her skin and stroked.

Her senses purred.

The taste of him spread through her, intoxicatingly male, dangerous yet tempting. Her lips felt warm as she returned his kisses, increasingly bold, increasingly sure.

Increasingly convinced that through this, she would find her answer.

She was hovering on the brink of stretching her arms up, twining them about his neck and stepping into him, wanting to touch, oddly urgent to feel the hard length of him against her, when he broke the kiss.

Not as if he wished to; when she lifted her strangely weighted lids, she sensed as much as saw his sudden alertness as he looked over her head out of the window.

Then his lovely, mobile lips tightened. Under his breath, he swore.

He looked at her, met her eyes. "Our sisters."

Disgust dripped from the words. She glanced toward the lake, and grimaced, her emotions matching his. Having circumnavigated the lake, the three girls were marching steadily nearer—heading for the terrace alongside the library. Any minute one of them would look ahead . . .

"Come." Charlie lowered his arms.

She felt oddly bereft.

His hand at her elbow, he turned her deeper into the library. "We'll have to go back."

He guided her to the door to the corridor; for one instant she considered suggesting they adjourn to some less visible room, but . . . she sighed. "You're right. If we don't, they'll come searching."

3

Neatly garbed in her apple-green riding habit, Sarah trotted down the manor drive on the back of her chestnut, Blacktail, so named because of the glorious appendage that swished in expectation as she passed through the gates and turned north along the road.

The day was fine, the sun shining weakly, the air cool but still. She was about to urge Blacktail into a canter when the sound of hoofbeats approaching from the south reached her.

Along with a hail. "Sarah!"

Reining in, she turned in the saddle; she smiled as Charlie cantered up. He was once again on his raking gray hunter; the horse's deep chest and heavy hindquarters made Blacktail, an average-sized hack, look delicate. As always, Charlie managed the powerful gray with absentminded ease; he drew up alongside her.

His gaze swept her face, lingered on her lips for an instant, then rose to her eyes. "Perfect—I was thinking of riding to the bridge over the falls. I was wondering if you'd like to come with me."

To spend some time alone with me. Sarah understood his intention; the bridge over the falls that spilled from Will's Neck, the highest point in the Quantocks, was a local lookout. She grimaced ruefully. "I can ride with you a little way, but Monday's the day I spend at the orphanage. I'm on my way there. We have a committee meeting at ten o'clock that I have to attend."

She tapped her heel to Blacktail's side. He started to walk. Charlie's gray kept pace while his master frowned.

"The orphange above Crowcombe?" Charlie recalled the discussion he'd overheard between Mrs. Duncliffe and Sarah outside the church. He dragged the name from his memory. "Quilley Farm." He glanced at Sarah. "Is that the one?"

She nodded. "Yes. I own it—the farmhouse and the land."

Inwardly he frowned harder. He should have paid more attention to local happenings over the years. "I thought . . . wasn't it Lady Cricklade's?"

Sarah's lips curved. "Yes. She was my godmother. She died three years ago and left the orphanage, house and land, as well as some funds, to me, along with the responsibility of keeping it functioning as she'd intended it should." She shook her reins. "I'll need to ride on or I'll be late."

Charlie set Storm to pace her chestnut as they shifted into a canter. "Do you mind if I come, too?" He glanced at Sarah, trying to read her face. "I should learn about the orphanage."

She threw him an assessing, rather measuring look, then nodded. "If you wish." Facing forward, she increased the pace.

He went with her, Storm matching the chestnut's stride easily. "So who else is on this committee?"

"Aside from myself and my mother—she doesn't always attend—there's Mr. Skeggs, the solicitor from Crowcombe, and Mrs. Duncliffe. Skeggs, Mrs. Duncliffe, and I are the core committee—we oversee things week to week. Mr. Handley, the mayor of Watchet, and Mr. Kempset, the town clerk of Taunton, attend once, at the end of each year, or if we summon them."

Charlie nodded. "How large is the orphanage?"

"We've thirty-one children at present, ranging from babes to a few thirteen-year-olds. Once they reach fourteen, we find employment for them in Watchet or Taunton." Sarah glanced at him. "Most come from one or the other of those towns. There's so many factories in Taunton these days, and therefore more accidents, leaving children without fathers and too often their mothers starve, or fall ill and die, too. And from Watchet and the coast, we get those left when fishermen and sailors are lost at sea."

"So you've been involved with the orphanage for the last three years?"

"For longer than that. Lady Cricklade was one of Mama's closest friends. Her husband died soon after they were married, and she had no children. She and Mama set up the orphanage many years ago. Lady Cricklade always intended to leave Quilley Farm to me, so she and Mama made sure I knew all about it—I've been going to Quilley Farm almost every Monday for as long as I can recall."

The roofs of Crowcombe appeared ahead. The lane leading up to Quilley Farm joined the road just before the first house. They turned up the lane; it was wide enough for them to ride side by side as it climbed steadily, until eventually it gave onto the plateau that was Quilley Farm.

"How big is the farm?" Charlie asked.

Now on flat ground, they trotted toward the farmhouse that rose before them. Built of local red sandstone worn pink with the years, its long front façade was planted squarely east, facing the Quantocks across the valley. It boasted two stories in stone, with the attics above half-timbered. The roof was gray slate, common in those parts. The structure looked old but strong, secure, as if over the years its foundations had settled into the earth under the weight of the thick stone walls. A wide cleared space, lightly graveled, lay before the house. Fields stretched to either side.

"To the south, the farm extends to that stream." Sarah pointed down a long slope to where a line of trees marked the banks of a small brook. "But to the north not so far, just to Squire Mack's fields two fences over."

She waved over the roof to the rocky hillside looming behind the house—a part of the western end of the Brendon Hills. "At the back, there are three wings, unfortunately not as solid as the main house. Beyond them, we've only got space for kitchen gardens and a narrow patch for animals before the hill rises too steeply even for grazing."

Sheltered by a shallow porch, the front door stood dead center in the long façade, with wooden-shuttered windows in perfect symmetry on either side. Sarah and Charlie dismounted and tied their reins to the rail set beside the porch. A gig with a placid mare dozing between the shafts was tied up at one side of the forecourt; Sarah nodded toward it. "Mrs. Duncliffe's already here."

Stripping off her gloves, she headed for the door. Charlie glanced back and around, at the village of Crowcombe nestling some hundred feet below, then at the rising face of the Quantocks. From this elevation with the valley hidden in the dip between, the hills appeared closer.

Sarah lifted the door latch. Turning, Charlie followed her through the door—into bedlam.

Or so it seemed. Eight small children, boys and girls both, had been traversing the front hall in a more or less orderly file, but the instant they saw Sarah, all order deserted them. Bright smiles lit their faces; as one they detoured to mill about her.

They all talked at once.

It took Charlie, also trapped in the knee-high melee, a minute to attune his ears to the high-pitched babble, but Sarah reacted with aplomb. She patted two heads, asked one boy if he'd lost his tooth yet—the answer was yes as he promptly demonstrated with a gap-toothed smile—then she waved her arms and effectively herded the gaggle back into the clutches of a thin woman who'd been following in the children's wake.

The woman smiled at Sarah; her eyes widened as she took in Charlie, but then she turned and shooed her charges down a corridor. "The others are in the office waiting," she said to Sarah as she passed.

"Thank you, Jeannie." Sarah waved to the last of the children, then made for a door to the right. Reaching for the latch, she glanced at Charlie. "Would you like to sit in on the meeting, or"—she nodded in the children's wake—"look around?"

Charlie held her gaze. "If you don't mind, I'd like to listen to the discussions. I can look around later."

She smiled. "I don't mind." Her lips quirked. "You might even learn something."

As he followed her into the room, he wondered how he should take that comment, but the truth was he did feel compelled to learn more about the orphanage. Although it lay beyond his boundaries, he was nevertheless the senior nobleman in the area; in certain respects it fell within his purlieu, yet he knew very little of it—how the orphanage ran, under whose auspices, where their funding came from, and so on. All were things he ought to know, but didn't.

That the orphanage was legally Sarah's, and she involved herself in the running of it, made his continued ignorance even less acceptable.

The room was a well-furnished office with two desks, one large, one small, and various chairs and cabinets. In the center stood a round table at which Mrs. Duncliffe and Mr. Skeggs sat; as Sarah entered they broke off what had plainly been a social conversation to smile in welcome.

When they saw him behind Sarah, surprise entered their eyes, but the welcome remained.

He knew them both; they exchanged greetings, shook hands, then he held a chair for Sarah. Once she'd sat, he lifted another chair and set it beside hers, a little back from the table. He smiled at Skeggs and Mrs. Duncliffe. "I hope you don't mind, but I'd like to get some idea of how the orphanage is run."

Both assured him they had no objection to his presence; while Mrs. Duncliffe certainly wondered over his motivation, Skeggs was almost touchingly delighted.

"The more locals of standing who associate themselves with our effort, the better." The anemic solicitor beamed. He straightened a small stack of papers before him and adjusted the pince-nez balanced on his thin nose. "Now . . ."

Charlie sat back and listened as the three discussed various aspects of the day-to-day running of the orphanage. He learned that they bought most of their perishables in Watchet, with vegetables, grains, meat, and fish brought in by cart twice a week. For manufactured goods they turned to Taunton; Sarah consulted a list and declared there was nothing urgent enough to warrant sending the cart south just yet.

As the meeting progressed, dealing with the children's requirements—clothes, shoes, books, and so on—Charlie detected no funding constraints over such matters, but when it came to the fabric of the orphanage, a different sort of limitation emerged.

"Now," Sarah said, "Kennett has had a look at the leaks in the south wing. He says the thatch is worn. We'll have to get the thatchers to come and fix it." She grimaced.

Mrs. Duncliffe sighed. "I do wish we could get the wings better roofed. This is the third time we've had to bring the thatchers in over the past year, and that thatch is not getting any younger."

Glancing at Charlie, Sarah caught his eye. "All three wings are thatched. We've had Hendricks, the local builder, in to look at replacing the thatch with slate, but he said that we'd need to replace the whole roof—all the timbers and joists—in order to support the weight of the slate, but then the walls won't hold the additional weight. The walls in the wings are mostly lath and plaster—only their foundations are stone."

Charlie nodded. "That's why so many thatched cottages remain thatched. No way to replace the roof without replacing the walls and lintels—which amounts to replacing the entire building."

Skeggs grunted. "So." He made a note. "I'll send for the thatchers."

"Meanwhile," Sarah said, "let's pray it doesn't rain."

The meeting continued; Charlie listened and learned. By the time the committee adjourned, he had a basic knowledge of the workings of the orphanage. He rose and followed the committee members from the room. Sarah farewelled the others in the front hall; with a nod to him, Mrs. Duncliffe and Skeggs left, Mrs. Duncliffe to drive the tall thin solicitor down to his office in Crowcombe before heading south to the vicarage at Combe Florey.

Closing the front door behind them, Sarah turned to Charlie. "It's almost time for luncheon. I usually stay for the rest of the day—there's always plenty to do, and it gives me a chance to catch up with the staff, and the children, too."

She tried to read his face but, as usual, his expression gave her no hint as to his thoughts. In the dim hall, his eyes were shadowed; she could, however, feel his gaze on her face.

"Would you mind if I stayed, too?" There was a touch of diffidence in his tone, as if he feared she might think the request too encroaching.

Instead, the evidence of sensitivity reassured her. She smiled. "If you're willing to endure luncheon with a tribe of noisy children, then by all means stay. But there's various things I must do later—it'll be hours before I can leave."

He shrugged, lips curving. "I'm sure I'll be able to find something to fill the hours." His smile deepened as they turned to the corridor leading to the dining room. The sound of the children filing in was already swelling to a cacophony. "Besides," he murmured as they neared the open door, "I'll have the ride home with you—alone with you—to look forward to."

He met her eyes as she glanced up, trapped them; she was suddenly conscious of how close they stood, coming together in the doorway. For one instant, despite the noise assailing her ears, she was more aware of him—of his strength, potent and palpable as with one hand he held back the heavy door, of his maleness, carried in the heat that reached for her as their bodies passed mere inches apart.

Her lungs had tightened, but she managed a smile—a light, gentle one in return—as she inclined her head in acknowledgment of his gallantry and stepped over the threshold.

Mrs. Carter—Katy—principal cook and chief caretaker, saw Charlie and quickly laid another place at the staff table at one side of the room. A motherly woman of middle age with no children of her own, left alone when her sailor husband had been lost at sea, Katy had been Lady Cricklade's choice to manage the orphanage; over the years, Sarah had had ample reason to bless her late godmother's judgment.

Sarah led Charlie to the table, indicated that he should take the chair beside hers, then introduced him to the others as, one by one, after herding their charges in and seeing them settled at the long refectory tables lined up across the room, they came to take their seats.

Miss Emma Quince, known as Quince to all, eyed Charlie severely, but bent enough to incline her head when Sarah explained that she kept the books and oversaw all repairs to the house, furniture, and furnishings. "Which," Sarah said, "in an establishment such as this is a rather more demanding role than the norm."

Quince smiled thinly, but thereafter kept her eyes on her plate.

"Quince spends most of her time looking after the babies," Sarah continued. "And Lily here helps."

Lily Posset, a bright vivacious girl, once a charge of the orphanage herself, beamed at Charlie, clearly appreciating his sartorial elegance. He smiled and nodded down the table to her. Although he didn't look her way again, Lily kept darting quick glances his way; Sarah pretended not to notice.

Jeannie joined them and took her seat with a quiet hello. She was followed by a lumbering ox of a man who subsided into the chair beside her.

Sarah introduced Kennett, the man-of-all-work, a beefy, brawny hulking man who hid his soft heart behind a perpetual scowl—which fooled no one, the children least of all. "Kennett also takes care of all our animals."

Charlie raised his brows at Kennett. "What do you run?"

"Only what we can use," Kennett growled. "Cows for milk, goats and sheep for wool and meat. Ain't no room for more. We use the fields for grains and cabbages—you wouldn't believe how much this lot can get through in a winter."

"And Jim here," Sarah broke in, indicating the youth who'd slipped into the chair next to Kennett, "is our lad about the house. He helps everyone with everything, errands, fetching and carrying, feeding the animals."

Jim beamed back at her; he nodded to Charlie, then gave his attention to the rich stew Mrs. Carter ladled onto his plate.

The last of the staff to join them was Joseph Tiller. Sarah smiled at him as, with a smile for her and a careful nod to Charlie, he drew out his customary chair next to Katy. Dark haired, pale skinned, Joseph was good-looking in a reserved and gentle way; despite his quiet reserve, Katy, Sarah, Jeannie, and Quince were convinced he was far gone in worship of Lily. They were all hoping that at some point he would get up enough courage to ask Lily, at the very least, to walk with him when they escorted the children to church.

"Joseph Tiller—Lord Meredith." Sarah waited while Joseph, after a second's hesitation, reached over the table and grasped Charlie's proffered hand. Sarah wasn't sure how Charlie had known Joseph was a gentleman, but . . . "Joseph comes to us from the Bishop of Wells. The orphanage operates under the bishop's auspices. Joseph helps teach the children, especially the older boys."

Charlie smiled sympathetically. "Not an easy task, I imagine."

Joseph's lips quirked as he sat. "Not generally, no, but there are compensations."

Mrs. Carter banged her spoon on the saucepan's lid and the children abruptly fell silent. Joseph bowed his head and said grace, his voice firm and sure rolling out over the bent heads.

The instant he said "Amen" a whoop erupted; noise exploded and engulfed the room. Reaching for his fork, Charlie raised his brows.

Joseph met his eyes and smiled. "Always happens."

The meal passed in the usual distracted fashion with various staff members having to rise and settle disputes and arguments among their vociferous charges. But neither maliciousness nor anger intruded; there was no tension, only a sense of fun and an undercurrent of content.

Every Monday when she sat among them for the meal, Sarah found reassurance in that supportive atmosphere; that was why her god-mother had established the orphanage, and why she continued to de-vote to it so much of her time.

As the last dollops of custard were scraped from bowls, Charlie turned to her and grinned. "They're a lively lot. They remind me of an enormous family."

She smiled back, then patted her lips with her napkin and laid it aside. "That's exactly what we work to achieve." She wasn't surprised that he'd grasped that; like her, he came from a large family.

Many of the children had already left, some of the staff as well. She rose and Charlie rose with her. "I have to speak with Quince—we need to do an inventory of the linens. It'll take a few hours."

He shrugged. "I'll just wander and wait."

Joseph, rising from his chair opposite, glanced at Sarah, then looked at Charlie. "I promised I'd organize a game of bat and ball for the older lads once they finish their arithmetic. That'll be in about half an hour. If you have the time, perhaps you'd like to join us?"

Charlie grinned. "Why not?"

Sarah excused herself and left them. She had difficulty imagining Charlie, always so precise and elegant, playing bat and ball, at least not the way the older boys played it. They always looked like they'd been dragged through a hedge backward when they came in after their game; even Joseph usually ended badly rumpled.

But, she reflected, Charlie could look out for himself.

Determinedly she mounted the stairs to the attics. She had Quince, and what would no doubt prove to be stacks of torn and worn linens, to deal with.

For the next hour, she and Quince worked through the various piles, checking and noting. They always used the big attic nursery for the chore; the cradles in which Quince's charges lay were neatly ar-ranged at one end—six of them at the moment, more than usual—but there was plenty of room between the cradles and the neat truckle bed on which Quince passed her nights.

While Quince, thin and bony, with her severe expression, tightly restrained hair, and outwardly acid temper, might have seemed an odd choice as nursemaid, Sarah had often seen her face soften, her eyes fill with a soft light when she rocked one of the tightly wrapped bundles. The babies responded to that glow, and cared nothing for her appearance. No one was better with infants than Quince.

In the quiet of the nursery, she and Quince sat and sorted.

Later they were joined by Katy and Jeannie. As "the linens" included all the napery as well as towels, sheets, and napkins, it was a major undertaking to examine each piece, placing those requiring mending to one side and those requiring extra bleaching in another pile, and reluctantly setting aside those beyond repair or resuscitation to be used for rags.

The size of the pile for mending was always daunting.

"Jeannie?" Lily's voice floated up the stairs. "Your lot are stirring."

"Coming!" Jeannie set down the towel she'd been folding and hurried out. She took care of the toddlers who'd been put down for their afternoon nap. Lily, who was working with the older girls, had been watching over them.

"I'd better get on, too." Katy hauled herself out of the old armchair she'd sunk into. "Time to get started on supper."

Sarah looked up from the mending pile and smiled. "I'll be leaving once I've finished stacking these. I'll ask Jim to drop them off at the manor tomorrow, and I'll share them out for mending."

"Aye." Katy nodded. Turning for the stairs, she glanced out of the window, and halted. "Well now, if that ain't a sight."

Sarah looked up, then rose and went to join her. She followed Katy's gaze to where the older boys, and some of those not so old—and two much older—were playing bat and ball on the forecourt.

"They usually play at the back," she murmured.

"Too many of 'em, today." Quince had come to stand beside Sarah. "Looks like they've made up proper teams."

Sarah watched as Charlie lobbed the ball, and Maggs, who was holding the bat, whacked it to the side. To much hooting and cheering, while fielders scampered after the ball, Maggs dashed to where a peg was stuck in the ground; rounding it, he hared back to touch another peg near where he'd started with the bat.

Retrieving the ball, Toby, another of the older lads, threw it to

Charlie. The throw went rather wild. Leaping high, Charlie plucked the ball from the air. He tossed it in his palm. He fixed Maggs with a fierce look—but he was grinning. He called something to Maggs, then bowled again.

Katy said something and with a laugh headed downstairs. One of the babies stirred and Quince went to tend it. Sarah remained by the window looking down. The nursery was high under the eaves, the lead-paned windows shaded by the overhang. No one in the forecourt could see her as she stood and watched. And wondered.

What she was seeing wasn't something she'd thought to assess as part of her decision whether or not to marry Charlie. Yet she wanted children—yes, definitely—and a husband who could give himself over to a simple boys' game as Charlie was . . . that was certainly a point she should consider.

Indeed, not only was he patently immersed in the game, sharing the moment with the boys and with Joseph, too—the other man was smiling more widely than Sarah had thought possible—but he'd sacrificed his elegance, it seemed, without a qualm.

He'd removed his hacking jacket. His shirttails were hanging out; he'd rolled his sleeves halfway up his forearms and his neatly tied cravat was nowhere in sight. Nor was his waistcoat.

It was a severely rumpled Charlie who bowled the next ball—who leapt into the air and cheered as Maggs hit it straight to Toby and was caught out. Sarah watched as the boys crowded around, as Charlie tousled Toby's hair and called some compliment to Maggs, who glowed even while he handed the bat to Toby.

Sarah watched for ten minutes more. When she eventually retreated to finish folding the linens, she was pensive.

They left the orphanage half an hour later. The game had been over by the time Sarah had gone downstairs. She'd found Charlie talking with Joseph while they watched the boys finish their chores in the kitchen garden.

Joseph had still been rumpled but Charlie had made an effort to regain his customary style. While his cravat, redonned, would never pass muster in any ton drawing room, it was neat enough for country fields. From the darkened curls about his face, Sarah had concluded that he'd washed; he'd certainly made some effort to smooth his ruffled hair.

Her fingers had itched to run through the heavy locks and disarrange them again.

Instead, she'd smiled, bid Joseph and the boys good-bye, then led the way around the house to where their horses waited.

Before she could lead Blacktail to the mounting block, Charlie took the reins from her gloved grasp, then closed his hands about her waist and lifted her up to her saddle.

Her breathing suspended. She looked down and busied herself settling her boot in the stirrup. That done, she looked up, managed a weak smile, and accepted the reins from him.

By the time he'd untied his gray and swung up to the wide back, she had herself in hand again. She pointed due south to the stream. "I usually ride home across the fields—it's faster."

Eyes narrowing, Charlie followed the faint line of a bridle path that led to the stream.

"There's a place where the stream's easy to jump." Setting Blacktail's nose homeward, she tapped her heel to his side. "Come on."

She went and Charlie followed. When they came within sight of the place to jump the stream, he ranged alongside her.

They jumped together, both horses fluidly covering the distance from one bank to the other. She laughed, gripped by unexpected delight, then veered to the west into the lee of the Brendons, following the bridle path as it skirted the backs of various farmers' fields, cutting along the lower levels of the slope rising to their right.

She kept Blacktail to a steady, ground-eating pace. The gray thundered beside her, equally surefooted. She glanced briefly at Charlie. "The path's clear—no holes or roots."

He nodded.

The afternoon was waning, the light fading. It was not yet dusk; at this pace, they would reach the manor before the light became uncertain, but Charlie had to ride another two miles more to reach the Park.

They swept on side by side. The dull thudding of hooves echoed the thudding in her blood, an insistent, steadily escalating tattoo. It rang in her ears, in her fingertips, while the wind of their passage whipped her cheeks and set them, and her, glowing.

She'd ridden this way countless times, and some of those times she'd galloped even faster. It wasn't simply the speed that was feeding the undeniable exhilaration within her.

Stride matching stride, they swung down off the path onto another leading to the back of the manor. They clattered into the stable yard, iron-shod hooves ringing on the cobbles, a peculiar delight bubbling in her veins.

Her senses were singing. She couldn't stop grinning.

Charlie swung down, came and lifted her down; for an instant he held her close, protected by his body as the horses milled about them. Then the stable lads were there, grasping reins.

"Just walk him," Charlie called to the lad gathering his gray's reins. "I'll be off again shortly."

His gaze hadn't shifted from her face. Releasing her, he took her hand. "I'll walk you to the house."

She nodded, unable to decide what the light in his eyes meant, what the tension she could feel through his grip on her hand portended.

The horses were led away. Charlie strode for the stable entrance, drawing her with him. Under the arch he paused, looking across the stretch of lawn shaded by large trees that separated the house from the stables.

Puzzled, she looked, too, wondering.

Beneath his breath he muttered an oath, and abruptly towed her in a different direction, along the front of the stables and around the corner. He ducked under the low-hanging branches of a fir—then he halted, turned, pulled her into his arms, and kissed her.

Ravenously.

The triumphant delight bubbling in her veins sizzled, fizzed and rose, rose to wreathe through her brain and pleasurably sweep her wits away. Leaving a sense of certainty in its wake.

His lips were hard, commanding. She met them, met his demands, thrilled that she could.

More, that he could want her like this—with just a touch of wildness in the wanting. That he could desire her as he so patently did . . .

She hadn't thought of that, hadn't dreamt of desire, of him desiring her, but she couldn't think now, could only appease the hunger in him, and let him seed her own.

Her lips had parted of their own volition; he'd taken advantage on the instant and claimed her mouth. Claimed her in some way; she felt the possessivness in his touch as he backed her, as she sensed the brick wall of the stable behind her and his hand rose to cradle her face, to hold it steady at just the right angle so he could deepen the kiss.

The steely arm about her waist tightened. Her toes curled.

She gripped his shoulders, clung, intrigued, and kissed him back, unrestrainedly following his lead.

Two heartbeats later, things changed. The tenor of the kiss altered, gentled, as if he were reining himself—them—in, as if what had already passed between them had taken the edge from his—their—hunger, and now that desperate edge was gone, he—they—could savor.

Could appreciate, could sink deeper into the kiss and wallow.

He didn't let her go; his hold didn't ease in the slightest. He continued to kiss her, to indulge her and himself with long, languid caresses.

Simply because he wanted to.

That last was clear, a truth undeniably etched in her mind when he finally raised his head, and on a sigh released hers. He brushed a thumb across her lower lip, then let her go and stepped back, retaking her hand.

He didn't smile. "Come. I'll walk you to the door."

She managed a wobbly smile in acquiescence, and let him lead her back into the world. Ducking under the fir tree's branches, she went with him across the lawn. Reaching the side door, he opened it, and stood back. She stepped to the threshold, then turned back to him.

He bowed over her hand, effortlessly graceful, then released it. He met her eyes briefly and saluted her. "I'll see you tomorrow evening."

He barely waited for her nod before turning and striding back toward the stable.

Sarah stood in the doorway and watched him go. And reflected that the revelations of the day had left her with quite a few things to ponder.

4

❧

Casleigh, Lord Martin Cynster's house, was a huge, rambling country mansion filled with antiques and furnished in exquisite luxury; on Tuesday night, Charlie moved through the guests gathered in its drawing room, and saw nothing of the house's beauties.

He'd spent Monday evening and most of that day clarifying in his mind the framework of the life he expected to live once Sarah agreed to be his—the months in London filled with endeavors similar to those he'd enjoyed for the past decade, broken by the occasional trip to the country to check on the Park and the estate. That was how he'd envisaged it would be, but how to fit Sarah's devotion to the orphanage into such a pattern was more than he'd been able to see. He'd paced, and considered, and in the end had consigned the problem to the future. To be dealt with later.

After Sarah had agreed to be his wife.

His impatience on that score was steadily escalating.

Pausing beside those who hailed him, while chatting and smiling with practiced ease, he raked the throng, searching for her. She was there, somewhere among the guests; they'd been seated beside each other at dinner, but neither then nor earlier, when she'd arrived with her family and they'd met in the drawing room, had they had any chance for a private word.

Or a private anything else.

That kiss behind the stable, driven by frustration as it had been, had served only to further whet an appetite that hadn't needed further whetting.

He heard her laugh. Without pausing to wonder how among the crowd of females encircling him he could so unhesitatingly identify a single laughing note, he changed course, and then saw her. She was standing to one side of the room smiling sweetly at a gentleman he didn't know.

The sight gave him pause. Stepping free of the milling guests, he stood by the wall opposite and over the sea of heads studied the gentleman. He was relating some tale to which Sarah, tonight gowned in blue silk the color of her eyes, was listening attentively, yet even from this distance Charlie could tell that she was being polite and welcoming, but nothing more.

When she looked at *him* . . .

He didn't need to be jealous, thank heavens, but in other circumstances the gentleman would have rated as one to discourage. He was . . . it took a full minute before Charlie realized that he was viewing a gentleman remarkably like himself.

Tall, broad-shouldered, a touch heavier in the chest, but the man was a few years older, late thirties, Charlie guessed, to his own thirty-three, accounting for that. The man's hair was a touch fairer, straight where Charlie's was wavy, but with a similar gilded sheen.

His manner was likewise assured, yet he appeared more reserved, a touch aloof, tending not to cloak his arrogance, born of superiority; he seemed unable, or unwilling, to summon the glib and ready charm Charlie habitually employed.

"There you are!"

Charlie looked around as his eldest sister—half sister to be precise—resplendent in figured amber silk, glided up and slipped a hand through his arm.

Alathea smiled as, beside him, she faced the room. "I need to have a word with you."

Charlie stiffened.

"Don't get on your high horse. I have some advice to impart that it would pay you to hear, but once you've heard it, whether you take it or not is up to you."

Charlie inwardly sighed. Alathea was ten years older than he and in many ways more alarming than his mother. Serena was comfortable; Alathea rarely was. Yet he would never cease to be grateful for all she'd done for him in the past, an emotion she exploited with feminine ruthlessness whenever he proved difficult. "What is it?"

"As it appears you've finally decided to choose a wife, I thought a simple stating of the obvious wouldn't go amiss, you being male and, of them all, peculiarly inclined to think you rule your world."

Charlie suppressed his frown. Arguing would only prolong the lecture.

"Indeed," Alathea murmured, her gaze on his face.

From the corner of his eye, he saw her brows had risen haughtily, as if she'd read his thoughts. She probably had. She was married to Gabriel, and he and Gabriel rarely differed—except on the subject she wished to discuss.

Girding his mental loins, he said nothing.

Eyes narrowing, Alathea again faced the crowd, and went on, "Regardless of the fashionable norm, there have never in living memory been anything but love matches in our family—and no, I don't mean the Cynsters, although the same is true for them."

Charlie noticed that her gaze had fixed on her husband, Gabriel Cynster, who had moved to join Sarah and the unknown gentleman. It was patently clear Gabriel knew him.

"All the Morwellan males"—Alathea's voice continued from beside him—"have for centuries married for love, and you would be well advised to think very carefully about the whys and wherefores of that before you plunge ahead and without due consideration break that tradition."

A moment passed. Charlie, his attention fixed across the room, eventually realized Alathea expected some response. "Yes, all right."

Even though his gaze was elsewhere, he felt her glare.

Ignoring it, he demanded, "Who's that speaking with Gabriel?"

Alathea glared anew, then looked across the room, then back at Charlie. "Some gentleman investor Rupert invited—a Mr. Sinclair. Apparently he's thinking of settling in the area."

Charlie didn't take his eyes from the group—Gabriel, Sinclair, and Sarah. Especially Sarah as her smile brightened; ever since Gabriel had joined them, she'd relaxed. Charlie narrowed his eyes. "Is that so?"

Alathea looked across the room, then back at him. He didn't meet her gaze; lifting her hand from his sleeve, he squeezed her fingers, then released them. "Excuse me."

He cut a determined path through the crowd.

Alathea watched him go. Watched as he circled to come up beside Sarah, between her and Sinclair, effectively cutting Sarah off from the man. Alathea continued observing as Gabriel introduced Charlie, and he and Sinclair shook hands, as Charlie glanced at Sarah and offered his arm—she saw Sarah's expression as she took it, saw Charlie's expression ease as, Sarah's hand on his arm, he turned to Sinclair.

Across the room, Alathea smiled. "Well, well, little brother. Perhaps you don't need that warning after all."

Satisfied, she returned to her duties as cohostess.

Charlie, meanwhile, was as intrigued as he sensed Gabriel was with their new neighbor. Gabriel's introduction—"Mr. Malcolm Sinclair, a major investor heavily involved in the new railways"—had been enough to grab Charlie's attention. It transpired that Sinclair had rented Finley House just outside Crowcombe and was considering relocating permanently to the district.

"I find it a particularly restful area," Sinclair said. "Gently rolling hills, green valleys, and the sea not far away."

"It's very pretty in spring, when all the hedges and trees are covered in blossom," Sarah said.

"I noticed the orphanage above Crowcombe—Quilley Farm, I believe it's called." Sinclair's hazel eyes rested on Sarah's face. "I understand you own the farm, Miss Conningham."

"Yes," Sarah replied. "It was left me by my late godmother. She had a great interest in such works."

Sinclair smiled briefly, polite and distant, and let the subject drop. Now he was close, Charlie felt even more reassured; Sinclair seemed a cold fish, at least when it came to young ladies.

On investments, however . . .

He caught Sinclair's eye. "I believe I saw you in Watchet. You were with Skilling, the land agent."

Sinclair's thin lips curved. "Ah, yes—I was interested in that parcel of land, but I understand you've been before me."

Charlie grinned. He searched, but there was nothing in Sinclair's eyes or expression to suggest any significant gnashing of teeth. Given Sinclair's reputation as a major backer of some of the new railways, he would no doubt have shrugged and moved on to consider the next item on his investment agenda.

Naturally, Charlie wondered what that was. "How do you read the potential of the district in terms of investment?"

"As I'm sure you know," Sinclair said, "there's every likelihood that the trade through Watchet will substantially increase. I understand there's talk of several new factories in Taunton, and . . ."

With a smile and a nod, Gabriel moved away. He could learn all he wanted to know from Charlie later.

Charlie continued to discuss the future with Sinclair, in general terms as investors were wont to do, not mentioning specific projects they themselves were considering; no sense tipping off the possible competition. The scope of the discussion rapidly expanded to include the country as a whole; Charlie was keen to learn more about the evolving railways—a subject on which Sinclair was both knowledgeable and willing to talk—but their discussion held no interest for Sarah. Her attention was wandering.

Despite his keenness to interrogate Sinclair, having Sarah so close left Charlie highly aware of her. And of their courtship, the wooing he hadn't yet managed to facilitate to any great degree.

If he was to gain anything out of the evening, then he had to act now.

He smiled easily at Sinclair. "I would dearly like to hear more about your experiences with the railways. It seems we'll have ample opportunity to further our acquaintance. I'll look out for you now that I know you're in the area."

Sinclair inclined his head. "Indeed, and I'll be interested in hearing your views on the local economy in due course." His gaze went past Charlie to Sarah; he bowed. "Miss Conningham."

Sarah smiled and they parted from Sinclair.

Charlie turned her down the room. She glanced at him, curiosity in her eyes. "Are we going somewhere?"

"Yes." He lowered his head and murmured, "I thought we should spend some time together in surroundings conducive to courtship."

"Ah." Facing forward, she nodded; her tone indicated she was entirely willing. He steered her to one of the drawing room's secondary
doors. "Where are we going?"

"You'll see." The only place that would ensure privacy was the ga-
zebo tucked away at the bottom of the garden, but it was late February
and her shawl was too lightweight. He opted for the back parlor instead.

When he opened the parlor door, the room proved to be unlit and
unoccupied. He stood back; Sarah walked confidently—even eagerly—
into the room. Winter moonlight poured in through the uncurtained
windows, crisp and silver-bright; it was easy to avoid the furniture.

Halting in the room's center, Sarah heard the door shut softly behind her. "So—what should we talk about?"

She turned—and found herself in Charlie's arms, found herself
drawn to him as they closed around her. Without thought she lifted
her face as he lowered his head—and their lips met.

Touched, brushed, then melded. Hers parted; he took advantage,
took control, and swept her, unresisting it was true, into a passionate
exchange.

An increasingly passionate encounter. Conversation was clearly
not on his mind, not a feature of his immediate agenda.

Exploration of a different sort was. Communication on another
plane.

And in that, she was as eager as he to know, to learn, to experience.
To test, to tempt, to feel and savor the subtle complexities of the kiss. Of
the intangible need as well as the tangible pleasure that swirled around
them, through them, when they kissed. When she gave him her mouth
and he took, claimed, then, deepening the exchange, settled to plunder.

If she wanted to know of him, of all that he offered her, then she
needed to know of all this.

All this. Charlie held her in his arms and some primitive part of
him gloated, delighted that this—she, her softness, her fresh innocence, her supple figure and alluring curves—would soon be his. All
his. That—

High-pitched voices, gay bubbling laughter cut through his fascination. He lifted his head, blinked, then quickly released Sarah as the
latch clicked and the door swung open.

Three children tumbled into the room. Charlie only just managed
to smother a curse.

He glanced at Sarah, through the moonwashed dimness saw her smile.

Although the children smiled in return—they all knew Sarah—it was he they had in their sights.

"Uncle Charlie!" the youngest, seven-year-old Henry, piped censoriously as his older brother Justin, a more circumspect twelve, shut the door. "You didn't come to say hello, so we came to find you."

Throwing himself at Charlie, Henry wound his arms about Charlie's waist and gave him a ferocious hug.

Juliet, just ten, bounced on her knees on the sofa. "Actually, we saw you slip away from the drawing room and thought we'd come and talk to you." She wrinkled her nose, glancing at Sarah as if sharing some discovery. "It's so noisy in there it's a wonder any of the older folk can hear themselves think!"

Sarah grinned, and exchanged a glance with Charlie. They were apparently not classed among "the older folk."

Justin came up to clasp one of Charlie's hands. "You brought your pair up from town, didn't you?" Wide gray eyes fixed on Charlie's face. "Jeremy said he thought you would. If you have, can I drive them?"

Charlie looked down at the upturned face—faces; Henry was also making huge puppy-dog eyes at him. "No." He gave them a second to digest the unequivocal nature of that answer, then relented, "But if you're good, I might—only might—take you up beside me for a drive."

"Yes! Oh, yes!" The boys, each hanging on to one of Charlie's hands, jumped up and down.

"Me, too—me, too!" Juliet bounced even higher on the sofa.

"Right." Charlie made a grab for the conversational reins. "Now—"

"Where will we go?" Justin asked.

"To Watchet!" Henry cried.

"No—up to the falls," Juliet said. "It's prettier that way."

"What about to Taunton?" Justin put in. "Then we can let them have their heads along the London road."

A spirited discussion ensued on the merits of the various suggestions; Charlie tried to curtail it, to exert some authority, but the task was beyond him.

He glanced at Sarah. She'd sunk down on the arm of the sofa and was watching him and his three persecutors; it was too dim for him to be able to read her eyes, but her expression said she was amused.

Her lips, soft rose in the moonlight, were certainly curved.

He stared at them, and felt an unprecedented rush of sheer lust streak through him.

Looking back at the children, he held up his hands. "Enough! I faithfully promise to come and take you for a drive behind the grays before I return to London, but it won't be until at least next week, so you can decide where you want to go among yourselves between now and then." He herded them toward the door; having gained their primary objective, they consented to leave.

Opening the door, Charlie waved them through. Justin and Henry left, still chattering about horses. Charlie was thanking his stars they were too young to wonder what he and Sarah had been doing in the parlor alone when Juliet swanned past—and caught his eye.

She smirked. Her eyes twinkled.

Charlie held his breath—but after that smug, distinctly female smile, she went out.

He exhaled and started to close the door—and heard the unmistakable sounds of departure drifting from the front hall.

Shutting the door, he stared at the panels. Thanks to his devilish niece and nephews, he and Sarah had run out of time.

He turned—and found her beside him.

Through the dimness she smiled, relaxed and assured. "We should return."

He heard the words, but his attention had fastened on her lips. Beguiling, tempting; he had to taste them one last time.

Lifting his hands, he framed her face; he didn't trust himself to take her into his arms, and then let her go after just one kiss. Tipping up her face, he looked into her eyes, wide soft pools of serenity.

He bent his head and tasted her—not just a kiss but a more explicit sampling, one that sank to his bones, that spun out, and on . . .

With a wrench, he drew back. Forced his hands from her face.

He waited until she met his gaze and drew in a shaky breath before he reached for the doorknob. "Yes. We have to get back."

Frustration had sharpened its spurs.

It had pricked before; now it jabbed. Hard.

Later that night, Charlie paced the unlighted library at Morwellan

Park, a glass of brandy in his hand. Wondering how many more prior claims on Sarah's time, more meetings in crowded social settings, more unanticipated interruptions he was going to have to endure.

In the lead-up to the London Season, before the departure of those intending to spend those entertainment-filled months in town, the local ladies hosted a range of events; he'd always viewed it as a form of practice, a testing ground for young ladies destined to make their mark on wider tonnish circles.

All well and good in its way, no doubt, but that meant that he and Sarah, despite neither being in need of such practice, would be included in invitations to countless dances, dinners, and parties, and expected to attend.

In town, he would consider balls and parties as opportunities to further his aim. Here, he knew such local events would prove nothing more than wasted time. The company was too small and the houses too limited in their amenities to allow him and Sarah to slip away—not for more than the few inadequate minutes he'd managed to steal at Casleigh. Casleigh was the largest house in the district, and look how that had turned out.

Halting before the fireplace, he stared at the tiny flames licking over the dying embers.

He wanted Sarah's agreement to their wedding. He wanted that agreement as soon as possible; the idea of dallying even for the period of courtship he'd agreed to didn't appeal.

She was the one—he was beyond sure of that. So . . . he needed a plan. Some scheme to ensure she happily accepted his proposal—and why not within the week?

He sipped his brandy and stared at the flames while the notion took shape, and crystallized in his brain.

Sarah would agree to marry him before next Tuesday night.

Bringing that about was the challenge he faced.

He'd always relished challenges.

Time and place were the first hurdles he needed to overcome.

"Perhaps . . . ?" About to take his leave of Lady Conningham, and Sarah, Clary, and Gloria, with whom he'd spent the last half hour chatting about local concerns—a very proper visit on his part—Charlie paused and glanced at Sarah, then looked at her ladyship. "Would you allow Sarah to walk with me to the stables?"

Naturally Lady Conningham gave her consent. Smiling, he took Sarah's hand. She joined him readily, a question—an eager one—in her eyes.

Holding the door for her, he glanced back, and inwardly winced. Clary and Gloria had "realized"; their eyes were round, the questions in them all but clamoring.

Closing the door on that pair of avid gazes, he told himself that Sarah's sisters' interest had been inevitable from the start. His only hope was that Lady Conningham was strong enough to keep them from following.

Sarah led him to the side door, then out onto the lawn. Ahead, the stable lay soaking up the afternoon sunshine.

Pacing beside her, he touched her arm. "Have you time for a longer walk?"

She smiled—delightedly; he'd just answered her question. "Yes, of course." She glanced around. "Where should we go? Mama won't be able to hold Clary and Gloria for long."

"In that case, let's get out of sight." He gestured to the path that wended away from the house, eventually leading to the stream that burbled along a short distance behind the manor.

Sarah nodded. He offered his arm and she tucked her hand in the crook of his elbow. They crossed the lawn to the path; passing down an avenue of rhododendrons, they were soon effectively screened from the house.

The path reached the stream and turned, following the rushing water. They continued on, leaving the house behind.

"I assume you'll be attending Lady Cruikshank's dinner tonight?" Sarah glanced at him. "There'll be quite a crowd."

"Indeed." Charlie looked ahead. If memory served, just beyond the next bend the stream flowed into a weir. The path hugged the shore; halfway down the body of water . . . a summerhouse used to be there, of white-painted wood, nestled into the lee of the rising bank behind. He remembered it from childhood summers when his mother and Sarah's had sat in its shade and watched their children play in the shallows or, as in his case, fish from the banks. "But yes, I'll be there tonight."

A stand of trees and a thicket of bushes blocked the view ahead. Passing the trees, they rounded the bend—and there stood the summerhouse.

Charlie smiled and steered Sarah toward it. "But as we've seen, getting any reasonable amount of time alone—time in suitable privacy so we can get to know each other better—is a tall order at this time of year."

"Especially for you." When he glanced at her, seeing his faint frown she smiled and looked ahead. "You're the earl now. Even being heir to the earldom doesn't equate with being the earl yourself—you can't avoid any of the gatherings, not at present. Not while you remain unwed, and while the gentlemen aren't yet sure what you might think about this topic or that."

He grimaced. "True." Although he'd been the earl for three years, he'd spent precious little time in the country; to many of the district's landowners he was still something of an unknown quantity.

"That, however"—he looked ahead—"brings me to my point."

The summerhouse steps were beside them. He turned her; side by side, they climbed up.

Looking around, he relaxed. The place was perfect. Wooden shutters closed off the rear archways, those facing the bank and the trees. The arches overlooking the weir remained open; in summer cooling breezes would lift off the water, but now, in winter with the weir full, slate gray beneath the massing clouds, the summerhouse was protected from the prevailing winds by the bank and the trees embracing it. The air beneath the ceiling was still and faintly warm, courtesy of the day's sunshine.

Sarah drew her hand from his arm and walked to where a thickly cushioned wicker sofa sat between two similarly padded armchairs, all angled to best appreciate the view.

Most helpful of all to Charlie's mind was the place's seclusion. It was hidden from the house by the intervening gardens, and in this season it was highly unlikely anyone else would walk this way.

One glance around as he trailed after Sarah confirmed that the place was kept swept and dusted. There were no dead leaves anywhere, no cobwebs strung between the rafters.

Sarah had stopped before the sofa, her back to it as she surveyed the view. He halted beside her, his gaze on her face. After a moment, she turned her head, searched his eyes, then raised a brow in question.

He reached for her, turned her into his arms, and she came. Readily, without uncertainty or hesitation. He looked down at her face for a moment, then bent his head and kissed her.

Long, deeply, as he wished. As the minutes stretched, he let his hunger reign, allowed himself to appease her curiosity to some small degree. Then, with an effort, he drew back, raised his head and murmured, "They're going to be watching us, all the matrons, all the other young ladies—even the gentlemen. Like your sisters, they've guessed, and as we've made no announcement they'll be avidly following every move we make."

Sarah reluctantly accepted he wasn't going to kiss her again, at least not yet. Opening her eyes, she looked into his, into the soft blue that so often screened his thoughts; he wasn't an easy man to read.

"You asked for a period of courtship," he said, "for us to get to know each other better, but our social surroundings are a real constraint."

For an instant, she wondered if he was going to ask her to decide and give him her answer now, before their two weeks were up, but before she could panic at the prospect—she had no notion what her answer should be—he went on, "We can accept those constraints—and a subsequently restricted courtship—or we can work around them."

Her relief was real. "How do we work around them?" Even she heard the eagerness in her voice.

He smiled. "Simple. We meet here." He gestured about them; his gaze lowered to her lips. "Each night, after whatever engagements we attend, we come here—to pursue our private, mutual agenda. We both want to, need to, get to know each other better, and we can only do that in the privacy this place, at night, will afford."

His gaze rose to her eyes. "Will you do it? Will you meet me here tonight, and every night thereafter, until you know enough, have learned enough, to give me my answer?" She blinked, and he went on, "Will you meet me here tonight after Lady Cruikshank's dinner?"

"Yes." To her mind there was no question; to clarify, she added, "Tonight after Lady Cruikshank's dinner, and every night thereafter, until I'm sure."

His smile held an element of triumph; she noted it, but then his arms tightened, and he kissed her again.

Another of his long, drugging, exciting and satisfying but curiously incomplete kisses; when he broke it, she had to battle a wanton urge to grab him and haul him back—to somehow demand ... she knew not what. The rest, but what was that?

That was one of the as-yet-undefinable things she needed to know.

He looked into her eyes, and seemed satisfied with what he saw. "We need to start for the stables, or your sisters will come searching." Releasing her, he took one of her hands and raised it to his lips. "Until tonight."

Entirely content, she smiled back. "Until then."

5

Later that night, Charlie tied Storm at the edge of the manor's gardens, then strode quickly down a narrow track that joined the path by the stream. Clouds scudded overhead; the moon was fitful, shining down one moment only to vanish in the next, dousing the path in unrelieved gloom.

Conscious of rising tension, of an edginess he ascribed to impatience to get their courtship moving in the right direction, he prayed Sarah wasn't frightened of the dark, that she wouldn't allow the inky shadows to deter her.

He reached the summerhouse, started up the steps—and saw her. She was waiting, once again before the sofa. She must have spotted him on the path; he detected no start on seeing him. Instead, as he neared, she smiled and held out her hands.

He took them, registering the softness of her skin and the delicateness of the bones between his fingers, then he lifted both her hands to his shoulders, released them, and reached for her. Sliding his hands about her waist, he gripped, and drew her to him. Not into his arms, but against him, simultaneously bending his head and covering her lips so that he tasted her surprise, that evocative leap of nerves, the first shock of sensual awakening as their bodies touched, breasts to chest, hips to thighs.

Sarah caught her breath, physically and mentally; she couldn't catch her reeling, whirling wits, but she didn't need to. Her will remained her own and she knew what she wanted. To know, to learn all she might from this.

From this and all subsequent engagements. From his kiss, that melding of their mouths that was no longer remotely innocent, from his embrace, different tonight—his hands remained at her waist, yet she still felt his strength surrounding her, potent, male, dangerous, yet so tempting.

She slid her hands up over his shoulders, felt the heavy muscles under her palms and tensed her fingers, savoring the warm hardness, then reached further, sliding her hands up the strong column of his nape; spreading her fingers, she ran them through his hair.

Fascinated, she ruffled the heavy locks, thrilling to the silky texture and the way he reacted, the kiss, and him, heating at her boldness.

She knew what she wanted—she wanted more. Wanted him to show her more, to let her see what lay behind his newfound desire for her. So she kissed him back, more definite, more demanding in her own right, inviting . . . he hesitated for an instant, then accepted, plucked the reins from her grasp and took control.

He swept her into some hotter, more urgent existence.

He kissed her more deeply, more thoroughly, more evocatively, until heat swamped her, threatening to melt her bones, until her wits were no longer reeling, but flown. Until her skin was flushed, until her body felt simultaneously unbearably languid and indescribably tense.

Waiting, but she wasn't sure for what.

Charlie reminded himself of her innocence, that she was all the word implied; she had no notion of what she hungered for, what she was inviting as her tongue boldly met his and stroked, caressed.

All her responses, enticing though they were, were instinctive, flavored with that distinctive fresh and heady taste he now associated with her. She was unlike any woman he'd encountered, something other than those on whom his experience was based; the difference logically had to be a symptom of the way she differed from all the rest—that singular quality was the taste of innocence.

He'd never expected to find innocence so addictive. So arousing.

So powerfully alluring that he had to battle, actually had to exert his will against his own inclinations, against a welling, remarkably strong desire to sweep her up in his arms, lay her on the sofa, and . . .

But that wasn't his purpose, not tonight. Tonight, and over those to come, he was, he inwardly reiterated, committed to playing a long game. Tactics, strategy, and how to influence a negotiation. She had something he wanted; tonight he was sweetening his price.

So he held her against him, his hands at her waist, too wise to tempt his baser self by taking her into his arms; it was not part of tonight's agenda to crush her to him . . . not yet. Not until she was ready, not until she yearned for that contact with a hunger even greater than his own.

He continued to kiss her evocatively, commandingly, letting passion rise, writhe and beckon—until she clung to his shoulders, the fingers of one hand sunk in his hair, until her body was heated, pliant, and wanting.

He drew back; he had to fight to do it but he held to his purpose and freed her lips. Felt her breath wash over his and had to battle the urge to sink back into the delectable cavern of her mouth and take. Taste. More.

He inwardly swore. He would, soon, but not tonight. Tonight . . .

Muscles bunching, he raised his head and eased her back. "Enough."

He wasn't sure whom he was addressing the command to—her, or himself. He waited until she lifted her lids, until the dazed haze faded from her eyes and she blinked, and refocused. On his face. She quickly scanned it as if trying to read his direction. He would have smiled, reassuring and calm, but his features felt graven.

"It's late." He forced his hands from her waist, reluctantly relinquishing the feel of her body supple and lithe between his palms. "Come. I'll walk you back to the house."

Sarah found the next day trying, and the evening was even worse, complicated by being able to see Charlie, being able to sense his impatience for their next meeting in the summerhouse, which in turn fed her own.

The evening dragged while her father played host to the other local landowners, using a dinner to consult over matters pertaining to the local hunt. By the time the gentlemen eventually rejoined the ladies in the drawing room, her frustration had reached new heights; as their neighbors milled and chatted, keeping a sweet smile on her face and polite and appropriate comments on her lips was a distracting irritation.

At last they all left, Charlie included. Surrounded as they parted in the front hall, she had no chance to learn whether he intended to drive home and then ride back, or whether instead he would drive the grays out of the gates and around to the weir through the fields. As she climbed the stairs behind her mother, she weighed distances and times against the likelihood of him leaving his precious pair in a field, and couldn't be certain; she remained unsure at what hour to expect him, at what hour he would reach the summerhouse.

Yet she was absolutely sure he would come. Sometime that night he would return, and she would be able to learn, if not all, then at least more.

Reaching her bedchamber, she sent her sleepy maid, Gwen, to bed, and regretfully changed out of her pretty silk evening gown and donned an old plain walking dress instead. If by some chance she was discovered wandering the gardens in the dead of night, she could say she'd been unable to sleep and had taken a short walk.

Selecting a woolen shawl that at least matched the gown, she blew out her candle and sat down before the dying fire to wait until her parents went to bed and the house quieted.

Half an hour later, she rose and slipped out. She crept down the side stairs and eased open the side door; exercising caution, she walked slowly, drifting from shadow to shadow across the lawn.

Once she gained the path and was out of sight of the house, she picked up her pace; drawing the shawl firmly about her shoulders, she allowed her mind to focus on what lay ahead.

Literally, and figuratively.

After last night . . . she'd returned to her room, her bed, and unexpectedly fallen into a sound sleep. But she'd had all day to mull over Charlie's actions, his direction; it seemed clear enough that he intended to tempt her into marriage with desire. With the promise of passion, and all that would mean.

Why else had he stopped? Why else had he drawn such a definite line at such a relatively early—and unrevealing—point? She'd sensed his control, the steely will he'd ruthlessly wielded in order to stop when he had; he hadn't stopped because he'd truly wanted to, but because it was part of his plan.

His plan wasn't, quite, what she wanted, but his direction suited her well enough.

She wasn't so innocent that she didn't appreciate that he could well make her so desperate to experience the ultimate pleasure that she would set aside all reservations and agree to marry him regardless of whether he loved her or not. In falling in with his scheme, she was taking a risk, yet against that stood the reality that in order to learn what she needed to know, his plan—essentially to seduce her into marriage—held out the best prospect of her gaining what she wanted, of revealing to her *why* he was so set on marrying her. Specifically her.

She'd asked, but he hadn't truly answered; he'd given her all the conventional reasons, but such reasons weren't enough for her, and, more importantly, she was quite sure they weren't—wouldn't have been—enough for him, enough to move him to offer for *her*.

He could have had his pick of every eligible, or even not-so-eligible, young lady in the ton, but he'd chosen her. And despite her ambivalence, her insistence on being wooed—her refusal to meekly fall in with his initial plan—he was still, indeed it seemed he was now even more, determined to marry her.

Which either augered well or was simply a demonstration of his ruthless habit of insisting on having his own way.

She rounded the bend in the path, and the summerhouse came into view. Whichever of those two options was correct, by following his script she would learn the truth. The truth of why he wanted her.

He was waiting; she saw his tall figure shift in the shadows, pushing away from the archway against which he'd been leaning. Lungs tightening, she lifted her skirts and climbed the steps.

Again they met before the sofa. He held out a hand as she neared; she gave him her hand, conscious of his strength as he grasped it.

Smoothly, he drew her closer; lifting her hand, he brushed his lips lightly, lingeringly, over the sensitive backs of her fingers, then, holding her gaze, he turned her hand and pressed his lips to the inside of her wrist.

Her pulse leapt.

They had no need for words; they both knew why they were there.

His lips, hot, trailed along the bare inner face of her forearm, sending sensation streaking through her, a prelude, a sensual warning as he raised her hand higher, releasing it to fall on his shoulder as he drew her to him.

Fully against him, as he had the previous night, but this time his arm went around her, a steely band that held her trapped, that caged her as he bent his head. Eagerly she lifted her face and met his lips with hers.

She inwardly smiled, savoring the firm pressure of his lips, then she yielded to his explicit demand and gave him her mouth. And let her wits slide away as sensation bloomed, as she sensed hunger flare, in herself and in him.

They'd waltzed only once, and that months ago; this was a waltz of a different sort, where their senses revolved in time to a beat orchestrated by sensation. By the heavy stroke of his tongue against hers, by the whirling, fractured pricking of her nerves, by the escalating tempo of her heart.

By the tensing of his fingers on her back as he tightened his grip on his control.

Engrossed, enthralled, she savored the sensual slide into the familiar passion of the kiss, and willingly followed his lead.

She was aware, yet not—acutely aware of him, his lips, his hands, his body, and the flagrant promise carried in his embrace, yet she'd grown strangely insensitive to the world around them, the shadows beyond his arms, the soft sounds of the night beyond the summerhouse, the distant babble of water over the lip of the weir.

Here, now, with him; her world had shrunk, senses intently, intensely focused. On the next stage in his plan.

She quivered, prey to building anticipation, to the shivery thrill of expectation. To the steady rise of a wanting she was coming to think must be desire.

Sunk in the warm pleasures of her mouth, Charlie tracked her responses. He knew to a nicety, to a single shaky breath, just when to ease back enough to slide one hand beneath her shawl. Setting his palm to her waist, he swept upward, lightly tracing her side, then the outer curve of her breast.

The shiver she'd been suppressing became a reality, a response that incited, that invited him to touch, to caress, so he did. At first gently tracing the swelling curves, then subtly stroking so that she heated and yearned; only then did he shape her flesh, curve his hand about the firm mound and gently squeeze, then more evocatively knead.

Her mouth surrendered, her hands once more gripping his skull, her fingers twining in his hair, she arched against his supporting arm, gratifyingly pressing her breast more fully into his hand, offering and inviting—even demanding—his further attentions. The movement set her hips riding more definitely against his thighs.

The latter caught him unawares, set fires where he didn't yet need them burning. For a moment, he teetered, then plunged back into the kiss, distracting his awakening demons long enough to catch his sensual breath.

Since when could a mere innocent override his will, tried and tested as it was, forged in the steamy, highly sensual world of the upper echelons of the haut ton? His rational mind scoffed, confident and assured. Reassured, he eased his focus once more from the delights of her luscious mouth; taking a firmer, more determined grip on his reins, he returned to the execution of his plan.

Responding to her clear invitation, he let his fingers find, circle, then gently tweak her nipples. Already furled, they tightened even more; he played, and made her gasp. Made her catch her breath and cling, not just physically but mentally, caught on that sensual hook between need and gratification.

But that wasn't yet enough. His rational mind once again intruded, reminding him that she hadn't proved to be as malleable as he'd expected; if he wished to succeed, then showing her more, introducing her to more passionate, and more addictive, delights, was only sensible.

As he was going to win—to win her hand and marry her—there was no reason, social or moral, that prohibited him from showing her a great deal more.

Thus went his rationalization, but even while his mind trod those paths, he was conscious, more conscious, of a primitive compulsion to touch her—not for her benefit but for his.

Not for the delight of her increasingly clamorous senses, but for his own.

As his fingers found the buttons closing her bodice, there was no thought in his mind beyond the need to touch her. Beyond satisfying that—his need, not hers.

He distracted her by engaging her in a more heated exchange, a brief duel of tongues to keep her wits whirling. The gown was old, well-worn; the buttons slid easily from their tiny toggles.

And then her bodice gaped; he pressed one side wide, and slid his hand beneath.

Through the heat of the kiss, she gasped, but then he set his palm to the fine silk of her chemise, sliding over even finer, much hotter silken skin, and she froze. Trembled. Tensed as he caressed, as yet undemanding but insistent, then he searched with his fingertips, found the ribbon he sought, and tugged.

The ribbon unraveled.

With a practiced flick, he hooked the chemise over her tightly furled nipple, and then her breast was in his palm.

Skin to hot skin. Sweet sensation and fire.

Both flooded him, and her.

He closed his hand, hungry, greedy, needing; expertise gentled his touch, kept the caress just this side of possessive, but that was sheer instinct.

His wits had suspended, submerged beneath a ravenous passion.

A passion that roared as the fire flared and spread through her—from his increasingly driven touch, through their kiss—and she melted.

She sank against him in wanton abandon, with flagrant promise and in blatant invitation.

As he wished, she wanted. Every instinctive response she made screamed that to his witless, wholly mesmerized brain.

Heavy and swollen, her breast burned his palm, the furled nipple a hot bead, one his mouth watered to taste.

He felt giddy, drunk on sensation. She was hot and so malleable within his arms, pliant, nubile, supple, and seductive. It was as if he embraced a steadily burning flame, a sensual being of heat and glory, an elemental creature lured forth by passion.

Steeped in it.

He drank her fire, supped it from her lips as she eagerly offered it. Plunged deeper into the beckoning flames, felt them lick over him as she arched against him, felt them spreading, urgent and compelling, beneath his skin, setting his own fires raging.

His arm at her back was tensing to sweep her up so he could lay her on the sofa behind him when his rational mind clawed back to the surface and stopped him.

Not cold. He still burned, ached, wanted; something within him raged at the suddenly jerked leash, but . . . this wasn't his plan.

He'd been derailed; like one of the new locomotives he'd rocketed off his intended track. As with a runaway locomotive, it took immense effort to pull back and regroup.

Enough to understand that if he wanted to rescue his plan, he had to end this now.

Now, before her passion again overwhelmed his will.

He had to steel himself, force himself to draw his hand from her breast. He couldn't hide his reluctance, even though he tried to conceal it behind his customary control, as if drawing back was what he wanted to do.

Abruptly pulled from the fiery depths they'd been exploring—she'd thought in perfect harmony—Sarah mentally blinked, but as his hand left her breast, as the arm around her eased, she realized that he wasn't intending to allow them to indulge in the rest of the symphony.

The analogy was apt; she felt the disappointment, the same unhappy wrench, from having something temptingly pleasant dangled before her, and then removed from her reach.

Even as he—albeit with obvious reluctance—lifted his head and broke the kiss, even as she moistened her lips, lifted her heavy lids and looked into his shadowed face, she was conscious of uncharacteristic anger stirring within her.

She studied his face; he was looking down as he did up the buttons he'd undone. She made no move to help him, but examined the angular planes of cheek and brow, the strong line of his jaw.

Every facet seemed harder, more sharply delineated. His breathing, while not as rushed as hers, was nevertheless no longer slow and even.

She hadn't imagined it. He'd been as affected as she, as drawn into the heated pleasure, but . . . of course he'd drawn back.

That was his plan. She resisted the urge to narrow her eyes at him, bit her tongue against an impulse to tell him she knew what he was trying to do. Calmed herself as he released the last button and, slowly, let his hands fall, reassured herself that, in letting him pursue his plan, she'd furthered her own.

Something had risen between him and her that had, at least temporarily, shaken his control. The knowledge allowed her to smile, smugly if a trifle dazedly, when his eyes rose and met hers.

"That was—" To her surprise her voice had lowered. She'd grown used to his doing so, but never before had she heard her own voice take on such a tone. She cleared her throat, lifted her chin. "I was going to say that was pleasant, but that's such an inadequate description perhaps I'd do better to say nothing at all."

He grinned, almost boyishly, and suddenly the air felt lighter. He glanced beyond her, toward the weir. Turning, she felt the night breeze as she'd never before felt it, sliding cooling fingers over her heated skin.

The sensation was evocative; she shivered more from remembered pleasure than from any chill.

"Come." He spoke from behind her. "I'll see you into the house."

He lifted her shawl from her elbows to her shoulders; with a nod, she tightened it about her, then gave him her hand.

He closed his about it, engulfing her fingers.

Without a word, they walked back to the house.

O nce again to her surprise, Sarah slept like one dead.
She woke late, and then had to rush. What with preparing to attend Lady Farthingale's luncheon and then traveling to Gilmore, her ladyship's house, she had no time to ponder what she'd learned the previous night before she laid eyes on Charlie across her ladyship's drawing room.

She walked in and there he was, chatting with Mrs. Considine beside the fireplace. She hadn't imagined he would be there, not at such a function; she had to battle not to stare.

The fact that all the other matrons and their daughters were staring avidly at her helped; clearly everyone knew of their courtship, unannounced though it was.

Facing the fireplace, Charlie sensed the expectant hiatus and turned. Their gazes met; both of them stilled, then, his lips curving in just the right degree of welcome, he held out his hand.

Leaving her mother and sisters to join what group they chose, she went to him, and prayed the sudden leaping of her senses didn't show.

Charlie took her hand and bowed, entirely nonchalantly; the touch of his fingers on hers made her pulse thud, her nerves skitter. He sensed it, or perhaps he felt the same shooting awareness. He met her gaze briefly as he straightened, then set her hand on his sleeve and turned back to his companion. "Mrs. Considine was telling me of the new breed of sheep her son has been trialing."

Despite the district being all but overrun with the beasts, Sarah knew little of them—the breeds, the herding, the pasturing, the shearing. She did, however, know a considerable amount about spinning and weaving.

Aware of that, Mrs. Considine fixed her with an inquiring look. "The new breed gives a much different fleece, dear. The wool is finer than the usual—if it were you, which of the mills would you send it to?"

Sarah considered, conscious of Charlie's interest—both as to why she'd been asked, and what her answer would be. "If the fleeces are thicker, which I assume they must be, I'd take it to Corrigan's in Wellington. They're a smaller concern, but they're better equipped to work on something that might need extra care. Most others would just put it through their regular process rather than developing the wool to its best."

"Corrigan's, heh?" Mrs. Considine nodded. "I'll tell Jeffrey—he'll be pleased I had the forethought to ask."

After recommending that Charlie try the new breed, Mrs. Considine moved away.

Shifting to face him, Sarah met his eyes. "What are you doing here?"

His expression turned grim, but the effect was limited to his eyes, which only she could see, rather than his features, which far too many of the surrounding ladies were monitoring closely. "I didn't realize it was this sort of gathering." He cast a glance around; only she was near enough to detect what seemed very like desperation. "I assumed there would be at least *some* gentlemen present."

He meant gentlemen like him; she refrained from pointing out that other than him, there were few in the immediate locality. "There are seven other males present, and all of them are gentlemen."

"Two ancient codgers and five still-wet-behind-the-ears whelps," he growled. "I feel like a carnival freak."

She smothered a chuckle. "Well, why did you come?"

He looked at her, met and held her gaze—and said nothing at all. But she felt his answer, could read the exasperated frustration in his eyes. Her breath caught. For an instant she wondered if he would—

Instead, he said, low, just for her, "You know why I came. I thought . . ." He grimaced. "Clearly I miscalculated."

She understood all too well. She felt the same, the same rush of eagerness to touch, better yet to kiss, to sink together . . . she still felt breathless. "Regardless, now you're here, you can't cut and run. You'll have to make the best of it."

"Precisely my conclusion." Retaking her hand, he set it on his sleeve, shifting to stand beside her, his gaze again passing over the interested onlookers. "Aside from all else, there's clearly no reason for us to pretend to polite indifference."

"That seems to be the case."

"So how is it that you know so much about wool processing?" He started slowly strolling down the room, she assumed to forestall any who might think to join them.

"I mentioned that when the children at the orphanage turn fourteen, we find them employment in the nearest towns. We take a close interest in the businesses to which we send our boys and girls, so we know the sort of work the children will be doing. That means learning about the business processes in some detail." She glanced at him. "I know a great deal about the workings of the mills and factories in Taunton and Wellington."

He digested that. "Do you know much about the warehouses and wharves in Watchet?"

"Not to the same extent. Mr. Skeggs takes care of those."

"I must remember to call on Skeggs." He caught her eye. "Or perhaps I could catch him sometime at the orphanage."

She grinned. "After that game of bat and ball, you'll always be welcome."

He smiled and looked ahead.

Despite the attention focused on them, he stuck by her side, chatting to those of the matrons it was impossible to avoid, then when luncheon was announced, holding her plate while she helped herself to salmon, then following at her heels along the board, sampling most of the dishes but with an idle, abstracted air.

They sat at a small table to eat. Clary and Gloria joined them; Sarah watched in some amusement as Charlie, resigned, responded to their sallies with a pointed patience that eventually had the desired effect. Her sisters retreated to look for jellies, and were distracted by friends on the way back.

Most of the company were likewise distracted. There were still eyes turned their way, but not the relentless covert observation that had initially been focused on them. For the first time, Sarah felt able to draw a free breath.

Unbidden, her gaze slid to Charlie; seated beside her, he was looking down unseeing at his empty plate, his mind elsewhere.

His attention focused, abruptly, on her. He didn't move, didn't shift so much as a finger, but a stillness came over him, and she knew.

Then he lifted his head, and his eyes met hers. There was heat in the blue, and a lure, something that beckoned, to which she instantly responded.

Her body warmed, came alive; her skin tightened, her nerves grew taut. Her nipples peaked, contracted.

She caught her breath, wrenched her gaze from his and looked away. Told herself this was madness. Swallowed, and still felt giddy.

Just that one look, and she could remember the feel of his lips on hers, of his hand on her breast. And he was remembering it, too.

Her lips throbbed.

He was there, near, and her treacherous senses remembered all too well, and wanted more. Now. That their surroundings were completely inappropriate didn't seem to matter in the least.

Unable to help herself, she glanced at him. He was looking at the table again, but once again not seeing. Again he felt her gaze, glanced at her, then abruptly rose, his chair scraping on the floor.

He held out a hand. "Come." With his head, he indicated the others all rising and making for the door. "It appears we're to be subjected to some music."

His tone made it clear he expected it to be torture; in all honesty, she couldn't reassure him. Giving him her hand, she got to her feet.

His grip, the way he moved his chair out of her way—all screamed of harnessed frustration. Of a tension not just equal to hers but greater.

While she didn't know, not in a practical sense, what lay ahead in his plan, he did. That was presumably what was feeding his mood, lending it such a sharp edge.

He led her to join the others as they filed out of the dining room and headed for the music room, keeping to the rear of the crowd.

Her nerves were still fluttering, flickering, wanting; she drew in a breath and firmly suppressed her distracting thoughts. Considered him, here and now, instead, and drew some small satisfaction that he was as affected as she.

All the others had entered the music room; for one moment they were alone in the corridor. He bent his head and murmured by her ear, "Tonight. Will you be there?"

She met his eyes. Very nearly said "Of course" in a surprised tone that would have made him think twice. Made him suspect.

Searching his eyes, she confirmed that he had no inkling that she knew what he was about, that she understood his plan. She opened her mouth, tempted to set him straight; instead, she merely said, "Yes. All right."

As if she'd needed to be asked. To be reminded.

He nodded and escorted her into the room. He found two chairs by the wall. Settling beside him, she reflected that there was a significant difference between being innocent and being naive, one he—never truly innocent, let alone naive—transparently didn't appreciate.

She might be innocent, but she wasn't naive.

He would learn soon enough. Night by night, as they met in the summerhouse, pursuing his plan—and hers.

She was waiting for him in the summerhouse that night. She reached for him as he reached for her. She framed his face as their lips met and they sank immediately into a heated kiss, as their bodies met, and pressed close, wanting, knowing, knowing enough to want more.

Heat flared, passion followed. In seconds they were caught in an untempered exchange, in a tempestuous, compulsive expression of their need.

For each other; that was the wonder of it, the point that reached her through their mutual urgency, sliding through her mind even as her wits sank beneath the surging sensations. It was a point that fascinated.

That lured and enthralled.

He wanted her, and not for a heartbeat did he—or could he—deny that. He couldn't hide it, not even from her, innocent though she was.

It was there, investing the hard lips that ravaged hers, investing every heavy, evocative stroke of his tongue. There in the unmuted hardness of his chest, in the strength in the arms that crushed her to him.

There in the hand that swiftly, expertly undid the buttons of her bodice.

She'd worn the same old gown; in less than a minute, the bodice gaped open.

She steeled herself to feel his hand close about her breast.

Instead, he stooped, swept her off her feet, up into his arms, then he swung around and sat on the sofa with her on his lap.

His hand slid beneath her bodice and closed about her breast; his lips covered hers and drank her gasp.

He held her cradled as he pandered to her senses, as he made them spin, made her arch and invite and delight in his skillful play.

But that wasn't enough. She wanted more.

She had to experience more to learn what was driving him.

Reaching up, she twined her arms about his neck, and kissed him back. And wantonly, with full intent, with lips and tongue and her restless body, issued a clear invitation.

She didn't expect him to refuse, and he didn't. But she hadn't foreseen what he would do. She'd had no real idea, so was only mildly surprised when he released her breast, raised his hand to her shoulder and pushed aside her gown.

Until her breast was bare, exposed to the night air, to his hot palm and hard fingers, to his too-knowing caresses.

She savored each one. Eyes closed, she let her head fall back, arching as his fingers closed, tweaked. His lips traced her jaw, then slid down the long curve of her throat to the hollow at its base, to place a hot, openmouthed kiss over the spot where her pulse thundered.

Catching her breath was hard, near impossible—and became even more difficult as his lips cruised her skin, trailing over the upper swell of her bared breast, then dipping.

His hot breath bathed her nipple, then his lips touched—a delicate kiss that sent a jolt down her spine.

The caress came again, barely there, and she gasped.

Arched.

He opened his hot mouth and took her nipple within.

She cried out as sensation—burning and wet—streaked through her, smothered another cry as he gently suckled. Heart galloping, she struggled to find some purchase in her whirling mind, to understand, to see—but for the moment she was blind.

Blinded by passion, by pleasure and delight.

He knew what he was doing; he sent all three racing through her, wreathing and beckoning and luring her to be even more wanton than before. Even more blatant.

Of their own volition, her hands had risen to grasp his head; her fingers tangling in his hair, she gripped, and flagrantly held him to her, arching beneath him, inviting more.

She heard—or was it felt?—an amused chuckle. She would have taken exception, but the sound was strained; he seemed every bit as driven as she felt, every bit as urgently breathless.

Then he complied with her request.

For long moments she knew nothing beyond piercingly sweet sensation. Minutes passed as she savored the pleasure he lavished on her—and it was such a giving. He delighted in her pleasure; she sensed that through his touch, through the kisses he paused to share with her in between his worship of her breasts, his carefully orchestrated educating of her senses.

Of her desires.

Knowing what he was doing, what he intended, gave her the strength to observe, to see more than perhaps he intended to reveal.

Gazing at his face, limned by the faint moonlight, she felt the knowing touch of his fingers, felt the sharper bite of the desire they called forth, but she also saw the hunger etched in his drawn features, sensed the quiver in his control as he looked down at his hand gliding over her bare flesh.

Reaching up, she drew his head down to hers, drew his lips to hers, and embraced him. Welcomed him, embraced the desire, and that other, too—his hunger, his passion—welcomed both, and drew them to her. Urged them nearer.

He kissed her, and she thought he shuddered, quaked, as if holding back his need, screening it, was causing him pain.

Another need welled and washed through her, surprising her with its intensity.

She held him to the kiss, tempting and luring and challenging, playing in the ways she'd learned most captivated him; drawing a hand from his nape, she slid it beneath his coat, found his waistcoat in the way, and quickly unbuttoned it.

Pressing the velvet aside, she laid her hand on his chest, felt the warm hardness of the muscles beneath the fine linen, then she laid her hand over his heart, and savored the heavy, thudding beat.

A beat that reached some primal part of her. It emboldened her, turned her brazen enough to slide her hand down, palm flat, between them, over his ridged abdomen, over his taut waist and belly, to caress the iron-hard ridge of his erection.

He stilled. With a predator's stillness that abruptly reminded her she held something capable of violence in her arms.

But then he broke the kiss and with a muttered oath reached down, manacled her errant wrist in a steely vise and drew her hand away.

Raising it to his shoulder, he turned back to her, clearly intending to resume the kiss. She pressed back, forestalling that. "Why can't I—"

"Not yet." His jaw was set.

"But I—"

He kissed her, hard, ruthless, determined.

She met him, just as determined, let him sweep her senses away—for a minute—then exercised her will and drew back.

Enough to make him reluctantly break the kiss.

She met his eyes from a distance of mere inches. Then she let her gaze lower to his mouth, and sent the tip of her tongue skating over her swollen lower lip. "Perhaps," she breathed, then looked into his eyes, "we've gone far enough tonight?"

He stared into her eyes; a moment ticked past, then he blinked, and glanced down at her breasts, bare, swollen, flushed, and peaked.

The effort it cost him to draw back and accede to her suggestion was palpable, but . . . easing back, he nodded. "Yes. You're right. Enough for tonight."

His diction was clipped and taut.

He helped her straighten her clothes and she let him, studying him, marveling at the tightness of his face, the inflexible control he imposed on his desire. Regardless, his reluctance—the fact that a very large part of him hadn't wanted to call a halt even if that meant letting her caress him—invested every movement.

He didn't speak as he walked her back to the house, traversing the night-shrouded gardens, but she walked beside him content enough.

He wanted her to caress him, but didn't want to risk it.

Why?

That, she felt, as they parted at the side door and she watched him stride away, was a very interesting question.

6

The next day was Saturday. Midmorning found Charlie cantering south along the road to Taunton, guiding Storm in the wake of Sarah's chestnut and inwardly cursing. How had he allowed himself to be roped into this?

This was an excursion to visit a traveling fair that was currently encamped outside Taunton. At Lady Finsbury's party he'd been invited to join the group of young ladies and gentlemen who had decided the fair provided the perfect opportunity for some innocent fun. He'd accepted, at that time viewing the jaunt in the light of a useful, entirely aboveboard—entirely innocent—opportunity to get to know his wife-to-be better.

That had been then. This was now.

Innocent outings, especially with Sarah, especially after last night, no longer featured on his agenda; he no longer viewed such encounters with equanimity, much less comfort.

After last night, having her close, even within sight, was enough to raise prospects his body yearned for regardless of the repressive instructions from his brain. Riding when half aroused had never been his idea of fun.

Yet here he was, in discomfort if not pain, condemned to spending the entire day by Sarah's side—in public. Worse, under the interested gazes of six others, three of them young ladies who were avidly curious over the purported link between himself and Sarah. He would have to endure, to literally grit his teeth and bear it, but he certainly wasn't happy about it, much less looking forward to the hours he would have to stand and walk beside her, watching over her while chatting and being sociable with the others.

He couldn't imagine any activity more inimical to his mood.

After last night . . . on one level all he wished was to get Sarah in suitable surroundings alone and take her a great deal further down their sensual road, sweep her deeper into desire until she surrendered and agreed to marry him forthwith. However, on another, less physical, more intellectual plane he was, if not uneasy, then certainly of the opinion that caution would be wise.

She'd surprised him. With one innocently sultry caress, she'd very nearly cindered his control. That wasn't something she should have been able to do, much less so easily. Consequently he kept reiterating to himself that in all future engagements, he would need to keep a firm hold on the reins.

An unbreakable hold on his reins.

Losing control in any sphere wasn't something he was comfortable even contemplating, much less doing. Not being in control, as he well knew, was, for a Morwellan, the road to ruination.

The roofs of Taunton appeared in the distance, materializing out of a wreathing mist of fog and woodsmoke that the light breeze and the weak sunshine were between them endeavoring to disperse. Charlie surveyed the sight, then considered the riders ahead of him. The four ladies were cantering two abreast; immediately ahead of him Sarah rode beside Betsy Kennedy, with Lizzie Mortimer and Margaret Cruikshank in the lead. Sarah was wearing her pale green velvet riding habit. For the occasion, she'd perched a small hat with a curling feather atop her shining hair.

The ladies, of course, were chatting, their light voices trailing over their escorts, following in similar pattern, two abreast. After exchanging greetings when they'd assembled at Crowcombe, other than a few desultory remarks, the gentlemen had held their tongues and simply enjoyed the ride and the views, both pastoral and feminine.

Behind Charlie rode Jeremy, his brother, another observer Charlie could have done without.

They all slowed to a trot as the first houses neared. When they reached the cobbles of Bridge Street, they reined in to a walk. The thoroughfare was crowded. Not only was the fair in town, but it was market day, too. Luckily, they didn't need to go through the town to reach the fair.

They left their horses at the Taunton Arms, a large posting inn just over the bridge, then strolled back across the river and down the gentle slope to the bright tents and caravans spread over a fallow field bordering the river Tone.

On the opposite bank, the high stone walls of the Norman castle rose, severe and brooding; against that silent backdrop, the richly colored flags and noisy gaiety of the fair stood in bright relief.

It was close to noon when they paid their pennies and entered the fairground beneath an arch resplendent with gaudy pennants and ribbons; the place was already crowded, the lanes between the booths and caravans bustling with people and children of every degree and station.

They halted just inside the gate to take stock. Jeremy, standing beside Charlie, glanced around, then said, "There's no way we'll manage to stay together. Let's meet back here at three o'clock. We'll have to start for home then if we don't want to be riding through the dark."

Everyone murmured their agreement; the clock in the tower of the nearby church could be seen from most of the fairground. Then the four ladies, eyes bright, determinedly set off for the first of the alleys lined with booths selling every conceivable trinket. Perforce, the gentlemen followed. This was not the sort of gathering in which their female folk could safely wander unescorted; there were a number of unsavory characters amid the crowds, and while the atmosphere was gay and said crowds were presently laughing and joking, one never knew what might occur.

Initially, the four ladies stayed together, moving from booth to booth, admiring ribbons and lace, calling to one another to point out items and compare opinions. But then Margaret Cruikshank dallied by a magic stall. Also mildly interested, Jeremy remained with her as the others moved on. Margaret and Jeremy were the youngest of the group, much the same age, and had been friends all their lives; Charlie knew he could rely on his younger brother to keep an eye on Margaret.

As the oldest of the group, he felt a certain responsibility toward the others, but that didn't mean he wished to spend the next three hours in their company. With Margaret and Jeremy occupied, that left Lizzie Mortimer and Betsy Kennedy, along with Jon Finsbury and Henry Kilpatrick, to deflect.

At the end of the first alleyway they came upon a bright purple and gold tent with a sign announcing the Great Madame Garnaut, fortune-teller extraordinaire. Lizzie and Betsy were keen, Sarah less so, but she allowed herself to be persuaded. The three ladies lined up and paid their sixpence, then waited to be summoned into Madame's presence.

Charlie had escorted females enough to fairs and similar diversions; with barely a sigh, he took a position by the side of another tent from where he could keep the entrance of Madame's garish abode in view. Younger than he, Jon and Henry grumbled, but nevertheless joined him, debating whether they would manage to find time to view the pugilistic displays being held in roped arenas on the other side of the field.

Charlie listened to their chatter; they politely included him, although he contributed little. They were five or six years his junior, and consequently viewed him with a certain awe; while Charlie found that mildly amusing, it created a certain distance between them. He turned his mind to detaching himself and Sarah from the other four.

Fate smiled, and first Betsy, then Lizzie, both rather flustered and sporting blushes, came out of Madame's tent. Sarah was the last of the three to duck beneath the richly colored flap. As it fell behind her, Lizzie and Betsy exchanged hushed confidences, then they bustled across to join their escorts.

Jon straightened and took his hands from his pockets. "So what did she say?" He directed the question impartially to both girls.

Lizzie and Betsy exchanged a glance, then Lizzie tapped Jon's arm. "Never you mind. That's for us to know and you to wonder about."

The girls looked along the next alley; they jigged, impatient to get on. They glanced back at Madame's tent; Sarah's consulation was taking longer than theirs had.

Charlie inwardly smiled. Outwardly, he grimaced. "Why don't you go on? I'll wait for Sarah."

The four looked at each other, wordlessly conferring, then brightly thanked him and bustled on to the next attraction—a line of booths selling ribbons and handkerchiefs.

Charlie watched them go, then smiled and settled to wait.

I nside the deep purple tent, Sarah sat staring into a large green glass globe. Her hands were cradling it, one palm pressed to each side as instructed. Madame had already pored over her palms, both of them, then frowned, shaken her head, and in a heavy accent informed her, "Is complicated."

That wasn't what Sarah had expected to hear. She didn't truly believe in fortune-telling, yet given she was, at that very point in time, working to discover whether Charlie loved her or not, or alternatively if he might love her once they were married even if he didn't yet, the appearance of Madame Garnaut and her services had seemed an opportunity too potentially useful to pass by. She was willing to pursue any reasonable avenue to learn what she needed to know.

But she couldn't see anything in the globe.

She glanced at Madame, seated on the opposite side of a small round table draped in deep blue velvet. The gypsy's hands, strangely cool, were clamped around Sarah's; she was peering, narrow-eyed, into the globe, a look of utter concentration etched on her much wrinkled face.

Madame's hair, black as a raven's wing, long and curly, seemed to lift and spread about her head. Then she slowly closed her eyes, slowly raised her head, and she exhaled. Into an eerie stillness, she spoke. "You wish to know whether this man can love you. He is tall, but not dark, and more than handsome. The answer to your question is yes, but the way is not clear. Whether you gain what you seek . . . that, in the end, will be up to you. It will be your decision, not his."

A long moment passed, then Madame exhaled in a long sigh. To Sarah's wide eyes, she seemed to deflate.

Madame removed her hands from Sarah's, then met Sarah's gaze. "It is the best I can do for you—the most I can tell you. So the answer is yes, but"—Madame shrugged—"the rest is complicated."

Sarah drew in a breath. Withdrawing her hands from the globe, she nodded. Pushing back from the table, she rose. "Thank you." On impulse, she dug into her reticule, pulled out another sixpence and placed it on the table. "For your extra trouble."

The gypsy took the coin and nodded. "You are a lady, but I knew that." Her old eyes, a disconcertingly bright black, met Sarah's. "I wish you good luck. With that one, it will not be easy."

Turning, Sarah lifted the tent flap and stepped out—into disorienting brightness. She blinked rapidly, then saw Charlie—*that one*—lounging by the side of a nearby tent. She walked across the alley, busying herself retying her reticule strings, using the moment to regain her composure.

It will not be easy. It will be your decision, not his.

Reaching Charlie, she looked up.

He was grinning. "So what was it—tall, dark, and handsome?"

She smiled with more confidence than she felt. "What do you think?"

He drew her hand through his arm and turned her along the next alleyway. "I think that demonstrates why you shouldn't believe the prophecies of fortune-tellers. They're all charlatans."

She'd thought the same. Now she wasn't so sure.

But the last person she wished to discuss Madame's revelations with was him. She glanced around as they strolled side by side, then realized the others were nowhere in sight. "Where are the others?"

"They headed this way."

She glanced at him, waiting, but he didn't add anything, no suggestion that he intended to find, let alone rejoin, the rest of their group. She thought, then inwardly shrugged. That suited her well enough.

Especially given Madame Garnaut's revelations. If matters were going to be complicated and if all would hinge on her decision, then the more she knew . . .

Her gaze fell on a portly figure, nattily dressed, promenading down the alley toward them. She leaned closer to Charlie. "I gather you keep abreast of changes in the industries around Taunton. Have you met Mr. Pommeroy?" With her head, she indicated the man approaching. "He's the owner of the new cider company—they've set up premises just outside town."

"Out to the west, isn't it? I've heard of it, but I rarely pass that way." Charlie drew his gaze from Mr. Pommeroy and met her eyes. "Do you know him?"

She nodded. "He's taken on two apprentices from the orphanage so far." Without waiting to be asked, she put on her best smile and angled toward Mr. Pommeroy.

Noticing her approaching, he beamed and halted. "Miss Conningham." He took her hand between both of his. "I have to tell you those two lads of yours have been working out very well—very well, indeed. If you have any more like them coming along, we'll be happy to have them join us."

"Excellent!" Retrieving her hand, Sarah gestured to Charlie. "Might I introduce Lord Meredith?"

Mr. Pommeroy was gratified. He bowed. "My lord."

Charlie nodded, precise and correct. Mr. Pommeroy introduced his wife, after which he and Charlie spent the next five minutes talking of factories, and yields, and transport. Sarah listened; she was always on the lookout for any new openings for the orphans—such as the increase in carting that, from Charlie's and Mr. Pommeroy's discourse, she realized must be occurring. She made a mental note to have a word with Mr. Hallisham, who owned the local cartage business.

Mrs. Pommeroy, however, despite the smile fixed on her face, started shifting. Taking pity on her, Sarah intervened; under cover of asking a more general question, she pinched Charlie's arm. He glanced at her, but fell in with her clearly concluding remarks, and they parted from the Pommeroys.

As they moved on, she murmured, "You can ride out and visit him sometime. It doesn't do to put up the backs of owners' wives."

Charlie's brows quirked, then his lips curved and he inclined his head. "I suppose not."

"Lady! Pretty lady!"

They'd turned into the next avenue of booths. An older man with a broad weathered face and gnarled hands waved Sarah to his counter.

"Come see! Just right for you—pretty as a picture." His head bobbed as, beaming, he beckoned her nearer. Curious, she stepped his way. He glanced down at his tray, thick fingers picking over his wares, searching. "Straight from London. Enamels from Russia. Perfect colors for you."

There was no harm in looking. Sarah towed Charlie to the booth, stopping before the raised counter.

"Ah!" The man looked up. Draped over his large fingers he displayed a necklet of interlinked enamels. A medley of bright spring greens and summer blues patterned on white decorated each shield-shaped piece. The strand looked ridiculously delicate against the man's huge hands.

Sarah's eyes widened. She reached to touch.

"Come." The trader whisked out from behind the counter. "You try it and see."

Deftly, he strung the necklet around Sarah's throat and fastened the catch.

Charlie watched, resigned; he had to give the man points for adroitness. He knew how to sell to ladies.

But the necklet did indeed suit Sarah. Head tilted, Charlie examined it, considered how it looked on her as, fingers lifting to stroke the enamel, she studied her reflection in a spotty mirror the trader had produced from beneath his counter.

The effect was . . . complex. The enameling appeared to be quite fine. The result was a piece that melded innocent simplicity with the decadence of vibrant color.

One look at Sarah's face was enough to tell Charlie that she appreciated the piece as much as he. He didn't need to glance at the shrewd trader to know the man was now watching him closely—ready to encourage him to indulge and impress his lady.

Charlie studied the necklet. The light seemed to corruscate with color when it struck. Despite an ingrained resistance to wasting any blunt on fairground gegaws, he raised a finger and traced the shields. In the mirror, Sarah glanced at him; he saw but didn't meet her gaze.

The work was smooth, as good enamels should be. Hooking a fingertip inside the strand, he flipped it so the underside showed.

And was impressed. The work on the reverse of the shields was of similar quality to that on the faces.

Alathea had a fondness for enamels—preferably from one of the Russian masters. From her he'd learned the rudiments of distinguishing good from bad. This piece wasn't from one of the masters' studios, but it was a significant cut above the average.

Having a business-trained face was so useful. His expression utterly impassive, he met the trader's gaze. "How much?"

Sarah blinked at him. She'd intended buying it for herself, he realized, but when he didn't look her way, and instead engaged the trader in a brisk round of bargaining, she closed her lips and let him buy it for her.

A small, almost insignificant victory, yet he felt it to his marrow.

By the time he and the trader exchanged nods and he and Sarah stepped away from the booth, he'd bought not just the necklet, but also a ring and three brooches. One brooch for Alathea in red, black, and gold, and one for Augusta in her favorite purple, amethyst, and mauve. Steering Sarah away from the counter, he halted her by the side of the booth and pinned the third brooch, a match for the necklet in blues and greens, into the lapel of her riding habit.

Lips gently curved, she brushed her fingers across the surface, then looked up into his face. "Thank you. They're very pretty."

He met her gaze for an instant, then looked down, found her right hand, and raised it. Slipping the matching ring onto her middle finger, he raised her hand and laid it at her breast so he could view all three pieces together.

He did, and felt his lungs contract. He knew he was looking at enamels, but that wasn't, in his mind, what he was seeing.

Lifting his gaze, he met her eyes. "Until you agree to let me give you something more valuable." Her lips quirked, but before she could speak he asked, "Have you seen the Morwellan emeralds?"

She blinked, then slipped her hand into his arm; they started strolling once more. "No." Frowning, she shook her head. "I can't recall ever seeing—"

"You might not have. Mama rarely wears them—they don't suit her. They're pale, clear, and flawless. The set—necklace, earrings, bracelet, and ring—contains the largest group of perfectly matched emeralds currently known." He glanced again at the woman on his arm—his countess. "They will suit you."

She glanced up and met his eyes. "If I marry you."

There was no "if" about it. The quiet challenge in her eyes provoked a quiet storm in him—an impulse to react and ruthlessly quash her resistance, to deny beyond doubt or even imagination that there was any other outcome possible. A muscle in his arm flexed. In something close to horror, he fought down the nearly overwhelming urge, primitive and powerful, to demonstrate the truth for her in simple, impossible-to-misconstrue actions, to make it plain that she was his.

His. He felt his jaw set. He fought and forced himself to acknowledge her words—her right to deny him—with an inclination of his head. Then he faced forward, unseeing, still struggling to subdue his reaction.

He wasn't, hadn't thought himself, a particularly possessive man. So where had such intensity come from? Why was it so strong, and what did that mean?

Regardless, if he gave in to it, if he in any way let her guess that in truth she had no choice—that she hadn't had any choice from the moment he'd stood in her father's drawing room and offered for her hand, quite aside from all that had passed between them since—if he gave her any inkling that their path was set regardless of her thoughts, he would run into a wall of feminine resistance.

One he knew well enough to avoid. Alathea had a similar defense, that construct of a steely female will, and so did many, if not all, the Cynster ladies. No sane male knowingly provoked such a defense.

There were some battles from which it was wiser to retreat.

He repeated those strictures until he calmed, until that prowling, lurking beast she'd pricked settled grudgingly back to watch, and wait.

Strolling by his side, Sarah pretended not to notice the tension that had flared, that he'd subdued and smothered, but that only gradually faded from the arm on which her hand lay.

Only gradually did the large hard body pacing beside her regain its customary loose-limbed ease, his signature grace.

Once it had, she breathed a little more easily. He definitely didn't like her even obliquely suggesting that she might not marry him. Which again raised the question of what it was that was driving him—why he was so *intent* on marrying her.

If only he would tell her, life—his and hers—would be considerably simpler, yet it was patently clear that he didn't wish her to know. So she'd have to keep pressing, holding to her line, until she learned enough to understand.

"Miss Conningham!"

"Yoo-hoo, miss!"

Sarah halted and turned. Smiling, she watched three lads—well, they were young men now—come pushing through the crowd. Reaching her, all three bowed their best bow, then grinned at her cheekily.

"I say, miss," Bobby Simpson said, "have you seen the half man—half woman? He's in a tent over there."

"He—or she. It's really amazing, miss," Johnny Wilson averred.

Naturally the boys thought that that was the most exciting side-show. Sarah swallowed a laugh. "What else is there to see?"

They were only too happy to pour into her ears a catalogue of the carnival delights to be found on the perimeter of the fair. They'd known her through their formative years and felt no constraint; they eagerly gave her their young male views. They'd noticed Charlie by her side—how could they not?—noticed that her hand lay on his arm, but from the quick, uncertain glances they threw him, none of the three had recognized him.

Eventually their patter ran out.

"Thank you. Now I know what there is to see in the remaining time I have." She indicated Charlie. "This is Lord Meredith."

All three immediately tugged their forelocks; they recognized the title well enough.

"Now tell me," Sarah continued smoothly, "how are you getting on at the tannery?"

They told her, but their eagerness in that was clearly not matched by their fascination with the fair. Smiling, she let them go. After quick bows to her and Charlie, they pelted off through the crowd.

Charlie watched them disappear. "There must be quite a few around here who know you through the orphanage." They started strolling again. "How many such do you release into the world each year?"

"It varies. And there are girls, too. They go into the major houses, most often as maids but sometimes in training as cooks."

They continued on down the alleyways of the fair, idly scanning the booths, resisting all inducements to draw near and sample the wares, or to view the numerous sideshows. The crowd of children before the Punch-and-Judy was considerable; they paused at the edge of it and watched for a time, more entertained by the children and their raucous reactions than the show itself, then walked on.

Nothing occurred to reinvoke their earlier clash of wills, for which Sarah was grateful. She saw no benefit in further prodding a point over which she knew he would react.

His uncanny, indeed ruthless and quite relentless habit of always getting his own way, regardless of his outward charm and apparently easygoing nature, was well recognized within his family and, courtesy of his sisters, had long been well known to her, too. Intriguingly, he hadn't attempted to charm her. A wise decision; glib charm never worked well with her, and in his case, she saw through his veneer as if it were thinner than a gossamer veil.

She knew what he was, underneath the glamor; the closer they drew, the more time they spent together, she realized that that was true—more true than she'd realized. That her vision of him was . . . as clear and flawless as his family's emeralds. She'd somehow always known him in a way she couldn't explain.

And as she wasn't yet able to tell him yay or nay, and from the occasional sidelong glances he threw her, his gaze sharp as a lance, studying her face, she knew that he was evaluating ways and means to bring her answer—the right answer—about, it was undoubtedly wise to let the question lie, unresolved and for now unapproached between them.

Tonight would be soon enough to push ahead with that.

Such were her thoughts. Her nerves and senses, however, were nowhere near as well ordered. As cool and collected.

She wished they were. Wished that her senses wouldn't leap and jump whenever the crowd forced them close, that her nerves didn't make her shiver with reaction when, in a sudden crush, his arm brushed her breast.

As the afternoon rolled on and the crowd grew denser, all Charlie's misgivings over the outing were borne out. Unfortunately, he derived no joy from having been right in his predictions. Not even a perverse joy from knowing that Sarah was equally susceptible, that her nerves skittered every time he touched a guiding hand to her back, that her breath caught, suspended, when in the press of bodies his thigh brushed hers.

Then a rowdy group of journeymen came caroling and leaping down the crowded alleyway, their rush forcing all others to give way, to draw aside and let them pass.

The sudden movement threatened to bowl over those walking at the edge of the alley.

Charlie reacted instinctively, whipping an arm around Sarah and half lifting, half sweeping her out of danger, into the protective lee of his body, and then into the cramped space between two booths.

The wave of jostling humanity rolled through the crowd and past. To the sound of curses, the pack of overexuberant young men disappeared, leaving those scattered in their wake to right themselves, dust themselves off, and resume their more sedate progress.

Leaving Charlie and Sarah upright, but close. Very close.

He'd been watching the young men disappear; as he turned his head to look at her, he felt a shiver of sensual awareness, of sheer sensual anticipation, ripple through her from her shoulders to her knees. Felt his reaction—not a shiver—race through him, hot, ardent, hungry, and greedy, even before his eyes met hers.

And he saw his own need, his own flaring desire, mirrored in the cornflower blue of her eyes.

Her lips were parted, her breath caught, her hands raised between them, suspended before his chest; she didn't know where to put them, knew well enough not to touch him, but she wanted to.

That last was a palpable, tangible thing, real enough to feel like a caress even without the contact. In response his own need rose in a surging wave, like a cat arching into that phantom caress. Wanting more.

For one definable instant, he teetered on the brink of surrendering— to his need and hers. Taking just one moment to let passion have its way—but it wouldn't be for just one moment.

Dragging in a breath and easing back, deliberately breaking the spell, was the hardest thing he'd ever done. It was a wrench, a pain, a denial that hurt. Both of them.

He managed to step back; taking her hand, he drew her, unresisting, out of the cramped space, back into the alleyway. Linking their arms, he turned; after an instant's hesitation, they resumed strolling.

Minutes passed before they were breathing freely again.

He drew a deeper, still not entirely steady breath. Eyes fixed forward, he said, "Tonight."

A statement, no question. He felt her gaze briefly touch his face; from the corner of his eye, he saw her nod.

She looked ahead. "Yes. Tonight."

Tonight they would deal with what had flared between them.

For now . . . "This crowd is getting too dense for comfort." Talk about stating the obvious. "Perhaps we should head for the meeting place."

She glanced at the clock tower; the time was two-thirty. But she nodded. "The crowd might be less thick over there."

To their mutual relief, that proved to be the case. Even more helpfully, the others had also found the increasing crowds off-putting; within ten minutes, they'd all arrived.

"How about a quick tea at the Arms before we take to the saddle?" Jon suggested.

The group agreed. They walked back to the Arms. After duly refreshing themselves, they mounted their horses, and headed north for their homes.

Sarah rode alongside Charlie and tried not to think. Not to dwell on that fraught moment between the booths, not to dwell on their interlude tonight. Tonight would be time enough to think of that. Until they were alone, there was nothing more they could do.

Nothing to quell the urgency driving them, or still the insistent pounding in their veins.

7

He wasn't there when she reached the summerhouse, sunk in the quiet of the night. She listened, but heard nothing beyond the soft slink of the water over the lip of the weir, no footsteps, no impatient strides approaching.

Pressing her hands together, straightening her curling fingers, she forced herself to calm; drawing in a steadying breath, she willed her wits from the whirl of anticipation they'd too eagerly allowed to claim them. She tried to think, to reason, tried to focus firmly on her goal, reminding herself of what that was and how she intended to pursue it.

How she intended to force him to reveal what lay behind his desire for her.

She'd barely formed the thought when a boot crunched on the path outside and he was there, taking the steps three at a time, an elementally male figure crossing the wooden floor in long, fluid strides.

And then she was in his arms, wrapped in their strength, and his lips were on hers. And she was swept away, into the beckoning heat, into the fiery furnace of their mutual desire.

Every night it burned hotter; every day the inevitable abrading of their senses, relief withheld until the dark of night, only stoked the flames higher.

And the urgency built.

Tonight she welcomed it. Tonight she had her own agenda and was relying on that driving pounding in their blood to give her the strength and the opportunity to pursue it.

She made no demur when he invaded her mouth and ravaged her senses, when he drew her flush against him, then evocatively stroked, one large palm gliding over the curve of her hip and derriere, then firming, cupping, and provocatively kneading.

Her breath caught as he molded her to him, her senses threatened to fracture as the hard ridge of his erection rode against the soft tautness of her belly. Heat flared; the furnace swelled. A hot empty ache yawned deep within her.

She only gasped when he tumbled them both onto the sofa; she landed beside and half under him, their legs tangled, hands grasping.

He flicked loose the buttons of her bodice. She wrenched the sides of his coat wide, ran her hands up to his shoulders to push the garment off. He muttered a curse, and pulled back enough to shrug free of the jacket. She fell on the buttons of his waistcoat; he muttered another oath and obliged.

But then he kissed her again and pressed her back against the sofa, rapidly dealt with buttons, bodice, and chemise—and then his hand was on her breast and she gasped again, louder, lungs tighter, tightening yet further as his palm cruised, stroked, then his hand closed and his fingers settled to play, to pluck her nerves, to orchestrate the pleasure that rushed through her. It was a swirling, mindless temptation of delight; she let it flow and wash through her, until she found her feet.

Until she could marshal and harbor and ultimately wield enough wit and will to kiss him back, to raise a hand and frame his face, meet his tongue with hers, and distract him.

Long enough to undo the buttons closing his shirt, long enough to slide her hand beneath the gaping linen, and touch him.

His reaction was instantaneous. He broke the kiss and sucked in a breath; his whole body hardened and stilled. But he didn't pull away. In the darkness she couldn't see his expression, yet his face seemed tight, lashes lowered, jaw clenched. As if her hand were burning him,

as if her touch were something it pained him to endure . . . but it was he
who was burning.

His skin felt like lava poured over solid rock, smooth, almost fluid,
yet beneath it nothing moved.

Determined to know, to learn, she caressed, for a long moment gave
her senses over to exploring the heavy muscles of his chest, sweeping
both hands across, then lower to slide over his ridged abdomen, to glide
farther and grasp his sides at his waist, to feel the naked skin like flame
beneath her palms.

For one instant she gloried, filling her senses with the perfection of
him, then he broke. He pressed her down into the sofa cushions, leaned
over her and recaptured her mouth—and without quarter ripped her
wits away.

Swept her will away, sent it spinning beneath an onslaught of feeling, of his actions and her reactions, of an exchange at a wholly different level of greedy rapacious need.

Of hunger more explicit, more definite, less controlled. She marveled and embraced it. Let herself slide into it, let it flow around and
over and through her, fascinated and enthralled.

This was what she wanted to see, to know, to examine. This—his
desire—was what she needed to explore.

Charlie kept her pressed into the sofa, kept her mouth locked with
his, kept her wits whirling while he grappled with a conundrum he'd
never before faced, not in this arena, not with any other woman. Contradictory compulsions rode him, each merciless and demanding—an
instinctive desire to appease her, to happily fall in with her blatantly
declared wishes and show her all she wantonly wished to know, if anything to encourage her even further, yet his plan called for something
else. Dictated a different line of play—of attack.

Her small hands had pushed beneath the back of his shirt; her fingers gripped and pressed into his skin. Urgent, needy.

The innocent touch seared him. Called to that hunger, the prowling ravenous beast that she so readily aroused and sent raging.

Every instinct he possessed was clamoring to take her, to finish
this strange wooing now and have done, yet . . . if he showed her all, if
he joined with her tonight, would she be sufficiently enamored of the
pleasures of the flesh to happily agree to be his forevermore?

If he joined with her tonight, would she agree to marry him

tomorrow? With any other young lady, the answer would be yes, but with Sarah . . . she'd already surprised him multiple times.

No. Safer by far to hold to his plan and give her time and experience from which to properly appreciate the splendors of pleasure. To learn of the delights to which he proposed to introduce her, and to subsequently enjoy with her for the rest of their lives.

How could she appreciate if she didn't truly know? If she didn't understand what the elements of pleasure were?

Teaching her, introducing her to pleasure step-by-step, as he'd planned, was the wiser course. The course more certain to succeed in convincing her to accept his proposal and agree to be his.

Despite the lure of her supple, soft body, so quintessentially feminine stretched half beneath his, despite the wanton encouragement of her kiss, of the way she gifted him with her mouth, the way she met and challenged him, and taunted and teased . . . not that she actually meant to . . . he had to remember what the course of wisdom was. He couldn't afford to forget.

Couldn't afford not to have her eager and willing to be his bride.

So he reined in his own desires, ruthlessly quelled his rioting instincts and resisted her lure, resisted the open invitation she was so blatantly issuing. Blotted it from his mind and drew back from the kiss, and set his lips skimming down her throat.

Down over her collarbone, tugging aside her gaping bodice to gain access to the rosy peaks of her breasts. Then he settled to show her what pleasure was. One element of it, at least.

One compulsive, giddy, dizzying facet; her responses were more intense than the previous night's, heightened by the last time and the frustrations of the day. Good. He focused on her, on her reactions, with lips, mouth, teeth, and tongue concentrated on immersing her senses in the heady, enticing delight.

As before, the taste of her awakening was sheer wonder to him. For every iota of delight he gave her, she reciprocated in a way he'd never before even imagined existed.

She writhed beneath his experienced caresses, the firm touch of his hands, the wet heat of his mouth, the shocking rasp of his tongue drawing gasp after smothered moan from her lusciously swollen lips. As he bent his head and drew one taut and aching nipple deep into his mouth, and heard her cry out, he felt a curious sense of honor warm him. It was not just that he was the lucky man who would introduce her to sensual pleasure, that he would be her mentor in this, the one to educate her senses in this intimate field, but that he was all that at her invitation. By her choice.

He had chosen her as his bride, but part of his unacknowledged reasoning had been that he'd hoped, if she were given the choice, that she would choose him.

In this, in this arena. And she had.

It was, he was discovering, an unexpectedly heady honor to be chosen by her—an honor conferred by her desire. He'd had no idea that such a thing would mean so much to him, that despite his frustrated needs, he would so enjoy these moments. These never-to-be-repeated moments when he opened her sensual eyes to passion and all its glory.

Entranced, nearly mesmerized by sensation, Sarah was nevertheless conscious of time passing; at some point, he would call a halt to their night, and she'd yet to make any real progress. Just a glimpse before he'd slammed a door on his desire, that was all she'd seen. She needed to see more.

The only way to succeed was to circumvent his control.

Gathering sufficient will along with sufficient strength required concerted effort, but eventually she managed to turn her mind from what her reeling senses were reporting enough to refocus on him.

Sliding her hands from his back, she tried to reach lower but discovered she couldn't reach even as far as his waist. Palms at his sides, she urged him higher, but he ignored such weak demands.

And tried to distract her by suckling more deeply—she had to pause, drag in a huge breath, hold tight to her wits as sensation sharp and powerful threatened to rip them away . . . she succeeded, managed to catch her mental breath, then even more determined, she tried again.

Drawing one hand from the warmth of his torso, she found his jaw, cupped it, and gently but insistently nudged and tipped until he complied, lifted his head and brought his lips to hers.

She was ready to meet them, ready to let their mouths meld, their tongues twine, then duel. Then she wriggled and slid beneath him, one quick shift so that their heads were closer to level. In the same movement, she drew her other hand from his back, pressed it between them, and found him, his erection hard and rigid beneath his breeches.

Boldly she stroked, then experimented and closed her hand.

His reaction was immediate. Despite the clamp of her hand on his jaw, he drew back from the kiss, a curse on his lips; half lifting from her, he caught her wrist in a viselike grip and hauled her hand from his straining flesh. "No." Raising her hand above her head, he anchored it against the sofa cushions; from a distance of shadowed inches, he met her eyes. His were narrowed.

She glared at him. "Why?"

"Because—"

He broke off on a hiss as she wriggled, squirmed, and managed to caress that most sensitive and, for her purposes, useful part of him with her thigh. His eyes closed, but his jaw set even harder. He swore, grabbed her other hand and anchored that above her head, too, as he shifted over her, then he lowered his weight and she was trapped.

Beneath him. Half a second's consideration informed her that that was not necessarily a bad thing. One of his legs lay between her, his knee sinking into the thick cushions so that the hard muscle of his thigh rode against the sensitive spot at the apex of hers.

The result gave her pause.

But then she remembered. Narrowing her eyes on his, she demanded, "Why?"

Each of her hands was locked in one of his; he was pressing both into the cushions above and to either side of her head. Their faces were close; he looked down into hers. "Because you're not ready for that yet."

Each word was bitten off. Grim frustration invested them.

She considered all she could see, all she could sense in the hard, taut, definitely aroused body above hers. "Why not?"

She made the demand a trifle less challenging, more a sincere question, but that she was not going to be fobbed off nevertheless rang in her tone.

He studied her eyes, then searched her face. A moment ticked past in which their heated bodies cooled not one whit, in which the passion trembling in the air about them subsided not at all, then his lips twisted, a resigned grimace.

The odd notion flitted across her mind that she wasn't certain the resignation was real. Charlie surrendering? That didn't seem likely.

"You can't—shouldn't—just plunge into this. It shouldn't be considered as a simple act, but an art. Not only in the execution, but in the enjoyment, too. So you need to learn, and at a reasonable pace."

In the shadowed dark, she could see his eyes but had no hope of reading them. But she wasn't witless; he wanted control of the pace. They would see. She shifted, just a fraction, beneath him, enough to draw his attention to her bare, swollen, tightly peaked breasts. "So, what's next?"

Her tone had once again found its sultry note.

He met her eyes for a heartbeat, then lowered his head. Whispered his answer to her unvoiced challenge over her lips. "If you think you're ready?"

She met his gaze as he drew back a fraction. "Oh, yes."

Then she kissed him, or he kissed her—all that mattered was that their lips met in a sharp exchange that set instant spark to the hungry flames that had simmered, held down by force of will while they spoke.

Now those flames roared anew. Compelling, driving.

What next? Her question rang in her mind while the urgent need to know filled her. His lips on hers, he drew her hands higher, then manacled both in one of his. Above her, he shifted his weight, so that while one thigh remained between hers, his weight rested beside her. She sensed him reach down, with his free hand grasp her skirt, then he flicked it up above her knees.

He reached beneath, his hard palm gripping and sliding over her bare thigh, and she shuddered.

And he stopped. His hand remained where it was, although she could sense the effort it cost to stop there, on the cusp of whatever came next.

His lips gentled; before he could draw back from the kiss and speak—ask her if she was sure—she arched and kissed him fiercely, and gave him his answer.

His grip on her thigh eased, his touch instantly assuming a more dangerous, more seductive intent. His tongue probed, stroked hers, then withdrew; with only the pressure of his lips to distract her, her senses slid down to focus on his hand. On the play of his fingers as they rose, trailing spiraling sensation upward to the crease between torso and thigh. One blunt fingertip traced it, forward, then back an inch, forward then back; totally caught, barely breathing, she waited to see, to know . . .

His palm slid along her hip, then pushed over and back as he rolled to his side, taking her with him. He released her hands; unthinking, she let them fall to his shoulders, caught in the shock of feeling his questing hand rove over her bare bottom. His other hand cradled her head, holding her mouth to his, his to plunder at his languid will while the hand beneath her skirts explored.

Also at his will. Under his complete and absolute control.

Despite the compelling, distracting sensations, the enthrallment of her senses, the shivery cascade of heightened awareness that slid over and through her and made her quake in anticipation, she was conscious to her bones of his concentration. Of the unwavering focus he brought to the moment. A commitment not only to maintaining that unshakable control, his bulwark and defense, but to her, to her pleasure, to, as he'd put it, teaching her this art.

To educating her senses in how it felt to have his hand idly fondling her bare bottom, to have him stroke, caress, then trace the cleft between the taut hemispheres, following it down to lightly, intimately, flirt in the hollow between her thighs.

She shuddered, and pressed nearer, turned her body to his, slid one hand to his nape and asked for more through their kiss.

He hesitated, then his fingers left the sensitive skin at the top and back of her thighs, skating down until he reached her knee, then he gripped and lifted, bending and wrapping that leg high over his hip. Briefly he caressed her knee, then his fingers slowly trailed back down the line of her thigh, to where the delicate flesh between her thighs was now open and exposed to his touch.

She shivered again, but he didn't stop; he reached and touched, lightly brushed her curls, stroked tantalizingly through them, then settled to not so much explore as map, to outline rather than probe. The light caresses made her nerves flicker and skitter, substantial enough for her to follow his intent, to track each caress to its end, yet every time be left hungry, waiting for the next.

Waiting for tactile fulfillment of some barely perceived desire. Her flesh heated, then throbbed; a strange restlessness gripped her. The yearning for him to touch her more intimately burgeoned and grew.

Swelled until it fed her desire, fanned the flames . . .

He seemed to know the precise moment when she was about to break and demand more; he drew back from the kiss, skated his lips along the line of her jaw to her ear, then murmured, "When we're wed, you'll open yourself to me like this, part your legs and wind them about my waist, and I'll fill you."

The words—the image they conjured—transfixed her. In the darkness, she focused on his face, his lips, so close, his eyes screened behind his long lashes. She licked her lips and he glanced at them.

His voice, when it reached her, was pure passion, the distillation of desire. "I'll fill that odd emptiness inside you." He spoke slowly, his cadence deliberate, the words direct. "I'll drive into you, over and over, and you'll never know such pleasure, and then you'll be complete."

Dipping his head, he brushed her lips, one long lingering touch. "As you need, and want, and were meant to be."

Mine. Charlie heard the word ring in his head, but kept it from his lips. He'd fought and managed to turn her unexpected insistence to his advantage. But enough was enough. Before she could snap free of the sensual web he'd woven, he withdrew his hand from beneath her skirt, framed her face, and kissed her—deeply, as deeply intimate as he wished.

"For tonight, that's enough." His growl bore testimony that that wasn't his body's wish any more than it was hers. His mind, however, was firmly in the ascendant.

She frowned at him. "Why?"

Her favorite word. He managed not to frown back. "Because if we let our horses bolt, we'll go too fast and you'll miss too much along the way." He capped those eminently sane words with a statement it was impossible to dispute. "And we need to get this right because there's only ever one first time along this road."

The next afternoon, Charlie stood in one corner of the high hedge bordering the vicarage lawn balancing a teacup on a saucer and, his expression as impassive as he could make it, considered his wife-to-be, sitting sipping tea in the diagonally opposite corner, as distant from him as she could possibly be.

Who would have thought it could be as bad as this? Charlie cursed the impulse that had prompted him to accept an invitation to the monthly Sunday-afternoon tea party at the vicarage; he'd heard that Mrs. Duncliffe had intended to invite Mr. Sinclair, and had accepted assuming Sinclair would be present, and that he'd be able to distract himself discussing investments while keeping Sarah in sight.

Unfortunately Sinclair had been otherwise engaged. Even more unfortunately, he'd underestimated the cumulative effect of his and Sarah's nightly interludes; said effect had made itself known immediately he and she had drawn close enough to touch hands.

Just one look, that one touch, and they'd both felt the jarring jolt, the fierce tug. The powerful, elemental, all but overwhelming need to be together in a physically explicit sense.

In mutual shock they'd retreated to the safety of opposing corners of the lawn, to preserve some semblance of acceptable behavior and not risk shocking everyone present—most of their neighbors and both their mothers—by giving in to some action too suggestive to mistake.

He'd taken cover with Jon and Henry and a small group of other gentlemen. And Sarah was surrounded by the other young ladies, yet many feminine eyes, young and old alike, were watching him and her, wondering at their separation, given what was now transparently common knowledge as to their direction.

Regardless of the speculation, being close in public was no longer wise.

Which was one of several points he found difficult to accept. Never in his life had he been affected to this degree—even close to this degree—by a woman. By the pursuit of a woman. He currently had more in common with some rabid adolescent in the throes of his first affair, than the suave, debonair, and sophisticated man of the world he unquestionably was. He was thirty-three, for heaven's sake! A gentleman of his ilk, of his age and experience, shouldn't feel as if his continued existence hinged on sinking his far too active erection into the hot haven of a specific female body.

He shouldn't feel as if possessing her was now the be-all and end-all of his life.

Yet he did.

Accepting another tea cake from the plate passed around, he bit into it and shifted his gaze from Sarah—why torture himself? this was the vicarage; there was no hope whatever of doing anything to ease their burning itch while here—and subjected Mrs. Duncliffe's rose garden to distant scrutiny while reliving again the events of the previous night.

He'd left the summerhouse satisfied and relieved. Relieved because he'd weathered the challenges, satisfied because from the battle he'd not just wrested control but had managed to establish a base, a rationale she understood, for pushing ahead with his plan.

While the relief had evaporated, the satisfaction at least remained.

Small comfort. No matter how he twisted the facts, what he couldn't understand or explain, but likewise couldn't dismiss, was that while he'd been seducing her, and succeeding, he'd somehow managed to seduce himself.

He could hardly blame *her*. Given the differences in age and experience, it simply wasn't possible to credit that she could seduce him. Yet time and again, he'd found himself driven if not out of control then temporarily beyond it. And time and again he'd adjusted and changed tack; he would draw a line, determined not to step over it, then she'd press, and he'd find himself rearranging his plan.

It might have been she making the demands, but it had been he who'd acquiesced.

She wasn't capable of controlling him, and there wasn't anything or anyone else involved, so it had to be him, something within him that for some godforsaken reason was pushing him, seducing him, into doing things that were making this courtship so much harder.

He didn't understand it, but he was determined to prevail. And he would.

His gaze returned to Sarah. She felt it, briefly met it across the expanse of the vicarage lawn, then she turned away. Lifting her cup, she sipped. He saw her hand tremble as she set the cup down on her saucer; he looked away.

The week he'd set himself ended on Tuesday night. Tonight he'd take her further, tempt her yet further, but every step of the way he'd remain on guard.

Against whatever it was that was invading his brain.

The moon hung suspended over the weir when she came to him that night. They were hungry, so hungry, both of them, that it was implicit from the first ravenously yearning kiss that tonight he would show her more.

Much more.

Sarah burned and wanted, but it wasn't simply the delights of physical pleasure she sought. She wanted to know why, and if she was starting to understand that it wasn't reason, cold and logical, that drove his transparent desire for her, she'd yet to grasp any firm comprehension of what that elusive something was.

Yet the physical was linked with the ephemeral; it was an outcome of it. If she explored one, she would at some point understand the other.

Her plan, such as it was, had been reduced to that. To take his hand and let him show her what he would, and then encourage him to show her more. Until she saw and understood.

And if she shivered when his mouth closed over her breast, cried out, a primitive sound in the night when he suckled fiercely, if her limbs melted and her nerves quivered, coiling and quaking, as he lifted her skirts and stroked, then touched her, cupped her, lightly probed that most intimate part of her until flames licked down her spine and heat pooled in her belly, then it was, she told herself, a willing and necessary exchange.

If she wanted to learn more of him, she had to surrender more of herself.

How much more she was willing to surrender, of that she'd had no clue, not until they were once more a tangle of tumbled limbs on the sofa, and she was hot and needy and urgently greedy, with her hands sunk in the softness of his hair, evocatively gripping, with her lips parted, hungry and wanton beneath his, with her tongue tangling with his, challenging and taunting, even demanding. With his hands on her body, long fingers stroking between her parted thighs, again and again caressing the slick swollen flesh of her entrance.

She had to have more, then and there, not later. Needed that next moment more than she needed to breathe. Needed . . . she wasn't entirely sure what, but she felt sure he did.

When he tried to hold firm to his invisible line and deny her more than that minimally greater intimacy, with lips and tongue, with her hands and her body, wordless in entreaty she begged.

Charlie discovered he wasn't proof against her sensual pleading. She wanted, and he gave; some unruly, rampant part of his mind had taken that as its code, and stamped it on his brain. No matter his determination to remain in complete control, and through that dictating each caress, each moment of pleasure, each new delight to which she was exposed, he couldn't deny her, couldn't hold back from appeasing her wantonly explicit need.

Couldn't deny himself that pleasure.

Driven by that passion he didn't entirely recognize, by that need he couldn't name, with one blunt fingertip he circled her slick entrance, then, when she clutched and begged, he pressed in, just an inch. But she was heated and urgent, lifting against his hand, inviting, enticing; he surrendered and gave her what she wished.

Felt her gasp through their locked mouths as he slid one finger deep into her sheath. Felt her virgin flesh ease, then contract, scalding velvet about his finger. He tracked her response, sensed and grasped the perfect moment when she'd absorbed that first shock to stroke, at first slow and deliberate, letting the full impact of the intimate penetration impinge on her whirling senses, then, at his direction, and hers, the beat gradually built.

Faster, harder, in time with their hearts, with the pounding in their blood.

She writhed, trapped half beneath him, her hips instinctively lifting into the intimate caress. Driven by her and his own compulsive need, he ravished her mouth, then settled to plunder there to the same escalating, undeniable beat.

He drove her onto the rising slope, then whipped her up it, higher and higher, until she found the peak, until she tensed, fingers sinking into his upper arms, until at last she soared, then fractured, shattered, and came apart in his arms.

The rippling wave died, faded away and left her; boneless, she relaxed beneath him, all tension released. He drew his hand from her, let her skirt fall. Hoped she was satisfied.

Breaking the now gentled kiss, he lifted his head and looked down on her face, pale and fine in the moonlight. An angel's face, one that hid a will to match his own.

That was one reason why he wanted her.

The thought strayed across his mind, then drifted away.

Her features had relaxed into the blankness of satiation, but as he watched, they came alive, vitality reinfusing them.

Her lashes fluttered, then she lifted her lids, and looked at him. She frowned. "I want you inside me."

The words were a sultry complaint. Although she didn't quite pout, the impression was there.

He drew a tight breath and pulled back, only just managed to slam a mental door on his demons, slavering in anticipation and only too ready and willing to fall in with her suggestion. "Not yet."

His accents were clipped, his voice strained.

He forced himself to sit up. Bludgeoning his unwilling body to his bidding, he lifted her and settled her, cradled across his lap.

Her hip rested against his erection, but there was nothing he could do besides grit his teeth and bear it. And sternly refuse to listen to his baser self report that he was so hard he was risking permanent injury.

He had to think, yet with her in his arms, the exercise seemed indescribably difficult; he concentrated, but all he seemed aware of, all he could find in his mind, was the sensation of the delicate swell of her cheek nestling against his bare chest.

She'd managed to rid him of his coat and waistcoat, and open his shirt, again. Managed to get her hands on his naked chest, skin to skin . . . perhaps it was that that had scattered his wits, although why that should be so he couldn't imagine. He'd never been susceptible in that way before, not with any other lady, yet with her, Susceptible had become his middle name.

His arms closed around her, supporting her. Holding her.

Unexpectedly, she gave a little laugh, wry, faintly cynical. "After our performance at the vicarage, my mother wanted to know if anything was wrong."

His mother hadn't asked, although she'd wanted to. He was curious. "What did you say?"

"That we were finding being the cynosure of attention for everyone around us a trifle unnerving."

Despite all, he smiled. "Excellent answer. Perfectly true as far as it goes." He made a mental note in case of later need.

They sat on the sofa as the moon slid away and the comfortable dark closed around them.

Eventually, she stirred. Lifting her head, she touched a hand to his cheek. "Charlie—"

"No." He caught her fingers, brought them to his lips, held her gaze as he kissed. His wits had returned; he'd started to realize what had—again—occurred. "Not yet," he murmured. "We need to proceed at a slow pace."

A *slower* pace.
    Heaven help him.

The next morning Charlie sat at the desk in his library, chin propped in one hand, staring unseeing at the Aubusson rug, entirely unable to understand how matters had reached such a convoluted state.

His plan was straightforward, its execution well within his abilities, yet somehow his and Sarah's interaction continued to escalate further, faster, propelled by some force he was unable to brake.

And now, even though he knew he had to—somehow—slow their sensual progress, a large, increasingly strident and powerful part of him wanted nothing more than to forge ahead. To simply dive into the passion that flared so hotly between them, to slake his ever-increasing lust, to gorge and drink his fill, then to revel and wallow.

Despite his long walk through the chilly night after he'd seen Sarah to the house, despite the ride home through winter's bleakness, he'd barely slept a wink, unable to free either his mind or his senses from the promise of passion she embodied.

From all that his experience knew he could make of it, all he knew he could gain from it.

From that elusive, enticing taste of innocence.

It was that, he decided, that had invaded his brain—an addiction to the taste of innocence. Addictions, like obsessions, could drive men to do things they wouldn't normally do, to behave in ways they normally wouldn't, but addictions, thankfully, could fade. As this one assuredly would.

Once she'd agreed to marry him, to be his forevermore, once they were wed, then her innocence would gradually fade. A few weeks, a month at most, and his curious fascination with it would be sated, and it itself would have dissipated.

So he didn't need to worry. This wasn't an obsession, as love could be. This was fascination to the point of addiction, nothing more.

He turned that conclusion over in his mind, and found nothing in it with which he wished to argue. He could, therefore, press ahead with his plan.

Except that it was Monday, the day Sarah spent at the orphanage.

Despite a very real compulsion to have Storm saddled and ride up to Quilley Farm, and trust to his undoubted talents to make hay of whatever opportunities the day might afford to ease the compulsive itch to hold her, kiss her, touch her, the notion of trying to keep his reactions to her concealed from all the bright eyes in that place—imagining the sheer amount of teeth-gritting, jaw-clenching wrestling with his demons that would require—was enough to keep him in his chair.

Was enough, ultimately, to make him refocus on the various estate papers spread before him. Grimacing, he picked up a pen, and forced himself to deal with what he could during the day, and leave the night's challenges until then.

"Tnere's a gentleman here to see you, miss."

Folding and sorting the freshly laundered clothes in the orphanage nursery, the perfect way to keep her mind from dwelling on other, infinitely more distracting things, Sarah looked up as Maggs stuck his curly head around the door.

"Mrs. Carter said as she'd put him in the office and could you come down and see him." Maggs grinned. "He looks like a shylock."

"I see." Sarah laid aside a pair of woolen socks, rose and went to the door. "Thank you for the message, and now back you go to your lessons—and no dillydallying along the way."

Maggs essayed an affronted look, which Sarah returned with a glance sufficiently pointed to have him heaving a put-upon sigh. "All right. I'll go straight back."

Sarah followed him down the stairs. At the foot, Maggs slouched into the corridor leading to the room Joseph used for his classes. Smiling at the blatant evidence of his reluctance, Sarah headed for the office.

Joseph had been exposing the older boys to Shakespeare. While she doubted that any moneylender had called to see her, she wasn't surprised when on opening the study door she discovered a thin, sharp-featured gentleman dressed in rusty black. With his small, deep-set dark eyes and blade-thin nose, he was clearly Maggs's vision of what a shylock should look like.

She hid her amusement behind a welcoming smile. "Good afternoon. I'm Miss Conningham."

The man had risen; now he bowed, a touch obsequiously. "Mr. Milton Haynes, miss. I'm a solicitor from Taunton, and I have an offer to lay before you from one of my clients."

Sarah gestured to Mr. Haynes to resume his seat in the chair before the desk while she stepped behind it and sat in the desk chair. "An offer?"

"Indeed, miss." All brisk efficiency, Mr. Haynes lifted a leather satchel onto his lap, opened it, and extracted a folded document. "If you'll permit me?" At Sarah's nod, he set down the satchel and, with a certain sense of drama, spread the paper on the desk before her. "As I will endeavor to explain, Miss Conningham, this is what I have no hesitation in describing as a very generous offer for the house and land described as Quilley Farm—you will see the sum proposed here." He pointed with a neat fingernail. "Now, if you will allow me to advise . . ."

Frowning even more, Sarah reached for the paper, drawing it from beneath the solicitor's finger; he was reluctant, but in the end lifted his digit and allowed her to pick up the sheet.

Although she was unfamiliar with such documents, a quick scan of the convoluted legal phrases confirmed that someone was indeed making an offer for Quilley Farm, house and land all together, and the sum offered was enough to make Sarah blink.

Mr. Haynes cleared his throat. "As I was about to say, this offer is extremely generous, certainly significantly more than you could expect on the open market in this area, but my client wishes to secure the property, so is willing to offer above the odds." He leaned forward. "Cash, I might add. Nothing questionable, no, indeed."

Sarah lifted her gaze to Haynes's face. "Who is your client?" According to the letter, the offer was made via Haynes's office.

Haynes sat back, his gregarious expression fading into primness. "I'm afraid I'm not at liberty to divulge his name. He's an eccentric, and prefers absolute privacy."

Sarah raised her brows. "Indeed?" She had no idea what to make of that. Were such anonymous transactions common? Regardless . . . "I'm afraid, Mr. Haynes, that your client has been misinformed." She stood; folding the sheet, she handed it back to Haynes who, face falling, was forced to rise, too. "I have no interest in, or intention of, selling Quilley Farm."

Seeing something like shock infuse Haynes's sharp features—perhaps understandable given the sum offered—she added, "The farm was bequeathed to me as a working orphanage with the clear assumption I would keep it operating as such. I couldn't break faith with such a legacy."

Haynes opened his mouth, then shut it. After a moment, he said, "Oh."

Deflated, he allowed Sarah to herd him out of the office and to the front door.

There he turned. "I'll report to my client, of course, but, well . . . I suppose there's no likelihood of you changing your mind?"

Sarah smiled and assured him there was no chance whatever. Shoulders slumping, Haynes mounted the cob he'd left tied outside the door, and, spirits dampened, trotted off down the drive.

Folding her arms, Sarah leaned against the door frame and watched him go. He disappeared for a while, shielded by the dip and the houses of Crowcombe, then reappeared, trotting as fast as the cob would go south along the road to Taunton.

She heard a footstep behind her and turned her head. Katy Carter appeared and came to stand by her shoulder; wiping her hands on her apron, she looked out—at the dwindling figure of the solicitor.

"Said as he had an offer to make you, one you couldn't refuse." Katy shot Sarah a questioning look.

She met it with a grin. "In that, he was mistaken. It was an offer to buy the farm, house and land, but I explained I had no interest in selling."

Katy nodded, turning back into the house. "Aye, well, I didn't think you would. Old Lady Cricklade would turn in her grave."

Looking out once more, Sarah chuckled. "She'd come back to haunt me." She smiled at the memory of the gaunt, autocratic figure she'd been so fond of, heard again her godmother's strident tones.

Glancing back as Katy headed for the kitchen, Sarah called, "Katy, if there is any talk of people wanting to buy the farm, do reassure the others—I won't sell."

Katy flashed a reassuring smile. "Aye, I'll do that."

Sarah looked out again, content to stand in the doorway and gaze across the valley to the rippling rise of the Quantocks. Behind her the orphanage hummed, full of life, full of hope. She'd been inducted into her caregiving role by godmother and mother, but she remained because she wished to, because the orphanage gave her something, too.

As the sun, slanting low, struck beneath the clouds to illuminate the opposite slopes, still cloaked in their winter drab, she tried to define what that something was; she concluded that the orphanage was one of *her* places, the places in which she had a role to fill, one that in turn fulfilled her, and as such it was a necessary part of her life.

It was, however, only one aspect of her life, one piece in a jigsaw. A jigsaw she'd yet to define, to find enough pieces and set them in place so that she could see the whole.

Her life revealed.

The thought brought her mind back to the subject that, over the past week, had consumed it. Charlie, and his offer. Two items, two pieces, but in reality inseparable; if she wanted one, she had to accept the other. Over all the countless hours she'd spent considering, the real question she'd grappled with was: Was he, and the position he offered, also an essential part of her life?

Should she gladly grasp what he offered, accept it and fit it into her jigsaw?

Would it—and he—fit?

That was the critical question, and while she still didn't know the answer, she knew a great deal more than when he'd so unexpectedly asked her to be his bride.

As he'd stated, they shared a common background, even to the countryside of their birth; contemplation had confirmed there was significant comfort to be drawn from that. Aside from all else, in moving to his home, she would still be surrounded by people she knew. While he would have friends and acquaintances she didn't know in London and elsewhere beyond the valley, here, at home, their acquaintance was in virtually all respects shared.

Much in their lives was already the same.

Overall, it was difficult to find anything in all that he was physically—as a person, a man, all his possessions and known habits—with which to cavil.

As for less tangible concerns, such as what he felt or might feel for her, she now knew his offer wasn't solely driven by logic, by the conventional reasons. That there was some other emotion influencing him, although exactly what that was she'd yet to learn. Regardless, it was patently one if not more of the emotions she would want to know he felt for her—passion, desire, even perhaps love. That last remained to be seen, literally, but . . . what he felt for her might be all she wished it to be.

She considered that, considered what he made *her* feel, and regretted that while she suspected that given the way he responded to her that what they felt toward each other was in many ways the same, reciprocal and matching, she'd yet to define to her satisfaction what she felt for him, whether or not she truly loved him.

Fascination, enthrallment to the point of sensual abandon, yes, but did that equate to love?

After a moment she left that point as it was—unresolved—and moved on. What else had she learned? While he obviously wished for children, that he liked them and could and would play with them was a definite bonus.

She scanned her mental list, and was surprised by how many ticks were now in place. Eyes on the road below, she saw another rider pass by, was reminded of Haynes and his client's offer . . .

Slowly she straightened, lungs tightening.

If she married Charlie, what would happen to the orphanage? It was a bequest to her, but was now part of her property and, as such, on her marriage, would pass legally to her husband.

She stood and stared unseeing at the rolling dips of the hills, then tightening her arms around herself, she turned and headed inside.

She would have to speak with Charlie.

8

That night the moon was full; riding a clear sky untrammeled by clouds, it cast a stark radiance over the hills, silvering the ripples on the weir and streaming into the summerhouse, where Charlie waited.

There'd been no social gathering to endure that evening; he'd come to the summerhouse early, hoping Sarah would do the same. Regardless, he'd rather wait here, close to her and the promise of the night, than in the confines of Morwellan Park under the eyes of his observant family.

He paced slowly, conscious, minute by minute, of the hardening of anticipation, of the sharpening of his desire, then he saw Sarah marching along the path—and immediately knew something was wrong.

Arms folded, her shawl clutched about her, she walked quickly along, her gaze fixed not on the summerhouse but on the path ahead of her.

Her attention wasn't locked on him, and what was to come; she was absorbed with some other concern.

Had she been any other lady, he would have been irritated that her focus wasn't on him, and all they might shortly do. Instead, his anticipation, his desire, smoothly, from one heartbeat to the next—at that simple sight of her—transmuted into something else.

He was waiting when she climbed the steps and walked into the softly lit shadows. "What is it?"

She'd raised her head. Drawing close, she blinked at his question, then accepted he'd seen her abstraction and replied, "I was at the orphanage today, and . . ." Halting before him, through the moonlight, she scanned his face, then, chin firming, continued, "If I accept your offer and marry you, the orphanage, as property I own, will pass into your hands."

It was his turn to blink. He hadn't considered that, yet what she said was true.

Pressing her hands together, she turned and paced. "What you may not appreciate is that, to me, the orphanage is considerably more than mere property. As I mentioned, it was left to me by Lady Cricklade, my godmother, of whom I was especially fond, and ever since I was young, both she and Mama encouraged me to take an active interest in the place, not simply oversee it from a distance."

Halting before one of the arched openings, she lifted her head and gazed out at the weir. "For some years now, I've been in charge of running the place." She turned and through the shadows looked at him. "That takes time, and effort, and care, but in return the orphanage gives me untold satisfaction on many levels."

She paused, then said, "If I marry, you or anyone else, quite aside from the obligation I feel to Lady Cricklade's legacy, I doubt that I could happily surrender all that—the interest and the consequent satisfaction. I certainly wouldn't do so willingly."

He walked to join her before the arch; she faced him, and the moonlight poured over her features. "There's no reason whatever for you to give up anything at all. It's a simple enough mattter."

He met her eyes, his mind racing, assessing the ways. "You're correct in thinking that when we marry ownership of Quilley Farm will pass to me, but we can stipulate as part of the marriage settlements that that title will form part of your dower property. We can arrange that the title, plus a suitable sum invested to provide income for the farm's upkeep, be set aside for your exclusive use from our wedding day, remaining yours as part of your dower property in the event of my death, to pass on your death to our joint heirs."

Pausing, he considered, then arched a brow. "Does that meet with your approval?"

Her approval, and rather more. Sarah nodded. "Yes." She'd known he wasn't marrying her for money, or for any property she might own, yet she hadn't expected . . . "The sum invested . . . ?"

His lips curved. "Consider it in the light of a wedding gift—one of the benefits that will accrue once you marry me."

She found herself smiling; he was incorrigible in pursuit of a goal, but of his determination she'd never been in doubt. Yet she was surprised—first that he'd been so attuned to her troubled thoughts before she'd said one word or even met his eyes. More, that he'd been so immediately focused on what was troubling her that not one iota of his customary sensual predatory intent toward her had shown through; instead, he'd been the embodiment of a chivalrous knight intent on slaying whatever dragons had dared to darken her path.

A fanciful thought, yet, as she studied him through the shadows, that image lingered. She stirred, then, wrapped in moonlit dark, moved to him; lifting her hands, placing them on his chest, she slowly slid them up to his shoulders as she stepped closer still.

As she boldly pressed herself to him, stretched up, and lightly touched her lips to his. "Thank you."

She drew back, just enough to focus on his face—to see the change in the austere planes as desire infused and etched his features. The tone he'd employed in discussing the orphanage, brisk, businesslike, his investor's voice, had reassured her even more than his words. She now knew all she needed to know on the physical plane. Only one question remained.

And she wasn't averse to grasping unexpected opportunity and turning it to her purpose—to gain the answer to that one remaining question.

Lowering her gaze, she let it fasten on his lips. "That's a very generous . . . suggestion." Hands on his shoulders, she pushed; he hesitated for an instant, then acquiesced and allowed her to steer him back—until the back of his calves hit the sofa. At her prodding, he sat.

She followed, one hand on his shoulder as she brazenly flicked up her skirt and lifted one knee, then the other, placing them on the cushions on either side of his thighs. Her shawl fell disregarded to the floor as she sat, then edged forward along his hard thighs, leaned in, breast to chest, and kissed him.

Flagrantly, blatantly enticing; she was sure she didn't need to specify that this was her chosen way of thanking him. Nor did she think, as their lips parted, then fused, as their tongues found each other's and dueled, as his hands rose to close firm and strong about her waist, that she needed to explain which path she wished to follow.

This time, however, she intended to reach the end.

Charlie sat back, content with her direction, perfectly content, with her lips ravishing his, to follow her lead, to let her lead for the moment. To let the taste of her innocence wreathe through his brain.

Between them, he opened her bodice, bared her breasts for his delectation, then closed his hands over them, heard her shattered sigh, felt her flesh warm and firm beneath his palms, and rejoiced. Her lips taunted and challenged. Inwardly smug, he drew her up, one arm across her hips; bending her back, he set his lips to her flushed skin, and heard her gasp.

He set about orchestrating a symphony from her, one of sensual, abandoned moans and short, breathy gasps, punctuated by near-sobs of entreaty. Each sound acted powerfully on him, fed and lured his prowling hunger, made it yearn and strain all the more to break free, so it could feast, so it could gorge on her and be sated. More deeply and completely than ever before.

Of that last he was certain, although how he knew he didn't know, yet instinct, sure and absolute, assured him it was—would be—so.

But that wasn't part of his plan, not tonight. Tonight was for twisting the sensual rack one notch tighter, for turning the screws of their sensual tension just a tad more—enough to make her wild with wanting, enough to make her agree to be his.

Soon. She had to agree soon.

That was the only real thought in his brain as he feasted on her flushed breasts, as her soft cries of delight fell on his ears, as he felt her fingers twine and tangle in his hair. She was responsive, and made no move to hide it, no effort whatever to conceal from him all that he made her feel.

Her eyes glinted from beneath heavy lids as he raised his head enough to look down on the rosy mounds he'd captured, enough to gloat over their beauty, enough to feel sharp, lancing satisfaction over their swollen roundness, their sumptuous weight, at the tightly furled nipples he slowly rolled between his fingertips.

She sucked in a tight, tortured breath. Her fingers, locked in his hair, tightened, then clenched. She tugged and he lifted his face—so that they could kiss again, so he could raise one hand and frame her face and sink into the luscious haven of her mouth. So he could taste her again and enjoy.

He did, then abruptly found his head reeling. Between them, she'd reached down and found him, hard as steel, as rigid as iron. She touched, then pressed her palm to his aching length, through the fabric of his breeches boldly caressed.

And he was lost. Caught and swept adrift on an upswell of sensual heat, on a sharply rising wave of burning desire.

Before he could catch his breath, before he could summon enough wit, let alone will, to catch her hand and remove it, she slumped against him, bare breasts to his now equally bare chest—when had she managed that?—and murmured, her voice low and sultry, a siren's whisper in the night, "You want me—why?"

He couldn't think, so he didn't answer.

Her hand shifted, fingers seeking, sliding. Eyes closed, he clung to sanity, tried to remember his plan . . . he'd had one, hadn't he?

"You don't want to marry me for money—I'm not that wealthy and you're already rich."

The words feathered over his lips as she supped, sipped, then let her lips drift to trace the line of his clenched jaw. All the while her fingers played. His tensed on her back, then slid to her sides and gripped; he should lift her away, at least enough to gather his scattered wits, but she was swaying, just a little side to side, against him—the feel of her breasts caressing his chest was too tempting. He hesitated, not wanting to cut short the feeling, not yet, not until his parched senses had drunk their fill.

"You're not marrying me for dynastic reasons, either." She purred the words into his ear, for one instant closed her hand, then eased her hold. "My family's not important enough for that. If anything, the Conninghams are a trifle low on the scale for an alliance with the earls of Meredith."

Her statements reached him through a steadily rising tide of desire; arguing was beyond him, not least because all she said was true.

"And you're certainly not marrying me for any cachet I personally might bring you—I'm not a diamond of the first water, no spectacular beauty, no toast of the ton." She raised her head and looked into his face. "I'm not and never have been a trophy to be won."

He tried to frown. That was wrong. He might not have seen her naked yet, but his senses in respect to womanly beauty had been educated to the highest degree; when he finally had her naked in his arms, she would be a goddess, skin pearly white, every curve a delight, every line of her body created just for him—solely and deliberately to sate his senses. "I—"

She laid a finger across his lips. "You want me." Her hand shifted, stroked; there was no point arguing. "But why?" She tilted her head, through the moon-washed shadows searched his face, his eyes. "*Why* do you want me?"

Then she waited. And he realized he would have to answer. That with her hand, small, warm, intensely feminine, cradling his rampant erection, with his senses reeling, with his hunger clawing so close to his surface, he no longer had any other option; he no longer possessed the strength to deny her, to turn her straightforward, direct, and highly pertinent query aside.

He also couldn't lie—not to her, not here and now with the heat of passion shimmering all around them. The lick of flame was almost palpable on his skin as he drew breath and managed, "Because you're you." His voice was low, a dark, gravelly rumble to answer her sultry siren's call. He looked into her eyes, then let his gaze fall to her lips. He licked his, and confessed, "*You* are what I want."

There were no other words he could find to express what she made him feel, what he felt for her. How he felt about her and only her. He wanted her more than he'd wanted any woman before. The feelings, now she'd forced him to look, were strange, different, not anything so simple as the customary desire a man felt for a woman, a desire with which he was amply familiar. This was something different, and if he were truthful, always had been. He'd told himself it was because she was the one he'd chosen to be his wife, but that begged her question. What was this he felt?

All he knew was that it was stronger, that the passion flared hotter, the desire ranging that much more deeply and widely, all-encompassing in its power.

It had continually surprised him, and now, sitting in the moonlit dark with her so close, so wantonly enticing, with her direction—the fullness of it—there in her eyes, he discovered that it was even stronger than he'd thought.

That it wasn't fueled solely by his need but by hers as well, and together, combined, their mutual wanting held power enough to turn his head.

She hadn't said anything, but had studied him; now she smiled her siren's smile, as if his answer had been sufficient to pay her price. That softly glowing smile stated that she was, if not completely appeased, then satisfied enough, more, that she wanted to go forward and yield more, seek more, learn more. Of him. And herself. Of them together.

Shifting sinuously, she swayed close, offered her mouth—and he took. Greedily, hungrily, he plunged them back into the heat that hovered, unabated. Cradling her head, he kissed her, increasingly explicitly, and she kissed him back, and the heat closed around them. Engulfed them, infused them.

The flames built, then roared and drove them.

Between them, she undid the buttons holding the placket of his breeches closed; her small hand slid beneath the fabric, and found him.

He sucked in a breath at that first innocent touch; his control quaked as her grip firmed, then her fingers eased and she stroked, and he felt like growling.

Releasing her waist, with a quick tug he raised her skirts and reached beneath. Found the soft flesh between her thighs and caressed, then lightly probed.

She shuddered, caught her breath, then her fingers trailed tantalizingly down his length. Closing her hand about his turgid flesh, she gently tugged.

Her meaning couldn't have been clearer.

And this time he had no ability, no thought in his head, to deny her.

Just a small adjustment of her body over his and he could draw her down and sheath his erection in her slick softness; despite the potent attraction, he knew that this time it couldn't be that way. Not for her. Not the first time. He was too large, too engorged, for her to take him easily that way; she might balk, and find it too difficult to go on . . .

Deftly he turned her and tumbled her down to the cushions. She went readily, reassured when he moved with her, willingly surrendering to the pull of one small hand gripping his shoulder. He settled between her thighs, spread wide on either side of his hips, the fingers of one hand still buried within her sheath, his other hand cradling her head, keeping her immersed in their kiss.

He hadn't intended their first time to be like this, on a sofa in the summerhouse with the night dark about them, a coupling accomplished beneath layers of clothes, his and hers. He would have preferred to be naked, to have her naked, too, but it was too chilly to undress; while the heat of passion had allowed him to bare her breasts, to not even notice that she'd bared his chest, the night was too cold for them to dispense with further clothes.

Beneath her skirts, she guided his erection to her entrance; drawing his fingers from her sheath, so hot and wet and ready for him, he caught her hand, twined her fingers with his, and drew them away.

And sank slowly, carefully, into her scalding heat.

Her breath hitched. She tensed, then through the kiss caught her breath and fought to relax, to reverse the instinctive tightening. Her fingers clutched his. He pressed in, steady, sure, not too fast yet not so slow that she had time to think too much. Then he reached the barrier that was her maidenhead; with one powerful thrust he breached it, with the movement forging deep into her body.

She cried out, the sound muffled between their lips, and tensed. He held still, giving her time to adjust.

Giving himself time to still his whirling senses. To assimilate the feel of scalding velvet gripping him so tightly. To grit his teeth and hold against the powerful, all but overwhelming urge to ride her, hard and fast. As some part of him had wanted to do for a very long time.

He'd told her it would be like this, with her legs spread, her knees clasped about his flanks, with her body open beneath his, with him sunk to the hilt within her, filling her.

His senses continued to reel, more affected than he'd imagined they could be. Rational thought was far beyond him, but snippets flashed over the surface of his mind. He was dimly aware that this wasn't his plan, that complying with her wishes had gone counter to his aim. Yet his plan no longer mattered—not as much as appeasing her, as satisfying the want, the desire that had risen within her, that he'd evoked, lured forth, and fed. In that moment *nothing* mattered as much as answering her call and filling her as she wished.

She wanted, her heightened desire now sharp and keen, and he wanted, fiercely, compulsively, to satisfy her need, to bring her to glory and share in her delight.

Her pleasure would be his; he knew that without thinking. He'd claimed her; his was the right to bring her that deepest pleasure, to take her and fill her and show her the golden glory of earthly paradise.

With a soft, evocative sigh she eased, her body giving, accepting. Instinctively she contracted the muscles of her stretched sheath, felt him there, and shivered.

Gritting his teeth against the inevitable effect of that evocative caress, he drew back just a little, then forged in again, filling her even more completely. Her breath left her and she clutched, both with her hands and her body. He eased back again, filled her anew; her breasts swelled as she breathed in, then she followed his rhythm.

He set the pace, slow, steady, only gradually increasing as he sensed her response, as desire rose, fresh and urgent, and the fires of passion reclaimed them, and the conflagration built.

And it was more, so much more, than the act had ever been. Reaching deeper, further, into some part of him he hadn't known could be touched, the intimate surrender and the possession sank to his bones. Her surrender to him, and his to her; his possession of her, and hers of him. This wasn't any simple joining, the usual trading of pleasure, but one intricate and involved, layered with meaning, coiled and twined with feelings and emotions he'd never before encountered, not in this arena.

Not between the woman who lay beneath him, so gladly and wantonly accepting him into her body, and him.

As if she were his goddess in truth, the keeper of his soul, and he could do nothing other than worship her.

Sarah rode with him and felt her body rejoice, felt her senses whirl and sing with pleasure. She was exquisitely conscious, to her fingernails aware of the shattering intimacy of their joining. Eyes closed, hearing suspended, her world condensed to just him and her, and another world came alive, a landscape filled with feeling, with heat and longing, with sensation and power and the promise of glory.

He moved within her and she rode out each thrust, met and matched him, welcomed and reluctantly released him again.

Pleasure and delight bloomed, welled, then spilled through her. The momentary pain had faded so fast it was already a dim memory, overwhelmed by the solid and immediate reality of him hard and strong and so elementally male, joining so deeply and inexorably with her.

His fingers slid from hers, sliding down and around to grip one globe of her bottom. He tilted her hips, and she gasped as the altered position let him penetrate her more deeply still.

The reined power behind each deliberate thrust sent a thrill arcing through her. A primitive sense of danger, the recognition of vulnerabilty; he was so much stronger than she, his body so much harder, so much more powerful than hers.

Yet he was careful. The realization slid through her, but she couldn't focus enough to think, then the heat of their passion rose another degree and claimed her.

Sent fire and a hungry, ravenous need sliding through her veins, making her writhe, making her gasp. It inexorably branded desire deep into her flesh, marking and searing, until she burned.

Until her body was aflame, until the flames coalesced and concentrated, burning fiercer and hotter until she sobbed and clung and desperately urged him on, and he rode her faster, harder, deeper.

Until with a rush, all heat and yearning, she found herself clinging to that final, dizzying peak. Felt him thrust one last time and shatter her, felt the furnace within her that he'd stoked and fed rupture, felt glory pour forth and sear her veins.

And rush through her.

She spiraled through a void, cushioned in heated bliss, her mind disconnected. Dimly, she heard him groan, long-drawn and guttural, was distantly aware that, joined deeply with her, he went rigid in her arms. She felt, from far away, the warmth of his seed spill inside her.

Buoyed by glory, cocooned in golden rapture, she smiled.

S he'd found her answer—several answers, in fact.

When she could think again, Sarah felt rather smug. Not only had she succeeded in reaching the end of the path, but the pleasure she'd found there had proved even more delicious than she'd imagined.

That, however, relatively speaking, was incidental. She'd had one principal aim in taking that path, one question she'd wanted answered, and if he hadn't given her that answer in clear and simple words, he had shown her. More than enough for her to grasp the truth. Actions, after all, spoke louder than words. Especially with gentlemen, or so she'd always heard.

And perhaps he was right; answering in words wasn't easy. Even now she found it difficult to describe even to herself what she'd sensed. A power, insubstantial, elusive, yet potent, an emotional imperative, something capable of overriding rational will, of directing behavior to suit its own ends, but those ends were focused on another.

That power seemed to exist solely in terms of another.

She'd given herself to him, yet his focus had been on giving her pleasure, and only secondarily in taking his.

Contrarily, her focus had been on him; much of her actions had been driven by an instinctive need to sate the desire she evoked in him. To pleasure him.

To agree to their wedding, her price was love, and of all the emotions that power might be, love was the only one that accounted for all she'd sensed, especially that compulsion to give, to lavish on the other all one could.

She now knew she felt that way about him; after the last hour, she accepted that she did, that when they were together and the world wasn't there to distract them, he and his needs and wants became the dominant focus of her mind. She now knew how that feeling, that power, compelled her to act, and his actions were the converse of hers.

Love might be hard to describe, but its symptoms were clear.

If what she felt for him was love, then presumably what he felt for her, what was driving him to marry her and only her, was the same.

She reached that conclusion as he shifted; the movement drew her back to the world. She lifted heavy lids to reorient herself. At some point he'd rearranged them; he was now sitting on the sofa with her in his lap, wrapped in his arms. Her head rested on his chest, one palm splayed over his heart. The heat of his skin, the warmth surrounding her, the solid beat of his heart beneath her palm reassured and more; there was, in that moment, nowhere she'd rather be.

Sensual consciousness drifted back to her; her body felt different—glorious and alive in a way it hadn't been before.

And then you'll be complete. So he'd told her, and now she understood. With him, she was whole. He was a necessary piece of the jigsaw of her life; she couldn't imagine feeling this way—behaving this way—with any other man.

His arm tightened; he bent his head and pressed a gentle kiss to her temple. "Are you all right?"

Charlie heard the concern in his voice; he felt it to his marrow.

He knew she'd been conscious for some minutes, but she'd remained so still, so silent. Had the pain been too much, or the pleasure too shocking?

He could barely form a coherent thought himself, and he was far more experienced than she. Not that being rendered all but non compos mentis was in any way usual for him; he still didn't understand how it could be, yet with Sarah everything, even those moments he'd lived through hundreds of times with dozens of other ladies, seemed intrinsically different.

To his relief, she moved her head and pressed a soft kiss to his chest—a caress that sank much deeper. "Yes. That was . . . *lovely.*"

Her tone, the sigh on which the word "lovely" floated, soothed his ego. The shimmery amazement with which she'd invested the word expressed something of what he, too, felt.

Regardless, he now had to readjust his plan—again. And this time, the variation was dramatic. He'd thought that once they'd indulged, he would no longer have anything with which to so strongly lure her, at least not on the plane of sensual curiosity, but given the intensity of what had just transpired, perhaps that wasn't the case. He was certainly curious, more curious than he'd been in far longer than he could remember. If they indulged again, would it be as glorious? As invested with deeper feeling, as intensely enthralling?

But would such questions occur to her? Unlike him, she had no previous encounters against which to judge theirs.

He didn't know whether she would think in such terms, didn't feel confident enough to base a strategy on that point.

Which left him considering the insistent chant his more primitive self was repeating, over and over, in his brain.

You have to marry me now.

He knew better than to utter those words. He had four sisters, three of them wed, and Augusta was eighteen. Such words would be met with scorn and derision, and subsequently entrenched resistance, even though they were true. He wasn't letting her go; she certainly wouldn't be marrying anyone else.

But surely there was some way he could use their intimacy to advance his cause? Without sparking resistance instead of acquiescence.

His mind balked. He mentally snorted. What was the use of having a honeyed tongue and charm enough to tame gorgons if he couldn't convince the lady lying so sweetly and utterly sated in his arms to be his?

"I've made up my mind."

The soft words jolted him. He looked down.

She lifted her head, looked up at him and smiled, the dreamy glory of satiation still hazing her eyes. "I'll marry you." She tilted her head, her eyes on his. "As soon as you like."

Sarah had remembered the gypsy's prophecy. It was her decision, not his. If she wanted love, it was she who had to make the declaration, to make up her mind, accept the risk and grasp the chance and go forward.

She understood that despite all, there was a risk—she might have read things wrongly—but if she wanted love, she had to take the offered chance and go forward to find and secure it.

So she would.

His eyes had widened, but his features were blank—truly blank as if she'd surprised him. Then he blinked, and she sensed he was searching for words. In the end, his eyes locked with hers, he drew in a huge breath, and, jaw firming, nodded. "Good."

If it had been left to Charlie, as soon as he liked would have meant the next day. Unfortunately, once apprised of their agreement to marry, Sarah's mother and his proved to have other ideas.

"Tuesday next week," Serena declared, her fine eyes steady on his face.

From his stance before the fireplace, Charlie stared back. Hard.

They were in the drawing room at the Park. As early as acceptable that morning, he'd driven to the manor to, with Sarah, speak with her parents; after the expected delighted outpourings, they'd all journeyed to Morwellan Park to consult with Serena.

Correctly divining the unvoiced protest behind his rigidly impassive countenance, Serena explained, "Sarah will need time in Bath to assemble her trousseau, and Lord Conningham and I will need to oversee a multitude of arrangements here. The wedding of the Earl of Meredith will, naturally, be a major event."

The look in Serena's eyes warned that resistance would be futile; he was her eldest son, and she wasn't going to allow his marriage to pass off without due pomp and ceremony. Indeed, she'd already acceded to more than he had any right to expect; she hadn't insisted he and Sarah marry in St. George's, Hanover Square.

"Very well." His jaw felt as if it were cracking, but he fought to keep his tone mild, in keeping with the celebratory atmosphere. He inclined his head to both Serena and Lady Conningham. "Tuesday next it is."

Seven full days away. Seven nights as well.

"Excellent!" Lady Conningham, seated in one of the large armchairs before the hearth, looked at Sarah. "We'll leave first thing tomorrow, my dear. We'll need all the hours we can muster in Bath, what with the girls' dresses to fit as well. Let alone all the rest." Her ladyship held up her fingers one by one, clearly mentally counting. "Dear me—we won't be back until Monday."

She looked not at Sarah or Charlie but to Serena, who dismissed her silent question with a wave. "I'm sure," Serena said, "that Frederick and I can take care of all the details here. And of couse Alathea will help."

That was the start of an avid discussion encompassing "all the details." Charlie listened with only half an ear; he was far more exercised by the thought of seven nights of enforced abstinence than with the question of which carriage they, as the happy couple, should use for the journey back from the church.

He looked at his wife-to-be, seated on the chaise beside his mother. Sarah was alert, paying attention, quick to step in and declare her preference if any potential option was offered. Better her than him, and it was wise of her to do so; he suppressed a shudder as she firmly quashed the idea of a platoon of flower girls and boys to precede her into the church. With such potential horrors threatening, he didn't try to distract her but waited with assumed patience until the discussion finally came to an end.

By then grooms were already flying hither and yon, delivering invitations for an impromptu dinner to announce their engagement to be held at the Park that very evening.

"Such a rush!" Lady Conningham declared. "But it simply has to be."

Serena shot him a warning look, but Charlie merely smiled, and kept his opinion to himself.

His charm came to his aid in conducting his prospective in-laws and his bride-to-be out to their carriage. He seized the moment as Lord Conningham helped his wife into the carriage to lean close to Sarah, on his arm, and whisper, "Tonight. As usual."

She caught his eye, hesitated, then nodded. "All right, but I might be late. They're going to want to talk for hours."

He grimaced, but nodded back. The look in her eyes was some consolation. As he helped her into the carriage, she met his eyes again. Her fingers tightened on his; he returned the pressure, then released her and stepped back.

The groom shut the carriage door. Charlie raised his hand in salute, and saw Sarah look back, and smile.

As resigned as he felt. The sight left him feeling just a little less frayed.

9

Put upon—that's how Charlie was feeling by the time he finally reached the summerhouse, only to discover Sarah still not there.

In the gloom, he cursed, then paced and waited.

The stresses of the evening had been many. Celia and Martin Cynster, along with Alathea, Gabriel, and their children, had descended on the Park; together with Sarah's sisters, her parents, and Jeremy and Augusta, they'd formed the family core of the gathering before which Lord Conningham had announced the engagement of his daughter to Lord Charles Morwellan, eighth Earl of Meredith.

Also present had been the vicar, Mr. Duncliffe, who would officiate on Tuesday next, Mrs. Duncliffe, and Lady Finsbury and Lady Cruikshank and their lords, among others from the local area summoned to bear witness. Given the latter-named ladies' propensities, Charlie had no doubt that news of the betrothal would soon be spread the length and breadth of the ton.

His mother, Celia, and Alathea would, of course, do their part, too.

The gathering had been joyous, the tone happy and relaxed; indeed, the whole had passed off better than he'd hoped, yet throughout he'd been conscious of building impatience.

In business dealings he'd never had this problem, the feeling he was constantly battling to restrain himself, to hold himself back, to make some powerful and quite primitive part of him toe a civil line. And there was no real reason for it now that Sarah had agreed to be his; logically he knew that, yet the driving insistence had yet to ease.

Indeed, if anything, it had grown more pronounced.

He could only attribute it to the unusual depth of his hunger for her, a depth he'd yet to sate; presumably once she'd been his, had given herself to him a few more times, the compulsive itch would fade.

He wished he could believe that, believe that the compulsion was purely physical, that its power arose from nothing more than as-yet-unslaked desire. He told himself that it couldn't be anything else, yet . . .

A light, fleeting footstep had him turning.

Sarah came running down the path, then pattered up the steps. She came quickly to him. "I'm sorry—it was as I said. They wanted to—"

He jerked her into his arms.

Sarah swallowed her next words as he kissed her, ravenously hungry and demanding. All thought of apology fled from her head, overwhelmed by the need to appease, to sate, to give him all he wished, all he wanted.

He transparently didn't want to talk.

In what felt like mere seconds, he had her beneath him on the sofa, her bodice open to her waist, her breasts swelling under the expert ministrations of one hand, while his other hand drew up her skirts, and slid beneath.

The fires between them had already flared and ignited; his seeking fingers found her entrance already slick and wet—he caressed, probed, and the flames roared.

Having weathered the storm once, she embraced it and gloried in it, thrilled to be wanted with such unwavering intent, with such concerted focus, with such . . . adoration. Despite the passion driving him, despite the desire that had hardened his body, that infused every caress with a driven edge, behind all was a care that never wavered.

A care that had him holding back, his breathing as ragged as hers, his kiss every bit as desperate, until his clever fingers sent her wits spinning from this world and submerged her senses in indescribable pleasure.

Only then did he shift, pin her beneath him, and thrust into her.

She gasped, arched beneath him, then moaned as he took advantage of her instinctive invitation and drove even deeper into her very willing body. She clamped around him and he paused, eyes closed, every muscle clenched and tight, on the cusp of quivering, then he drew in a labored breath, withdrew and thrust anew, and she lost touch with the world.

And once again all she knew was the heat and the flames and the steady, relentless possession. The giddy pleasure and delight, and beneath and through it all threaded the elusive evidence of his loving.

It was there in the catch in his breath when she shifted, rose beneath him and moved against him, letting the fascinatingly crinkly hair on his chest abrade her excruciatingly sensitive nipples.

There in the way he slowed, metaphorically gripped her hand and drew her back from the brink so that she didn't rush ahead and end the pleasure too soon, but instead caught her sensual breath and joined again with him in that primitive and evocative dance. An extended measure, more detailed than the first time. More all-consuming, all-absorbing. More intimate.

Love was there in the guttural whispers of encouragement he fed her when she once more started that inexorable climb, when passion roared and she suddenly found it upon her, near and so intense.

There in the way in which he held her, cradled her, all the while moving so relentlessly within her, stoking the flames, sending her senses careening.

There in the moment when ecstasy claimed her and he held her close, and held still, muscles quivering with restraint, prolonging the moment until she wept with simple joy.

There in the final helpless moment when he lost himself in her.

Because she was looking, and now knew what to look for, and when, she saw.

Sarah set off the next morning with her mother, Twitters, Clara, and Gloria for five days in Bath, sleepily content, convinced that she'd made the right decision.

Whether Charlie knew it or not, whether it was love full-blown or merely the first tender shoots of a plant they would take a lifetime to fully cultivate, she didn't know. But the potential was there, beyond question, beyond doubt, and that was all she needed to know.

With a sigh, she closed her eyes, settled her head back against the squabs, and relived, yet again, the events of the previous night.

Where was his control? Why, when faced with her, did it simply evaporate?

That and similar questions wreathed through Charlie's brain as, two days later, he guided his grays down the slope into Watchet.

He'd spent the time since Sarah left immersed in business, not only that of estate and fortune but also the business of marriage. He and Lord Conningham had agreed on the marriage settlements; they were presently being drawn up. His lordship had been surprised by his stipulation regarding Quilley Farm, and had commented on his generosity and understanding. He'd held his tongue, yet the urge to admit that generosity had had little to do with it, but that understanding of Sarah had indeed driven the matter, had been strong.

Quilley Farm had been a small price to pay to ensure that she became his.

Which brought him once again to the vexed question of his passion for her, his wife-to-be. With no prior experience to guide her, she couldn't know, and with any luck would never guess, that his . . . desperation—he had no other word for it—when he was with her was not the usual, customary way of things for gentlemen such as he.

Never before had passion ruled him, not like this. Not to the extent that when he was with her, driving her to the pinnacle of earthly bliss, preferably while he was buried deep inside her and subsequently, as his reward, joining her, became to all intents and purposes his single overriding aim in life.

It was . . . faintly shocking. Even harrowing. Such a connection was certainly not what he'd expected, not with sweet innocent Sarah.

Yet sweet innocence seemed to be his sensual drug. How could he have known?

The archway of the Bell Inn appeared before him. Slowing the grays, he told himself, as he had a hundred times over the past forty-eight hours, that his reaction to her was an addiction and, once sated, that addiction would fade.

He simply had to see it through, and that would certainly be no hardship. A month or so of married life, and all would be well. He just had to stay the course.

Leaving the grays at the inn, he walked up to the shelf of land on which he intended to build his new warehouse. Sarah had been right; a warehouse twice the usual size would be a better investment on numerous counts than two normal-sized structures. The local builder he habitually employed, Carruthers, was waiting to meet with him. They discussed the project at length, then parted, Carruthers to liaise with the local draftsman over plans and costs while Charlie wandered back to the docks and thence to Jones's office.

The agent was pleased to see him. "I don't know what's in the air," Jones said, "but there's a number of outsiders sniffing around."

Charlie raised his brows. "Sinclair?"

"He's one. But there's another man about, not a gentleman but he's asking questions for someone." Jones grinned. "And if the latest news from the shipping lines is anything to go by, they're onto the right scent."

By which Jones meant the scent of increasing traffic in goods through Watchet. Charlie smiled back. "Excellent news for us, then, as I've decided on the new warehouse." He filled Jones in on his decision; the prospect of a double-sized structure quite made Jones's day.

After discussing when the new warehouse might be usable, and matching that with the seasonal traffic of goods and thus which merchants Jones should approach, Charlie left the agent juggling figures and stepped back into the High Street.

He paused on the narrow pavement, looking down toward the harbor.

"Lord Meredith. Well met."

Charlie turned. Smiling, he held out his hand. "Sinclair. And it's Charlie."

Returning his smile, Malcolm Sinclair shook his hand. "Malcolm. I was about to adjourn to the Bell Inn for luncheon. Will you join me?"

"I'd be delighted."

They crossed the cobbled street and entered the inn; the advent of two such customers, both tall, well set-up, elegantly accoutred gentlemen, brought Matthews, the owner, scurrying. He bowed them to the same table Sarah and Charlie had shared, set in the nook with a view of the harbor.

Malcolm nodded toward the cargo vessels undulating on the waves. "I've seen many small harbors around the coast, but this one's always busy."

"It's an excellent alternative to Bristol, especially for certain cargoes." They sat and Matthews hurried to serve them a first course of soup and fresh crusty bread.

When the innkeeper withdrew, Charlie glanced at Malcolm. "Are you intending to stay in the area?"

Malcolm sampled the soup, then admitted, "I'm definitely looking to settle in the locality."

"You don't have a residence elsewhere?"

While they ate the soup, Malcolm explained, "I was orphaned at an early age with no close relatives. Consequently it was Eton, Oxford, and my guardian's house in London—and London is home to all Englishmen after a fashion—so no, I never formed connections to any region. Now, however, I feel the lack of a place to which I can retreat, and of all the counties of England, and I've traveled over them all, this area appeals to me the most."

Malcolm met Charlie's eyes. "You might not notice it, having been born to it, but the countryside hereabouts is uncommonly attractive and simultaneously restful. Not spectacular so much as soothing. I've been looking around for just the right estate."

Charlie smiled. "If I hear any useful whispers I'll pass them on."

"Do," Malcolm said. "But one question I wanted to ask of you. Given that you are, as I am, involved in investing to a high degree, how do you find doing business from here? How reliable are communications with London, for instance in winter? Is this area cut off? And if so, for how long?"

"In that, we're uncommonly lucky." Charlie sat back as the soup plates were removed, then outlined the various modes of communication with the capital, explaining why they were rarely disrupted. From there, they moved to a discussion of investments, which types each favored long-term, and so to their current personal interests.

While both avoided naming specific projects, Malcolm let fall enough for Charlie to realize that the man was as inherently cautious as he and Gabriel were; not one of them liked to lose money. However, Malcolm had plainly found ways in which to make investments that were inherently risky, and which therefore, if successful, gave commensurately greater returns, somehow acceptable to his cautious soul.

That intrigued Charlie. While he'd never had any difficulty resisting the lure of risky investments, not sharing in the success—and those commensurately greater returns—nevertheless irked. Gabriel felt the same.

"I do much of my investing through the Cynster funds—those managed by Gabriel Cynster." Twirling a goblet of red wine between his fingers, Charlie grimaced. "But I have to admit we tend to stick to the tried and true—it's mostly funds themselves, and the financing of projects, rather than the direct development of new ventures."

Malcolm nodded. "I spent some time chatting with Cynster the other week. Everyone knows of the Cynster funds, of course, and they have been hugely successful over time. That, however, is the long-term approach, and while one can hardly criticize, there is a lack of . . . excitement, I suppose. Of real involvement with the frontiers of new business."

"Exactly." Charlie grinned. "The long-term is sure, but hellishly dry. While ever-increasing figures in ledgers are always nice to see, they rarely inspire victorious delight."

They paused while the main course of roast beef was laid before them. They picked up their knives and forks; silence reigned for some minutes, then Charlie asked, "Tell me, how did you get involved with the railways?"

That was clearly a question Malcolm had frequently been asked. "I was lucky. I was about in '20 when Stephenson was doing the rounds trying to drum up backers for the Stockton-Darlington. While there was a lot of interest in the concept, most preferred to sit on the sidelines until there was some evidence the business would work. At the time, I had the cash and, of course, it was only a short stretch, the trial as it were. So I bought in. There was only a handful of us, and once the line opened and the proof was there to see, that small group became the first port of call as potential backers for every new line. Out of that, I went into the Liverpool-Manchester, and I've bought into the extension to London, too."

"So you've done well out of your investments in the railways." Charlie patted his lips with his napkin, then pushed aside his plate.

"Yes." Malcolm frowned. "But I haven't taken positions in any of the other—so very many other—projects currently proposed."

"Oh? Why?"

"There's too damned many of them for a start. Everyone's jumped on the bandwagon, and proposals are being floated for every conceivable connection. There's commercial sense in joining London with Manchester and Liverpool. I'm less sure of the wisdom, in terms of solid and quick returns, in the Newcastle-Carlisle, yet they've started laying track. And I know the London-Bristol is in the wind, and that makes commercial sense, but—and this is the problem with so many proposals being touted these days—when will it be running, when will the returns eventuate and will they be sufficient to cover the time taken between investment and the first flow of returns?"

Charlie understood. "You're saying the time frame has blown out."

Malcolm nodded. "Consider Stockton-Darlington. We paid in in early '21, they started immediately, and the first stock rolled in '25, with a defined and ready market to run to capacity, more or less indefinitely. A relatively short span of time for a very sound return. The Liverpool-Manchester took from '27 to '30. Again a reasonable time for a solid return. The extension to London, however, will take many more years to complete. Since I realized that, I've been much more careful and, frankly, none of the proposals currently doing the rounds will see any return for . . . it might be more than a decade."

Sitting back, Malcolm met Charlie's eyes. "That's not the sort of project I'm comfortable with." He held up one hand. "Don't mistake me—I'm sure most of these railways will eventually be built. But the time in the capital phase is no longer in an investor's favor."

He paused, as if considering, then added, "In addition to that, too many of these proposals are being floated by the same small set of senior investors. They need others to buy in to make the projects fly, but they themselves are too financially stretched to allow each project to proceed at the proposed pace. I wouldn't be surprised if over the next decade a number of syndicates founder."

Eyes narrowed, Charlie said, "So it's a case of trying to do too much, too quickly, and with too little overall available capital—at least capital available for such distant returns."

Malcolm nodded. "There's also precious little attention being given to the difficulties of construction that some proposals face. Yet another reason to steer clear of railways, at least in terms of investing."

Charlie's brows rose. "Indeed!"

The meal completed, they pushed back their chairs and rose. After settling with the innkeeper, they walked out onto the pavement. Charlie turned to Malcolm. "Thank you for your insights—they were fascinating."

"Not at all." Malcolm offered his hand; Charlie gripped it. "It was a pleasure to talk to someone with similar interests."

Charlie felt the same. "We must get together again sometime, and explore our mutual interests further."

Malcolm inclined his head and they parted, both well pleased.

Charlie looked down at the harbor. The wind had risen, whipping the waves to whitecaps. Not good sailing weather. And the last time he'd been out, he'd had Sarah with him . . .

Turning on his heel, he headed for the inn yard. Better he drive himself home, and then find something else to occupy his mind.

The wedding preparations proceeded apace under his mother's and Lord Conningham's direction; there was little for Charlie to do— indeed everyone was of the opinion he should simply stay out of the way. Consequently, two evenings later, after spending the day driving about the county with Jason, Juliet, and Henry, he was hiding in the library reading the day's news sheets, quietly desperate to find some topic of sufficient interest to see him through the evening, when Crisp, his butler, entered to announce, "Mr. Adair has called, my lord."

Charlie blinked, sat up, and laid aside the news sheet. "Show him in, Crisp."

Curiosity stirring, he wondered what Barnaby was doing in the neighborhood, and at such an hour. Something had to be afoot.

One glance at Barnaby as he came through the door confirmed that. His expression was serious, his blond curls rumpled, his cravat rather limp; he was still the same well-dressed and handsome gentleman of the haut ton, but he appeared distinctly travel worn.

Rising, Charlie met him, shaking his hand and clapping him on the shoulder before waving him to the armchairs before the blazing fire. "Sit and get warm." Barnaby's hands were chilled. "Have you dined?"

Barnaby shook his head. "I drove directly from town."

Charlie raised his brows. "You're staying, I take it?"

Sinking into an armchair, Barnaby's lips twitched. "If you have room."

With a grin—the Park was huge—Charlie turned to Crisp and gave orders for a substantial supper for Barnaby, and for a room to be prepared. Crisp departed. Charlie strolled to the tantalus. "Brandy?"

"Please." Barnaby leaned back in the chair. "It's bitter out there."

Charlie glanced at Barnaby. More than the weather was affecting his friend. His face was uncharacteristically grim and set, as if it had been that way, unrelieved, for days.

Strolling over to deliver a tumbler of French brandy, Charlie then crossed to the other armchair and sat. He sipped, taking in the strain in Barnaby's face. It eased as he, too, sipped the fiery liquid. Charlie leaned back. "So—what's up?"

"Dark doings, of an especially exercising sort."

Charlie waited. Eventually Barnaby went on, "The pater and the other commissioners have asked for my help—official, but on the quiet—to investigate, and if at all possible bring to justice whoever's behind a particularly nasty series of cases of land profiteering."

Barnaby's father was one of the peers overseeing the recently instituted metropolitan police force. Charlie frowned. "*Series* of cases?"

Barnaby sipped and nodded. "That's part of the nastiness. That individual cases of minor profiteering might occur from time to time would surprise no one, and indeed it's no crime, but these cases—and I'll explain in a moment why they're different—have been happening up and down the country for years. Literally for about a decade. Everyone's horrified that the villains have been so active, and for so long, all apparently in perfect safety, but because the cases have been so geographically spread, no one realized."

He paused to sip again. "Until recently, there was no central authority to whom such crimes would be reported." He humphed. "Mind you, the first week and more of my time has gone in hieing up and down the country, dragging full accounts of all the known cases from magistrates and sheriffs and lord lieutenants."

Barnaby sighed. Leaning back, he closed his eyes. "I stopped in Newmarket on my way back to town and stayed with Dillon and Pris. When he heard what I was about, Dillon called Demon in and we sat down and put together all I've learned. It's clear the situation is both serious and very difficult to pursue. We tossed around various avenues, and in the end we agreed that the best bet was to come to you and Gabriel."

Charlie's frown deepened. "I haven't heard any tales of land profiteering hereabouts, or elsewhere, and I'm sure Gabriel hasn't, either."

Wearily Barnaby waved his glass. "That's one of the neat things about profiteering—no one ever learns about it until long after the deed is done. If then. Even with these particular cases, it was only because some of these new railway companies have senior investors in common, and said senior investors have been deuced unhappy, not to say apoplectic, over the extortionary prices their companies have been and are being forced to pay for certain parcels of land, that they approached the police with a list of properties their companies have paid huge sums for, wanting the matter looked into—and *then* the pater called me in."

"Ah." Cynical understanding colored Charlie's tone. "I see." Many of those senior investors were peers and similarly wealthy individuals, the sort the authorities would wish to placate. "So the bit are biting back?"

"So to speak." Barnaby paused, then continued, "From Newmarket I went to London, and consulted with the pater and our old friend Inspector Stokes. The long and short of that was that they thought our best bet lay with you and Gabriel, too."

Charlie's brows rose high. "I don't see why, yet, but you have my complete attention."

Barnaby grinned fleetingly. "First, why these cases are different." He broke off as Crisp returned with a loaded tray.

Charlie sipped his brandy and waited while the tray was set up on a small table before Barnaby, and his ravenous friend started eating.

Without prompting, the instant the door shut behind Crisp, Barnaby continued between mouthfuls of roast beef. "Every case in this series involves a particular, very specific parcel of land. In every case, that parcel of land has been critical for the completion of a canal link, or a new toll road, or in recent years, one of the new railways."

"Critical how?"

Barnaby chewed, then swallowed, his gaze on his plate. "The cases with the railways are the easiest to explain. Steam locomotives can't handle steep gradients. When the track needs to climb or fall steeply, then they must ascend or descend slowly through a series of curves to keep the gradients low. The land around those steeper points is critical for the construction of the track. Often there is no alternative path. There are other places that are critical, too—like a natural pass between high hills. Tunnels and bridges can sometimes be used, but are significantly more expensive. And in the cases I'm investigating, regardless of all options, there hasn't been any alternative but to buy the land."

"So the land is being chosen—targeted if you will—by someone who knows a good deal about the construction of canals, toll roads, and railways."

Barnaby nodded. "More, whoever they are they've also had knowledge of the routes of future canals, toll roads, and railways long before they've been announced. These cases involve land bought literally years ahead of any announcement of proposed routes, even of any private proposal being canvassed."

Charlie raised his brows. "Guesswork?"

"Damn good guessing if that were so, but I don't think it can be. Every case I've uncovered has been . . . well, if I were a villain, I'd say it was a jewel, perfectly chosen for the purpose of profiteering. *Every* case—I can't believe anyone could guess that well."

"How many cases?"

"Twenty-three so far."

"You said these were a *series* of cases. I'm assuming they follow the customary pattern—locals unaware of potential increase in land value are presented with an offer for their acres that seems too good to refuse. They accept and ride happily to the bank, and then sometime later—years later in these cases—the new owner sells to the development company at a hugely inflated price, in these cases verging on the extortionary." When Barnaby nodded, Charlie asked, "What's your reason for imagining these twenty-three cases are the work of one villain?"

"Or villains." Barnaby's grimness returned in full measure. "The persuasion."

Charlie blinked. "Persuasion? To sell?"

Barnaby nodded. "It always starts innocently—an offer for the land made through a local solicitor. If the owners accept—and remember most would and then there's no crime—then all passes off smoothly. The original owners don't make the money they might have, and the development companies end up paying through the nose for land they might have had much cheaper, but, at least up to now, that's been considered a risk of the business.

"However, in sixteen of the twenty-three cases reported by our senior investors, the original owners refused that first offer, and a subsequent increased offer, too. That's when the persuasion started. Initially, it was mild—like cows straying if it's a farm, or fences down. You know the sort of thing. Anonymous irritations, but they built. And then came another, slightly increased offer."

Barnaby reached for his glass. "The persuasions escalated. Step by step, steadily more aggressive, punctuated by increasing offers, but the two appear unconnected. Indeed, in some cases, renewed offers were made in the spirit of assisting in a time of trouble. Often, the owners gave in and sold. However, there are at least seven cases where the persuasion progressed to injury, and at least three where the injury proved insufficient to move the owners to sell, and so the persuasion escalated to the ultimate level." Barnaby met Charlie's eyes. "Death."

Charlie held his gaze for a long moment. A log cracked and hissed in the grate. "Who are these people?"

Barnaby replied, "That's what I, and Stokes and my father, want to—and are determined to—find out. Because the reason behind the offers for the land was never obvious until so much later, even to this date the accidental injuries and even the supposedly accidental deaths haven't been connected to the subsequent buyers of the land. Each case has only turned up on my list because of the railway companies' directors' ire, and the crimes only became obvious as crimes once I looked into the sequence of events.

"And this is not the usual investigation where I can follow someone's trail. You'd think the new owners would be traceable, but I've tried, and very quickly got ensnared in a horrendous web of land companies and solicitors, and then more companies." Barnaby set down his empty glass. "Only Gabriel might be able to see some way through the maze. However that may be, that's not the principal reason I came to see you."

"How can we help?" Now every bit as grim as Barnaby, Charlie drained his glass.

Barnaby studied his face. "Tell me if this makes sense. The only way we can catch these villains and charge them with any crime is if we catch them actively coercing someone to sell a parcel of land. Criminal coercion is the only legislated crime involved. But to catch them at it, for our particular villains we need to look—"

"In an area where a development hasn't yet occurred, but is likely to in the next decade." Charlie's gaze grew momentarily distant, then he refocused on Barnaby's face. "I assume you mean the railway line that will, at some point, be laid between Bristol and Taunton, and from there most likely to Exeter and Plymouth?"

Barnaby nodded. "I talked to some of the railway-company directors. Taunton may well end as something of a railhead, years from now." Slumping back, he studied Charlie's face. "This is your country—yours and Gabriel's. What are the chances you'd hear if something untoward was afoot?"

Charlie thought, then grimaced. "Not as good as you might think. People don't generally talk of offers for their property, not until after they sell—or unless they believe there's real coercion involved. And as you've found, often not even then. Our villain hasn't targeted land held by major landowners, or if he has, he's been careful not to overly persuade them, and ordinary farmers don't air their affairs. It's likely neither Gabriel nor I would hear until long after the fact, and then most likely via the local gossip mill."

Barnaby sighed. "I was afraid you might say that."

Charlie held up a hand. "There might, however, be another way, or ways, we can learn more about these villains. And you're right about this area being among the most likely to be targeted at some point—there's lots of hills to navigate around. If we can find out more about our villains' modus operandi so we'll be able to search for their activity more effectively, then searching in this area is indeed a good bet."

He looked at Barnaby. "We'll need to speak with Gabriel . . . and the others." He blinked. "I sent you a card—an invitation. Did you receive it?"

Barnaby shook his head. "I stopped in briefly at the pater's—I haven't been back to my lodgings. Why? What's the event?"

Charlie grinned. "I'm getting married. In three days' time. You're invited. So are all the others."

Barnaby's smile dawned, sincere yet faintly taunting. "Congratulations! That's Gerrard, Dillon, and now you—I'll have danced at all your weddings."

Charlie arched a brow. "No thoughts about joining us?"

"None whatever. I have other interests to pursue. Namely villains."

"Indeed, but as it happens, attending my wedding will advance your cause. We're expecting not just Gabriel, but Devil, Vane, and all the others, Demon and Dillon included. It'll be the perfect opportunity to enlist our collective aid and pick our collective brains. Between us, we'll find some way to trace your villains."

"Amen to that," Barnaby replied. "One thing—keep all this firmly under your hat. At this point, we have no idea who our villains might be."

S arah returned to Conningham Manor in the carriage with her mother, her sisters, and Twitters early on Monday afternoon.

She'd found the long journey a trial, enlivened as it had been by Clary's and Gloria's innocent but unnecessary speculations on the morrow. The instant they were indoors and had greeted the various relatives and connections who'd arrived for the wedding, she seized on the orphanage as her excuse, and escaped.

Galloping north on Blacktail's back, she dragged in a huge breath—it felt like her first free breath in days. She rode quickly, conscious that her time was limited, that she would have not much more than an hour in which to accomplish all she normally did over a whole day.

After tomorrow, she'd have farther to travel to reach the farm; she would have to allow more time for the ride up from the Park, two miles south of the manor. After tomorrow . . . she hoped that would be the extent of the change, that all else would remain more or less the same.

Reaching the farm, she tied Blacktail up by the door, smiled and waved to the children playing in the front yard, then hurried inside. She went straight to the office to look over the books and arrange any payments or orders that were urgent. Katy found her there, and laconically brought her up to date on the doings of their small world.

Sarah discovered that the staff had rallied around, and there were only the books to quickly check, and Skeggs's and Mrs. Duncliffe's decisions of the morning to approve.

"Thank you!" She smiled gratefully at Katy as she shut the main ledger.

"Aye, well—we all thought that you should start married life without anything dragging on your mind." Katy grinned.

Quince appeared at the doorway. She met Katy's eyes, then looked at Sarah. "There's something here you ought to see."

"Oh?" Rising, Sarah joined Katy and together with Quince they went out into the hall.

"*Congratulations, miss!*" The assembled inmates of the orphanage, lined up neatly in the hall, chorused their message with the hugest of smiles.

Ginny, the eldest girl, stepped forward, a package wrapped in brown paper in her hands. Beaming, she dipped a cursty and offered the package to Sarah. "For you, miss. We hope your wedding goes smashingly!"

Sarah looked around at the platoon of bright faces; she'd been the recipient of many such wishes over the last days, but this was unquestionably the most touching. "Thank you." She blinked rapidly, then smiling, took the parcel; it was surprisingly heavy and solid.

The children's expectations rose another notch; they jigged, waiting for her to open their gift. Sarah noted that Maggs was uncharacteristically sober, gnawing at his lower lip.

Looking down, she pulled apart the wrappings—revealing a nearly foot-high gnome with a frog, attentive, at his feet. "It's . . . *lovely.*" And it truly was; there was a certain wordly wisdom in the gnome's expression as he considered the frog; the piece demonstrated remarkable attention to detail.

Maggs edged closer, checking her face. What he saw there reassured. "I made it," he confessed. "We had it fired at the potter's over Stogumber way, and Ginny painted it mostly. We thought you could take it to your new home and put it in your garden so you'd think of us when you saw it."

Sarah glowed and briefly hugged him, then Ginny. "I will. It's perfect." She made a mental note to make inquiries among the local potters for a place for Maggs when it came time for him to leave. She looked at the other children. "I'll always treasure . . . Mr. Quilley."

She held up the gnome and the older children cheered, delighted with the name; the younger ones stared round-eyed and jigged. It was time for tea; the staff herded the group into the dining room, where a special tea was laid out in honor of Miss Conningham's marriage.

Sarah spent the next half hour celebrating with the children and staff. Once the children reluctantly returned to their lessons, she thanked the staff warmly, accepting their personal congratulations, then tied Mr. Quilley securely to her saddle, mounted Blacktail and headed home.

There was still such a lot to do, yet she deliberately put all thoughts of gowns, flowers, ribbons, and garters out of her head, and looked around her as she rode. Let the countryside soothe her as it always did. Let her thoughts settle, let her mind refocus on the important things.

For the past three days, uncertainty had gnawed at her. Had she made the right decision? When she'd been with Charlie, she'd felt confident, convinced that marrying him was the right thing to do, that becoming his wife was her correct path forward. That when she married him love would be there, underneath all, the cornerstone of their union.

Love had been her price, and he'd convinced her that love was theirs for the taking . . . or rather, she'd convinced herself, which was the root cause of her present unsettled state.

What if she'd imagined it? What if she'd simply convinced herself that she'd seen what she'd wanted to see—the promise of love in his touch, in his caring? What if all she'd seen was in truth nothing more than a figment of her imagination?

He hadn't said the words, but she hadn't, and still didn't, expect him to. He wasn't the sort of gentleman given to flowery phrases, to poetry and the like; passionately declaring "I love you" aloud just wasn't him.

She'd known and accepted that, so she'd looked for other, more certain signs—actions, his reactions—and found them. Or so she'd thought.

Over the last days, away from his presence and plagued by uncertainty, she'd relived all the moments they'd shared in the summerhouse and elsewhere, all she'd seen and learned of him, and still wasn't sure; she'd ended with a headache and an upset stomach.

But she couldn't step back from the altar, not now. She'd accepted his proposal, agreed to be his wife, and the whole world knew it.

And marrying him *might* be the right thing to do. Perhaps seeing her decision through was the aspect Madame Garnaut had referred to as "complicated"?

The manor came into sight; Sarah looked at the house, and sighed. From tomorrow it would no longer be her home.

Perhaps all brides felt this unsure?

10

~~~

Unsurprisingly, she couldn't sleep. Donning her old gown, Sarah slipped out of the house, reflecting that this time, her prepared excuse— that, unable to sleep, she'd decided on a walk in the gardens—was true. She and Charlie had made no arrangements to meet tonight; tradition held that they shouldn't meet again until they came together before the altar.

Tomorrow, at noon, she'd become his wife. A suffocating sense of uncertainty swamped her. She tried to put the entire subject from her mind, tried to focus on the here and now, on the gardens in the dark, on the still chill of the night, on the shadows that appeared denser and more encroaching in the weak illumination of the waning moon, yet her feet took her, unresisting, to the path along the stream, to the weir and the summerhouse.

The white structure appeared solid and stark against the dark backdrop of the trees. Perhaps there she would find reassurance, some lingering trace of what her memories insisted had been present, would still be present, between her and Charlie.

Walking to the steps, she went up, stepped into the dimness, and saw him. Seated on the sofa, leaning forward with his elbows on his thighs, hands loosely clasped between his knees, he looked at her through the shadows; she felt his gaze, hot and wanting, instantaneously heating.

She paused, then slowly, deliberately, walked to him.

Charlie straightened as she neared. He hadn't expected her; for one instant when she'd stood on the threshold limned in faint moonlight, he'd wondered whether his mind was playing tricks and she was a phantom, a figment of his dreams.

But it was no specter who halted before him. His gaze on her face, he reached and took her hand, felt the delicate bones between his fingers.

Through the dimness, she met his gaze. He tensed to rise, but, moving with steady deliberation, she placed her free hand on his shoulder and held him back, then she stooped and kissed him.

He kissed her back, not as ravenously as he wished but as he sensed she wanted. Hungrily yet not hurriedly, taking time to explore anew, to taste, to savor. For long moments they communed with lips and mouths and stroking tongues, with wanting and heated yearning on display, openly acknowledged, yet for the moment held at bay.

Familiar, yet different. The desire, the hunger, the passion were there, ready to flare at their call, yet, it seemed, that wasn't all they had to share.

Her hand on his shoulder gripped, pushed; obediently he leaned back until his shoulders met the back of the sofa. She followed, not ready to break their kiss, then she released his shoulder and raised her skirts so she could place first one knee, then the other, alongside his thighs, nudging them closer together. Then she sat, flicked her fingers free of his as she slid slowly, languorously, closer, and brazenly straddled him.

As she had once before, but again, this time was different. This time, as he raised his hands and closed them on her sides, long fingers flexing over her supple back, feeling her body between his hands again, so alive, so much his, he felt that other emotion, the one he couldn't name, rise through him, effortlessly claiming him, submersing him in need of a different sort, a need wholly and completely focused on her.

On her wants, which she made abundantly clear through her slow, thorough and determined kiss. He sat back, content to let her lead, not passive—he could never be that—but prepared to let her script the scene; she was no longer truly innocent, and it was patently clear, as her hands rose between them and she undid the buttons closing his shirt, that this time she knew what she wanted.

As she spread the halves of his shirt wide, then laid her hands on his chest, small feminine palms to his heated skin, the only thought in his brain was to appease her, to give her all she wanted, every last little thing.

So he let her play as she wished, let her explore his chest, held his reaction, powerful and primitive though it was, in check, even when she discovered his nipples under the light pelt of hair, and tweaked.

He jerked; it felt as if she'd twanged every sexual tendon he possessed. Even through the kiss he sensed her smile, sensed the warm glow of her satisfaction. Mentally gritting his teeth, he suppressed the instinctive urge to react, to pay her back and take control, and waited.

Her hands skated over his chest, then lower. Through the kiss, he tracked her responses; focused wholly on her, he sensed she was filling her mind with him, and some dark part of his being exulted.

He followed the slow, inexorable rise of her passion; for once he made no move to drive it, to actively evoke it. Instead, fascinated, he watched it burgeon and grow of its own accord, simply because she was there, in his arms, and he was in hers.

Only when she grew restless and needy did he let his hands slide up and around and close them over her breasts. She gasped, lightly arched, and it was her turn to actively encourage—one of her hands rose to close over the back of one of his, urging him on. Smiling, knowing she would sense it with her lips on his, he complied, deftly undoing the now very familiar buttons, opening her bodice enough to slide his hand beneath, with a quick tug and a sliding caress to dispense with the barrier of her chemise, and close his hand about her swollen breast.

Just the touch made him ache.

It made Sarah burn. Made her feel not frantic as it had before, but fully aware of the fierceness of her desire. Of its strength, of the passion that flowed from it, of the flames of need that now burned steadily in her veins.

His fingers shifted, both hands now cradling her breasts, fingertips finding and tightening about the aching peaks. She broke the kiss on a gasp, grabbed his shoulders for balance as she tipped her head back, struggling to breathe while simultaneously absorbing, savoring, and reveling in the pleasure he gave her.

Unstintingly gave her; she let her senses whirl, deliberately letting go and glorying in the delicious delight as he bent his head and set his lips to her sensitive flesh. She shuddered when he licked, then tortured one tightly furled nipple; when he drew it deep and suckled, she moaned.

Her hands closed about his head, fingers splayed and spread in his hair as he pandered to her senses. As she wanted, as she wished.

Until she was burning so strongly, so passionately, her inner self would no longer be denied. She grasped his face and drew his head up, leaned into him and kissed him, met his lips, found his tongue with hers and stroked.

And felt the ripple of pure desire that coursed beneath his skin, the tensing, the readiness, the eagerness, the hunger locked in muscles that had turned to rigid steel. Beneath the heat, the licking, tantalizing flames, she sensed just how potent, how powerful was the passion he held leashed, at her command. His control was there, unwavering and complete, but it wasn't her he was controlling. And it was she who held his reins.

Joy flooded her, an emotional exultation that had her mentally gasping, that had her heart singing. Her lips on his, his mouth all hers, she reached between them and grappled with the buttons closing his breeches. He helped, shifting beneath her, but didn't take over. He let her free his staff, let her close her hand about it and stroke.

And make him shudder.

Her fingers curled about him, she did as she wished, and sought for the ways in which to pleasure him. Experimented, not in a rush, a few seconds seized before he took control, but deliberately and wantonly held him in her palm, and caressed, and learned . . . and felt his control quake.

She didn't stop but pressed on, pressed him on until she sensed he was struggling to hold on to that control, fighting, his breathing ragged. Wrapping her fingers about his rigid length, hot silk stretched over iron, she shuffled closer still, pushing her knees deep into the cushions past his hips, plucking her skirts from between them, positioning herself over him, guiding him . . . she thought it would work.

Mentally reeling, driven beyond any point of sensual desperation he'd previously reached, Charlie released her breasts, closed his hands about her knees, then swept up the line of her quivering thighs to seize her hips. Felt her scalding slickness brush the engorged head of his erection.

Felt the pent-up passions within him roar.

He drew her down, nudged into her tight sheath, tightened his grip on her hips—

She broke from the kiss on a gasp, head rising, spine instinctively arching. "No—let me!"

It was a cry from the heart; soft, intensely female, it rocked him to his core. His fingers tensed, bit into her flesh; his jaw clenched, ached as he battled to halt the all but ungovernable urge to pull her down and thrust upward and impale her.

He was entirely certain he was no longer in this world. He couldn't focus, not on anything beyond the need to be inside her . . . but then she touched his cheek, leaned in and kissed him softly, gently. Her other hand was locked around one of his wrists; using that to steady herself, she lowered herself upon him.

And he discovered there was so much more to lovemaking than he'd experienced before.

That her giving, rather than him taking, was the true measure of earthly bliss.

Bit by bit, inch by inch, she enclosed him, sank lower and engulfed him in her body, and showed him a new road to paradise.

His chest was locked; breathing was beyond him as on a tight exhalation she sank the last inch. And paused. Carefully, experimentally, he eased the taut leash he'd jerked so ruthlessly to harness his baser self, and discovered that self swooning.

With pleasure.

Ready to lie down and let her ravish him.

She was monitoring, discovering, learning as he did; through their kiss, she seemed to sense both his wonder and his unformed wish. As his grip on her eased, she relaxed a fraction, then rose a little way before sinking down again.

He let her set the pace for long enough to catch his breath, then when she sank down again, he thrust upward and filled her.

Sarah gasped, stilled for a moment to savor the fullness of him, the physical reality of having him so deep inside her, then she rose again,

again used the intimate slide of their bodies to pleasure him, and herself.

The link between them had grown stronger. She felt it now in every touch of his hands, investing every kiss be it driven or gentle. It was there in the way he forced himself to accept the slow pace she set, so that she could savor every step of the way, savor every nuance not just of their joining but of his commitment to her pleasure, to her need. There in the way he stood firm against his own desires, with every muscle in his body screaming for a much more active and immediate release.

He fought, and held to that line, to give her what she wished.

Charlie was conscious of every second of that battle; he knew she was, too. Knew she saw and followed, that she was aware of his devotion to her needs, that she appreciated every iota of the strength he wielded for her.

That alone made it worthwhile. Made the moment shimmer with emotion, and gave him the strength to hold to that road when his passions rose to near ungovernable heights.

It was worth the battle to restrain them to hear her increasingly ragged gasps, to feel the desperation mount within her and know it wasn't him driving, wasn't him orchestrating and controlling her that made her so.

As they moved together, her riding him, him thrusting just enough to appease them both, to let passion flow unimpeded on its course, as the familiar landscape of sexual delight flowered around them, as passion wound through them and tightened its snare, he was distantly aware of how different the familiar was.

How much more layered with feeling, with meaning. With emotion.

The end, when it came, was an implosion of sensation, finer, sharper, reaching more deeply than any such moment before.

With a cry, high, triumphant, and primally female, she shattered in his arms; the contractions of her sheath caught him, drew him on. Release swept him, and he cried her name, held her down, his grip unforgiving as he shuddered beneath her.

She collapsed upon him, into his arms. He closed them around her; eyes shut, he rested his cheek against her hair. And gave thanks that he'd lived to experience the glory she'd shown him, and the wonder they'd just shared.

．　．　．

Different. With her it was always so different, so familiar yet so rarely what he expected.

Slumped on the sofa with Sarah a warm and deeply sated bundle of female limbs and curves in his arms, Charlie stared at the dim ceiling of the summerhouse and let his mind find its way back to the world.

A world wherein, thanks to her, the landscape was changing. Again.

He puzzled over what had made this time so different from the last. Perhaps it was simply that she'd made her decision and had already agreed to be his, so having gotten what he'd wanted he hadn't had any driving motive other than to enjoy her.

That was true enough. He hadn't come to the summerhouse expecting to meet her; he'd been driven here purely by a nebulous feeling that, as he couldn't sleep, this was the place he should be. Here, waiting, in case . . .

In case she'd needed him. In case she'd come, searching, for what he didn't know, but she had come. And she had needed.

Him. Something he could give her.

He wasn't, even now, at all sure what that something was. But he'd sensed her need and had responded, as some part of him now claimed the right, the honor, to do. As it had transpired, she'd wanted to follow a sensual path he hadn't known existed, one that had demanded a great deal from him—yet part of the glory, much of the challenge, had been to give her what she'd wanted, to lavish on her whatever pleasures she wished, to make whatever sensual sacrifices that called for.

She stirred in his arms. He placed a gentle kiss on her temple, and she relaxed once more, unable as yet to summon the strength to rouse. He smiled, more than a trifle smugly. When she regained her bed he was sure she'd sleep soundly.

Settling his head against the sofa back, he thought of the next day—of the next night. Finally, he'd have her naked in his arms. The vision . . . brought to mind his thought that she would be a goddess— his goddess.

She was already that.

Somewhere inside he knew that was true, that some element of worship, of reverence, had already crept into his view of her, already colored the way he dealt with her. It was partly from that that the glory he felt in their physical union flowed; it was that that fed his devotion to satisfying her wants and demands. Her needs and wants now governed him. He expected to be shaken by the mere thought; instead, he felt sanguine, as if some part of him, his baser self certainly, felt that was only right, more, that it was his due.

Curious, but that was how he felt.

Perhaps it was simply another symptom of his addiction to the taste of innocence.

An addiction he felt confident would gradually fade.

The thought of that addiction drew his mind back to her, to her body, warm, sated female flesh still sheathing his staff . . .

His senses refocused. Confirmed that they must have been lying slumped for some time, that she was returning to full awareness, to command of her senses, limbs, and wits, then she contracted about him, and he didn't need to think any further.

Shifting, half lifting her, he tumbled her onto her back along the sofa, following her down without breaking their connection, beneath her rucked skirts rearranging her limbs so that her knees gripped his flanks.

Then he thrust into her.

And felt her immediate response. Saw her eyes glint from beneath heavy lids as her body arched beneath his.

He lay upon her, hands gripping her hips holding her immobile, trapped beneath him. "My turn," he murmured.

Her lips curved, swollen and sheening. Smiling like a cat drunk on cream, she tipped her face up so those luscious lips met his, reached up and twined her arms about his neck, and wordlessly invited him to take what he wished.

He wasn't sure which of them was more drained, more sated and ready for sleep, when an hour later he saw her to the manor's side door. There couldn't be that many hours left before they'd have to rise and plunge into the chaos of their wedding day, yet he doubted either of them cared.

Her hand on the doorknob, she glanced back at him, raised one hand to touch his cheek and smiled her madonna's smile. "Thank you."

He leaned in and kissed her. "It was entirely my pleasure." Drawing away, he met her eyes. "I'll see you at the altar."

Letting her fingers slide from his, he saluted her, then turned and walked away into the night.

At noon the next day, Sarah paced down the nave of the church at Combe Florey in a daze of happiness. Eyes locked on Charlie's as he waited for her on the shallow steps before the altar, she literally felt the glow that her mother, sisters, and all others who had seen her that morning had remarked on.

It came from somewhere deep within her, fueled by the absolute certainty that Charlie loved her as she loved him. That even if today was only the beginning for their love, love was unquestionably there.

Last night had been more than an affirmation; it had been a promise enshrined in bliss.

Reaching the steps, she gave her hand to Charlie, into his keeping, and stepped up to stand by his side.

And so they were married, with the Reverend Mr. Duncliffe officiating, and their familes, immediate and extended, looking on. Clary, Gloria, and Augusta had followed her down the aisle; Jeremy stood on the other side of Charlie, along with two gentlemen Sarah hadn't met before.

Beyond the fact that the church was packed, that was all she took in. The rest of her awareness was focused on the ceremony, on the words of the vow she made, and the one Charlie made in return.

To honor and obey. To honor and cherish.

He placed a golden wedding band on her finger, and they kissed to seal the pact, a caress that lingered longer than it should have. Their lips parted and their eyes met—for one instant there was just her and him and the joy between them—then reality returned, they smiled, resigned, and stepped apart. As one they turned and gave themselves over to their respective roles for the day.

Arm in arm they walked up the aisle, laughing and smiling, acknowledging the congratulations of all those packed inside the church. Once outside, they braved a shower of rice, but rather than simply climb into the carriage waiting to whisk them away, they paused in the crisp sunshine to receive the wishes of the crowd of locals who had gathered, to let the women coo over the exquisite pearl beading and Brussels lace adorning her white silk gown, while the men shook hands with Charlie or nodded respectfully.

Everyone beamed. It was a moment of golden fairy-tale-like happiness.

Both of them were locals; they'd lived most of their lives—in her case all of her life—within a few miles of the church. There was a small host of people lining up to wish her well, and she couldn't find it in her to cut the moment short.

She half expected Charlie to grow restless and perhaps drift to where his groomsmen loitered beside the ribbon-draped carriage. Instead, he remained beside her, his arm linked in hers, and employed his ready charm, leaving all those who spoke with them feeling gratified.

Mr. Sinclair appeared out of the throng to bow over her hand. "My congratulations, Countess." He smiled, debonair and sincere, then, releasing her, turned his smile on Charlie and held out his hand. "You're a lucky man, my lord."

Shaking his hand, Charlie inclined his head. "Indeed," he murmured, his eyes on her. "So I think."

Sarah felt herself blush; how she knew she didn't know, but she knew precisely what Charlie was thinking. They parted from Sinclair, and she looked around for distraction. To one side of the milling throng she spied Maggs's carroty-red head, then saw that Lily and Joseph had brought the older children to the church. She glanced at Charlie, but he'd already followed her gaze.

He caught her eye, smiled. "Come. Let's go over and greet them."

She caught the resignation in his eyes, yet there was something else in his demeanor, too—the something that had him so readily acquiescing to all the social demands of the day. She wasn't sure what that something was, but she smiled and let him steer her to the children.

After they'd chatted with the group, all round-eyed, letting the girls ooh and aah over her gown, Jeremy came and whispered that they really had to leave.

"I'll see you next week," she promised the children. They waved as Charlie led her away.

Reaching the open carriage, he handed her in, then to cheers and huzzahs and a swelling chant of "Meredith!" he joined her. He sat, and his coachman flicked the reins. They smiled and waved, then as the carriage carried them away from the church and through the town they sighed and sat back. It was only a minute to the impressive gates that gave onto the long drive leading to Morwellan Park.

She breathed in, catching the scent of budding things on the faint breeze. Spring was on the brink of bursting through; the sense of a fresh, joyous start found an echo within her.

She would soon arrive at her new home; today was the start of the rest of her life.

Beside her, Charlie took her hand in his, conscious that, as so frequently happened when he was with her, this day was unfolding somewhat differently than he'd thought.

He hadn't expected to actually enjoy his wedding, yet the instant he'd laid eyes on her, a vision in white gliding up the aisle toward him, he'd felt as if the sun had broken through and since then had been shining, glowing, on him. On them.

She was now his, and while part of what he felt was relief, a more solid part was pride. Pride in her, that he'd secured her as his bride, that he'd been so lucky even if he hadn't fully understood her worth when he'd first offered for her hand. He'd thought her an excellent candidate for the position of his countess, but he hadn't known then just how very true that was.

Seeing her moving through the hordes outside the church, smiling and knowing just what to say to the most crusty, tonnish beldame, and also to the miller's wife, and to the orphans, had brought the point home. She interacted with all levels of society easily, as did he, but that wasn't an ability shared by all young ladies. Others would have shrunk from what to them would have been a mere duty, and would have relied on him to deploy his charm and see them through. Sarah, instead, had a sincere interest in all who lived in the area; she'd done most of the talking, leaving him to play the relatively easy role of proud groom and local noble lord.

He looked down at her as, eyes briefly closing, smiling, she lifted her face to the sunshine. She looked radiant, and she was his. A warm glow suffused him, and settled in his chest.

A pleasant, very comfortable feeling.

Many of those invited to the wedding breakfast had driven ahead; a crowd was waiting in the drawing room to greet them. Within minutes of entering to joyous applause, they'd separated as friends and relatives claimed them. He was surprised to find himself highly aware of Sarah's absence from his side, but he'd attended fashionable weddings enough to know the ropes without thinking. Independently, they circled the room, chatting, then, at Crisp's announcement, came together again to lead the assembled host into the ballroom for the wedding breakfast.

They sat at the long tables draped in white linen, with silver and crystal glinting in the weak sunshine pouring through the long windows. Flutes of champagne were already waiting at each place; it should have been his father who proposed the first toast, but his father was dead. Gabriel Cynster had largely stood in loco parentis, but in deference to Charlie's title, it was Devil Cynster, Duke of St. Ives, who rose and proposed the first toast to the happy couple, welcoming them into the congregation of the wider family.

Everyone rose, lifted their glasses, echoed, "To Charlie and Sarah," then drank. His hand covering Sarah's as she sat beside him, Charlie smiled at the company, then glanced at her. And felt that odd feeling in his chest lurch, then intensify.

She was so happy it nearly hurt to look at her; the sight made him blink several times, and feel strangely humbled.

But then with much talk and laughter everyone sat again, and the meal was served. There was talk on every side. The majority present were now related in some fashion. With the Season yet to start and Christmas more than two months in the past, there was much to catch up with. Noise rose all around, yet it was the pleasant, embracing, congenial sound of shared familial happiness.

The next hour passed unmarred by any incident or consideration. The customary toasts were observed, predictably with some hilarity. Good humor and unalloyed gaiety were palpable threads twining through the gathering as guests stood and started to circulate.

Turning from chatting with Lord Martin Cynster, Charlie found that Alathea had captured Sarah. They sat together at a nearby table, engrossed in discussion. He suspected he should listen in to whatever "wisdom" his eldest sister was imparting; instead he simply stood and drank in the sight of Sarah's face. The sight of her transparent happiness.

It was a glow that radiated from her fine skin, that seemed to light her from within and shine from her cornflower-blue eyes. They seemed brighter, more sparkling, than he'd ever seen them.

For one instant alone within the whirl, he grasped the moment to wonder just what he was feeling, why that sight stirred something so deep, so profound inside him. Why his response was so strong, so powerful that it momentarily cramped his chest.

And left him faintly dizzy.

He raised the glass he held and sipped. And recalled his reasons for marrying. Recalled Sinclair's and others' comments; he was indeed a lucky man. He studied Sarah's face and heard again in his mind the vows he'd so recently spoken: to honor and cherish.

Unbidden, unintended, his mind supplied another vow, one he silently made as he watched her: He would do all he could to defend and protect the happiness shining in her eyes.

He would do all he could to make her anticipation of future happiness as his wife a reality.

"There you are!"

Charlie blinked and turned as Jeremy, looking faintly harassed, appeared at his shoulder.

"Who would have imagined getting my older brother wed would prove such a trial?" Jeremy resignedly but pointedly glared at him. "The musicians—you did remember we had musicians, didn't you?—have been waiting, not patiently, for you to give the signal for the first waltz."

"Ah." Charlie drained his glass, and handed it to Jeremy. "In that case, consider said signal given."

Jeremy rolled his eyes, heaved a put-upon sigh, and turned to wave to the musicans stationed at the other end of the room.

As the first chords sounded, Charlie crossed to take Sarah's hand. Catching her eyes, he smiled and drew her to her feet. "This is our dance, I believe."

Her smile, her joy, visibly brightened.

As he led her to where the central part of the floor was clearing, he felt her fingers tremble in his; turning her into his arms, he caught her eyes and murmured, "For this moment at least, it's just you and me."

She held his gaze; as he stepped out and swept her into the dance he felt her relax, losing the sudden nervousness that had assailed her at being the sole focus of everyone's complete attention. She followed his lead without hesitation, her skirts flowing about his legs as they twirled; he smiled, and drew her closer as he whirled them through the turn, then set them revolving back up the room.

"It's over," he murmured, smiling down into her eyes, keeping her close as, their lap of honor completed, Alathea and Gabriel, then Dillon and Pris and Gerrard and Jacqueline, took to the floor. Other couples followed.

Smiling back, Sarah sighed. She searched his eyes. "It's been . . . perfect, hasn't it?"

He felt his smile deepen. "Yes." And the day wasn't over yet. He didn't utter the words, but the direction of his thoughts must have shown in his eyes because she blushed, then looked away.

Inwardly grinning, he glanced around at the numerous couples now circling about them. Martin and Celia whirled past, laughing. Charlie had seen Devil sweep his duchess, Honoria, onto the floor; they whirled past with Honoria lecturing Devil about something, transparently to no avail. From the expression on his starkly handsome face, Devil seemed to be enjoying it.

Charlie wondered if he and Sarah would be like that after they'd been married for years. He looked into her face, and again felt the warmth inside him resonate with what he saw there.

The music ceased and the dancers re-formed into various chatting groups. Sarah remained on his arm and showed no inclination to desert him.

She glanced at the corner where the older ladies had congregated on a collection of chaises. "Should we . . ." She waved at the gathering. "Do you think?"

He didn't. "We spoke with all of them in the drawing room before." Lady Osbaldestone was there, and the old tartar's pointed comments had only grown sharper with her advancing years. With her sat Helena, Dowager Duchess of St. Ives, Lady Horatia Cynster, the Marchioness of Huntly, and various other grandes dames, all of whom shared one scarifying attribute; they could be counted on to see far too much— such as his unexpected response to Sarah's happiness in becoming his wife—and there was no power on earth capable of preventing them from commenting when and wherever they chose.

"We don't need to give them another chance at us." Charlie turned his new wife toward less unnerving guests. "There's the twins— Amanda and Amelia. You know them, don't you?"

"Yes, of course." Sarah was delighted to join the group clustered about the two bright heads.

They were greeted with delight, then the group separated into two halves. The female half—Amanda, Countess of Dexter, her twin sister, Amelia, Vicountess Calverton, and Sarah, now Countess of Meredith—became engrossed in a discussion of children (the twins now had three each and had apparently decided to call a halt to their unintentional rivalry) then turned their attention to the upcoming Season, and the likelihood of them meeting in London shortly.

The male half—Charlie, Amanda's husband, Martin, Earl of Dexter, and Amelia's husband, Luc, Viscount Calverton—exchanged long-suffering glances and instituted their own conversation about matters politic. The three of them were linked in that Devil and Gyles Rawlings, Earl of Chillingworth, had acted as sponsors and mentors in steering each of them through the process of taking their seats in the Lords, and guiding them into the sometimes confusing political arena.

Politics was an aspect of life the five—Charlie, Luc, Martin, Devil, and Gyles—as peers of the realm shared, keeping abreast of the vissicitudes that shaped the country, making sure they were in London to take their seats and vote when necessary, even though none of them harbored political aspirations.

Regardless, all of them accepted they had political responsibilties; that was part and parcel of who they'd been born and raised to be.

However, as Parliament wasn't sitting and there were no major upheavals threatening, there was little they had to discuss, unlike their ladies. But before they'd been reduced to feeling redundant, Barnaby approached from one side, while from the other, Reggie Carmarthen, a longtime friend of Amanda's and Amelia's, and his wife, Anne—one of Luc's sisters—joined them, along with Penelope, Luc's youngest sister.

Sarah greeted the newcomers with delight; thanks to Alathea's having married into the Cynster fold, and Sarah's family's being invited to all the major gatherings at the Park and also at Casleigh, the Cynsters' house, she'd met all these ladies before. While no one had guessed she would marry Charlie, now that she had, Amanda, Amelia, and all the rest were intent on embracing her and wholeheartedly welcoming her into that unfailingly warm and supportive set.

Their interest and the promise of evolving friendships added yet another layer of joy to her day.

Barnaby Adair was one gentleman she hadn't met, but when Charlie introduced him, he smiled and charmingly complimented her.

Blond, exceedingly handsome, and understatedly sophisticated, he was clearly another of this group, unrelated maybe but transparently a part of the circle.

Charlie introduced Barnaby to Penelope, the only other lady he hadn't previously met. She regarded him seriously through her spectacles, then offered her hand. "You're the one who investigates crimes—do I have that correctly?"

Taking her hand, Barnaby admitted that he did, but glibly turned the conversation to other, less sensational avenues. Penelope narrowed her eyes, then, retrieving her fingers, turned to Sarah and the other ladies.

As they stood in a loose group at one side of the ballroom, with the sunshine streaming over them, chatting and talking of this and that, the looming uncertainty Sarah had felt over managing Charlie's London house and all the tonnish entertaining his position necessitated evaporated. With friends like these, she had nothing to fear.

Both Amanda and Amelia insisted she call on them for any help she might need. "We've been through it all," Amanda said. "And while it's daunting at first—"

"It's the way our world is," Amelia cut in, "and once you've survived hosting your first ton ball you can manage *anything*."

The assembled ladies laughed, then Amelia and Amanda firmly collected their spouses and led them, unresisting, away.

Charlie, Reggie, and Barnaby resumed their discussion of horseflesh. Sarah turned to Anne and Penelope, neither of whom she'd spent much time with before.

Her gaze direct and fearless, Penelope met Sarah's eyes. Unlike Luc's other sisters—the softly feminine Anne and the eldest, Emily, and the strikingly attractive Portia—Penelope always appeared rather severe, with her thick, dark hair tightly restrained and her spectacles perched on her straight little nose. She spoke very directly, too. "Mama mentioned," she said, "that you manage an orphanage nearby."

Sarah smiled. "Indeed. I inherited it, you might say as a going concern, from my godmother." Penelope's glance was openly inquiring; Sarah glanced at Anne and found her interested, too. She briefly outlined the scale and scope of the orphanage, and their aim to give their children a future trade.

"Aha!" Penelope nodded. "That's what I need to hear about. You see, together with Anne and Portia, and others, of couse, I manage the Foundling House in London. We face much the same difficulties as here, but we've yet to institute any real program to help the children once they're old enough to leave." Penelope glanced around at the wedding guests, but refused to be deterred. "Would you mind terribly taking a moment to explain how your system works?"

"No, of course not. The orphanage is my principal interest." Sarah paused, then amended, "Well, after my household."

"I know Portia's around here somewhere. She should hear this, too." Stretching on her toes, Penelope scanned the room. "Can you see Simon Cynster?"

"Why?" asked Anne, looking, too. "Was he with her?"

Penelope snorted. "No, but if you find him, I'll lay you odds he'll be scowling at her." When Sarah frowned in question, Penelope shrugged. "In gatherings such as this, he always does."

At that moment, Charlie caught Sarah's eye and raised a brow. Deciding it was, perhaps, not the wisest of moments to become engrossed in a discussion of the orphange, Sarah turned to Anne and Penelope. "Perhaps I can introduce you to Mrs. Duncliffe, the vicar's wife. She's on the orphanage committee and knows even more than I about the history of our placing boys and girls in various positions."

Penelope's attention was immediately deflected. "Mrs. Duncliffe—which lady is she?"

Luckily, Mrs. Duncliffe was seated on a chaise not far from where they stood. Sarah led the sisters over and introduced them, then left the three ladies to share their experiences.

She returned to Charlie's side just as the strains of another waltz floated over the room.

"Good." He captured her hand, raised it to his lips and kissed. "I've missed you."

The murmured words were just for her. They warmed her, buoyed her, and then she was in his arms, circling down the room, and for those few moments nothing else mattered.

Nothing else could gain any foothold in her mind, not when she was surrounded by his strength, not when she was whirling down the floor lost in his eyes.

Eventually, he said, "One definite benefit to being married is that we can waltz whenever we wish, as many times as we wish."

She smiled and replied, "There's no one I want to waltz with but you."

His eyes widened fractionally; she got the impression she'd surprised him in some way, yet her words were the simple truth. As he searched her eyes, clearly checking, she let that fact show. Let her smile deepen.

He drew breath, then looked ahead and whirled her through the turn. They spoke no more until the music ended and they halted with a flourish in the middle of the floor.

"Who now?" she murmured.

Charlie closed his hand, tight, about hers, then forced himself to ease his grip. He had hours yet to endure before they could slip away, before he could further explore and savor that fascinating tenderness he'd glimpsed in her eyes. "This way." He glanced at her. "I want you to meet my closest friends."

Sarah had met Gerrard and Dillon only briefly in the church. She hadn't met their wives, but from the instant he introduced her to Jacqueline and Pris, it was obvious to him, Dillon, and Gerrard that their only concern henceforth would be separating the three. There seemed to be an amazing range of subjects on which their ladies needed to speak and exchange opinions.

Some of those subjects, such as the balls and dinners each lady was considering giving during the upcoming Season, were topics their husbands felt it was best not to hear of; leaving their spouses avidly talking, the three edged to one side.

"Thus ends your freedom," Dillon advised Charlie, distinctly smug. "I recall, at my nuptials, you crowing about being the last man standing." He grinned evilly. "How did it feel to fall?"

Charlie grinned back, unrepentant. "Actually, it was rather less stressful, and distinctly more pleasurable, than I'd expected."

Gerrard arched a brow. "So we've seen. Mind you, you need to understand you're starting from well behind. We've both got ourselves heirs—you'll have to hustle if you intend catching up."

Charlie chuckled; he met Gerrard's eye. "I'll bear your advice in mind."

They'd lowered their voices, yet, as one, they turned to verify that their respective ladies hadn't heard.

All three of them stayed staring for rather longer than a glance;

eventually dragging his eyes from Sarah's animated face, Charlie noted that both Dillon's and Gerrard's gazes, too, were lingering on their wives' faces.

There was a softness in both men's normally hard gazes that he never saw except when they looked at their wives and sons.

He glanced again at Sarah, and finally understood, felt again the welling sensation of warmth, and yes, of curious softness, that blossomed inside him when he looked at her. That only deepened and intensified at the thought of seeing her with his child in her arms.

Drawing breath, he turned away, a trifle unsettled by the strength of that feeling. From Gerrard's and Dillon's experience, it seemed it was only to be expected . . .

He inwardly frowned. His situation wasn't the same as theirs.

Before he could pursue that disturbing thought, Barnaby wandered up. He glanced at the three ladies.

"Don't you think," Gerrard murmured provocatively, "that it's time you took the plunge and joined us?"

Barnaby turned from his contemplation of their spouses and smiled, charmingly glib. "I think not. My fascination, I find, lies in other spheres."

Dillon laughed. "We all thought that—until we learned otherwise."

Barnaby's easy smile remained. "I suspect my 'otherwise' might never eventuate. I'll be eccentric Uncle Barnaby to all your sprigs—all children should have an eccentric uncle, don't you think?"

"Why think your 'otherwise' will never appear?" Charlie asked.

Barnaby met his eyes, then grimaced. "Can you honestly imagine any lady of the ton understanding what I do—how I increasingly spend my time? Would any lady countenance my commitment to criminal investigations in preference to the social round?"

The others exchanged glances, then grimaced, too.

But Gerrard shook his head. "Be that as it may, I still wouldn't tempt fate by thinking this won't happen to you."

"*Be* that as it may," Barnaby replied, his eyes going to Charlie's, "this seems the perfect time to have our little meeting."

Reminded of their prearranged plan, Charlie glanced around. "Very true." The gathering was still absorbed; the ladies would talk for hours yet and the gentlemen had topics enough to pursue. He turned to Gerrard and Dillon. "Barnaby's in pursuit of some rather nasty criminals and there's a chance we can help." He dipped his head to Dillon. "You've heard some of it, but Barnaby and I thought today the perfect opportunity for him to explain to the whole lot of us at once. Why don't you two head for the library"—he glanced at Barnaby—"while we round up the others?"

Dillon's and Gerrard's eyes had widened; they readily nodded. With one swift glance at their ladies, confirming they were still engrossed, they strolled away across the ballroom.

Charlie met Barnaby's eyes. "You take that side of the room—I'll take this."

Barnaby nodded and they parted, prowling, apparently unhurriedly, through the assembled guests.

11

When Charlie led Gabriel into the library, all the others were there.

Devil had taken the chair before the desk, leaving the one behind it for Charlie; Vane Cynster, Devil's cousin, was lounging against the bookshelves nearby. Vane's brother Harry, known as Demon, along with Alasdair Cynster, Gabriel's brother and commonly known as Lucifer, had appropriated the chaise from the other end of the room, and set it before the desk.

Gyles, Earl of Chillingworth, close friend and honorary Cynster, had pulled up a chair across from Devil, while Simon Cynster, the youngest present and other than Barnaby the only one unmarried, leaned elegantly against the raised back of the chaise.

Dillon, Gerrard, and Barnaby had fetched straight-backed chairs from around the room and sat interspersed between the others, while Luc and Martin stood shoulder to shoulder with their backs propped against the bookshelves, their long legs crossed at the ankles and their hands in their pockets.

Every handsome but hard-planed masculine face bore a serious and in most cases expectant expression. Gabriel went to sit between Luci-fer and Demon on the chaise. Charlie felt every eye tracking him as he moved to his chair behind the desk.

He sat, then looked around, briefly meeting every eye. "Thank you for coming. Barnaby's on a mission and he needs our help."

With that, he looked at Barnaby, who succinctly yet comprehen-sively explained the crux of his investigation.

Throughout, no one moved or even shifted. Charlie felt certain he would have heard a pin drop on the Aubusson rug. No one interrupted or even humphed.

Barnaby ended his exposition with, "While the pater and the other peers overseeing the force, as well as all the senior members of the force itself, want this game stopped, given that there are so many other peers, parliamentarians, wealthy individuals, and other gentlemen of influ-ence involved in the various railway companies and therefore poten-tially implicated, any investigation has to be discreet."

He fell silent. The others finally shifted, exchanging glances. As a group, they were powerful in many ways—wealthy, influential, titled, every one of them born to the elite.

Gabriel mumured, "Everyone here would have some dealings, some financial exposure, to the companies that have been targeted by this . . . let's call him an extortioner. So we're potentially all victims, albeit not in a way that will personally hurt us. But this sort of activity may well result in some of those companies going bankrupt, and a consequent loss of confidence in that whole area of endeavor, which will in the short term impinge on our investments."

Devil shifted. He exchanged a glance with Chillingworth, then said, "There's a wider issue here—one that reaches much further than any individual investments involved." He glanced around. "All of us here ap-preciate how much the future of this country is going to depend on the successful introduction of the infrastructure of the future—specifically the railways. The introduction of the canals last century ushered in a minor boom, but the railways are vital to the next stage. If it becomes widely known that investing in a railway company carries a risk of the company being subject to such extortion, and consequently bankruptcy, the small investors essential to fund each project will take flight. They're the ones with least stomach for danger."

"And least ability to withstand it," Lucifer put in.

Devil inclined his head. "Indeed. And yet further, if it becomes widely known that having land close to or beside the proposed route of a railway can result in becoming the target of such tactics as our extortioner has used on farmers and the like, then we can expect whole areas to rise up in arms and refuse to allow tracks to cross their counties."

"The fact that it's only specific parcels of land that are being targeted won't make any difference," Chillingworth said. "Panic pays precious little attention to logic."

Barnaby's gaze had grown distant; his face paled as he envisioned the scenario they were painting. "Great heavens." His voice was weak. "I don't think the pater and the others even thought of that."

Devil grimaced. "They probably did—they just didn't see any reason to spell it out. They know you'll be discreet."

Barnaby looked grim. "Indeed. But such prospects make it even more imperative that we identify and stop this extortioner."

"Are you sure it's all the same man, or group?" Martin asked.

Barnaby nodded. "I came to that conclusion after trying to trace the profit from some of the extortionate land sales, reasoning that the profit must eventually find its way back into the villain's hand. What I discovered was that each property is initially bought by a unique land company, and sold by that company. But after the sale, that original company is dissolved and its profits, the money from the sale, transferred to two other land companies. In turn, those second-string companies each pay their profits to two or more other companies, and the further I tried to push, the web of companies just proliferated.

"And *that* was the situation in all instances where I tried to chase the money. Every initial land company leads into a web of other companies, and while all the companies are different, the strategy is exactly the same. It's so complex yet effective I can't imagine that two people independently thought of it."

Vane looked at Gabriel. "Is there any way we can find our way through the maze?"

"There *should* be," Gabriel replied, "but if this extortioner has been clever enough to use a network of companies in this way, then we're likely to find ourselves running in circles. Until the government legislates for companies and their owners to be registered, tracing the legal owners, and more importantly the *beneficial* owners of such a web of companies—especially when that web has been intentionally created to conceal the identity of the ultimate beneficial owner—will almost certainly be an exercise in futility."

Gabriel glanced around the ring of faces. "My recommendation is that we reserve our efforts for some avenue more likely to succeed."

There were grimaces all around. For a long moment, silence reigned.

"Very well." Luc looked at Barnaby. "Our estates, collectively, are spread all over the country. We should at least keep our ears open for any hint of coercion going on in the areas we each know best."

Barnaby nodded, rather glum. "You all know your own areas—think of where railways are likely to go through, about where they'll need to climb or descend, and if you hear of people in those areas being approached to sell, let me know. I've spent the last few days looking over the land between Bristol and Taunton, and a little farther west. Given the topography, it seems likely our villains will make some attempt in this region, so we'll keep a tight watch here."

He sighed, then slumped back in his chair. "At present that seems to be all we can do."

"Actually," Charlie said, tapping one finger on his blotter, his gaze fixing on Gabriel, "I think there's one other avenue we've overlooked—and it's just possible that our villain may have overlooked it, too."

Gabriel held his gaze for a moment, but then, with a ghost of a smile, shook his head. "If it's finance, I can't see it. What?"

"I'm not sure, but . . ." Charlie glanced around, then looked again at Gabriel. "Our villain has been terribly clever about concealing where the money goes. But has he been equally clever about concealing where the money came from?"

All the others became alert; the tension in the room abruptly heightened. Glances were exchanged as they all saw the point, then everyone again looked to Gabriel.

He nodded slowly, his gaze locked with Charlie's. "Excellent point." Gabriel's drawl had taken on a predatory edge.

Charlie grinned, equally predatory. "Wherever the money came from, in the end, the profit must find its way back to the source—such is the nature of investing."

"Oh, yes," Gabriel averred. "And while he might have thrown up a web of companies to obscure the movements of the profits back, looking in the other direction, at where the money to buy the land came from in the first place, even if he's using a web of companies again, it's unlikely to be as complex, and at some point funds must have entered the web."

"Funds from outside the web—from the source, our villain." Devil arched a brow at Gabriel. "How hard will it be to trace the initial incoming capital for a land company?"

Gabriel didn't immediately answer; eventually he said, "It won't be straightforward"—everyone present knew that by "not straightforward" he meant it would involve employing questionable means—"but we should be able to do it."

"We might find ourselves faced with a similar web," Charlie said, "but if we concentrate on one land company, and look only for the original funding, even if he's moved it through various companies, it'll still be one lump we're tracking. One identifiable sum. It's unlikely he'll have thought to pay the initial sum in smaller amounts."

"Regardless, the initial capital will have come from him by whatever roundabout route." Gabriel nodded. "That's eminently worth pursuing." He looked at Barnaby. "We'll need all the details you have of the land company used to buy the most expensive parcel you know of. The larger the sum the better, the easier it will be to trace. With that"—Gabriel looked at Devil—"Montague will be able to focus on the land company, learn when it was set up, and then search for the source of the seed capital through the movement of that sum through the banks. With any luck at all, he should be able to follow the trail back, ultimately to our villain's accounts."

Devil nodded. "Will you instruct him?"

"I'd rather you did." Gabriel looked at Barnaby, then Charlie. "I agree that this area, of all the regions in England, is the ripest at present for our villain. I think I'll be more valuable here, helping to keep watch for him."

Their meeting broke up. They drifted back into the ballroom in twos and threes, their reappearance sufficiently staggered to conceal the fact that any meeting had occurred. In that they seemed successful; none of their mothers, sisters, or wives appeared to have noticed their collective absence from the still-considerable crowd.

Relieved not to be called to account, each returned to his spouse or, in Simon's case, to his perennial irritation with Portia Ashford. Charlie found Sarah chatting with that young lady about the orphanage. He nodded to Portia, took Sarah's arm, and waited beside her.

On reentering the ballroom, he'd signaled to the musicians that the airs and sonatas he'd instructed them to play before he'd slipped away to the library were no longer required and could be replaced by the waltzes they'd been hired to provide.

Throughout the day he'd suppressed the inevitable effect of the previous night, tamped down his impatience to test his hypothesis and assure himself that his addiction to Sarah would inevitably wane once she was legally his. He'd performed as required of a nobleman of the ton on his wedding day, but he'd—they'd—now done all that was needed; his impatience, temporarily deflected by the meeting in the library, had returned in full force.

Two minutes later, the strains of a waltz filled the room. He whispered in Sarah's ear, then glibly excused them both to a grinning Portia and led Sarah onto the floor.

"Where were you?" Sarah asked, once they were pleasantly revolving.

Charlie looked down at her, then looked over her head as he steered her on. "I was talking to a few of the others about some business dealings—we went out where it was quieter."

"Oh." She was a trifle surprised that his mind had strayed to business at such a time.

As if guessing her thoughts, he caught her eye and smiled—his private smile, lacking the gloss of his sophisticated charm, more honest and sincere. "It filled the time."

Tilting her head, she studied his eyes, trying to see what he was telling her. "The time . . . ?"

"Until . . ." He steered her through another turn, then drew her out of the throng of dancers; he halted by the side of the room where an ornately carved sideboard created a sheltered nook between its side and the room's corner.

Taking her hand, he captured her gaze. "Until we can do this"—reaching out, he twisted a knob in the paneling and a concealed door popped open—"and quietly slip away."

Her heart—along with every nerve she possessed—leapt, but she cast a swift glance at the guests swirling about the floor.

"Don't worry," he murmured. "The majority will be more surprised if we stay." His arm circling her waist, he urged her to the doorway; with no real reluctance, she stepped through into a narrow service corridor.

He followed, closing the door behind him. Retaking her hand, he drew it through his arm and led her on.

She glanced up at his face. "Why would they expect us to leave like this—slipping quietly away?"

"So that we avoid the awkward alternative, especially the 'farewell' Jeremy, Augusta, Clary, and Gloria have doubtless spent the last few days devising." He raised a brow at her. "Do you really want to learn how inventive they've been?"

She laughed and shook her head. "I believe I'll survive perfectly well without knowing."

"Thank heavens—I know I will."

She heard the note of real relief in his voice and inwardly grinned, but then she remembered where they were going. And why. A species of nervousness threaded through her. She looked around, trying to get her bearings, as he led her down an intersecting corridor, then up a narrow flight of stairs to a landing.

He opened a door; he glanced at her as he guided her through. "Have you been in this wing before?"

Stepping into a wide, richly decorated corridor, clearly one of the major corridors of the house, she looked around, then glanced out the window to orient herself. All sound from the ballroom had faded; all about them was quiet. "No. This is the west wing, isn't it?"

Nodding, he retook her hand, engulfing it in his. "The earl's apartments are in this wing. You reach it from the gallery off the main stairs." He waved behind them as he led her on.

Her lungs started to tighten.

It was nonsense, she told herself, to feel like this, as if they'd never . . . but that had been in the summerhouse, in the silent depths of the night, not here, not . . . This was very different.

The corridor ended in a circular anteroom. A highly polished round table stood in its center, upon it a tall chinoiserie vase holding a massive arrangement of hothouse blooms. They stepped into the room. Charlie let go of her hand and turned back. Looking up, Sarah blinked and went slowly forward, staring up at the huge circular skylight above the table.

Hearing a click behind her, she swung around and saw Charlie bolting a pair of huge doors, sealing the room from the corridor.

Stepping back, he surveyed his handiwork. "That should hold them."

Turning to her, he smiled, then, closing the distance, he saw her eyes, saw her sudden nervousness. His smile eased, became more gentle—personal and reassuring.

Reaching her, he took her hand, cruised his thumb over her knuckles. Simply said, with total sincerity, "I don't want us to be interrupted."

He looked into her eyes, then raised his other hand and framed her face. Slowly, he tipped her chin up, equally slowly bent his head, and kissed her.

A gentle, easy kiss, asking nothing more from her than her instinctive response, a response she gave without thought, without hesitation.

His lips firmed and she yielded, parted her lips and waited. His tongue found hers, caressed, and she sighed.

Long moments passed while his lips moved on hers, while with his tongue he engaged in a slow, unhurried exploration, a claiming renewed by one who had the right. His fingers traced her jaw, then slid lower to firm over one side of her throat, his thumb beneath her chin keeping her face tilted as he wielded his considerable expertise and lured her to him; his other hand rested at her waist, anchoring her before him.

His.

When he raised his head and looked into her eyes, studied her face, she was already immersed in the web of sensual pleasure she knew would intensify over the minutes to come.

As he'd intended.

His lips curved, but only faintly, his face already set in the sensual mask she now knew well. Releasing her face, he retook her hand and turned to the double doors across the anteroom.

As he led her to the earl's bedchamber, she understood that what had passed between them in the summerhouse would be as nothing compared to this—to the moments that were to come.

She was now his wife—that's what was different.

Opening one door, he ushered her through. Eyes widening, nerves stretching, she walked in and looked around. Behind her, she heard the door shut; lips faintly throbbing, her breathing already shallow, she gazed at the huge ornately carved four-poster bed, hung with blue silks and covered with blue satin.

She felt his gaze on her face; he paused, watching as she took in the sumptuous furnishings, the tasseled gold cords holding back the bed curtains, and the long blue velvet curtains at the windows. The entire room was decorated in shades of blue; even the wallpaper was ivory figured with blue fleurs-de-lis. Against the blue, the richness of golden oak shone and glowed. The wood of the bed, the tall armoires against the walls, the dressing table with its oval mirror sitting between two long windows, the frame of the comfortable armchair set nearby, balanced and contained the blue, keeping it from being overwhelming.

Glancing down, she saw the same pattern repeated, the rich medley of blues, ivories, and golden browns in the Persian rugs framed by the polished floorboards.

Every item on which her eye alighted was elegant, expensive, yet not overpowering. Every lamp, every wall sconce, every dish, seemed to fit within the overall scheme so that the totality exceeded the sum of the parts.

Enchanted, she drifted to the dressing table, and found her brushes laid out. The sight made her nerves quiver, why she didn't know.

She moved to look out the windows. The view was to the south, over the western end of the wide south lawn to the ornamental lake. Massive ancient trees edged the lawn, their canopies still bare and brown but with the first glimmer of green buds appearing.

It was late afternoon; the day was closing in, the sun starting to wane, but enough light remained to clearly see. To see, as he joined her before the window and she drew in a tight breath and faced him, his features, his eyes.

He stood before her with less than a foot between them, and looked down at her. Banked desire etched the angular planes, giving them a sharpness, an edge she now recognized. His blue eyes were intent; he was studying her, his eyes searching hers, her expression, trying to read her thoughts.

She wished him luck; she couldn't have told him what she felt in that moment—there simply weren't words for such a medley of feelings.

After a moment, he said, "I could picture you in the blue. I hope you like it, but if you don't, you can change it."

His voice was low, his tone private, undisguised.

Looking into his eyes, she realized what instinctive understanding had made her shiver. He'd created this place for her—here, in this room, she would be his wife in the most private and fundamental way. In the most intimate way.

Echoing her thoughts, he took her hands, one in each of his. His eyes locked with hers, he lifted first one, then the other to his lips, placing a kiss on the sensitive backs of her knuckles.

"All you see," he murmured, "is now part of your domain. Yours to rule."

She looked at him, and felt the power that had welled between them in the summerhouse flare anew, sensed that it was now a part of them, steady and true.

That it would only grow and burn brighter, here in this room, between them.

It was she who slipped her fingers from his grasp and reached up, slid her hand about his nape and stretched up, and kissed him. Offered herself to him, to that power.

His arms went around her; he drew her to him. Lips firming on hers, he effortlessly took control of the kiss and whirled them into the flames.

It was like waltzing on some sensual plane; the thud of their hearts, the building, artfully driving rhythm of passion provided the beat, the kiss, hot and ardent, in this setting unrestrained, provided the power to swing their senses around and around, and leave them giddy.

Their hands took turns removing their clothing. She dispensed with his cravat while he started on the tiny pearl buttons trailing from her nape down her spine. There were dozens of them; she interrupted him to wrestle free his tight-fitting morning coat, seized the moment to discard his waistcoat as well.

He hauled her back against him, his hands busy at her back, his lips and tongue increasingly insistent and demanding. Increasingly distracting.

The familiar heat had welled and rushed through them by the time she managed, with her hands all but trapped between their bodies, to open the front of his shirt. In the same moment, he flicked the last pearl free and with a frustrated growl released her to strip away the heavy silk gown.

She pulled her arms from the long tight sleeves; beneath his hands, the bodice slid to her waist, then the skirts fell with a swoosh to the floor. He took her hand, steadying her as she obediently—eagerly—lifted her petticoats and stepped free of the stiff skirts.

One step away from the window, one step closer to the bed.

Aware of that, of the intense burning in his blue eyes, she let him tug her back to him, but raised her hands and pushed the shoulders of his open shirt wide—off his shoulders, down his arms.

The cuffs were still fastened. He muttered an oath and reached around her, fumbling with the closures behind her back while with his arms he urged her against him, bending his head to kiss her—to kiss her witless she had no doubt, but this time she wouldn't be denied. Palms to his chest, she pushed back, held him back enough to allow her to do as she wished.

He, after all, was a part of her domain.

One she wanted to explore.

Fully. More fully than she'd been able to in the restricted amenities of the summerhouse. Now, in the clear if fading light of a winter's day, she could appreciate the muscled expanse of his chest, the sculpted sweep of each muscle band, the heaviness, the harnessed strength. Spreading her fingers, she explored, palms pressed to warm skin stretched over what felt like heated steel. A band of crinkly brown hairs adorned the width, tangling with her questing fingers. Beneath that pelt her searching fingers discovered the flat discs of his nipples and boldy caressed.

He stilled, breath suspending, muscles tightening; delighted, she pressed her hands wide, and let her fascination show. Intuitively she knew he liked seeing it, that the sight of her absorption in turn fascinated him.

How far would his fascination stretch? How far would it tempt him? Lifting her gaze from his chest, she trapped his eyes, and skated her hands down, over his ridged abdomen, lingering to savor the muscles tensing beneath her touch, then she reached his waistband and the buttons fastening it.

The planes of his face tightened, the edges growing harder, more defined. His jaw tensed as she slipped the buttons free, but, his eyes locked with hers, he let her.

Let her disrobe him until he stood naked before her, until there was no distracting clothing to detract from his male beauty.

Her lungs locked, her mouth dry, she gazed, wantonly amazed; he was even more handsome, more sculpted, more elegantly and intensely male without his clothes than with. She longed to step back, to take several steps back to get a better perspective, but she instinctively knew he wouldn't allow that. That just holding still and letting her look her fascinated fill was taxing his control to its limit.

A limit she fully intended to break, but not yet.

Dragging in a breath, she reached out, with the fingers of one hand touched the side of his waist, then slowly she moved to the side, letting her fingertips trail over his stomach, across to his hip, and around as she circled him.

As she passed beyond his shoulder, she saw his eyes shut, saw his jaw tip upward and clench. His hands fisted, but with her hand on his skin assuring him she remained close, near, he allowed her to slowly circle him. She did, marveling at the long graceful lines of his body, the smooth hard planes, the lean muscles flickering and flexing in his shoulders and back, cording his legs.

He could have been a sculptor's model; every line of his body seemed fashioned by the gods.

Behind him, she paused, her fingertips resting in the hollow of his spine; she sensed the tension thrumming through him, in reaction to her touch, to her gaze.

She went on, continuing to look, to savor, as she rounded him. His eyes opened as she did. The instant she returned to face him, before she even had a chance to lift her gaze, he reached for her. Gripping her waist, he turned her around—so he could more swiftly deal with the ties securing her petticoats.

She felt the near-violence in his quick, impatient tugs. Thanks to their earlier step back and his turning her, they now stood in line with the dressing-table mirror; in the reflection she saw him behind her, head bowed, his attention focused on unraveling the knots. On undressing her.

A sultry chuckle escaped her. He lifted his head, in the mirror met her gaze—and heat flared and swamped her.

What she saw in his eyes stole her breath.

Stole her wits, or rather focused every one she possessed, and all her senses, on him, on them.

She was completely and utterly caught when he looked down; with a final jerk, the pressure about her waist eased. With a tug, he sent the ruffled petticoats falling, sliding down her legs to pool about her feet.

Leaving her clad in chemise, stockings, garters, and wedding slippers. For the occasion, her chemise was of the finest silk, translucent, nearly sheer. His hand closed about her waist, and the fabric was no more substantial a barrier than spider's silk between his skin and hers.

Her skin heated beneath his hard hand. He looked up, in the mirror trapped her gaze. "My turn."

His voice was low, gravelly, laden with male emotions she couldn't name. His gaze roved her silk-clad body. Eyes wide, she waited, breath bated, to see what he would do.

Bending, he reached around her; grabbing the dressing stool, he drew it closer, setting it before her.

Straightening, he stood behind her, close, his heat like a flame down her back, one hand at her waist, holding her. In the mirror he met her eyes. "Put one foot on the stool and take off your stocking."

Her nerves shivered, tensed, tightened to a knot. She drew breath, and complied; slipping her left foot free of her satin wedding slipper, she raised it to the top of the stool. Her toes on the velvet, she reached to where her chemise had drawn back, revealing the antique garter holding up her silk stocking.

As her fingers touched the richly embroidered garter, his palm made contact with the back of her thigh, which with her leg raised was fully exposed. A long slow comprehensive caress made her lungs seize. Giddy, she gripped the garter; his blunt fingertips helped her ease it down. His palm followed her stocking to her knee, tauntingly caressed the sensitive spot behind it, then slowly, provocatively, retreated up the back of her leg as she removed stocking and garter, then set her foot down.

Gathering the strength to repeat the exercise, knowing what would come, took a moment. "The garters were your mother's, did you know?" She sounded breathless, hoping to distract him and gain another minute to steel her nerves. "They were my 'something borrowed.'"

"Indeed?" The word was a low growl. His fingers tightened on her waist. "Other leg."

She hauled in a breath, and did as he asked, unable this time to quell a shiver as he stroked, not just down but, once her stocking fell, all the way up past the top of her thigh to caress her bottom.

Her knees weakened, nearly buckled.

He removed his hand unhurriedly and stepped nearer.

So his chest touched her shoulders, so she could feel his rampant erection riding against her back. His hands gripped her waist; she refocused on the mirror, wondering what he planned, but although he was surveying her in the glass, he wasn't looking at her face.

He raised his hands; with the side of his thumbs, oh-so-lightly, oh-so-tantalizingly he brushed the underside of her already taut breasts. A sensual shudder racked her; from beneath suddenly heavy lids, she saw his lips curve, just a little.

He turned his hands and cupped her breasts, hands closing, unrestrainedly possessive, then he bent his head, brushed her ear with his lips, and murmured, "Now this."

He plucked the ribbon tie of her chemise, unraveling the bow tucked between her breasts. Curling his fingers into the gathered top, he drew it slowly out, then slowly down, away from her breasts, down past her waist; then he flicked his fingers and the fine silk floated down her legs to the floor.

Leaving her as naked as he.

She didn't truly know what he would see, what he would be expecting. It was a battle to draw breath, to steady her whirling wits, to find courage enough to lift her gaze to the mirror, to his reflected face, and see . . . the same enthrallment she felt with his naked form laid like a tattoo across his features.

Delight was a drug surging through her as she watched his eyes trace her body, watched his gaze heat and devour, then rise to her face.

In the mirror, she met his eyes, let him read in hers her joy that he found her as pleasing as she found him, then his gaze lowered to her lips.

She tensed to turn, but his hands at her waist tightened.

"No. Wait." His gaze on her body, he released her and stepped back. She felt the heat as he focused on her shoulder blades, then his gaze swept down over the planes of her back, with a touch like flame lingered on the swell of her bottom, on the backs of her legs, before he reached out, grasped her hand, and slowly, very slowly, turned her.

She felt as if she were moving through heat, toward some potent fire. She halted when she faced him fully. His gaze was on her toes.

It rose, slowly, unhurriedly; confident yet enthralled, he drank in every inch of her.

She was battling inward shudders when his eyes finally reached hers. Impulsively, she stepped closer—he stopped her, with his grip on her hand held her back.

"No. Not yet." He drew in a breath as ragged as hers. Clearly clinging to his control, he murmured, husky and low, "You have no idea how long I've waited to see you like this."

The tone of his voice, its cadence, fell into her mind, bearing a message much deeper, much more primitive and evocative than his words. She swayed, but through his grip on her hand he held her steady.

As he raised his other hand and, with the lightest of touches, brushed the backs of his fingers down the swell of her breast, then around and across the underside.

She shuddered and closed her eyes.

"Just like this." His words reached her in the same mesmerizing tone. "Waiting for me to take you. Wanting me to take you."

His fingers drifted, flame on her skin, tracing powerful patterns over it.

She heated with every touch, every evocative caress.

His fingers rose to her hair, searching, pulling free and discarding the pins restraining the heavy mass of gilded brown. Slowly, reverently, he drew the tresses out and laid them over her shoulders.

He moved near and she felt his breath on her cheek, sensed his willing enthrallment as he said, "You're a goddess and an offering, both at once. You're the woman I worship, and the woman I must have. The woman I will take, but in the taking . . . I, too, willingly yield."

Charlie didn't know where the words came from, only that they were true; he felt them resonate deep inside him. Deep, where only she—sweet innocent Sarah—had ever reached.

Those words encompassed the truth—the truth of him and her, and what had grown between them, the truth of them in the here and now, and in the ever after. Worshipping her was a passion he embraced willingly; he set his hands, his lips, his mouth, his body, to the task.

Set himself to hold her there, naked before him, while he worshipped each curve, each evocative line of her slender form. While he awakened her to more intimate delights, to the pleasure of being touched without touching. From their earlier interludes, he'd learned those spots that most inflamed her desire—the sensitive underside of her breasts, the even more arousing lower curve of her bottom. Slowly, steadily, he applied the knowledge, arousing her to a passion to rival his own.

He took his time, ruthless in his need to worship her, to draw out every last minute of that curious hunger; he only took her in his arms and drew her against him when she could no longer stand.

They came together, skin to skin, flesh to heated flesh. She gasped; he quelled a long shudder. She shifted against him, silken limbs caressing his harder, hair-dusted frame, her soft belly cradling his aching erection. He sank one hand into the mass of her bright hair, gripped and held her as he bent his head and kissed her, hard, ruthless, and demanding.

This time he was determined to remain in control throughout, not to weaken and cede to her at any point; given their past history, reducing her to mindless need seemed a wise idea.

There were levels of fire, degrees of sensual flame. Under his practiced caresses, growing harder, more urgent, increasingly driven, at the center of his unwavering attention she heated, slowly but surely under his guidance progressing from one level to the next, from one degree of heated yearning into ever deepening flames.

He went with her, but he was more accustomed to passion's heat, to its beat, to withstanding the compulsion that lay within it.

Until the sensual conflagration captured them, him as well as her. Until their embrace grew so hot it cindered all thought and left no other awareness but of him and her, and the need to come together.

Desire flared ever hotter; passion roared through the flames.

He stooped, swung her into his arms and carried her to the bed. Laying her on satin sheets the color of her eyes, laying her hair, a bright veil, over the pillows, seeing her writhe and reach for him, heated, wanton, almost desperate in her need, he paused for one second to savor the sight of her, naked, aroused, and all his, and sensed, as he moved to join her, a spark of something like triumph, obscured by the storm of desire raging through him.

That moment of lucidity was enough to let him grasp the reins again, as he stretched beside her on the bed to consider how much further he could push her into mindless wanting, how much higher on passion's peak he could drive her before he let her dive off the edge.

The higher, the more pleasure, for her and for him.

He caught the hand that reached for him, leaned over her, deliberately letting his chest abrade the tight peaks of her breasts as he kissed her deeply, unrestrainedly, letting her taste how wild for her he was, filling his own senses with the evocative taste of her.

Sweet innocence and passion.

The combination was an unbelievably heady mix, but now his mind had fixed on his plan, the execution required no further thought.

Only action.

He held her down in the cushioning billows of the bed, kissed her, fondled and provocatively caressed until she arched, with her body begged; breaking from the kiss, he trailed hot, wet, openmouthed kisses down the taut line of her throat, over the creamy upper swell of her breast, and gave her the first course of what she'd asked for.

He feasted on her breasts without quarter, licked, suckled, and laved as she writhed and gasped beneath him, as her hands gripped and tightened on his skull as he drew every last gasp and moan he could from her, then moved on.

Over her midriff, down over her waist, pausing to pay homage to the sensitive indentation of her navel, then he shifted still lower.

Trapping one of her long legs beneath him, lifting and draping the other over his shoulder, he held it there, held her steady as he pressed an ardent kiss to the curls shielding her mons.

He heard her breath hitch, felt her body tremble, then tense and coil. Glancing at her face, he caught a glimpse of intense cornflower blue burning beneath her heavy lids, saw her lips, slick and swollen from his kisses, parted in shocked disbelief. Deliberately he slid lower, bent and set his lips to the slick, swollen flesh between her thighs.

She jerked, moaned. He licked and she screamed. She reached for him, but could only touch his head. Her fingers twined in his hair, tightened; she tensed to tug, but he licked again, then slowly, expertly probed, and she didn't move.

Panting, eyes shut, she waited.

Inwardly smug, he settled to worship her in that way, too, to taste her, to fill his senses with her, and hers with him.

She let him have his way, let him taste her as he wished, let him try her with his tongue and drive her mindless.

He asked, and she surrendered; he took, and she gave. In return, he pleasured her with unwavering devotion until she sobbed and cried his name.

Rising, he rolled her fully onto her back, trailed kisses like fire up her belly and breasts as he loomed over her, spreading her thighs wide, settling between. He held himself over her, arms braced as he kissed her, tasted her desperation on her lips. Then with one single, powerful thrust he joined them.

She closed about him like a glove, and he gasped; like the goddess he'd named her she welcomed her servant into her temple and embraced him.

He moved, and she moved with him, fluidly meeting him as they gave themselves up to the now familiar dance. His thoughts fractured, ripped from him as a whirlpool of sensation rose up, drenched, then drowned him.

And there was no longer any such concept as control, no restraint whatever in the world they'd finally reached. There was only him, and her, and the power raging through them, seeking its long-denied release.

Through the tempest of their passions, through the wild turbulent ride, Sarah was conscious only of sensation. It buffeted her, overwhelmed her mind, etched itself on her awareness. So that despite the heat and the delirious pleasure of his body moving over hers, despite the powerful thrusts that physically rocked her, despite the impossible clamoring urgency that had her tilting her hips to take him yet more deeply, that had her scoring his back urging him desperately to ride her yet more forcefully, the one element that shone through the raging veil was his hunger for her. It was every bit as deep and powerful and demanding as her hunger for him.

No—more.

For him, in him, that hunger was so potent, so deeply ingrained that she had no doubt he would give every last gasp to sate it—to consummate it, to give it life, here with her in their bed. It drove him, and controlled him, and drew her into the maelstrom, too, until she was as passionate as he in finding the way to appease it, to sate it, to discover the way into its temple and sacrifice herself at its altar.

And at the last, in the final mind-shattering moment when she clung by her fingernails over the sensual void, the veils ripped apart and she saw that hungry power clearly—saw, felt, with her own senses knew what it was.

Unquestionably, beyond doubt.

Then he thrust one last time and with a cry she shattered; with a sob she lost her grip on reality and fell. Weightless for that moment, that briefest of journeys, falling from heavenly pleasure into satiation's soothing sea.

Bliss closed around her, suffused her, buoyed her, softening her limbs, eradicating every last iota of tension. Then the glow brightened, flared as with a guttural groan he stiffened in her arms.

From beneath her lids, she looked up, in that telltale moment saw his face stripped of all sophistication, of all veils and screens. In the instant when he lost himself in her, when he shuddered and completion racked him, there was only one emotion etched on his face.

One she felt in her heart, recognized in her bones.

He slumped across her, as boneless as she; she let her lids fall, felt her lips curve. Remembered his words. All she saw here, in this room, in her domain, was hers.

Hers to rule in the physical dimension perhaps, but hers to be ruled by in that other dimension, in that other world given reality by their love.

Hers, and his. She'd felt hers, felt, sensed, and seen his.

No more doubts.

He lifted from her, slumped heavily beside her, and drew her into his arms. She went gladly, pleasured and joyful beyond her wildest dreams.

Here, with him, was her life, her future, the right path for her. With him, she would find the satisfaction she sought. Together with him, all would be well.

She'd made the right decision.

Her mind was drifting, her brain hazed with pleasure. Secure in his arms, her cheek on his chest, she whispered, "I love you."

Even though her mind was sliding through sleep's veil, she heard the faint surprise in her tone, and smiled. "And I know you love me, too."

Sleep enfolded her in rapturous arms, and she sank into bliss-filled dreams.

Sprawled on his back, her gentle, almost ethereal whispers sighing through his head, Charlie lay sunk beneath her soft weight, his arms loosely around her, his body too sated even to tense.

He stared up at the canopy, blue silk the color of her eyes.

And wondered how his wonderful plan had gone so terribly wrong.

. . .

He roused her as dawn was sliding across the sky. As rosy glory streaked the horizon, he dipped his fingers into her swollen softness and lured her from sleep with slow caresses, until, flushed like the morning, she sighed, and he slid into her body and she smiled.

He rode her slowly, totally controlled, rigidly watchful, desperate to convince himself that the addiction, and his raging hunger, had muted. That the power that drove him, that fueled his mindless need—that regardless of his guard inexorably rose within him, whipped through him, wrested control from him and wrenched him from this world—had abated.

It hadn't. Not in the least.

If anything, that power had only grown.

He held her until she slid back into sleep, then turned onto his back and, staring upward unseeing, faced the cold hard facts as a cold hard dawn broke over his lands.

Alathea had been right; until him, love had invariably captured every Morwellan male. It had caught his sire, and driven him, obsessed him, had compelled him in its name to take risks that had nearly destroyed their family, the earldom, and everything he'd held dear.

With that example engraved on his mind, he'd chosen a different path. By arranging a conventional marriage, he'd sought to shut out love, and thus remain in absolute control of his life, safe from that dangerous emotion.

Instead . . . fate had set her snare, and he'd walked unheeding—arrogantly—into it, and tripped the trap himself.

He'd married Sarah—sweet innocent Sarah—and now he faced the one prospect he'd fought, and thought he'd arranged never ever to meet.

He was in love with his wife.

There was no point pretending he wasn't, not any longer, not with the clutch of that power still so tangible in his chest, not with its claws sunk in his heart. There was no value whatever in denying its existence, not to himself.

He should have seen . . . but he hadn't. Perhaps he should have guessed what it was that had made her different—to him so different from all other women on virtually every level—but he'd had no experience from which to judge; the notion that the reason she was so unarguably his was because he loved her hadn't even crossed his mind.

So now he loved. He'd fallen victim to that ungovernable emotion, and now and forever would be subject to that irresistible force, that power that could so easily fuel obsession.

That same power that, in his father, had led to the brink of ruination.

Instead of being the bulwark he'd intended, the salvation he'd sought, his marriage had transformed into his worst nightmare.

How on earth was he to manage? What could he do?

12

The closing of a door, followed by the hesitant patter of feet across the floor, woke Sarah. She blinked, and looked around, and remembered where she was. She struggled up onto her elbow; the bed beside her was rumpled, but empty.

Sunlight streamed in through the windows, bright and sharp, but Charlie was nowhere to be seen.

Gwen, who had come with her from the manor, carefully set a steaming pitcher on the dresser; reaching for a door in the paneling, she glanced at the bed. Seeing Sarah awake, she grinned. "Thought I'd best come and wake you, miss—m'lady, I mean. I've brought your washing water." She opened the door, and nodded. "Your dressing room's through here—have you seen it?"

"Ah, no." Sarah pushed back her hair. She hadn't seen anything beyond the bed since Charlie had laid her upon it. She went to throw back the bedclothes, then realized she was naked. She blushed.

So did Gwen. "I'll just pop this pitcher on the washstand in here and bring you your robe."

Sarah peered over the side of the bed, and saw her beautiful wedding gown lying where it had fallen. Remembering the look in Charlie's eyes as he'd peeled it from her, she grinned. Then Gwen brought her robe and she shrugged into it. Leaving Gwen to deal with her discarded clothes, she went into the dressing room, discovering that it matched the bedroom, decorated in blues and glowing golden oak.

She quickly washed. "What time is it, Gwen? What's happening about breakfast?" To her surprise, she felt ravenous.

"It's just gone eleven," Gwen called from the bedchamber. "Breakfast was held back—they're just gathering in the breakfast parlor now."

"Oh. Good." Sarah grimaced at her reflection in the mirror. Her first morning as lady of the house, and she'd be the last down to breakfast. More, she'd have to face various sets of curious eyes, and have to conduct herself as if it were just another day—all while Charlie was in the same room.

It was a prospect to tie her stomach in knots, but when she consulted that organ she discovered she was still too relaxed, too inwardly languid in the wake of Charlie's so-expert attentions, that she really couldn't summon the tension to manage knots at all.

Pondering that unexpected ramification of her wifely duties, she left the earl's apartments and followed the corridor to the gallery, and thence to the stairs; descending, she gained the front hall and the areas of the house with which she was familiar.

The breakfast parlor was a sunny room off the conservatory. A rectangular table sat in the room's center with places laid along its length; a heavy sideboard stood against one wall, all but groaning beneath a profusion of serving dishes and warming pans. Both table and sideboard sported vases brimming with white blooms from the day before, an appealing touch.

The instant she appeared in the open doorway, chairs scraped as all those seated rose to greet her. She hesitated, smiling but unsure just what to do; Serena, whom she'd known all her life and who was now her mother-in-law, came bustling forward, a smile wreathing her face.

"There you are, dear." Serena embraced her warmly, lightly touching cheeks, then ushered her to the chair at the end of the table. "This is now your place. Of course you know everyone here." With a wave she indicated her children and their spouses. Nudging Sarah into her chair,

Serena subsided into the one beside her. "We're all absolutely delighted to see you in that seat."

"Thank you." Sarah settled into the high-backed, ornately carved chair.

Her gaze traveling around the table, she nodded a smiling good morning to Mary and Alice, Charlie's sisters, and their husbands, Alec and George, and Augusta and Jeremy, all transparently pleased both with her presence and how yesterday had gone.

Alice leaned forward; with a swift grin, she continued to relate a tale gleaned from a guest that Sarah's arrival had interrupted. The others' attention deflected to Alice—all except Charlie's. He sat opposite Sarah at the head of the table, coffee cup in one hand, a news sheet in the other, but his eyes weren't tracking the print; they were on her.

She met his gaze and smiled—just for him. Relieved, happy, and content, she used the gesture to convey how she felt.

His expression remained impassive; at this distance, with the windows behind him and the sun shining outside, she couldn't read his eyes. But then he inclined his head to her, lifted his cup, sipped, and returned to his perusal of the news sheet.

Sarah inwardly frowned. She studied him, puzzled that he wasn't smiling—although perhaps that was due to the others' being about—yet he wasn't relaxed; he wasn't anywhere near as relaxed as she was.

"Tea, ma'am?"

A second passed before Sarah realized the sonorous question was addressed to her. She glanced up at Crisp, hovering by her elbow. "Oh—yes! Thank you, Crisp. Tea and . . ." She glanced at the sideboard.

Crisp shifted and stood ready to draw back her chair. "If I could suggest, ma'am, the deviled eggs are excellent. Cook's specialty."

Sarah threw him a smile as she rose. "I must try some, then."

For the next fifteeen minutes as she ate and sipped, then refilled her plate and ate some more, the familiar warmth of a large and happy family closed around her.

"The other guests left last night or early this morning." Serena turned to her, her words sliding beneath the general conversation. "Indeed, if it wasn't for wanting to catch up with Mary and Alice and their broods, all of us would be gone, too. Every young couple needs a few weeks alone in which to settle into life together."

Sarah's eyes widened; she hadn't thought . . . "You don't need to leave—this is your home, and I wouldn't dream of trying to supplant you."

Hazel eyes brimming with understanding, Serena patted her wrist. "But *you* are now mistress here, my dear, and believe me when I say that I'm beyond content to consign the care of this house and household into more youthful hands. We'll stay long enough for me to explain all you need to know, then we'll be off to Lincoln with Mary and Alec, and from there Augusta and I plan to visit various family members I haven't had time to call on in years, before joining you and Charlie in London once the Season gets under way."

Serena studied her, then reached out and tucked a stray strand of hair behind her ear. And smiled somewhat mistily. "Believe me, my dear, everything is set to work out just splendidly."

Sarah wasn't entirely sure what that "everything" encompassed, but true to her declaration, Serena embarked on a description of various matters of household management.

At the other end of the table, Charlie, outwardly involved in a discussion of corn prices with Alec and George, watched Sarah, without fuss, bother, or further fanfare, begin to assume the mantle of his countess. He'd presumed she would find it easy, given she already knew them all, but it wasn't only familiarity that eased her way—that made Crisp hover so, or allowed Serena and Augusta to so swiftly explain what she needed to know.

She fitted. She was, as he'd foreseen, the perfect lady to fill the position.

That he'd been so right, so clear-sighted in that, only served to deepen his disquiet over all he hadn't, in his arrogance, understood.

The sounds that rose around him, his sisters' voices, the deeper rumblings of his brothers-in-law, the comfortable, usually undisturbing cacophony of his family at breakfast, for once did nothing to soothe his soul.

Quite the opposite.

Then Alec started describing the antics of his and Mary's son, just old enough to sit his first pony, and the goad became too sharp to bear.

His expression uninformative, Charlie pushed back from the table. "If you'll excuse me, I must see to some business." He stood.

Alec and George looked up, smiled vaguely, then continued chatting. He stepped away from the table; Jeremy glanced at him, then returned to teasing Alice.

As he strode down the room, all the ladies broke off their discussions and looked at him expectantly.

He inclined his head to his mother, then to Sarah. "I'll see you later."

She smiled, transparently content, but her eyes swiftly searched his face.

His stride unhurried, he passed her chair and continued to the doorway, certain that she would read nothing of his thoughts no matter how sharp her gaze. There were times when the facial control necessary to conduct business at the highest level was an unlooked-for boon.

He just hadn't imagined deploying that shield against his wife.

Night had fallen. Wrapped in a silk negligee, another part of her trousseau, Sarah paced before the fire in the earl's bedchamber and wondered where her earl was.

The velvet curtains were drawn against the dark; outside rain fell steadily while the wind rattled the bare branches of the nearby trees. Candles stood on the mantelpiece and on the small tables flanking the bed, their steady glow contributing to the cosy warmth that enveloped the chamber.

She'd had a busy, information-packed day. From the breakfast table on, every one of her minutes had gone in learning the myriad details of how to run Morwellan Park, and of the numerous other tasks that would fall to her now she was Charlie's countess.

Not one of those details or tasks had been unexpected, yet she'd concentrated; if Serena and Augusta were shortly to leave and not be present to consult for several weeks, then she needed to ask all the relevant questions now rather than later be caught unawares.

Her absorption had distracted her from Charlie's ... distance. The distance he seemed intent on preserving between them, somewhat formal and stiff. His behavior in the breakfast room had been only the beginning; he'd been the same at the luncheon table, and his stance had been even more pronounced over dinner and during the short time he'd spent in the drawing room afterward, before he, Alec, George, and Jeremy had taken themselves off to play billiards.

Admittedly, throughout, she'd been surrounded by his mother and sisters, all talking more or less constantly, imparting facts and advice, all of which she'd needed to hear. Yet . . .

She grimaced. Perhaps his unexpected, rather formal reserve was simply a reaction to having his family there, watching his and her every move. Despite his outwardly easygoing nature, he was a private man, and his family were unquestionably the most aware of observers, the ones most able to read him and his reactions easily.

Perhaps he was simply uncertain how to publicly acknowledge the connection that was growing between them, or was, as yet, given its recent genesis, uneasy about doing so.

Indeed, she wasn't yet sure herself how to relate to him when others were about; it was hardly any wonder if he felt the same. The same sense of feeling their way.

Halting before the fireplace, arms crossed beneath her breasts, she stared into the flames. Then the handsome clock on the mantelpiece chimed the hour; she looked at it and frowned. Eleven o'clock. Where was he?

As if in answer, she heard a footstep on the anteroom's tiles—a familiar stride. Lowering her arms, she lifted her head, swinging to face the door as it opened and Charlie entered.

He saw her, hesitated for an instant, then closed the door. And came toward her.

She studied his face, searched his eyes as he neared . . . and sensed a hesitation, an uncertainty, one that echoed in her heart.

She also saw, more clearly, more definitely, the falling of the curious barrier that had seemed to stand between them through the day. Saw intent return to his eyes, replacing his impassivity, saw desire rise and edge his features.

By the time he halted before her, the firelight playing over him, glinting gold in the waves of his hair, there was no doubt in her mind that at least between them here, nothing had changed, that all was as she'd thought.

His gaze lingered on her face; he searched as she had, then his gaze lowered to her shoulders, all but bare beneath the diaphanous silk, slowly fell further to her breasts, then to the indentation of her waist, to her hips, her thighs, clothed tantalizingly in ivory silk and lace . . . his lids fell.

He drew breath and raised his head. Eyes closed, jaw tight, he mumured, "You are so desirable it hurts to look at you."

The words grated, as if they'd been dragged from him. She smiled. "Then keep your eyes closed."

She moved nearer on the words, her voice sultry again as she responded to him, his transparent desire awakening hers. "Keep your eyes closed and let me guide you."

Ease you. Her hands on his chest, she stretched up, and kissed him. For a moment, he let her, then he responded, his head angling over hers, his arms rising to close around her. To hold her against him as he supped from her mouth, as he tasted her, and let her taste him. She inwardly sighed and sank against him; reaching up with one hand, she cupped his nape, then slid her fingers into the softness of his hair and gripped, urging him on. For long minutes, she savored their play, the confident, assured give-and-take, then she drew back, broke the kiss.

"Keep your eyes closed." She whispered the words against his lips; as she drew back, she saw them quirk. Smiling, she set about divesting him of his clothes.

Although he obediently left his lids down, his long lashes casting crescent shadows over his high cheekbones, he didn't keep his hands still; as she wrestled him out of coat, waistcoat, and shirt, his hands roved over her silk-clad body, touching here, tantalizingly caressing there, making her nerves leap and tense, then tighten in anticipation. In reply, she gave her fascination full rein, running her hands over the acres of muscled chest she uncovered, glorying in the heavy muscles and bones of his shoulders, the taut ridged lines of his abdomen. Their interaction became a sensual game, one that heightened their senses, and left them both breathing rapidly, yet still very much in control.

Aware, and intent.

He reached for her again as her fingers found the buttons at his waist; she stretched up and once more covered his lips with hers. The kiss was hotter, desire escalating, the passion more intense; she felt the heat spread beneath her skin, felt the flames of need flare deep within her, yet for once in this arena, she had a definite aim.

She pulled back from the kiss. "Don't forget—eyes closed."

He shifted, lips thinning, fingers tensing on her back, but he acquiesced. He had to ease his hold on her and let her slide down, out of his arms as, trailing a few brief kisses down the center of his chest, she crouched before him, drew his trousers down, then turned her attention to his stockings and shoes. She dispensed with all swiftly—then grasped her chance.

She'd overheard Maria and Angela, her two older married sisters, whispering; she'd understood enough to leave her wondering. Now she had her own husband, she was curious as to whether he, too, might like . . .

There was only one way to find out. Bracing her hands on the taut muscles of his lower thighs, she went to her knees before him, then slid her hands up, following the heavy bands of muscle to where his erection stood proud, angling stiffly from its nest of curls, as if begging for her attention.

Even before her hands closed about his length, he guessed; he sucked in a breath. But then her fingers curled about his rigid flesh and he jerked. And couldn't seem to breathe. "Sarah?"

The word was weak, equal parts shock, astonishment, and question.

"No looking, remember." Leaning her forearms against his rock-hard thighs, she paused to study what she held for only a second, then she bent her head, parted her lips, and slid them slowly, lovingly, over and down the hot silk rod between her hands.

He groaned. His entire body locked, every muscle rigid as, recalling her sisters' words, she used her imagination to interpret them. Liberally.

His breath hissed in through his teeth. His hand found her head, his fingers tangled in her hair; for a moment she wondered if he would tug her away, but then his fingers firmed. Seconds later, she realized he was directing her, teaching her . . . what he liked.

A rush of giddy happiness rose through her, and she eagerly applied herself to learning, to discovering how best to pleasure him in this way. A brief glance upward revealed his head held high, features tight with fierce pleasure; no sight could have pleased her more.

Delighted, she devoted her full attention to her ministrations, to learning all she possibly could.

That last was implicit as the minutes stretched, and Charlie clung by his mental fingernails to some semblance of control. How? *Where?* A very large part of him didn't care. Had no interest whatever in how she'd known, but was avidly, greedily, hungrily absorbing every last iota of pleasure she was so unexpectedly and intently lavishing on him.

The wet heat of her mouth, the gentle, increasingly bold suction, the tantalizing flick and glide of her tongue, the soft caress of her hair against his thighs as her head moved so evocatively, so erotically, effortlessly commanded every wit he had. He was her sensual captive, wholly and completely ensnared in her web.

Yet even though his eyes were closed, his lungs tight and aching, even though every muscle he possessed was locked and straining, it wasn't solely physical reaction that held him at her mercy; the mental impact of her actions was infinitely more devasting. The implication of her going so willingly to her knees, taking him into her mouth, and so patently delighting in pandering to his senses, in learning of his darker desires and fulfilling them, resonated through him.

She and that power, the power she now wielded, or that wielded her, that functioned through her, was seducing him. And succeeding. She and it operated on so many levels, he was helpless to counter, to shield himself against her, and it. Against all that she and it together made him feel.

Passion and desire he'd weathered often before, but with her both were shockingly heightened, infused with that power and therefore more potent, infinitely more intense. More addictive.

And into the mix, arrogant possessiveness had swirled. He'd never felt the like, not with any of the countless women he'd bedded, but with her, his wife, possessiveness didn't just hover, it raged. And drove him.

Tonight . . . until he'd walked into their bedchamber, he hadn't known how he would behave, how their interaction would play out, to what level.

Some part of him had hoped, prayed, that tonight he would be able to suppress his reaction, to step back, to draw a line and hold to it, to continue the process he'd started that morning to get their relationship back on the track of a conventional marriage.

Throughout the day, he'd managed to hold aloof, but just the sight of her standing waiting for him before his fire, the flames flickering over her, lovingly revealing her figure beneath the translucent gown, had been enough to overwhelm his determination and shatter the guard he'd hoped to maintain.

As for this . . .

His chest hurt, tight, lungs seizing as her lips firmed and slid, as her fingers rose, sliding upward on his thigh. Sunk in the wet heat of her mouth, his erection was one massive, throbbing ache.

He dragged in a shuddering breath and forced his lids up. He looked down, at her on her knees, leaning into him, her glorious hair rippling over her shoulders, gilded in the firelight, shifting as her head moved and she pleasured him. He saw his fingers locked on her head, felt hers slide higher, circle the base of his staff, and tighten.

For one instant, he let his senses drink it all in, let that inner self he so rarely let loose glory in her and her devotion, then he gathered his will, fought and drew his strength to him.

Breathing was a battle; his head was swimming as he forced his hand from the golden silk of her hair, followed the curve of her jaw, then slipped his fingers beneath the gilded veil to grip her chin.

"Enough." The word was weak; she complied more with the pressure of his fingers than the command.

Releasing him, she sat back; hands resting on his thighs, she looked up the length of his body to meet his eyes.

Her expression, the glow in her eyes and her face, held him silent for a heartbeat; had any madonna ever looked so content? Then he reached for her; closing his hands about her upper arms, he drew her to her feet.

"You opened your eyes," she murmured.

He met her gaze for an instant, then holding her before him, bent his head. "My turn."

He kissed her. Not as before, not with any veil or screen, nothing to mute the raw hunger she evoked in him, the staggeringly powerful mix of passion, desire, and need—the need to possess her.

Completely and utterly.

To possess her body and soul, as she already possessed him.

That's what she and that power demanded.

So be it.

Sarah relished the passion raging through his kiss, inwardly gasped when he deepened the caress, ruthlessly commanding, his tongue probing, then retreating, only to return, echoing the possession she knew was to come.

Senses unfurling in the spiraling heat, she thrilled when his hands, curved about her shoulders, eased their grip—to reach for the edges of her silk and lace robe. He stripped it from her; it slid down her back to the floor. With two quick tugs he had the shoulder ties of her matching nightgown undone; it whispered down her body to pool about her feet.

As his hands slid about her waist, gripped, and he drew her forcefully against his naked length. Hot, hard, so male, the promise in his body affected hers like flame, melting, softening, heating anew. Sending fire down her veins to pool low in her belly, feeding her hunger, making the odd empty ache within her burgeon and grow.

He held her trapped in the kiss, yet she wanted to reach for him, to use her palm to caress that part of him she longed to feel inside her, filling her, stretching her, feeding that empty ache, satisfying the desire that beat heavily in her veins. But when he'd pulled her into his arms, she'd gripped his shoulders; as his arms tightened, then his hands slid down her back, molding her to him, she couldn't find the strength or will to push him back enough to reach between them.

Then he angled her and did, his fingers finding the curls covering her mons, and playing. Deliberately, evocatively. His touch was more intense, more openly driven; as he pressed further and found the soft flesh between her thighs already swollen and wet, his caresses grew ever more demanding, more intimate, more invested with a possessiveness that thrilled her.

His lips on hers, holding her wits captive, with one kneee he nudged her thighs apart, and slid first one, then two long fingers into her sheath. She felt the heat from the fire playing over her skin as his hand worked between her thighs, feeding the conflagration within.

Her body was no longer hers but his to command, her senses wholly caught, trapped in the moment. In the escalating desire, in the tension that rose through the fire and gripped her.

Then he buried his fingers inside her and she shattered. She gasped through the kiss, but he pressed her on; instead of falling weightless through the familiar void, she found herself riding a crest of incendiary passion. It swept her high, then he withdrew his fingers, gripped her waist, and lifted her up against him.

She broke from the kiss; from under heavy lids, breasts heaving, her hands gripping his shoulders, she looked down at his face, tipped up to hers.

His expression was graven, a mask of urgent desire. "Wrap your legs around me."

She could barely make out the gravelly command; it took an instant to register that his palms had slid beneath her bottom, supporting her weight, then to make her muscles obey her enough to obey him.

Immediately her thighs clamped about him, he lowered her hips, and she realized—felt the broad head of his erection nudge against her entrance, then he pressed in, and drew her down.

As he thrust upward.

Head falling back, she gasped as he impaled her, as the sensation of him riding hard and high into her body engulfed her senses, and dragged them down.

Into a whirlpool of seething desire, of passion so hot it scorched, of a need so fiery it melted her bones. He lifted her, and brought her down again, thrusting upward as he did, and every nerve she possessed shook, shuddered.

With a need he understood; legs braced, he held her in his arms before the fireplace, the heat from the flames dancing over her flushed skin as he gripped her bottom and held her to him, held her body against him and filled her again and again.

She wrapped her arms about his neck and clung, senses stretched almost beyond bearing, sensual delight buffeting her mind, then she lowered her head, he lifted his, and their lips met.

And hunger raged.

Not hers, not his, but theirs. A force stronger than either of them, able to compel both of them. Powerful enough to fling them both into a state of mindless, dizzying, clawing need—into intimacy unrelenting, to where there was no him or her but only their single, desperate quest.

Until they touched the glory. Until it rose in a burning wave and battered them, shattered them, caught them and cindered them.

Destroyed them.

Unmade them.

Then re-fused them and completed them.

When the storm retreated and they returned to the world, they found themselves slumped, limbs tangled, on the rug before the dying fire.

Sarah drew breath, with one hand traced his face, close, lit by the glowing embers as he gazed down at her, and marveled anew at what she saw there. Passion, desire, and need had faded, leaving behind,

stark and unmistakable, the one emotion that drove those lesser emotions, that gave them such intense life.

Mistily, she smiled up at him; there was no need for words.

He searched her eyes, then bent his head and kissed her gently, the
simplest of benedictions.

Then he drew back, lifted her in his arms, rose and carried her to
their bed.

W arm, sated to his toes, Charlie lay beside Sarah, listening to her
steady breathing, and to the wind gusting restlessly beyond the
windows.

The two sounds echoed his thoughts of her and him; she'd accepted what had flared, grown, and burgeoned between them without
a qualm, while he . . . couldn't.

The glow of aftermath that had claimed him, that still held him despite his restless thoughts, had never been this intense, this deeply satisfying. He couldn't pretend otherwise, couldn't deny the fierce triumph
he'd felt when she'd finally shattered in his arms, when his last vestige
of control had vaporized and he'd plundered her willingly surrendered
body to gain his own release—any more than he could deny the deeply
rooted pleasure of sharing those indefinable, ephemeral moments afterward with her.

She was different, and always would be, and no matter how he
might wish otherwise, he wasn't going to walk away from all she represented. All she gave him.

In some fundamental way—a primitive, primal, possessive way
he'd never imagined would apply to him—she was his rightful mate.
His. Claimed, willingly surrendered, she who would be the mother of
his heirs.

Where this aggressive, possessive, even more arrogant than usual
part of him had sprung from he didn't know. All he knew was that it
was integral, an inescapable part of him, that she called it forth, that
only she could sate it—and that was that. All unhelpful, potentially
obsessive powers aside, that was the situation he now faced.

When he was here, alone with her in this room, there was nothing
he could do—could even imagine doing—to avoid or hide that truth,
the truth of what he felt for her, how he felt about her. When he was

here, alone with her, the need to possess her was simply too powerful, the ache to pleasure her an unexpected spur. Taking her was no longer a simple focus, if it ever had been; the impulse to give, not just to sensually delight her but to teach her, and even more strongly to protect her, to care for her in each and every way, was irresistible. Compelling.

He saw it as a duty.

But . . . his duty, when all was said and done, did not lie solely with her. Indeed, their marriage had come about because he'd bowed to a greater duty. And that greater duty still remained, commanding his loyalty, his observance and devotion. His care.

He was the defender and protector of his title, his land, his people, his the duty to watch over all, to ensure both the safety and the future of the earldom. That was an ineradicable part of who he was, his birthright, and through that his inalienable duty, one he couldn't, and didn't wish to, walk away from, or even to jeopardize, not even for her.

Certainly not for him, in order to pursue his own pleasure.

Two duties, both commanding. Not precisely contradictory—for any other man observing both would pose no difficulty—but for him there existed one serious, potential, even likely problem. Yet he was going to have to accommodate both—the power that flared between Sarah and him, and his obligation to remain in control of all decisions, and not let love control him. Not let love become an obsession with the capacity to rule him.

Eyes narrowing, he stared across the room into the deepening shadows, and considered the past day, and the night that had followed.

When all was said and done, he never made professional decisions in bed.

He turned his new plan over in his mind, studied it, wondered.

It might be difficult, but it wasn't impossible.

It was what he would have to do.

S arah began the second day of her marriage more settled, more confident, than the day before. While Charlie maintained his aloofness over the breakfast table, and later the luncheon table, after the revelations of the night she no longer harbored any doubt over the nature of their marriage.

His family were still present, very much in evidence throughout the day; it seemed plain that their presence gave him pause. It seemed equally clear that he would take some time to ease into the way of things, to become accustomed to her and to learn how to react to her. Although he had the examples of his sisters' marriages, and even more that of Alathea and Gabriel, let alone Serena and his father before that, he was, after all, indisputably male; he had doubtless not thought to pay any real attention to how those gentlemen interacted with their wives.

But he was sharply intelligent; he would learn soon enough. And time was one thing they had an abundance of—the rest of their lives, in fact.

So she went about her day with a smile wreathing her face, with no worries clouding her mind, but with anticipation buoying it.

After lunch, Charlie, Alec, and Jeremy went riding. Leaving Serena and her daughters catching up in the parlor that Serena had, years ago, made her own domain, Sarah went to unpack her things in the room she'd chosen as her sitting room.

Every countess, it seemed, was expected to have a private sitting room. That morning, Serena had shown her around the reception rooms of the huge house, many of which weren't in regular use.

"This house is so large," Serena had said, "there's no reason for you to feel constrained to use the room I chose when I first came here."

When they'd reached the morning room on the ground floor at the end of the west wing, the room below the earl's bedchamber, Serena had explained, "This was traditionally the countess's sitting room. It was Charlie's father's first wife's sitting room. Even though she'd passed on years before I married Charlie's father, I didn't feel I could use this room. Alathea was still young, and I didn't want her to feel I was supplanting her mother, or worse, trying to eradicate her memory."

Sarah had wandered into the room, noting the long windows, and the pair of French doors opening onto the terrace overlooking the south lawn. The light was wonderful. It was a good-sized room, as were all the rooms in this wing, and was decorated as befitted a countess's sitting room in damasks and brocades, all golds, browns, and greens on an ivory base. She'd swung back to Serena. "Do you think Alathea would have any difficulty over my using this room?"

Serena beamed. "Oh, no—quite the opposite. I think she'd feel it only right that you should claim this room as yours."

And so it had been decided. Sarah had informed Figgs, the redoubtable housekeeper, of her decision. Figgs had instantly ordered a bevy of maids in to mop and dust. "It'll be ready an hour after lunch, my lady. I'll have Crisp get the footmen to bring your boxes in, then you can settle."

So this afternoon, with the sun streaming in through the long windows, she was settling, quiet and alone and more content than she felt she had any right to be.

As well as comfortable chaises and armchairs, the room was well supplied with bookcases, small tables, and an escritoire with a matching chair set against one wall. With the smell of beeswax hanging in the air, she'd left the double doors to the corridor open, and propped the French doors wide.

Finally finishing unpacking the three boxes of her books and setting the tomes neatly on the shelves, she stood, one last slim volume in her hand. Studying it, she turned; in the beam of sunlight slanting in through the doors she examined the silver plates that served as front and back covers. A heavy spiral of steel formed the spine. Smiling fondly, with one fingertip she traced the engravings covering the silver plates, then stroked the large oval cabochon amethyst set into the front cover.

A shadow blocked off the sunlight.

She looked up, her heart leaping; for one instant, she thought it was Charlie framed in the doorway, silhouetted by the winter sun, but then she saw the differences. The paler hair, the heavier chest, the different features.

Her initial, instinctive smile of delight had faded; she replaced it with one of suitable welcome. "Mr. Sinclair. How delightful of you to call."

With the sun behind him, his face in shadow, she couldn't be sure, but he seemed to have frozen—perhaps as surprised to come across her as she was to see him.

Her words, however, recalled him. He visibly relaxed, and smiled his easy smile. "Lady Meredith."

He stepped into the room and she offered him her hand. He bowed over it, then released her. "I was looking for his lordship." He held up a sheaf of what looked like news sheets. "I told him I'd drop these by. Investment news about the railways."

"Ah—I see." Sarah had no idea Charlie was interested in railways, but he was involved with investing. "He rode out some time ago. He should return soon."

"Actually," Sinclair replied with a brief smile, "that's why I came this way—the stable boy said he'd returned, and I saw the windows . . . I understood this was the library wing."

"It is. The library's a few doors down."

"Ah." Sinclair glanced down at the silver-backed diary she still held; again he seemed to go strangely still. Then his pale lashes flickered. "That's an unusual-looking book. Are there many like it about?"

"This?" She raised it, displaying the front cover with its amethyst. "I imagine it's one of a kind. It's a keepsake. My late aunt, my mother's oldest sister, had a large set of such diaries made up, each one with a different-colored stone. When she died, all her nieces were given one to remember her by."

She glanced at the book fondly, flicking through a few pages. "I have to admit I haven't read it yet, but Aunt Edith was a great one for recipes and useful hints—as I'm now in charge of my own household, I daresay I might find something useful."

"I daresay."

She inwardly frowned at Sinclair's tone, which was flat and oddly strained. But then footsteps sounded in the corridor. She and Sinclair turned as Charlie appeared in the doorway.

"There you are, my lord." She smiled, but Charlie's gaze had fixed on her unexpected visitor. That gaze was strangely hard . . . challenging? She hurried to add, "Mr. Sinclair's brought you some papers."

Sinclair smiled; he moved to join Charlie, assurance in every line of his large frame. He brandished his sheets. "Those investment reports I mentioned."

Charlie's odd tension eased. "Ah—thank you." He smiled. "Come into the library and you can guide me through them." He looked past Sinclair to her. "If you'll excuse us, my dear?"

A rhetorical question. She plastered on a sweet smile and bobbed a curtsy in acknowledgment of Sinclair's bow and Charlie's brief nod. They left and she turned away. Crossing to the escritoire, she opened it, and slipped the diary into the rack within.

Closing the lid, she stared at the escritoire, and inwardly humphed.

Swinging around, she surveyed the room—the subtle elegance, the understated richness—now overlaid with an element of herself.

It was a lovely room, and now it was hers.

Damn Sinclair—that was not how she'd wanted Charlie's first sight of her new sitting room to go.

Still . . . she could enthuse to him tonight, when they were alone. And perhaps she could think of some novel way in which to convey her appreciation.

Imagining it, she smiled, and walked over to shut the French doors.

Charlie's family—Serena, Augusta, Jeremy, and his sisters and their husbands—departed the next day. Everyone gathered in the forecourt midmorning to see them off.

With laughs and smiles, the ladies calling admonitions to one another and their husbands, and to the footmen and maids rushing back and forth with boxes and bags, the party piled into the three traveling carriages waiting, horses stamping.

Standing on the front porch ready to wave them away, Sarah was sorry to see them go, but also grateful; Serena had been right. All newly married couples did, it seemed, require a few weeks alone to settle into married life.

The last to quit the house was Serena. She wrapped Sarah in a warm, scented embrace and whispered, "Be patient, my dear, and all will be well."

Returning the embrace, then drawing back, Sarah met her mother-in-law's wise eyes and smiled, happy and confident. "I will." Regardless of whether Serena had been alluding to Charlie, the household, or both, Sarah was quite certain all would indeed be well.

Serena turned to Charlie; she gave him her hand and allowed him to lead her down the steps to her carriage.

She halted a yard away and looked up at him.

Charlie faced her. And saw, as he'd expected, a slight frown in her eyes. She studied him for a moment, then raised a gloved hand to lay it alongside his cheek. "She's everything you deserve—take care of her." Her expression remained gentle but serious, then her lips quirked. "And take care of yourself, too."

He smiled easily back. "Take care of yourself" had been Serena's parting words to him since he'd been in short coats.

Patting his cheek lightly, she lowered her hand and turned to the open carriage door. He helped her up the steps, then stood back as the footman shut the door.

With a salute to Serena and Augusta, and a nod to Jeremy, who'd elected to start the journey beside the coachman, Charlie returned to the porch to stand beside Sarah and wave the three carriages off. As the last rumbled away down the drive, he realized he was aware of her softness and warmth beside him. His necessary role high in his mind, he stepped back.

She turned to him, happiness shining in her eyes. "I thought, seeing as you haven't yet gone riding this morning, that perhaps we could ride together? I haven't had Blacktail out in days."

Charlie looked at her, and literally felt a good half of him leap to accept her offer, to seize the chance to relax with her, and laugh and ride and celebrate simply being together and alone, but . . .

He fought and succeeded in keeping his expression impassive. "I'm sorry—I have various business matters awaiting my attention." He turned to the house, then remembered Serena's words and looked back. "If you do go out, take a groom."

With a vague nod in Sarah's direction, without meeting her eyes, he continued into the house and headed for the library.

Sarah stood on the porch and watched him go, a frown replacing the happiness leaching from her eyes.

13

She told herself it wasn't a rebuff, that he was indeed involved with all manner of business dealings. When instead of joining her for lunch in the family dining room he elected to have a plate of cold meats in the library, she reminded herself that such behavior was perfectly normal between husbands and wives in their circle.

Husbands and wives did not live in each other's pockets. Nevertheless, she'd expected . . .

Inwardly frowning even more, she left the luncheon table. Feeling somewhat deflated, she retreated to her sitting room and spent the afternoon making a start on the long list of thank-you notes it fell to her to pen.

Charlie apparently made a habit of going riding around the estate immediately after breakfast. As he was also developing a habit of leaving her slumped, deliciously exhausted, in their bed in the morning, by the time she stirred and emerged for the day, he'd already broken his fast and was gone.

The next day she possessed her soul in patience, and was rewarded when, returning from his ride, he joined her at the luncheon table. He was happy to volunteer where he'd been, what he'd seen, to discuss the estate matters he'd been dealing with.

All well and good, as it should be.

She listened, learned, and responded encouragingly.

The previous evening, their first alone, had been spent companionably over the dinner table, with a short stint in the drawing room afterward. The night that had followed, once they were alone together in their bedchamber, had only confirmed, yet again, that there was patently, demonstrably, nothing whatever amiss between him and her. That he and she were as one in what they felt for each other.

Reassured, she waited until they'd risen from the luncheon table and were strolling into the corridor to suggest, "Perhaps this afternoon we could go for a drive?" It was Saturday; surely he could spare a few hours away from his investments.

Halting, she swung to face him, letting eagerness light her eyes.

His impassive mask was back in place. He met her eyes for the briefest of moments before, looking ahead, he shook his head. "I'm afraid I can't. There are some matters I must attend to." He hesitated for a second, then inclined his head. "If you'll excuse me?"

He didn't wait for any acknowledgment but strode away—heading for the library.

She stood and watched him go, eyes narrowing on his back, her lips slowly firming into a thin line.

She was starting to resent the very existence of his library.

By late afternoon her spurt of unaccustomed temper had cooled. A few rational hours spent in the calming ambiance of her new sitting room had suggested that perhaps this awkward attitudinal difficulty that seemed to exist between them during daylight hours was simply the outcome of his having different expectations—conventional expectations—over how they would spend their days.

Although she might wish it otherwise, in that light his behavior was understandable. If she wanted something different, then it was up to her to reshape his ideas.

Knowing his temperament, and his temper, she didn't expect that to be easy, but, given their continued closeness in the nights—she could almost see him relax, see the aloof barrier he held between them through the day fall away when he joined her in their bedchamber—she wasn't about to retreat from the task.

The following day was Sunday, which meant they went to church. It was odd to sit in the pew to the left of the aisle, rather than the one on the right, from which her mother, father, and Clary and Gloria smiled brightly at her.

Clary and Gloria especially; she hadn't seen them since the wedding and had little doubt of the thoughts humming in their minds as they pretended to listen to Mr. Duncliffe's sermon.

At the end of the service, Charlie took her hand and drew her to her feet; he ushered her up the aisle in the wake of Mr. Duncliffe, ahead of all the others in the church. It was now her place to be the first to take Mr. Duncliffe's hand.

He beamed at her. "My dear countess!" He squeezed her hand between both of his, then glanced at Charlie, by her shoulder. "What a glad day, my lord, that sees you here with your new bride."

"Indeed." Charlie offered his hand, rescuing her from Mr. Duncliffe's warm clasp.

"Your mother and sister?" Mr. Duncliffe inquired.

"They've gone to spend some time with Lady Mary in Lincoln."

"Excellent! Excellent!"

Before Mr. Duncliffe could embark on further queries, Charlie took Sarah's elbow, smiled, nodded, and guided her on.

She stifled a giggle as they walked slowly down the path. "He was so pleased to have married us, he would have kept us on the step for as long as he could just to enjoy the memory."

"Probably."

They paused on the lawn a little way on to allow her family to catch up with them. The next few minutes passed with Charlie and her father engrossed in county matters, while she satisfied her mother's maternal curiosity over how she was faring. The rest of the congregation streamed past, heads nodding, hats raised, smiles shy. She and her mother smiled in acknowledgment without breaking the stride of their conversation. Her older sisters, Maria and Angela, and their husbands had come only for the wedding and departed the next day, so there was news to be heard from that quarter, and she passed on good wishes from Mary and

Alice, and a reminder from Serena that she would meet them all in London in a few weeks.

She did nothing to assuage Clary's and Gloria's curiosity, however, no matter that it glowed in their eyes.

Seeing it, too, her mother bent a stern look on them, then gathered her spouse and departed.

Clary hung back, her eyes on their mother's back. "Can we come and visit?"

Sarah fought not to grin. "Mama will bring you when it's appropriate." Which wouldn't be for at least a week or more. "After that, you can visit whenever you like."

Clary's lips formed an O, then she nodded and hurried to fall in behind their mother.

Charlie turned to her, brows arching.

Smiling, she slipped her hand into his arm; telling him the reason behind Clary's and Gloria's wish to visit her would serve no good purpose. "Perhaps," she said as they turned toward the lych-gate beyond which their carriage waited, "we could go for a walk when we get back? I haven't been over the gardens at the Park, not for years, and you know them better than anyone."

She turned to look up at him—and could almost sense the wall of his aloofness growing and thickening.

His face gave nothing away. They reached the gate; he held it open for her. "It would probably be better if you asked the head gardener to show you around."

Better for whom? Passing through the gate, she turned to stare at him.

Following her through, he didn't meet her eyes. "I know Harris is eager to conduct you over his domain and discuss beds and bulbs and such. You'll do better without me."

That *might* be true; the gardens were ultimately her domain, her responsibility, and Harris might well feel confused by his master's presence, yet . . .

"Meredith—glad I caught you."

Sarah turned as Malcolm Sinclair opened the gate and joined them.

He smiled and bowed over her hand, greeting her elegantly and deferentially, then he turned to Charlie. They shook hands, and Sinclair said, "I've had some news from London. Drop by sometime and I'll tell you about it."

Sarah would have sworn the man intended to doff his hat and move on, but Charlie was slow to release his hand. His gaze, she noted, had sharpened on Sinclair's face, then he glanced briefly at her, his expression as ever unreadable.

Then he looked again at Sinclair, his easy smile dawning. "Why not come to lunch? You can tell me then. I'd like to have the opportunity to sound you out about some ideas I've had about the prospective Bristol-Taunton connection."

"Well . . ." Sinclair glanced at Sarah.

Charlie looked at her, too, and there was something in his eyes that made her feel this was some test. Summoning her own version of his easy—meaningless—smile, she turned it on Sinclair. "Indeed, Mr. Sinclair, do come. Your presence will enliven the occasion." She returned her gaze to Charlie's face. "We're rather quiet at present."

Sinclair glanced between them, but when Charlie raised an expectant brow at him, he accepted the invitation. Sarah couldn't fault Sinclair's manners.

Her husband's manners were another matter entirely.

She was not pleased, but an afternoon exploring the extensive gardens with Harris, listening to him expound on the intricacies of shrubberies and arbors, trading views on the colors most appropriate for the flower beds edging the lawns, then enlisting his aid in finding a suitable location for Mr. Quilley, the gnome, had a calming effect. She regained her customary equilibrium, enough for her thoughts to fire her determination rather than her temper.

Charlie was being difficult, but she knew what she knew, knew what she wanted, and was resolved to get it—to secure love as the daily as well as nightly basis of their marriage—for both their sakes.

Over a quiet dinner and the hour they spent in the drawing room afterward, he reading a novel while she embroidered—the very picture of matrimonial domesticity—she covertly watched him, but could find no clue to his strange attitude in his perennially inscrutable face.

She had no idea why he was being difficult, why he shied so completely from letting any hint of his true regard for her show outside

their bedchamber, but wisdom suggested that with simple perseverance he would eventually come around.

Consequently, after another sultry winter's night in their chamber
during which she found not one thing in his attitude with which to cavil,
she forced herself out of bed at a decent hour, hurried herself through
washing and donning her riding habit, then rushed downstairs—just in
time to run into him, literally, as he left the breakfast parlor.

"Oh!" She bounced back.

He caught her elbows, steadied her, then released her.

She smiled up at him. "I caught you. I wanted to ask if you would
ride to the orphanage with me today. Some of the boys have been
asking—"

"I'm sorry." He stepped back, his face turning to stone. "I . . . made
plans to ride to Sinclair's. He has some papers I need to see."

"Oh." She couldn't keep her face from falling, could literally feel her
happiness draining from her, along with her smile. But she quickly
drew breath, tamped down her rising temper, and reminded herself:
Persevere. "Well"—she forced herself to brighten—"as Mr. Sinclair's
house is just beyond Crowcombe—Finley House, didn't he say?—then
at least we can ride that far together."

His gaze briefly touched hers, then shifted away. "I have to deal
with some letters first. I can't say how long it'll be before I'm ready to
set out. Your meeting's at ten, isn't it?"

He glanced over his shoulder at the clock on the parlor mantel; she
followed his gaze—it was nearly nine o'clock.

"You'll have to hurry as it is." His voice was devoid of any real
emotion. She felt his gaze touch her face, then he stepped away and half
bowed. "If you'll excuse me, I'll leave you to your breakfast."

She remained standing in the doorway staring at the clock as his
footsteps faded down the long corridor.

Charlie hadn't made any arrangements to visit Malcolm Sinclair,
but it was easy enough to manufacture an excuse to go calling.
Indeed, given that he was steadily steering their discussions ever deeper
into the subject of railway companies and their financing, any excuse
for another meeting was welcome; he could push such a discussion
only so far at one sitting.

He rode into Crowcombe at eleven o'clock, an acceptable time for one gentleman to call on another. Finley House, a classical Georgian gentleman's house, was set a few paces back from the Watchet road just past Crowcombe.

Dismounting before the gate, he walked Storm, reasonably docile after the ride, through and across the narrow stretch of grass separating the house from the wall bordering the road. A tree with solid low-hanging branches provided a useful place to tie the gelding securely, then Charlie paced up the flagstone path to the front steps.

The front door and hall were flanked by two good-sized rooms. Charlie listened, wondering if Sinclair had seen him arrive. Hearing no sound in the hallway, he raised his hand and knocked. And waited.

He'd considered telling Sinclair of their quest; the man was, after all, a renowned investor in railways, one of those senior investors who, even if he hadn't been one of those who'd approached the authorities, had been financially harmed by the extortioner. Yet while he didn't imagine Sinclair had any involvement with the villain, he knew only too well how investing "information" got around. If he told Sinclair, even if he swore him to secrecy, Sinclair would feel perfectly justified in telling someone he trusted, who would then tell someone *he* trusted, and so on, until the secret information was common knowledge and someone had whispered it to their villain.

So he quashed any moral niggles over picking Sinclair's brains while concealing his true purpose.

Footsteps approached, coming from the rear of the house. The door opened and Malcolm Sinclair looked out.

He smiled. "Charlie."

Charlie returned the smile. "Malcolm." They shook hands and Sinclair waved him in.

He led him to a library-cum-study at the rear corner of the house. "My sanctum, such as it is."

Charlie entered, glancing at the bookcases lining the walls, filled with leather-bound tomes that hadn't been disturbed in years, the neat order of desk and chairs, an armchair and side table before the fireplace, French doors looking out to a small paved courtyard at the rear. Malcolm gestured; Charlie sat in the chair before the desk as his host resumed the admiral's chair behind it.

"Now." Malcolm caught his eye. "To what do I owe this pleasure?"

Charlie smiled and trotted out his perfectly genuine query. Sinclair thought, then replied; they were soon involved in a detailed assessment of the way the original Stockton-Darlington project had been funded and, in Sinclair's opinion, how such funding arrangements could be improved, both from the point of view of the investors, and also the project itself.

It took very little prodding, subtle or otherwise, to get Malcolm talking on that subject. After they'd been conversing for some time, Charlie glanced at the clock on the mantelshelf, and was shocked to discover more than an hour had passed.

He blinked, and straightened. "I must go—I had no idea I'd taken so much of your time."

Malcolm followed his gaze to the clock; his brows rose in patent surprise. Then he smiled, a gesture Charlie instinctively recognized as more sincere than the one he deployed socially; this smile seemed a trifle rusty around the edges. "That just goes to show. I had no idea, either, but I've rarely . . ." Malcolm paused, then met Charlie's eyes. "Met someone else with such similar interests, and"—his lips quirked—"such a similar facility for understanding finance and all its ramifications as I."

His smile deepened as Charlie got to his feet. "I thoroughly enjoy our talks—please do call whenever you wish."

Charlie prowled to the French windows and stood looking out. He knew just what Malcolm meant. In the last hour they'd jettisoned a great deal of the customary reserve men such as they maintained when discussing any subject involving money. He wouldn't have done that, and nor would Malcolm, unless . . . it wasn't so much a matter of trust as that they recognized in each other a very similar man. A degree of similarity greater than the norm.

Charlie couldn't pretend the unexpected association wasn't welcome. He glanced briefly at Malcolm, who was still seated behind the desk, watching him, then turned back to the window. "I'll take you up on that."

The moment stretched, then Malcolm asked, "How are you and your new countess getting on?"

Charlie inwardly stiffened, but remained outwardly relaxed, his hands in his pockets as he stared out at the straggly garden beyond the courtyard. The query had been couched entirely diffidently; he could acceptably turn it aside with some clichéd phrase and leave it at that.

Instead . . . "Women . . . ladies, often have ideas about married life that are somewhat different to those we gentlemen are prepared to countenance."

"Ah." Malcolm said no more, but sympathy, empathy, and understanding rang in the single syllable.

Charlie shifted, his gaze still locked on the bushes outside. "All I can do is hold firm—she'll accept and come around in the end."

Or so he prayed.

After a moment, Malcolm said, again in that diffident, incurious tone, "She seems a sensible lady. Mrs. Duncliffe mentioned she—Sarah—has lived all her life in this area and has various . . . interests."

Charlie's expression turned grim. "The orphanage." He tipped his head toward the front of the house, in the direction in which the orphanage lay. And felt his stomach contract.

That morning . . . his instinctive reaction to her bright, bubbling invitation to join her had nearly had him accepting with a smile. He'd caught himself just in time; her mention of the boys had jerked him to attention. He liked children, of almost any age; he always had. He responded to them and they to him. But children always, always knew when one was being false; if he was surrounded by them and she was there, he'd never be able to hide what he felt for her.

And just the thought of seeing her surrounded by them, with the little ones hanging on her skirts, her madonna's face alight as she reassured them . . .

No. He couldn't ever go with her to the orphanage again.

"Still," Malcolm murmured, "I imagine once you and she set up your own nursery, her interest in the orphanage will wane."

Charlie thought of Sarah with his son—or daughter—in her arms, and felt his knees weaken, felt his resolution simply dissolve. Dear God! How would he cope with that?

He drew in a deep breath, and stiffened his spine; he had a year, at least nine months, in which to figure out how to deal with that eventuality. How to deal with his wife while keeping his love for her locked safely away.

"I'd better be getting back." He turned, met Malcolm's faintly concerned gaze, and smiled. Returning to the desk, he held out his hand. "It's purely newly married jitters. I'm sure they'll pass with time."

His words, his smile, were a great deal more confident than he felt, but they served to put Malcolm at ease. He rose and clasped Charlie's hand; together they walked back through the house.

He paused on the front step, looking up and across to where the orphanage lay on its elevated ledge above the village. He glanced back at Malcolm. "I'm expecting some banking reports from London, news on the latest developments in general—they'll reach me tomorrow morning. Why don't you come for luncheon and we can go through them?"

Malcolm raised a brow. "One of the ways you keep abreast of things while buried in the country?"

Charlie nodded. "Just so. About noon?"

Malcolm hesitated, his hazel eyes on Charlie's face, then he nodded. "Very well. Thank you. I'll see you then."

With a nod and a smile, Charlie walked to Storm; untying the reins, he led the gray into the road, then swung up, and, with a salute, rode away.

Malcolm Sinclair stood in the open doorway, eyes narrowing as he stared after Charlie, then he looked up at the orphanage. After a long moment, he turned inside and closed the door.

W hile she washed and dressed the next morning, Sarah considered the developments of the day before. And felt increasingly confused. It was almost as if she were married to two men—the warm loving man she shared a bed with, and the cold aloof nobleman she met in the corridors of the house.

But not even that adequately described what she'd sensed.

Yesterday . . . his dismissal of her invitation, his clear avoidance of spending any time whatever in her company, had hurt. He'd refused even to ride four miles with her. On horseback, for heaven's sake! Not even in a carriage where they would be close.

What was the matter with him?

Her temper had spiraled, but she'd been forced to suppress it in order to deal with everyone at the orphanage. Charlie and his irrational behavior might be driving her to violence, but she couldn't—wouldn't— allow that to color her dealings with others, and most especially not the children.

That enforced exercise of restraint had been helpful; by the time she'd returned home in the waning afternoon, she'd had herself well in hand.

Nevertheless, through the evening, her temper had been simmering, just waiting for some act or word from him to trigger it. Instead . . . he'd seemed subdued. Not warm and loving, but also not quite so cold and distant; throughout the quiet hour and a half they'd spent, not in the formal drawing room but at her suggestion in her cozier sitting room, she'd felt his gaze on her face, on her, countless times, but whenever she'd glanced up from her embroidery, he'd been reading his book.

What did those surreptitious glances mean? Was he weakening over this silly state he seemed determined to force them into?

Wondering what the day might bring, she headed downstairs.

As she'd expected, the breakfast parlor was empty, devoid of earls; he'd already gone out riding. He'd been as attentive as ever before he'd left their bed, so she was, as usual, rather late. Or more accurately, rather later than she'd used to be before she was wed; ten o'clock was fast becoming her customary breakfast time.

That she could adjust to. But as for the rest . . .

Munching toast, sipping tea, she narrowed her eyes on the empty chair at the head of the table, and felt resolution well.

She thought of how she would wish things to be. While she could appreciate that gentlemen of Charlie's ilk would never willingly wear their hearts on their sleeves, that in public he would always be more reserved, when they were in their own house, there was no reason whatever for him to insist on the distance he seemed intent on preserving between them.

That had to go. And it wasn't as if they didn't have examples enough of successful love matches to learn from. Their wedding breakfast, attended by so many Cynster couples, not to mention Charlie's closest friends and their wives, had proved beyond doubt that all she wished for could come to be.

Her problem, it seemed clear, was how to convince Charlie of that. Of the desirability of that.

By the time she rose and headed for her sitting room to whittle away at the list of thank-you notes, she'd decided that the most sensible way forward was to simply behave, consistently and constantly, as she thought they should. If she played the role of loving wife diligently, then at some point, he'd fling his hands in the air, give up his silly stance, and start being the husband she wanted him to be.

The loving husband he truly was.

Marriage was like a dance—partners had to move together, responding to each other, to make it work. Perhaps he just needed to learn the steps?

She applied herself diligently to the thank-you notes. Halfway down her list, she sat back in the chair before the escritoire and straightened her spine; she was about to bend to her task again when she heard a distant knock.

She listened, and heard Crisp's heavy stride cross the front hall. A moment later, voices reached her. Glancing at the clock, she confirmed it was just noon. Wondering who had called, she rose and headed down the corridor.

Stepping into the front hall, she saw Mr. Sinclair handing his hat and gloves to Crisp. Plastering a smile on her lips, she went forward. "Good morning, Mr. Sinclair. Are you looking for his lordship?"

Sinclair took the hand she offered and bowed gracefully. "Indeed, Lady Meredith." He hesitated, eyes swiftly scanning her face, then added, "His lordship invited me to call."

Sarah blinked, and realized what Sinclair, with suitable delicacy, was telling her. If it was noon, and he had called in response to an invitation . . . Smoothly, she turned to Crisp. "Mr. Sinclair will be here for luncheon, Crisp."

Crisp bowed and withdrew.

Ruthlessly suppressing the spurt of temper that news had evoked, she smiled easily—the situation was certainly not Sinclair's fault—and with a wave invited him to join her in the drawing room. "As Crisp no doubt told you, Charlie has yet to return from his morning ride . . ."

She let her words fade as footsteps—long striding boot steps— sounded on the tiles, heading their way. She drew herself up, clasping her hands dutifully before her; she could manage her expression— unperturbed—but could do nothing about her eyes. If her temper showed there, so be it.

Poised before the drawing room door, she and Sinclair turned as Charlie emerged from the corridor leading to the side door and the stables.

His hair was windblown, a ruffled crest of spun gold. He was wearing an olive-green hacking jacket, a neckerchief tied loosely about his lean throat, a brown waistcoat over an ivory linen shirt tucked into tight buckskin breeches. His riding boots were brown.

Sarah absorbed his appearance, all the details, absorbed the full impact of his presence on her senses, in one swift glance. And wondered as she realized that although she'd seen Sinclair for rather longer, she had no idea what he was wearing beyond that he was dressed as a gentleman.

Given the situation, her sensitivity to her husband was more irritation than comfort.

He'd been looking down, tugging off his gloves; he glanced up, saw them, and his stride hitched. But then he came on, his cool, detached mask in place, his negligent, easy—entirely worthless—smile curving his lips.

She marveled that she'd ever thought that smile charming.

"Malcolm." Charlie offered his hand and Sinclair took it. "Sorry I'm late—I was with one of my tenant farmers."

His smile in place, Charlie turned to her. "My dear, Malcolm and I have much to discuss. You'd find us boring company, I'm afraid. If you could send lunch in to us? We'll be in the library."

He inclined his head and turned away, with a gesture indicating that Sinclair should accompany him to the library.

But Sinclair didn't immediately fall in. He looked at Sarah, then turned to her and bowed. "Thank you for your time, Lady Meredith."

Sarah drew breath, and inclined her head politely. As Sinclair straightened, she saw unexpected understanding and a degree of compassion in his hazel eyes. She was aware, too, of the sudden frown that leapt to life in Charlie's eyes as he noted the glance she and Sinclair exchanged.

As Sinclair turned away, she lifted her gaze for a brief instant to Charlie's eyes, then she turned and let her feet carry her into the drawing room, not glancing back as Charlie and Sinclair walked away down the corridor.

Stopping in the middle of the room, she drew in a huge breath, and held it.

She wasn't, definitely wasn't, going to lose her temper in front of Sinclair.

. . .

T wo nights later, she was lying in bed on her side, facing the windows, the covers around her shoulders, the candles doused, when Charlie entered the room.

It was late; the wind outside was howling.

She lay still, biting her lip to stifle the unwise words that rose to her tongue. She wanted to tell him what she thought, what she felt—wanted to rail at him over how stupid he was being with his present tack—but what would that achieve? Absolutely nothing; he was nearly as stubborn as she was. If she was going to succeed and gain all she wished, she needed a plan, not just anger. Not just pointless pleading.

Come what may, she wasn't going to plead.

That morning she'd reached the breakfast table to find a note by her plate. From Charlie. He'd apparently made arrangements to spend the day at Watchet with Mr. Sinclair, sharing with the latter his knowledge of the local shipping and warehousing businesses.

She'd sat and stared at the note for a full minute, wondering why he'd neglected to mention his daylong appointment with Sinclair last night. Last night, when she'd swallowed her earlier ire and responded to his honest warmth, his transparently genuine desire when he'd joined her in their bed, she'd wanted to encourage his affection, his love, rather than allow his stilted behavior outside the bedroom to spill into it.

Eventually setting the note aside, she'd grimaced, then gone about her day's work alone—as her husband clearly intended.

Until Mrs. Duncliffe called in the afternoon. Just a courtesy visit, but given that shrewd lady's knowledge of her, combined with the fact that although she was no gossip, Mrs. Duncliffe knew her mother extremely well, Sarah had been forced throughout to play the part of delighted and blissfully happy new wife; by the time Mrs. Duncliffe had left Sarah had a headache.

Luckily, it was unlikely that any other of the neighborhood ladies would call until the following week, such was the general custom; her position as vicar's wife gave Mrs. Duncliffe special dispensation.

Feeling unusually wrung out, Sarah had actually retired for a short nap. She'd awoken to the sound of the wind rising, to the softening late afternoon light, then she'd heard Charlie's booted feet on the terrace below the bedroom windows. He'd clearly just returned; she'd wondered, caught between sleep and reality, in the realm of waking dreams, whether he'd come looking for her, whether, when he didn't find her in her sitting room, he would come looking for her up there.

Of course he hadn't.

He'd retreated to the library and hadn't emerged until it was nearly time for dinner. Their evening ritual remained the same; she'd asked and he'd told her what he'd done in Watchet, how he and Sinclair had met with various merchants and agents, and also with the aldermen to discuss their visions for the future of the town. Later she'd embroidered and he'd read. Then she'd retired and climbed the stairs to bed.

She felt as though a weight were pressing down on her chest, making it difficult to breathe. He seemed determined to deny what she knew to be true; if he denied love long enough, would it die, converting his version of the truth into fact?

Listening as he crossed to his dressing room, hearing him move about as he undressed, she tried to define her way forward, a way to claim the love she *knew* existed between them, to force him to acknowledge it . . .

He never had.

Staring through the darkness softened by the dying fire's flames, she realized, quickly scanned her memories and confirmed, that he never, not once, had said that he loved her.

She'd said the words for him, once, and he hadn't denied them.

But he'd never acknowledged them, or their truth.

He came out of his dressing room; she heard the shush of his robe as he let it fall. Then the bed bowed as he climbed in beside her.

Something inside her tensed, the deadening weight coalescing to a hard tight knot in her chest, yet her traitorous senses stretched and reached for him. She continued to lie still. He shifted closer—and through the darkness she caught the scent of the sea.

He'd been sailing. While in Watchet, he'd taken Sinclair out on his boat. She hadn't thought to ask, yet neither had he mentioned it.

The hard knot in her chest grew colder, sank deeper.

For the first time in their marriage, she didn't turn to welcome him into her arms. Instead, she pretended to be deeply asleep, until he turned away and settled, and then fell asleep himself.

She lay still and stared into the night.

Outside the wind howled, as if winter were returning.

The following morning, Charlie felt his chest tighten as he laid another note on the breakfast table beside Sarah's place.

Lips compressing, he turned and strode from the room; going out to the stables, he swung up to Storm's back, turned the gelding's head south, and let him have his head.

He was riding for Casleigh; Gabriel was there, along with Barnaby, who'd elected to use the more southerly house as his temporary base while he and Gabriel covertly examined the possibilities for profiteering and extortion along potential routes for a Bristol-Taunton rail line.

It was time he caught up with Barnaby's and Gabriel's findings, and doing so was the perfect way to spend another day away from Sarah.

He forced himself to ease his tightening grip on the reins, but neither the thunder of Storm's hooves nor the rush of air past his face could distract him from the uneasy, unsettling thoughts circling ceaselessly in his brain.

Over the last days he'd done his best to do what he felt increasingly certain he had to. With every night that passed, he experienced the power of what had come to be between him and her, and it was too strong—it could so easily rule him. If he let it. If he let it out, let it flow through his life, and not only the hours spent in their bed.

And despite all, his tack seemed to be working, at least in the sense that she seemed to be gradually coming to accept that during the day, beyond their bedchamber, there would always be a wall between them.

But then last night . . . he tried to tell himself that she'd simply fallen deeply asleep before he'd reached the room, yet some more primitive, instinctual part of him knew she'd been awake. That she'd chosen . . . to remain apart.

One part of him, that same primitive part, railed and roared, cut and insensibly hurt. Yet that's what he wanted, wasn't it? At least during the day.

He wanted distance between them, wanted her to understand and accept that. What right had he to complain if she took his stance one step further?

Yet that wasn't what he wanted. Not now. Now love had come to be, now he'd sampled it, he couldn't bear to cut himself off from it entirely.

The wind bit through his hacking jacket and stroked icy fingers down his chest, yet the chilled tightness he felt inside owed nothing to the elements.

He needed to build the wall higher, needed to make it thicker. Perhaps then he wouldn't feel this peculiar cold pain.

Containing love was proving very much harder than he'd thought.

14

She felt betrayed.

Not, admittedly, as many ladies did, married to a philanderer, but betrayed in an even deeper sense.

She felt deceived. Knowingly, deliberately, and *senselessly* deceived.

The following morning Sarah completed the task of writing thank-you notes to all those who had sent formal congratulations and good wishes for their wedding. She stacked the neatly addressed notes, then, lips thin, carried them into the library—and sat them in the center of Charlie's blotter.

As usual, he was out riding. She stepped back, considered the teetering pile, then turned and marched out, leaving the notes for him to frank.

She returned to her sitting room, but with no immediate occupation offering, restlessness claimed her. Peering out the window, she assessed the day; the weather had turned finicky, patches of bright sunshine interspersed with gloom, but the skies appeared clear enough to risk a walk in the gardens.

Going out via the French doors onto the terrace, she descended the steps and walked briskly to the rose garden, an area between the shrubbery and the lake where neatly paved paths ambled between curved beds. Harris was particularly proud of his roses, so the paths were always well tended and swept; even in winter with the roses pruned back to collections of stumps and sticks, it was the perfect place for ladies to take their constitutionals.

She stalked down the paths, stared at the stumps and sticks, and prodded experimentally at her bruised heart.

The ache within was intensifying.

She hadn't wanted to marry without love; she'd only agreed to wed Charlie because, even if he hadn't *told* her he loved her, he'd *shown* her that he did. She hadn't been some silly ninny placing too great a reliance on a gentleman's promises; she'd waited until she'd *seen* that he loved her. And he did.

Still did.

She'd taken every precaution possible. What she hadn't known was that despite loving her, Charlie had had no intention of allowing love into their marriage. That despite his vows, in the very *teeth* of his love, he was refusing to allow it . . . loose. Refusing to allow it free rein in their lives, refusing to let it be a source of support and strength for them both, as instinctively she knew it could be, and indeed should be.

All but scowling, clasping her hands behind her, she paced on, at the end of the path kicking her skirts around so she could turn and pace back.

He'd shown her his love but had never intended to properly share it, to live up to love's implicit, age-old promise; betrayal and deceit darkened her mind, yet what set spark to her temper, what made her so angry she had to grit her teeth against a frustrated scream, was *why*.

Because there was no reason why.

None she could logically conjure; none she could understand.

He was set on his path, inflexible, determined, and as ever ensuring he got his own way, simply because . . . he thought that was how things should be?

She had no idea, but whatever his excuse, it wasn't good enough.

Hurt and anger warred within her, but the latter was stronger; far from retreating to lick her wounds, she wanted to . . . grab Charlie by the shoulders and shake him until he woke up and saw what he was so wantonly turning his back on.

If only she'd been a man . . . but of course that wouldn't have worked. She was a woman, a female . . .

Blinking, she halted, and stared unseeing at a dormant bush. She was a female, a woman, ergo Charlie, her temporarily demented husband, assumed she was weaker, less strong, and, most important, less stubborn than he.

Her scowl faded; her lips, until then compressed into a thin line, eased. He would assume that if he held firm, she would in the end, without any real struggle, accept his dictate and let their marriage become the hollow entity he wished, one without love at its heart. But there was no reason she had to follow his script.

No reason she couldn't fight for what she wanted, a marriage based solidly on love.

Standing amid the stumps and sticks, she savored the prospect of such a battle, one necessarily waged with actions, not words, and found it considerably more palatable than simply giving in. Whether she could change Charlie's mind, whether she could force him to see their future through her eyes, whether he would wish to join her in making it a reality even if she could, she had no idea, but that was her goal.

A footstep on the path behind her had her whirling. Her senses leapt, then abruptly fell flat; once again it wasn't her errant husband who was coming toward her. She drew in a breath, summoned a smile, and extended her hand. "Mr. Sinclair."

"Countess." Clasping her hand, he bowed gracefully, then released her. He glanced around at the winter-dead beds. "I saw you walking here . . ."

"I've been taking the air." She waved at the paths. "The lawns are so wet, it's safer here." She noted the papers he carried in one hand. "Is the earl expecting you?"

His expression easy but his eyes on hers, Sinclair raised the papers. "He asked to see these—they arrived this morning from London."

Sarah inwardly sighed; clearly she would get no chance to battle Charlie over luncheon, or for the rest of the afternoon. "I'm afraid he's still out riding, but he should be back soon."

Sinclair hesitated, his eyes searching her face, then he said, "In that case, if you don't mind, I'll walk with you."

She was surprised, but her duty as hostess was clear; with a light smile, she inclined her head and turned to pace down the path.

It was easy to make social conversation, to ask how he found Crowcombe and his rented house, about his thoughts on the bucolic amenities of the neighborhood.

"The bridge across Will's Neck falls is the best spot for appreciating the Quantocks." She glanced at his face. "Have you been there yet?"

"No." He met her gaze. "How does one reach it?"

She smiled and told him. As they walked, she was conscious of his size—he was nearly as tall as Charlie and somewhat heavier—but although he was classically handsome, well set up, and graceful, although in many respects he was an older version of Charlie, Sinclair stirred her senses not at all.

But her senses did leap when another heavy footstep rang on the path behind them. She turned, her usual welcoming smile on her lips—no matter the situation between them she doubted her instinctive greeting for Charlie would ever change—and found him regarding Sinclair, an odd, hard, distinctly challenging look in his eye.

For a fleeting instant, she saw Charlie as a knight, armored and ready to do battle.

Then she blinked, and Sinclair, smiling easily, transparently unaffected by the menace she'd sensed, stepped forward.

"Meredith." He held out his hand.

Charlie blinked, then, moving more slowly than usual, grasped it. "Sinclair." His gaze slid past Sinclair to her, but she couldn't read the expression in his eyes. His face wore its usual impassive mien.

"The countess was kind enough to keep me company until you arrived." Sinclair brandished his papers. "I brought those reports you wanted to see."

Charlie's gaze went to the papers. After an instant, he nodded. "Excellent." He looked at Sarah. "If you'll excuse us, my dear, we'll be in the library."

Of course. Her new purpose in mind, she smiled tightly and replied, "I'll send luncheon trays in to you."

He wasn't sure what to make of that. "Thank you."

With a nod and a bow, both men took their leave of her. She watched them stride to the terrace, then disappear into the library.

She allowed herself a grimace. Her gaze fell on one of the oldest rosebushes, the gnarled trunk as thick as her arm. She thought again of that odd reaction of Charlie's, relived again that momentary impression . . .

Had he been *jealous*?

Was that what had made him so menacingly stiff? Just for that instant until Sinclair had reminded him why he was there—subtly assuring Charlie that he had no designs on her.

Her eyes narrowed, her gaze sharpened—on the rosebush. And she noticed the slight bulges, the first signs of buds forming on the otherwise dead-looking branches.

Perhaps their marriage was like the rosebush—dormant, but with the right amount of sun it would come into bloom. Indeed, with the right attention it would bloom spectacularly. Perhaps what she'd just glimpsed in Charlie was the first hint of a bud? A sign that no matter the image he was striving to project, she might yet win through and secure all she sought.

She stood staring at the rosebush for a few minutes longer, then she turned and headed back to the house.

She was not giving up on her version of their marriage.

It took Charlie a few minutes to lose his stiffness, to let his idiotically instinctive hackles subside; he could only be grateful that Malcolm gave no indication of noticing, although of course he had. The very idea of having reacted in such a primitive—and revealing—way to Malcolm's plainly innocent presence by Sarah's side irked; he shut all thought of the moment out of his conscious mind as rapidly as he could.

He led Malcolm into the library and they settled to pick apart the information contained in the investment reports Malcolm had brought. Crisp duly appeared with a repast laid out on two trays; they continued to discuss the flow of funds into various types of projects while consuming slices of country bread piled with cold roast beef and pickles.

A footman eventually came and cleared away the trays, giving them space to spread the reports over the wide desk.

He was slouched in his chair, listening to Malcolm's explanation of the funding arrangements that had operated with the Liverpool-Manchester rail line, when Crisp unexpectedly entered carrying his silver salver.

"A solicitor from Taunton to see you, my lord. I informed him you were occupied, but he requested you be given his card and informed he brings a business proposition that he wishes to lay before you."

Crisp proffered the salver. Charlie picked up the card. "Thomas Riley, of Riley and Ferguson, solicitors, with an address in Taunton High Street." Lifting his gaze, he raised his brows at Malcolm. "I confess I have no idea what this is about. Do you mind if I see him?"

"Of course not." Malcolm made to rise.

Charlie waved him back. "Stay, please. At least until I learn what this is about." He glanced at Crisp. "Show Mr. Riley in."

Riley proved to be a typical country solicitor, self-effacing and prone to speak in low-voiced, convoluted phrases.

Charlie cut off his lengthy introduction and invited him to pull up a straight-backed chair and sit, which he did. Malcolm had retreated to stand by one of the windows, looking out. "Now, Mr. Riley." Charlie leaned forward, elbows on the desk, hands loosely clasped. "I would appreciate it if you could get straight to your point in requesting an audience."

Riley, singularly unprepossessing in a dark and dusty suit, swallowed. "Indeed, my lord. I'm only too aware of the—"

"Your point, Mr. Riley?"

"Ah—I have a client who wishes to make an offer for a parcel of land of which you are the owner." Riley reached into the battered leather satchel he'd balanced on his knees and extracted a sheaf of papers, along with a pince-nez he perched on his nose. He glanced at the papers, then at Charlie. "It's the Quilley property outside Crowcombe."

Charlie let his surprise show.

Riley hurriedly continued, "My client wishes to add Quilley Farm to his already considerable holdings in the area, and given that the farm is well beyond your boundaries, he hoped you would be willing to entertain his offer."

Curiosity prompted Charlie to ask what the offer was, and who was making it, but there was really no point. He leaned back. "I'm sorry, Mr. Riley, but there's no question of my selling that property."

Riley's eyes widened, fear rising as he saw his fee disappearing. "But my client is willing to be most reasonable—"

"It's not that." There was no purpose in prolonging the solicitor's visit; Charlie itched to return to his discussion with Malcolm. "I can't sell that property because it's not mine to sell. You've been misinformed, Mr. Riley."

"But . . ." Riley's wide eyes made him look like a squirrel. An aghast squirrel. "The farm belonged to Miss Conningham, and as she married you—"

"Indeed." Charlie paused for an instant, letting his tone—hard and discouraging—impinge on Riley. "Miss Conningham became my countess and ownership of the farm passed to me. It is, however, no longer mine."

Riley's lips formed an almost comical O of surprise.

Charlie debated whether to tell Riley who was now the owner of Quilley Farm, but Sarah was his wife and it was his duty to protect her from unnecessary pressure from the likes of Riley and whoever his client was. Nothing would be gained by referring Riley to Sarah; Charlie knew what her response to any offer to buy Quilley Farm would be.

"You, ah, couldn't perhaps tell me who the new owner is?"

Charlie shook his head. "You can, however, tell your client that the new owner has no need of funds, and is therefore unlikely to entertain any offer for that land, regardless of the amount."

Riley deflated. His expression turning glum, he stuffed his papers back into his satchel, then rose, bowed to Charlie, and took his leave. Crisp, who'd remained by the door, followed him out.

"Interesting." Malcolm had turned to watch the solicitor leave; returning to the chair before the desk, he raised his brows at Charlie. "That was quick work, arranging for the sale of that farm so soon. I had no idea the orphanage had changed hands."

Charlie grimaced. "Not so quick because it hasn't, in truth, changed hands at all. The title was passed back to Sarah via the marriage settlements." He shrugged. "Her interest in the orphanage runs deep."

He should have pressed to learn who Riley's client was, although the solicitor almost certainly wouldn't have revealed his name. But . . . "A client wishing to add the farm to his 'already considerable holdings in the area'—I suspect that's solicitor code for one of the farmers on either side." He thought, then nodded. "Both probably would like to get their hands on the property."

"Ah, well." Leaning forward, Malcolm picked up one of the reports. "Where were we?"

"The financial structure behind the original funding of the Liverpool-Manchester line."

"The farm was reverted back into the countess's hands, so it's her we need to approach."

"You still want the property?"

"Oh, yes. Absolutely. It's one of the best I've ever found."

"If that's the case, I'll get on with it."

"Indeed, but be discreet, and be prepared to take your time."

A few seconds passed, then, "Why?" Honestly puzzled, not challenging.

The answer took a moment in coming, and even then was clearly reluctant. "Because at present there's some strain between the earl and the countess. It's not her doing, and it's making her . . . sad."

"More likely to sell then, surely?"

"No—more likely to cling to something she knows. Something that's hers. However, the earl is far from stupid—I'm sure, given time, he'll come to his senses. Once he does, the countess's mood will lift, she'll become distracted with other things, and . . . I'm quite sure, then, that she'll be more amenable to selling."

A minute ticked by. "So—do you want me to wait until the earl makes the countess happy again?"

Low laughter filled the room. "Oh, no. I might appreciate the earl's acumen, but I'm certainly not prepared to subject my plans to his whim. You may proceed, but as I said, be careful and be patient. One way or another, I'm sure we can ensure that I'll have Quilley Farm in good time."

Sarah proceeded doggedly with her plan. If she behaved as if love were openly acknowledged between them, and refused to waver no matter his aloofness, his distance, his too-formal acts, then ultimately, in time, even he would have to admit that embracing their love was more rewarding than denying it.

Given Charlie's stubbornness, such a plan was akin to using water to cut stone, but perseverance, she hoped, would win through.

On Sunday, strolling away from the church on his arm, she was inwardly congratulating herself on a credible performance as a lady in love, one she felt confident had passed Clary's and Gloria's scrutiny, and even that of Twitters, confirmed romantic that she was, when Charlie informed her that Malcolm Sinclair would be calling after luncheon. Again.

She bit back an acid comment, then remembered. She raised her brows. "Mr. Sinclair seems . . . an interesting gentleman."

From the corner of her eye, she caught Charlie's slight frown; a minor triumph. At the moment, minor triumphs were all she'd garnered, but it was early days yet.

Resigned to the afternoon being lost to her campaignwise when, after luncheon, Charlie retired to the library to search out some details he and Sinclair intended to study, she retreated to her sitting room.

The day outside was cool. She looked out the windows, then drifted about the room; she wanted to forge ahead with her campaign, but at that moment there was nothing she could sensibly do.

With a frustrated sigh, she sat on the chaise and reached for the basket of mending she'd had fetched from the orphanage. The staff there did all they could, and Twitters helped, occasionally convincing Clary and Gloria to assist, but there was always so much to patch and darn, so many rips to stitch together again.

She was thus employed when she heard a footstep in the corridor. As usual, she'd left the sitting room doors propped wide; she looked up as Mr. Sinclair glanced in. He was obviously on his way to the library, but he stopped, smiled, and entered to greet her.

Smiling, she held out her hand; Charlie using him as a shield wasn't Sinclair's fault, and there was nothing to take exception to in his manners or his person. "Good afternoon, sir. Pray excuse me for not rising—I'm temporarily weighed down."

By the blanket she was darning.

Sinclair bowed over her hand, but as he straightened, his gaze fastened on the blanket; she could almost hear him wondering why the Countess of Meredith was darning at all, much less such an old thing.

"It's from the orphanage," she explained. "I help as I can."

"Ah." His face cleared. He glanced briefly around, taking in the room. "You've made yourself at home here—it suits you."

"Thank you."

He looked again at the basket of darning. "I'd heard that you were involved with the orphanage." He tipped his head at the nearby arm-chair; intrigued, she waved him to sit.

Gracefully doing so, he continued, "I've seen Quilley Farm—it's visible from my front steps. As you know, I'm thinking of settling in the district. I've never lived outside London, and . . . well, I thought that taking an interest in some endeavor like the orphanage might be a good way to fill some of my hours and build bridges with the local community."

If he hadn't added that last phrase, Sarah would have suspected him of bamming her; instead, she saw nothing but sincerity in his eyes.

He leaned forward attentively. "I wonder if you could tell me something about the place?"

She smiled, and obliged. The words came readily to her lips; she was comfortable describing the institution her godmother had established, having done it so often before.

But she knew better than to enthuse too long. She concluded with, "Given the increasing number of factories in Taunton and the increase in shipping, too, no matter how much we might wish it otherwise there's likely to be a corresponding increase in the need to care for children left behind in the wake of accidents and tragedies."

Sinclair had been listening intently. Now he nodded. "I see." He smiled briefly, confidingly. "I was present when his lordship dismissed the offer for the orphanage on Friday. Now I understand why he said your involvement runs deep, and that you would have no interest in selling."

Sarah blinked. Ice slid through her veins. "Offer? To buy the or-phanage?"

Sinclair's eyes locked on hers, swiftly—almost disbelievingly—searching. A faint flush rose in his pale cheeks. "I . . . apologize. I . . . assumed his lordship would have mentioned the matter."

Sarah's features felt stiff. She waved aside his embarrassment. "No need for apologies."

Sinclair rose. "Nevertheless, I hope you'll forgive me."

The tone of his voice—as if he were irritated, but not at her—kept her silent as she looked up at him.

He held her gaze for a second, then his lashes flickered down over his hazel eyes and he bowed. "If you'll excuse me, I really should join Meredith in the library. I daresay he's expecting me."

"He is," Sarah affirmed, her tone not as harsh as it might have been; none of what she felt was Sinclair's fault.

She could do little about her expression, however; it was stony as she inclined her head. Sinclair turned and left. She watched him disappear down the corridor.

His footsteps faded, then she heard a door close. She sat unmoving for a full minute, then she lifted the blanket in her lap and reapplied herself to the patch she'd been darning.

There was no point even trying to think until her temper cooled.

He should have told her—as even Sinclair, a confirmed bachelor, understood.

An hour and a half later, Sarah strode across the lawn, then swung onto the paved paths of the rose garden. Arms wrapped around herself, she paced. Her jaw remained clenched; a sense of cold that had nothing to do with the weather had sunk to her bones.

How could she engage with him, make headway against his foolish dictate, when he continued to push her away? When he refused to engage with her even on the subjects he should engage with her on, but rather erected a barrier—a wall that increased in breadth, width, and solidity by the day—between them.

At least he'd dismissed the offer; in that, at least, he'd kept faith with her.

Yet keeping faith with her on the subject of their marriage, of their love, was what he was otherwise so adamantly *not* doing. *Refusing* to do.

Although her temper had calmed somewhat, she only just managed to suppress a frustrated scream.

She walked briskly, pointlessly, back and forth; rosebushes offering the promise of spring today provided no distraction. Today her mind wasn't inclined to seek encouraging analogies. Today, she was engrossed in feeling cold.

In feeling unbelievably alone.

She'd grown up with four sisters, and Twitters; she'd rarely spent an hour alone. Yet now, in her new home with her husband in residence, for the first time in her life, she felt loneliness bite.

Sensed its emptiness.

Quelling a shiver, she swung around to pace back toward the house. A faint sound reached her; she looked up.

And saw Sinclair leaving via the terrace, Charlie seeing him off at the library's French doors. Sinclair hadn't stayed as long as he usually did. Even from this distance, she detected a certain stiffness in Charlie's stance, in his nod as he parted from Sinclair. She couldn't make out his expression, yet it appeared her husband was not best pleased.

Sinclair turned to follow the terrace past her sitting room and on to the stables; Charlie retreated and shut the French doors.

Sinclair strode along, then caught sight of her. Halfway along the terrace, he hesitated, glanced back at the library windows, then walked quickly down the steps and strode her way.

Surprised, she halted and waited. Like Charlie's, Sinclair's face was usually unreadable. His expression rarely gave any hint of his thoughts, let alone his feelings, yet she was growing used to dealing with Charlie; she was growing more adept at looking elsewhere for clues.

By the time Sinclair joined her, she was puzzled. He appeared to be bridling an intense irritation. "Lady Meredith. I wanted to inform you that, after my earlier gaffe, I felt compelled to mention my indiscretion to his lordship."

She raised her brows. She hadn't expected that.

"While he seemed entirely unconcerned that I'd told you, I . . ." Sinclair paused, then drew in a breath; his lips thinned even more. "In short, his attitude over his lack of consideration in not having informed you of the offer for the orphanage fell far short of my expectations."

Abruptly, Sinclair focused on her face. His sharp hazel eyes searched hers; Sarah struggled to place the emotion coloring his eyes, his voice . . . and was amazed to realize it was concern.

Apparently perfectly genuine concern.

"I realize, my dear, that I have no experience in such matters. I've lived my life almost entirely alone." His tone had softened, but his grim dissatisfaction remained. "I don't wish to pry, but I can see—appreciate— that matters are a trifle strained between you and . . . Charlie. Perhaps that's a normal thing, so soon after your wedding—as to that, I don't know. Nevertheless, I wish to most sincerely apologize if I have in any way contributed to that strain. Such was not my intention."

She held his gaze, savored the sincerity in his words, then inclined her head. "Thank you." She hesitated, then looked past his shoulder at the house. "I . . . it would be inappropriate to say more, but I most sincerely appreciate your understanding."

Neither moved; a moment passed, then he said, his tone quieter, more gentle, "He . . . is a lot like me. In many ways, he strikes me very much as a younger version of myself, with his fascination for finance and investments."

She glanced at him; he was looking at the library. His lips quirked ruefully. "As I mentioned, I've lived all my life alone. Enough to hope, for his sake, that he . . . comes to his senses." He looked back and met her eyes. "And realizes what he has in you."

She was astonished that he had commented on such a personal subject, let alone managed to do so while remaining within the bounds of polite conversation.

Before she could gather her wits to respond, he bowed. "Good-bye, my dear countess. I wish you better tidings. Until next we meet."

With that, he was gone, striding away across the lawn. Reaching the terrace, he climbed the steps, then headed toward the stables.

Feeling oddly comforted, Sarah wrapped her arms once more about her; turning away from the house, she paced deeper into the garden.

Buoyed by Sinclair's unexpected championing, she considered going in and bearding Charlie . . . but if she'd read Sinclair's disapprobation, Charlie would have, too. His stiffness in farewelling Sinclair suggested he would be in no good mood over that point or, indeed, any point to do with her.

Eyes fixed unseeing on the path, she grimaced. Sinclair might have meant well, but Charlie was Charlie—masculine, arrogant, and likely to turn as inflexible as iron if pushed. It was highly unlikely that prodding him at the moment would advance her cause.

The burden of loneliness that Sinclair's advent and his unexpected support had lightened slowly sank back onto her shoulders, weighing her down. A shiver too sharp to suppress had her turning around; loneliness wrapping ever tighter about her, she walked back to the house.

She returned via the terrace to her sitting room. She'd just closed the French doors on the dying day when Crisp appeared bearing a taper to light the candles and dispel the gathering gloom.

He also carried his salver, which he proferred. "A note, my lady."

She lifted the plain folded sheet. "Thank you, Crisp." She opened it and scanned the lines within, and frowned.

"Is there a problem, ma'am?"

Crisp's question brought her back to herself. She looked at him. "No . . . that is, I'm not sure." She glanced again at the note. "Mrs. Carter at the orphanage writes that there was a strange disturbance last night, but she doesn't say what." She contemplated the note, then forced a quick smile. "Whatever it is, I'll learn the details when I go there tomorrow, and as Mrs. Carter hasn't requested any help, I suspect this is purely to keep me informed."

"No doubt, ma'am. As is proper."

It took an instant or two for Crisp's last sentence to penetrate her distraction. She glanced at him, but with his usual butlerish mien in place, he was circling the room, lighting the candles she'd placed here and there; she couldn't catch his eye.

He bent to light the lamp on the side table; once he'd adjusted the wick so that it was burning steadily, he turned to her and bowed. Then he straightened and spoke to a spot above her head. "Mrs. Figgs and I . . . well, we realize that as matters fell out we did not have occasion to receive you in the manner in which a new countess is traditionally welcomed to the Park. And indeed, introducing you to the staff would have been redundant as you were already acquainted with us all. However"— Crisp drew himself up to his full imposing height—"Mrs. Figgs, I, and all the staff wish to assure you of our fondest welcome and our hopes to serve you faithfully for many years to come."

Sarah had to blink back tears. "Thank you, Crisp." Her voice soft, she added, "Please assure Mrs. Figgs and the staff that I appreciate their wishes and their willingness to serve me."

"Indeed, my lady." Crisp bowed deeply, then turned on his heel and left her.

Sarah dragged in a huge breath, then dropped onto the chaise. A second unexpected declaration of support. She thought back; Crisp had been shooting concerned glances her way for a few days. Figgs, too. They must have detected . . . how had Sinclair put it? Ah, yes, that matters were a trifle strained between her and Charlie.

She should have guessed that the staff would notice, yet it seemed they, too, had declared for her. That they, too, appreciated what she was offering Charlie, the promise and the power of it.

It seemed the only one who didn't appreciate that was Charlie.

Her impulse was to take the bull by the horns, but she knew him too well; wisdom insisted no good would be served—not now, not this evening.

Her fingers clenched; the rustle of paper drew her gaze to the note from Katy. It was puzzling, and worrying, but Katy was an experienced and competent woman; if she'd needed help tonight she would have asked.

Tomorrow was Monday; as usual Sarah would ride to the orphanage. She planned to spend the entire day there.

Better than spending her entire day here. Alone.

The clock struck the hour. She looked up at it, then stirred. Rising, she walked to the escritoire. She'd fallen into the habit of leaving the lid down; this was her room, after all. Folding the note, she placed it in the pigeonhole reserved for orphanage business. She glanced once more around the room, then with a sigh, headed upstairs. A long soak in a hot bath could only help.

H er aunt Edith's diary was gone.

Later that evening Sarah stood before the open escritoire and stared at the empty vertical gap where the diary had been. After a largely silent dinner, as had become their habit she and Charlie had retired to her sitting room. Charlie had settled in the armchair by the hearth and become absorbed in some text on engineering; tired of the incessant mending and seeking comfort, she'd decided reading more of her aunt's observations might divert or even help her. But nothing whatever reposed in the rack where the diary had been. She scanned the various spaces in the escritoire, but no glimmer of silver plate winked from anywhere within it.

"But . . ." Frowning, she ran her fingertips down the edge of the empty rack. "I *know* I left it there."

She'd put it there the day she'd moved her things into this room, and hadn't retrieved it since. "Where on earth could it have gone?"

And how? Perhaps the maids had moved it. She set about ransacking the escritoire's lower drawers; finding nothing there, she glanced around, then moved to the side table nearby. The drawer in that contained candles and tapers, but no diary.

She continued around the room, searching high and low, anywhere the diary might have been put. Increasingly frantic, trying to deny the growing conviction that the diary was no longer there to be found, that it had been stolen. Over the last week she'd frequently left the terrace doors propped wide. But this was an earl's private estate, and the house was a long way from any boundary.

Disturbed by her efforts, Charlie glanced up. She felt his gaze on her, but didn't turn to meet it. Although she was sure her agitation was showing, she noticed he hesitated, that he actually debated whether or not to speak before asking, "What is it?"

Facing away from him, she pressed her lips tightly together for a second—to suppress the words soaring temper set on her tongue— then evenly stated, "My aunt Edith's diary. I left it in the escritoire, but now it's gone." Something close to despair colored her tone.

She suddenly wanted to be held, to be hugged and told everthing would be all right. She sensed Charlie tense as if to stand and come to her, but then he hesitated; when she glanced his way, she saw him re-settling the book on his knee.

"No doubt you've misplaced it." The words were cool, dismissive— distant. He didn't bother glancing at her but refixed his gaze on his text.

For a moment, Sarah stared at him, stunned by the emotional slap.

Then she drew in a deep breath, clenched her jaw, and turned away. *I didn't!* she screamed at him in her mind, but refused to let her fury loose—refused to weaken herself by so doing. Not yet.

Clinging to the more important issue, sensing again that inner conviction that the diary truly was gone, that it had by whatever means vanished, she drew another deep breath and, with awful calm, entirely ignoring Charlie, crossed to the bellpull that hung beside the mantelpiece.

She tugged, then, clasping her hands before her, waited.

Crisp answered her summons, bearing the tray with the silver teapot and delicate china cups. Seeing her standing, he quickly set the tray down on the side table by the chaise. "Yes, ma'am?"

Head high, Sarah met his eyes. "I left my late aunt's diary in the escritoire, Crisp, but it's no longer there."

Crisp glanced at the escritoire, a frown forming. "The silver-plated one, ma'am? Mandy, the maid who dusts in here, did mention it."

"Indeed, it's an unusual design, probably unique." Sarah paused, then, fingers twisting as she struggled to hold down her welling emotions, said, "I was very fond of my late aunt, and therefore value the diary highly—it was a keepsake. Could you please ask the staff if they've seen it elsewhere in the house?"

Crisp's gaze had traveled to the French doors, then to Charlie, eyes on his book, apparently totally disinterested. When Crisp's eyes returned to her face, his sympathy was clear. "Of course, ma'am. We'll search for it. And I'll check with Mandy when she saw the book last. I believe she dusted in here the day before yesterday."

His decisive response brought some relief; at least she'd soon know if by some chance the diary had been moved. She inclined her head. "Thank you, Crisp. Please let me know what Mandy says, if she remembers if it was there."

"Indeed, ma'am." With another swift glance at Charlie, eyes on his book, unmoved and unmoving, Crisp bowed and departed.

Sarah's gaze fell on the teapot. After a moment, without looking at Charlie, she moved to the side table and poured herself a cup. Charlie didn't drink tea at this hour if he could help it; lifting her cup and saucer from the tray, she carefully sat, sipped, then gave her attention to the basket full of linens.

On impulse, she turned the basket out and searched through the blankets, sheets, and towels, but there was no silver-plated book buried among the folds.

L ater that night, Sarah blew out the candle by her side of their bed; burrowing down into the soft mattress, she pulled the covers up over her shoulder—and tried to relax. Tried to compose her mind for sleep, but with so much hurt and anger roiling inside her, she knew it would be hours before she achieved any degree of calm.

Charlie. What was she going to *do* about him? She hadn't missed his instinctive response to her distress, any more than she'd missed his deliberate suppression of same. Yes, he loved her, but he was refusing— *refusing!*—to let his love show.

She might have been able to brush his behavior aside, to ignore it as just another example of what she knew his dogged direction to be, as nothing more than she might have expected given that he'd yet to surrender and cease his senseless denial of his love, except that it was Edith's diary she'd lost.

She felt the loss keenly, like a wound in her heart. Edith had been far more than just an aunt; she'd been someone very special, someone who'd understood, who had taught her so much, who had shared her wisdom and her counsel. It was Edith who had educated her mind and opened her eyes to life—and so to love.

Her distracted mind tripped over that point. If it hadn't been for Edith and her insights, would she have married Charlie? Or would she years before have followed her older sisters' and mother's path and settled for a simple, undemanding union?

Her lips twisted at the irony.

Outside, the wind howled, a ravenous creature bent, it seemed, on rattling the sashes. Denied, it turned its fury on the massive trees, cruelly raking, cracking branches one against the other.

Sarah shivered, snuggled deeper under the covers and closed her eyes. And tried not to think of the ache in her chest. Just like the weather, life had turned unexpectedly cruel.

She told herself it wouldn't last, that it would blow over and she'd see sunshine again. But with her heart already bruised, and now aching more deeply from the unexpected blow of the diary's loss, when she heard the door open and Charlie's footsteps cross the room, she lay still, feigning sleep.

Ten minutes later the bed bowed at her back and he joined her beneath the covers. She kept her limbs relaxed, kept her breathing slow and even—and battled to wrestle down the anger that rose, unbidden, to swamp her.

If he reached for her, if he touched her . . . she might very well hit him.

Instead, propped on one arm, he watched her; she could feel the weight of his gaze even through the covers. The silence stretched, punctuated by the slow heavy tick of the clock on the mantel.

Then he shifted, and turned away. He slumped on his back; she thought she heard him sigh. Then his breathing slowed, became more even; she felt sure he'd fallen asleep.

With a mental sniff, she vowed to do the same.

Charlie lay on his back and stared up at the dark canopy, and wondered what on earth to do. He knew she wasn't asleep, but with matters between them like this—with cold stony silence enveloping the bed—he felt powerless to change things. Unable to act, uncertain what to do.

Helpless.

He wanted to comfort her. But he no longer knew how.

Or, perhaps, was no longer certain he had the right.

Yet every instinct he possessed—the very instincts he'd had to battle to suppress, to keep within reasonable nonrevealing bounds in her sitting room when he'd realized she was upset, the same instincts that had squirmed when Sinclair had mentioned the offer for the orphange, a matter he'd hoped, somehow, to broach that evening and soothe any hurt his lapse had caused, but again he hadn't been able to fathom how—clamored to comfort her, raged and fought against his restrictions. Against the tight rein he insisted on keeping over them outside this room, and now inside it, too.

He wanted to ease that rein, at least here, in the safe dark of their bed, but was no longer sure he should.

He'd never felt so torn in his life, so cut up and clawed inside, as if one part of him, a fundamental, primitive, but essential part of him had declared all-out war with his rational mind, with those more cautious, careful traits that were the province of self-preservation, the patterns of behavior defined and imposed not by instinct but by intellect.

And he could see no resolution. No way, no path, no course of action that would bring that conflict to any acceptable end.

Not for her.

Or him.

He knew she didn't like, approve of, or in any way agree with his decision, his way of coping with the reality of their marriage. But he could see no other option. If he found one, he would take it.

Because he no longer liked, or approved of—and he certainly wasn't enjoying—what was happening between them, the morass of pain and hurt in which his way had mired them.

15

Sarah's consciousness rose through the veils of sleep, tugging at her mind. She resisted the pull; it might be morning, but it was early yet and she was so snug and warm, her cheek resting on firm, resilient flesh, on a hot swell of hard muscle lightly dusted with curling hair, her body cradled in a pair of steely arms . . .

She opened her eyes, then drew in a slow, careful breath. She lay sprawled over Charlie, held securely in his arms. Naked, he lay on his back. Her fine lawn nightgown had ridden up to her waist; her bare legs were tangled with his amid the rumpled covers.

A peek at the distance to her edge of the bed confirmed that this was not his doing. He hadn't moved; she had.

She mentally cursed. From the slow cadence of his breathing, she thought he was still asleep, but from the morning light filtering into the room, she judged it was close to—indeed, possibly past—the time he usually awoke.

Drawing in a shallow breath, she held it, and tried to inch out of his arms.

They tightened. "No." Two seconds ticked by. "Just let me hold you."

His tone made her blink; this was not Charlie the arrogant but Charlie the vulnerable—a being she hadn't met before. She couldn't see his face without pushing back from his embrace and lifting her head, and with his arms lying heavy over her back she'd have to fight his hold to do that—and she was sure he wouldn't let her, not before he'd found his impassive mask and stuck it firmly in place. Curious, she let her tensed muscles ease; sinking back onto him, senses at full stretch, she waited.

He shifted his head; his lips pressed against her hair. "I'm sorry about your aunt's diary. You were close to her, weren't you?"

She focused on her hand, resting beside her face, her fingers spread over his chest, over his heart. "Yes." When he said nothing more, just waited, she went on, "She was . . . special to me, and that book was all I have to remember her by, and I'd only read the first pages—it starts in January 1816, so I expect it covers that year. She didn't use it as a diary so much as an occurrence book. The entry I read described a party at Lord Wragg's country seat, followed by a recipe for quince jelly extracted from his housekeeper."

"Daily life. The bits and pieces."

She nodded, her cheek shifting against his chest; she felt insensibly comforted by the simple nearness. The closeness. "I meant to go back and read it all when I had time . . . when the mood gripped me." At the time, her mind had been too full of her own thoughts to absorb anyone else's. She sighed. "But now it's gone and I'll never . . . never be able to use it to connect with her again. I feel like I've lost my last link to her."

Never again, she vowed, would she let the chance to connect with another soul slip through her fingers.

"But you haven't." His tone was gentle, soothing. Again his lips brushed her hair. "You loved her and she loved you—the diary was a symbol of that, but your love remains. You haven't lost that. Isn't that the real link?"

Sarah blinked. How ironic that he, so stubbornly determined to ignore their love, could see that, let alone put it into words.

Her lips firmed. If there was one thing Edith had taught her it was that when it came to people and emotions, there were symbols, words, and actions—and of those three, it was actions that spoke the most clearly, and most truly.

Her palm on his chest, she pushed back enough to lift her head and look at him. Enough to search his eyes and read his sincerity.

Enough to confirm that the vulnerability she'd sensed in him was real. That what she'd been fighting for, that link between them, hadn't been lost. That no matter what else, neither she nor he could lose it.

Wriggling her arms free, she reached up and framed his face. "Yes. You're right." She studied his blue eyes for one instant more, then she stretched up and kissed him.

With all the pent-up passion in her soul. There was no point in pretending, no point in holding back. She knew what she felt for him, and what he felt for her; that knowledge infused her actions, every languorous sweep of her tongue against his, every artful shift as she rose above him the better to share the kiss, the better to give her love free rein and incite and enjoy his.

He responded as she knew he would, and if on one level she gloried in his helplessness in that, in his inability to remain apart from her and their love at this level, she also appreciated every subtle nuance, every evidence of his desire, every scintilla of delight she felt as his hands gripped her waist, supported her, steadied her, then drifted to her breasts to pleasure her.

Until she drew her legs up, pressing her knees into the bed on either side of him, straddling his hips. Between their bodies, she reached down, and found him hard and ready, hot and heavy in her hand. Her nightgown had slithered down over her hips; his fingers left her breasts to tangle in the fine fabric, pulling it up again, then slipping beneath. His palms cruised her naked flanks, then curved about her bottom. Breaking from the kiss, one hand braced on his chest, she pushed back, with her other hand guided his rigid staff to her entrance.

Feeling him there, the blunt head caressing her slick flesh in blatant promise, made her shudder with sheer anticipation. From beneath her lashes, she watched his face, his eyes, as she rose a fraction higher, edged back a little more, and slowly, savoring every hot steely inch of him, impaled herself on him. Filled her body and her senses with him.

The raw hunger in his face told her all she needed to know; the all but quivering restraint he held so ruthlessly over his own strength, his own impulses, allowing her her way, allowing her to take the lead and script their engagement as she wished, was evidence enough of his commitment.

Lids falling, she leaned forward, braced both hands on his chest, and gave herself over to riding him. To savoring all, every last iota of the pleasure she derived from him, pleasuring him in return. Eyes closed, senses heightening, she concentrated on the heavy slick slide of his body into hers, on the alien but welcome penetration, on the repetitive rocking of her body over his, the rhythmic flexing of her thighs against his flanks. The burgeoning, building, overpowering physicality of their joining.

His hands had returned to her breasts, caressing, sensually massaging, tweaking her nipples into tight buds. Then her nightgown was open and he rose beneath her; she gasped as his hot mouth closed over one aching nipple while his clever fingers ministered to the other, sending shards of delight streaking through her, followed by waves of heated pleasure that pooled and coalesced low in her body. In her womb.

For long moments, head back, slowly riding him, she let sensation rule, let her senses expand and fill her mind. All but overwhelmed by sensual delight, by an awareness of her body and its potential for pleasure more extensive and more compelling than ever before, she slowed.

He growled, a guttural sound that sparked a completely different awareness. An instant later, even before she could lift her lids, he rolled, taking her with him, trapping them both in a welter of covers. Cushioned in the billows of the bed, he held her beneath him and thrust—hard, deep. With a cry, she arched; as he thrust again, even deeper, she desperately caught her breath, then wrapped her arms about him, lifted her legs and gripped his flanks, and raked her nails across his back as she joined him in frantic urgency as he rode her.

Hard, fast, desperate for fulfillment, willing to surrender all just to reach that peak.

And then they were there, panting, wanting, reaching, *stretching* for the glory.

It broke upon them, swept them up, shattered them, then on a gust of deep, mindless pleasure, surged through them and left them wracked.

Wrecked with pleasure. Smiling sillily, dizzy with delight, softly laughing, they slumped in each other's arms, and let the moment cradle them.

. . .

A bare hour later, dressed in her riding habit, Sarah clattered like a hoyden down the main staircase on her way to the breakfast parlor to catch Charlie before he had a chance to ride out. He, his resistance to their love, was weakening; now was the time to push just a little harder, and she'd realized how to do it.

She'd ask for his help. Charlie *always* responded when anyone asked for help; that response was an intrinsic, inherent part of his nature. If there was some trouble at the orphanage, who better, or more natural, for her to turn to?

Running down the main corridors wasn't ladylike; her habit's train over her arm, she hurried as fast as she could—and through the open doorway ahead saw him setting aside his napkin and rising from the table.

He was later than usual; the knowledge that he'd stayed in bed longer than the norm to hold her and comfort her over the diary—and to make love to her—buoyed her. Smiling brightly, she met him in the corridor outside the breakfast room. He met her smile with his usual cool demeanor, but she couldn't believe he'd already forgotten why he was late.

"I was hoping that you could ride out with me to the orphanage." Tilting her head, she looked into his eyes. "There's something going on there, and while I don't know what the problem is, I know I'd value your opinion."

Not a glimmer of the gentle smiles they'd shared only an hour before showed through his expressionless mask. "I don't think that's wise."

She blinked. Oh, no, no, no—they *weren't* going back to this. To his distant, coolly aloof attitude to her, and everything to do with her. She drew in a deep breath. "Charlie—"

"I don't think, my dear, that you comprehend the situation."

His tone brought her up short. This was the earl speaking, not Charlie, her husband, the man who regardless of his wishes loved her, but the feudal lord accustomed to being obeyed without question.

He went on, calmly, the steel in his voice unsheathed, "I have no interest in the orphanage. It's specifically yours and as such is no part of my life, not part of my responsibilities." His eyes held hers, and she couldn't see past the soft summer blue. "I have no connection with it, have had none in the past, and do not wish to involve myself with it in the future." He paused, then softly said, "I trust I make myself plain."

Her temper erupted; chill fury slid through her veins. She raised her head. *"Eminently."* She held his gaze, let him see her rage. Her muscles were quivering with the need to swing on her heel and storm off—before she said something she'd regret—but this time, she wasn't leaving so meekly. This time, she wasn't letting him escape.

She drew breath, and even more coldly than he, stated, "I understand perfectly. However, I had thought—" Her thoughts literally choked her; she broke off, then went on, if anything the ice in her voice even more intense. "I suspect you recall that in agreeing to marry you I insisted our marriage be a passionate one. If I remember aright, your answer was that you saw no impediment to that. Fool that I was, I believed you. I honestly believed that our marriage—*all* of it—would be more than a *hollow shell*."

He'd held her gaze throughout. His lashes had flickered once; his already clenched jaw had tightened even more.

She sensed the effort it cost him to maintain that rigid control. She quivered on the brink of saying more—of lashing out even more—but sanity returned enough to remind her of her aim—her unwavering goal.

Lips setting, she swung on her heel and stalked slowly, regally, away.

Charlie watched her go, and for the first time in his life understood what having his heart break felt like. His chest literally ached, as if some sword had cleaved him in two. His mind seemed detached; he realized she was heading for the stables—his immediate thought was that she hadn't breakfasted and should eat before riding out . . . but what was he going to do? Call her back and order her to eat?

He'd just resigned his right to care for her, or at least she would think he had.

Hearing a clatter behind him, realizing that Crisp was in the breakfast room and would without doubt have heard every word, he forced his legs to carry him to the library. Opening the door, he entered, and shut himself in.

Familiar comfort surrounded him, but brought no ease to the wounds inside. He felt as if his heart had been scoriated, clawed, and ripped. He knew—had lectured himself for the past hour let alone all the hours before—that this was how things had to be in order for him to function as he must . . . but increasingly some part of him, some surprisingly strong and fundamental part of him, was refusing to accept that. Refusing to make do with that.

Refusing to make her make do with only that.

Walking to the long windows, he stood and looked out. Unseeing. He'd known that she held a different, as he'd thought more feminine and flowery, expectation of their marriage; he hadn't known, when he'd told her he saw no impediment to theirs being a passionate marriage—that he was prepared to give her that, a passionate union— that by "passionate" she'd meant a union where love was freely and openly acknowledged.

He understood that now. Then . . . when she'd spoken of excitement, thrills, risks, and satisfaction, he'd thought she'd been referring to sexual passion.

Yet even if he'd understood her meaning, completely and clearly, at the time—and how could he have when he hadn't, then, understood what love was?—even if he had comprehended her meaning, he would still, regardless, have married her. Because by then he'd already known that she was his—his rightful wife, the lady he needed as his countess.

She still was. Nothing had changed; if anything, his conviction had only deepened. His commitment to her was deepening by the day— witness his difficulty with his feelings yesterday, and this morning. They—those emotions she stirred—were only growing stronger, more powerful, less governable.

Yet his first duty wasn't to her, but to the earldom. He'd been taught that from infancy, conditioned to, should any clash arise, place his own comfort and needs second to that duty. But . . . what of the vows he'd made before the altar in the church at Combe Florey?

To honor and cherish. As most would translate that, to love and protect. In part, he'd made that vow in bad faith, never intending, never imagining adhering to the first part of it. But regardless of his battle on that front, the second part of that vow was a promise he couldn't not keep—was incapable of not keeping. He couldn't not cherish her, and he certainly couldn't subdue or subvert the imperative to keep her safe. He hadn't comprehended how it would be before they'd wed, but now she was his, cherishing and protecting her were such fundamental instincts that he could no more stop himself from reacting in that way than he could stop the sun.

Letting out a painful, frustrated sigh, he dropped his head back and stared at the painted ceiling. This morning, after the hours they'd spent in their bed, he'd steeled himself to rebuff whatever renewed effort she might make to, figuratively speaking, open their bedroom door and weave love into their daytime interactions. He'd suspected she'd read those hours as proof he was weakening in his resolve to keep a sensible distance between them, and she had.

But the orphanage. Of all things to hit him with, she'd chosen that. His heart had literally leapt to accept her invitation and join her, to take care of whatever little problem they had—to see her with the children again, to join in . . . but he'd never be able to corral, to keep close and under guard, what he felt for her in that setting.

The effort to deny her—and his other self—had nearly slain him. He literally felt as if he were two men—that she and all he felt for her had driven a wedge through his heart, mind, and soul and split him in two. And the two halves were now locked in battle.

It couldn't go on. Aside from all else, the balance between those two halves was shifting, changing. The part that wanted her love and would surrender all and anything to secure it was growing stronger. He no longer knew what was right—what he should fight for, which half of him should triumph. He didn't even know which half he wanted to win.

He couldn't remember ever feeling this way, and there was no one he could turn to for advice. He was lost, adrift.

Completely and utterly at sea.

By the time Sarah reached the orphanage, she'd managed to, somewhat grimly, suppress her temper and all thoughts of he who had provoked it, but the news that awaited her was so strange it temporarily drove all other thoughts from her head.

"Ghosts?" Seated at the meeting table, flanked by Skeggs and Mrs. Dunstable, she stared at Katy.

Who grimaced. "That's what the children said. And more than a few of them heard it, and saw it, both on Saturday night and last night, too."

"What did they hear—and see?" Skeggs asked.

"A whooing noise, and chains clanking. Some of the older ones peeked out. They say it was all white and flapped about."

"Village lads," Mrs Dunstable stated. "Some old chains and a sheet."

Katy nodded. "Aye—so I suspect. But the younger ones are frightened, and some of them aren't sleeping. We've a few of them still in bed, poor mites, catching up now the sun is up and everyone else is around and they feel safe."

"A nuisance." Skeggs frowned. "The question is how to get rid of it."

Not an easy task. Sarah let the others discuss who they thought it might be, and if they might have a word with various elders, while she imagined . . . thought of the lads she knew and what might discourage them.

When the others concluded that there was precious little they could do without knowing which lads were involved—from Watchet, Taunton, Crowcombe, or any of the other villages dotted about the hills—she tapped the table. "I have an idea."

She outlined her plan. Katy grinned. Skeggs chuckled dryly. Mrs. Dunstable nodded. "Ingenious, my dear. Just like belling a cat."

As soon as they finished their meeting, and Skeggs and Mrs. Dunstable departed, Sarah summoned Kennett and together with Katy they walked around the house, studying the areas where the "ghost" had been seen, examining the various approaches to the house and the trees and bushes that grew nearby.

Eventually Kennett stood back and scratched his head. "Aye. I reckon that'd work. Fishing line'd be best, and we've enough cowbells in the shed to hook up. Jim and I'll get onto it. If that blighter comes back tonight, he'll get a right surprise."

Sarah smiled; she and Katy left Kennett to it, and headed back to the house. Once she was inside, the usual pandemonium engulfed her; she was drawn into this and that, and luncheon, then the afternoon, sped by.

Charlie called in at Finley House late that afternoon. He'd spent the day trying to find something to distract him from the sensation of cold iron lodged in his chest; given the stiffness that had invested their last meeting, calling on Sinclair was a last resort.

Yet business had always been a consuming interest, and Malcolm welcomed him readily, without any sign of constraint. They sat in his study and pored over the latest news sheets, reading between the lines of numerous business announcements. But even that no longer possessed sufficient power to quell Charlie's restlessness. While Malcolm read on, he laid down the sheet he'd been studying, rose and walked to the window.

At least the study looked onto the Quantocks rather than Crowcombe and the orphanage beyond.

Behind him he heard the muted crackle as Malcolm laid down the sheet he'd been perusing. Charlie felt Malcolm's gaze on his back, then Malcolm asked, "How is the countess faring?"

He managed not to stiffen. The inquiry had been careful, diffident, as if Malcolm knew he was treading on uncertain ground yet felt compelled to inquire.

Charlie started to shrug but stopped; thrusting his hands into his breeches pockets, he fixed his gaze on the scene outside. "She's well enough . . . but some diary of hers has gone missing. A keepsake from an aunt. She's upset, but there's nothing I can do about it." Even though he wished it were otherwise. The sense of helplessness irked, prodding him where he was still sensitive. "Then this morning she wanted me to go to the orphanage with her—as if I have the time."

Silence lengthened, then Malcolm said, "Perhaps . . . a new bride and all that. Spending some time with her might be in order . . . not that I'd know, of course, but that does seem to be the way of things."

Again he'd spoken almost warily, choosing his words, watching his tone. Charlie grimaced. "She and I have known each other for literally all her life. We don't need to learn about each other in the way most couples do."

Once again silence stretched, then Malcolm cleared his throat, and murmured, "You may be right, but . . . I was thinking more along the lines of what we all know so often occurs when attractive and still young married ladies such as your countess are not paid sufficient, and appropriate, attention by their husbands."

Charlie didn't—couldn't—move. It took every ounce of his considerable willpower to suppress his reaction—violent and instinctive— to the scenario Malcolm had painted. Sarah wouldn't, he told himself. Was Sinclair suggesting . . .

But then he heard again the diffidence in Malcolm's tone; he'd been trying, as any friend might, to make Charlie see . . .

Drawing his hands from his pockets, he faced Malcolm. "I'd better be going. The light will be fading soon."

Malcolm's expression was as inscrutable as his own. He rose and accompanied Charlie to the front door; they shook hands, then Charlie strode to where Storm was tied to the tree. Freeing the reins, he swung up to the saddle. With a curt salute to Malcolm, he turned down the road.

He clattered through Crowcombe; by a feat of will, he kept his gaze from the orphanage perched above. But he couldn't stop himself from wondering if Sarah had already started for home. Regardless, she'd take the track across the fields. The instant the last houses fell behind, he urged Storm into a gallop. He wanted to get home, to reassure himself that she had returned, that she was there, unharmed and well, once more within his keeping.

The following day, Sarah returned to the orphanage to learn whether her trap had been sprung during the night. It had. At just before midnight, the bells had pealed; Kennett, Jim, and Joseph had rushed outside, but all they'd seen was a white-clad figure fleeing across the north field, then he'd jumped on a waiting horse and ridden away.

The children were relieved and happy; many had seen the ghost turn tail and run. Most now viewed the incident as a performance put on for their titillation; there would be no more sleepless nights.

She was back on Blacktail and riding home to the Park before she allowed her mind to refocus on what awaited her there. She wasn't happy, yet her hours at the orphanage, both today and yesterday, had calmed her—their need of her, their appreciation of her contribution and abilities and the success of her plan, had been balm to her bruised soul.

Reaching the Park, she rode into the stable; leaving Blacktail with the stable boy, she walked to the house, turning over in her mind the one point in the recent drama that didn't quite fit. They'd been certain the culprits would prove to be local lads, but when she'd questioned Kennett, Jim and later Joseph more closely, the figure they'd described was that of a man. An adult male, heavily built, thickset—very definitely not a youth.

Why would an adult male cavort around the orphanage pretending to be a ghost?

The others had all shrugged. Kennett had suggested the man might be "touched in his upper works." Yet Sarah didn't think so. The sheet, the chains, the careful approach at midnight, all suggested planning, which wasn't a hallmark of those "touched in the upper works."

Still puzzling, she entered the house and went to her sitting room. Stripping off her gloves, she rang for tea. It arrived promptly. To her immense surprise, Charlie came with it.

Under her openly bemused gaze, he sat in the armchair he occupied in the evenings and accepted a cup.

Taking her own cup and saucer, she sat on the chaise, sipped, and wondered.

The footman retreated. Charlie balanced his cup on his saucer. Without looking at her, he asked, "How are matters at the orphanage?"

Ah-a. Despite all, she was tempted to pour out the story of the ghost, and see what he thought of the oddity of man rather than youth, yet his words of the morning before replayed all too clearly in her head. They still stung. Eyes on her cup, she shrugged. "Well enough."

She sipped, then drained her cup. Setting it aside, she reached for the mending basket and pulled it to her. Finding another blanket with a hole to darn, she lifted it into her lap, and gave her attention to the task.

Charlie glanced at her; she felt his gaze on her face. A minute ticked by, then he finished his tea. He rose, set the cup and saucer on the tray, and without another word left her.

Head bent over her mending, she listened to his footsteps fade down the corridor; then the library door opened, and a second later, it shut.

On Saturday morning, Sarah had just finished arranging the week's menus with Figgs when Crisp entered her sitting room, bearing his silver salver.

"This note arrived from the orphanage, ma'am. The young lad, Jim, is waiting in case you wish to send a reply."

Sarah took the note, suppressing a frown and an instinctive "Oh, dear, what now?"

One glance through the few lines Katy had penned confirmed her instincts were sound. "Good Lord!"

"Is there some problem, ma'am?"

Sarah looked up into Crisp's concerned, and willing to be helpful, face. "Some . . . *blackguard* has salted the orphanage well."

She could think of a few other names to call him, but "blackguard" would have to do.

"Dear me." Crisp frowned. "But why?"

"Indeed." Sarah folded the note and slipped it into her pocket. "It appears we have someone intent on causing problems for the orphanage. I'll have to go and see how bad it is. Please tell Jim to wait until I change into my riding habit."

Crisp bowed as she left the room. Ten minutes later, on Blacktail's back with Jim on a stout cob keeping pace, she headed north. By the time she reached the orphanage, she'd thought of how to meet the most immediate requirement.

"We'll have Wilson bring up water in barrels," she said to Katy as she tied Blacktail's reins to the rail outside the orphanage's front door. Wilson was the carter in Crowcombe. "I'll stop in on my way home. I'll tell him he can draw from the well at the manor, then I'll stop in there and see my parents—I'm sure they won't mind, and there's barrels there aplenty, so at least we'll have water to see us through."

Katy nodded. "Aye—you'd best come and see. Kennett says it's not as bad as it might have been, yet bad enough."

Walking through the house, smiling reassuringly at the children she passed, Sarah followed Katy to the stone-walled well that lay beyond the back of the northernmost wing.

Kennett was standing over it, glumly staring into the black mouth of the deep shaft. He looked up as Sarah joined him. "Poured a ten-pound bag of salt in, he did." He pointed at a jute bag lying beside the well. "Left it for us to find, the so-and-so." He kicked it. "Luckily, with the weather so cold we've got snow still on the hills. Water table's already rising, but once the thaw hits, this well'll flush—we're high, so although the well is cut deep, there's a lot of seepage from the sides. See?"

He pointed at the inner wall of the well. Sarah saw that the stones were indeed wet, even though at present the water level was fathoms lower. "So the salt will wash away?"

"Bit by bit. The water should be drinkable after a month or so."

She kept her sigh of relief to herself. "We can manage until then." She explained her idea of supplying drinking water from the manor.

Kennett nodded. "That would be the closest good source."

And they wouldn't have to pay for the water. Sarah turned for the house. "I'll get onto organizing it right away. As for who did this . . ."

"It'll be that idiot we chased off Monday night," Kennett said. "Didn't like being made a fool of, I'll be bound."

Katy nodded. "Aye—that'll be it, right enough. Tit for tat. Still, after this bit of maliciousness, he'll have had his revenge. I doubt he'll bother us again."

Sarah frowned. She wished she could feel so confident, but salting a well seemed a very deliberate act, rather than a simple lashing out. Yet what else could it be?

The question niggled, but she had more than enough to occupy her for the rest of the morning organizing the supply of water to the orphanage; by the time she headed home for luncheon, the niggle had slid to the back of her mind.

On Monday morning she rode up to the orphanage, and saw Doctor Caliburn's gig outside. She tied up Blacktail, telling herself it was surely just one of the usual illnesses or accidents associated with a large group of children . . . she strode inside and pounced on the first member of staff she met.

"What's happened?"

Jeannie grimaced. "Quince." She spoke softly, trying to hide her worry from the children about them. "You'd best go up and see."

Eyes widening—Jeannie's worry very effectively conveyed—Sarah walked quickly to the stairs, and hurried up them.

She rushed into the attic and found Doctor Caliburn repacking his bag. And Quince sitting in her armchair with her arm in a paisley sling.

Katy, hovering over Quince, looked up, and grimaced. "Iced steps. That blackguard must have slunk close during the night and poured water over the back steps."

"I went out first thing, like I always do, to fetch the milk for the babies." Quince's voice was gruff. "My feet went sailing from under me." She pointed at her cradled arm. "I cracked this on the way down."

Doctor Caliburn shut his black bag. "It's a clean break, but it'll be slow to mend. You mustn't put any stress on that arm until it's fully healed."

Although he spoke to Quince, his eyes meaningfully touched Sarah's. She turned to Quince. "You'll have to take care, Quince. You're the best with the babies—they need you healthy and well. Lily can come up and be your hands for you until your arm heals."

"Aye, well, she's already had to feed them this morning, and they do sleep for hours, but there's the preparation and cleaning—the poor girl can't do everything."

"I'll get someone from the village to come up and help. We'll sort something out." Exchanging a glance with Katy, Sarah turned to see the doctor out. "I'll come back in a moment and we'll plan."

Doctor Caliburn waited until they were on the stairs to say, "I'm quite serious about her being extra careful. She's not young, and old bones knit slowly."

Ahead of him, Sarah asked, "How is she otherwise?"

"Badly shaken, I'd say, and she must be bruised, although she'd have none of the laudanum I suggested. Said she had to wake at the first cry from one of her charges."

Sarah nodded. "I'll have them move another bed up there for Lily, so Quince won't have to cope alone, even at night."

"Good." Reaching the bottom of the stairs, Caliburn bowed over her hand. "And if you want someone extra who's reliable, you might try Mrs. Cothercombe's Lizzie. She's a steady soul and good with children."

"Thank you. I'll stop by at the Cothercombes' and ask if she can help."

S arah did, then rode slowly home. She was starting to feel like the Dutch boy plugging leaks in the dike; where and what would their next "leak" be?

More importantly, who was behind this? Could it really be a deranged simpleton now bent on revenge? Regardless, had they seen the last of the accidents, or were there more to come?

Those questions revolved in her head, following her through the rest of the day and into the evening.

Charlie couldn't help but notice her absorption, her concern. Yet what it was over, what was so troubling her, he didn't know; he didn't even know if it involved the orphanage or something else. But the impulse to aid her, to ask and do and set things right, was eating him alive.

It was, quite literally, like a beast burrowing under his skin; he couldn't ignore it.

But after his so-unwise words about certain aspects of her life not being of any interest to him—undoubtedly the most stupid remark he'd made in his life; how could he cherish and protect her if he didn't know what was happening in her life?—he could do nothing to soothe the burning, incessant itch. On such matters, he could no longer ask and expect to be answered; he had to wait for her to tell him—if she ever did.

He'd lied, but he couldn't take back the words, any more than he could admit the falsehood. If he did, he'd open the floodgates . . . and he was very sure he couldn't handle what would ensue.

One thing she'd demonstrated over and over again was that their love was stronger than he was. Stronger than his will, powerful enough to override his determination. It could and assuredly would control him, and that he could never risk.

So . . . as the evening closed around them, he stared at the pages of his book, and tried to keep his attention on it, rather than on his wife, sitting on the chaise mending some threadbare towel, a frown deeply etched on her face.

By Friday morning Sarah was close to biting her nails, both anxious and frustrated, wondering when the next message from the orphanage would arrive and what news of disaster it would bring.

On Wednesday had come the news that the fences keeping the animals from the fields and the kitchen garden had been broken, and their small band of livestock had spent enough of the night trampling through the crops and vegetable plots to have ruined much of what was in the ground. Luckily, it was winter, and other than some early plantings in the kichen garden, they'd lost little more than cabbages, easy enough to replace.

Nevertheless she'd ridden north again, and spent most of the day soothing and calming, getting both the staff and children involved in redesigning the kitchen garden prior to replanting, then organizing with Kennett and Jim to have the fences repaired.

The unbudgeted expenditure wasn't her primary worry. What would happen next was. Fences and wells were one thing; after Quince's broken arm, she lived in dread that someone else would be hurt.

She'd spent the hours since wrestling with the question of what to do, if there even was anything they could do. She'd consulted with Skeggs and Mrs. Duncliffe, but no more than she could they imagine the constable in Watchet taking much notice of this sort of "crime," let alone being of any practical help.

Sitting at her escritoire, she tapped a pencil on the blotter and grimaced. Meekly waiting for the next blow to fall went very much against her grain.

The sound of Crisp's measured footsteps reached her, then he appeared in the sitting room doorway. Although he was carrying his salver, to her relief it bore only a card, no note.

Crisp advanced, bowed, and offered the card. "A solicitor from Taunton to see you, ma'am."

Sarah lifted the card and read: *Mr. Arnold Switherton, Switherton & Babcock, Solicitors, East Street, Taunton*. She frowned. Charlie had, of course, noticed her concern and her extra trips to the orphanage; over the last days he'd developed the habit of informing her where he was going when he rode out. Today he was visiting Sinclair. She couldn't imagine what Mr. Switherton wanted. She looked up at Crisp. "The gentleman asked to see me? Not the earl?"

"He specifically asked to see you, ma'am."

Brows rising, she laid down the card. "Show him in." With a bow, Crisp withdrew.

Sarah considered, but elected to remain seated before her escritoire. Was this about the orphanage again? But it was a different solicitor; a different office, too.

And the man Crisp ushered into her sitting room was cut from a distinctly different cloth than the hapless Haynes. Mr. Arnold Switherton had a long thin nose with pinched nostrils, and his face bore an expression of perpetual distaste. Sarah found it hard not to dislike him on sight, and his opening speech did nothing to endear him.

"Countess." His bow was stultifyingly correct. "I am here to present an offer for a property to which I understand you still retain title." His brows contracted. "Most unusual in light of your recent marriage. I would have preferred to discuss such matters with your husband, however, I have been instructed to lay the offer before you."

Sarah did not invite him to sit. She waited, silent and unresponsive, while he fished in his leather satchel and drew out a slim sheaf of papers.

He glanced at them. "Yes—this is all in order." He offered her the papers and she took them.

"As you will see here"—reaching over the top of the sheets, Switherton pointed—"the offer is for Quilley Farm, house and land, and the sum offered is here." He pointed farther down the sheet.

Sarah looked at a sum that had grown significantly since Haynes's offer. She scanned down the page, then turned over to the next, and the next, ignoring Switherton's surprised frown. After scanning the last page, she looked up at him. "Who is your client?"

"Ah—that, my dear countess, is not something you need to know."

"Indeed?" Her icy hauteur and the cold fury behind it made Switherton blink. "And I am not your dear anything, Mr. Switherton."

He swallowed, carefully inclined his head in apology, but then rallied and drew himself up. "My client insists on complete anonymity. I comprehend you would, of course, have no experience in such matters, but such a stance is not unknown when buying land."

"I daresay." Sarah had had enough of Mr. Switherton. "Regardless, I have no interest in selling Quilley Farm. You may tell your anonymous client that." She held out the papers.

Switherton stepped back, refusing to take them. "This offer is a very generous one, Lady Meredith. I strongly advise that you seek your husband's counsel before you act rashly only to later repent. I'm sure the earl will see the sense in capitalizing on my client's whimsical caprice in offering such a patently ridiculous sum for such a property. Ladies cannot be expected to understand such matters—I urge you to lay this matter before your husband. He will know what's best."

Sarah let a moment pass in utter silence, then quietly said, "Mr. Switherton, what is beyond my comprehension is that you have failed to perceive that the title to Quilley Farm remains in my hands *for a reason*. In part, that reason is so that I can refuse all such offers as *this*"—she flung the papers at Switherton; he gasped, clutched, and caught them to his chest—"saving my husband, the earl, from having to deal with the importunings of solicitors such as yourself. Such refusals are not rash—they are entirely deliberate. Quilley Farm will remain in my hands—for reasons that do not concern *you*, that will not change. And I assure you the only repenting I am likely to do is that the earl is not here to deal with you as, in my view, you deserve—there are, indeed, instances where being a lady is restricting."

She held Switherton's gaze for a pregnant minute, then calmly said, "Crisp—show Mr. Switherton out."

"Indeed, ma'am. This way, sir."

Sarah hid a smile at Crisp's tone, one that effectively conveyed that, in the earl's absence, should Switherton give him the slightest excuse, Crisp would be only too happy to demonstrate what she and her household deemed Switherton deserved.

The thought laid her temper to rest. She glanced at her escritoire, but there was nothing more to do there. Rising, she returned to the chaise; there was mending—as always—waiting, but . . .

She was contemplating a walk in the gardens when Crisp returned to report Switherton's departure and to ask if, in the earl's absence and as she'd eaten so little at the breakfast table that morning, she would like an early luncheon on a tray in the sitting room.

"Thank you, Crisp. That would be lovely." She smiled as he departed; Crisp and Figgs, and indeed all the staff, were being very kind. Attentive but not intrusively so. They'd learned her routine and were fitting in with it, rather than imposing that of their last mistress, Serena, on her. That had made filling the position of Charlie's countess much easier, at least on that score.

As for all the rest that the position entailed . . . thoughts of that occupied her mind while she ate. Revived by the succession of light dishes Cook had prepared—she'd been unable to stomach more than tea and toast over the last few mornings—she decided a walk in the rose garden would complete her restoration.

Pacing along the paved paths, insensibly heartened by the sight of buds—real buds—pushing out along the sides of otherwise dead-looking sticks, she'd completely put aside the vexed question of the strange occurrences at the orphanage, and quite banished Switherton and his offer from her mind, when a horrible, unexpected, unlooked-for thought slipped into her head, and connected them.

"Good God." Halting, she stared unseeing across the lawns. What if . . . ?

What if there really was a connection? If after being refused once—no, twice; after they'd married, someone had approached Charlie to buy the farm, and it was after that that the accidents at the orphanage had started. What if the anonymous buyer had decided to make life difficult for the orphanage and her, to irritate and aggravate her and even Charlie, and then offer a "patently ridiculous" amount to prompt her to wash her hands of the place and sell?

Surely not. She shook herself; her mind was playing morbid tricks.

Yet once the notion had taken root, it wouldn't die. She paced on, examining the idea; it was only the relative timing of the accidents and the offers that suggested such a heinous connection—and the timing of the offers could be explained perfectly innocently. Anyone not acquainted with her might well imagine that after a few weeks of wedded bliss her interest in her "hobby" would wane, and she'd be more amenable to selling.

There was, she told herself, no per se reason to link the accidents with the offers to buy the orphanage.

16

Except . . . she couldn't get the possibility out of her mind.

Saturday afternoon found her back in the rose garden. The place was quiet, with no one to see her as she paced and occasionally muttered to herself. In her sitting room there was always the chance that Charlie, Crisp, or one of the footmen or maids would pass by and see her—and grow even more concerned for her than they already were.

Since her horrible thought the previous day she'd been distracted, consumed with trying to disprove and thus dismiss the notion of a link between the accidents and the offers. Despite her best efforts, she'd yet to succeed.

Indeed, she'd given up, and was now trying to decide what to do—from whom to seek advice. Her father? Despite all he knew of her, he would probably think—as in some part of her mind she herself still thought—that she was drawing far too long a bow and worrying herself for no reason.

Gabriel Cynster? While with his business background he no doubt would accept that such things might occur, he didn't know her personally all that well, and her account of the accidents and her suspicions might sound . . . well, a trifle hysterical. And he would certainly wonder why she was speaking with him and not Charlie.

Which left her with one obvious person to approach—Charlie. She'd snubbed his earlier inquiry when she'd believed she'd succeeded in dealing with the "ghost." Since then matters had gone downhill, but he hadn't asked again and his earlier disavowal of all interest in the orphanage still echoed in her mind, still cut. So she'd avoided saying anything, but . . . he knew something was preying on her peace, just not what.

And he did want to know. Indeed, he seemed absolutely tormented that he didn't know.

She grimaced; arms folded, she turned and paced on. If she walked into his library and said she needed his opinion on problems with the orphanage, she'd immediately have his full attention. He wouldn't mention his earlier words, or hers. It would all be so terribly polite but, to her mind, also terribly unsatisfactory.

It was all so *stupid*. In their bedchamber, no matter the constraint between them—his careful wariness, her irritation—neither of them could deny what happened there, that no matter his feelings or hers, love ruled—absolutely and completely, without quarter. But the instant they left that room, a wall went up between them, and she'd yet to find any way under, over, or around it, much less through it.

She wanted to knock it down, to shake its foundations so it came tumbling down and it was impossible for him to rebuild it. She still had no idea how to accomplish that, but giving him a way to soothe his increasingly abraded protectiveness without acknowledging that said protectiveness was there, so painfully present, *because he loved her* seemed a very bad move, a seriously backward step.

If she did such a thing, he would see it, and cling to it, as evidence that his way—with his daytime wall intact—could, and in time would, work. It couldn't, it wouldn't, but he was a man, and almost as stubborn as she was.

Yet if she didn't seek his help, help he could and would give . . . ?

What if she were right, and the accidents and offers for the orphanage were linked?

"Damn!" She halted, wrestling with the notion that she owed it to the orphanage staff and the children to swallow her pride and seek Charlie's help now, immediately, before anything more happened, before anyone else got hurt. Yes, approaching him would harm her personal position, but . . . she was stubborn, more stubborn than he. She would come about.

Jaw setting, she breathed in and lifted her head, looking toward the library. A movement at the other end of the terrace, near her sitting room, caught her eye.

Barnaby Adair, coming up from the stables.

Everything she'd heard about Barnaby raced across her mind—all Charlie had said of him, all Jacqueline, Pris, and others had let fall. Penelope's questions. She didn't give herself time to question her judgment, but hailed him and waved.

He heard, then saw her. When she picked up her skirts and hurried across the lawn, he halted and waited.

"Sarah." He took the hand she offered and bowed over it.

Disregarding all formality, she clutched his hand. "I need your opinion—it's quite urgent. Can you spare a few minutes?"

Intelligent blue eyes searched her face. "However many you need."

She gestured to her sitting room. "Come in and sit down."

They went in; at her wave, he sat on the chaise. She stood before the hearth, pressed her hands together, then drew in a breath and commenced. "I own a farm—Quilley Farm—just outside Crowcombe, a little way north of here. The farm's just a house with a few fields, not large, but it's run as an orphanage." Briefly she explained about her godmother's legacy, then went on, "Early last month, a solicitor called on me at the orphanage to present an offer from an unnamed client to buy the farm. I refused. That seemed to be that, but later, after we married, a similar approach was made to Charlie—they, whoever they are, knew the farm's title had passed to him on our marriage, but although it did, he passed it immediately back via the marriage settlements."

Barnaby's blue eyes were fixed on her face, his expression a testimony to utter concentration. He nodded, the lines about his mouth a trifle tight. "Then what?"

"Then . . ." She drew in a deep breath. "Accidents started happening." She began to pace, and succinctly described each incident in order.

"So you see, things seem to be escalating. I can't believe, as the staff do, that these are just the acts of some unhinged man. And *then*." Halting, she fixed her eyes on Barnaby's face. "Another solicitor called on me here yesterday morning. Charlie was out, and the man asked to see me specifically. He brought another offer—an even larger offer, one even he admitted was patently ridiculous—for the farm. He was high-handed and arrogant, but before I turned him away, I demanded the name of his client, but he insisted that was confidential."

Barnaby had proved a good listener, yet as Sarah paused and looked more closely at him, she realized his eyes had grown round, that he was sitting amazingly upright, utterly still, that his blue gaze had grown distant, as if he were seeing something she couldn't.

Then he blinked and met her eyes. "Ah—sorry. I just . . ." Again his eyes got that glazed, dazed look. "You said the orphanage was to the north . . . did you mean in this valley—between Watchet and Taunton?"

She frowned. "Yes."

He suddenly stood up—so abruptly she took an involuntary step back. He held up his hands placatingly. "Just wait."

She realized it was excitement—excitement so intense he was all but vibrating with it—that choked his voice.

"I need to check something with Charlie. Just stay there—I'll be back in a moment—and then we'll decide what to do."

Astonished, Sarah watched him rush from the room. His footsteps strode—almost running—down the corridor; she heard the library door open, then shut.

"Well." She stared at the open doorway for a moment, then moved to the chaise. He'd said "stay there," but presumably she could sit.

At his desk in the library, Charlie stared at the pen poised between his fingers. The ink had dried on the nib. On the blotter lay a concise, as-yet-incomplete summary of all he'd learned regarding railway finances from Malcolm Sinclair. He'd started writing it as something he could actually do that might be useful, to distract himself from what he wasn't able to do—ease whatever burden Sarah was laboring under.

The fact that he couldn't—that courtesy of their current situation, he was unable to protect her, his wife, as every instinct he possessed insisted he should—wasn't just a source of unease. His inability to act was eating at the foundation of who he was, of the man he knew he should be.

Underneath all, of the man he wanted to be.

His push to lock her, and all he felt for her, out of his daily life had resulted in his being locked out of her life. He hadn't foreseen that, hadn't considered what it would mean. How it would cut him off from something he now realized was vital.

Jaw clenching, he tapped the nib on the page, leaving small, smudged dots. This—their life as he'd scripted it—wasn't working; there was too much that was wrong, too many emotions weighing on him. He had to find some way to change things . . . but how?

He had no idea. Especially as, when it came down to it, he was still, despite all, unwilling to allow love free rein in his life.

He heard hurrying footsteps outside the door an instant before Barnaby burst into the room. A transformed Barnaby; Charlie blinked at the glow in Barnaby's face as he rushed to the desk.

"I've just been speaking with Sarah—tell me it's real?" Leaning on the desk, Barnaby fixed his eyes on Charlie's, excitement pouring from him. "After all our searching, I can barely believe it's been under our noses all along. And what better case to flush out our villain?"

A chill swept through Charlie. He stared at Barnaby, uncomprehending but with premonition solidifying second by second to icy certainty in his veins.

Seeing his blankness, Barnaby paused. "But perhaps I'm leaping to conclusions. Is this farm a target? Will it be crucial to a railway line?"

What farm? But Charlie knew. Slowly, he laid aside his pen. "Quilley Farm."

Barnaby registered his odd tone, tried to read his eyes and failed. "Sarah just told me about the accidents. They sound like the work of our villain, and combined with the offers for the property—"

"Offers? Plural?"

Lips tightening, Barnaby nodded. "But it all hinges on whether this farm is critical to a future railway line. Is it?"

It took effort to suppress his emotions enough to think. He drew in a breath. His control was shaky, tenuous, but he knew the land, the topography. It took only a second's consideration to see it. "Yes." His jaw clenched. "*Absolutely.* Once the Bristol-Taunton line is in, a spur from Taunton to Watchet would be not just obvious, but a commercial gold mine. And the valley narrows where the farm is—the property includes all of a shelf of land over which the railway would have to go."

His mind already elsewhere, he rose, went to a set of drawers and opened the lowest. "Have a look at the map. The land beyond Crowcombe rises sharply and there's nowhere—no space—to put in curves. The rail line would have to rise earlier, from before Crowcombe via the long upward slope south of the farmhouse, then go straight across the ledge and on through the fields to the north. That would be a clear run, easy engineering."

Dragging a large map from the drawer, he turned and flicked it out over the desk. "Running a line along the valley bottom, you could get as far as just past Crowcombe, but there's no way to go farther."

Barnaby flattened the map and bent over it. "So—no option but to buy that farm."

Charlie didn't bother nodding. He pointed out the farm on the map. "If you'll excuse me for a moment . . ."

He didn't wait for any acknowledgment, didn't care what Barnaby was thinking; all he knew as he opened the library door was what he was feeling. A species of horror beyond anything he'd ever known. And on its heels a black fury.

Perched on the chaise, Sarah was debating following Barnaby when she heard the door to the library close and a man's deliberate footsteps head her way.

She recognized the stride as Charlie's an instant before he appeared in the doorway. His eyes pinned her where she sat, but the distance was too great for her to read their expression; he hesitated, then turned and reached to either side, and ominously quietly—with ruthlessly controlled strength—closed both doors.

A ripple of reaction slithered down her spine. It prompted her to sit straighter; instead, declining to be intimidated, she leaned back against the chaise and watched as he drew near.

Stride slow and deliberate, he crossed the room; halting before the hearth, he looked down at her.

She studied his face, pale, set, every plane, every line unforgivingly harsh. His expression for once wasn't impassive; it was strained, almost tortured.

His eyes trapped hers, held them. He drew in a tight breath. "I just learned, from Barnaby, that there have been accidents at the orphanage.

And that you've received offers for the property—offers you suspect might be linked to the accidents." His gaze held hers, ruthless and hard. "In short, you believe you as the orphanage's owner are the target for some villain intent on forcing you to sell."

She said nothing, simply watched him.

Suddenly his eyes blazed. *"Why didn't you tell me?"*

It was a cry from the heart—tormented and true. He flung away. "You're my *wife*!" He paced away, then swung back. "It's my *duty* to protect you—I took *vows* to cherish and defend you. How can I do that if I don't even know when some villain has you in his sights?"

He shot a furious look at her; she met it with outward calm. Her temper had risen, but it was his she found intriguing; her rigidly controlled husband didn't lose his temper.

"You *knew* the accidents were serious—you've been worrying about them for weeks. Yet you wouldn't tell me—I asked, but no, you brushed me aside." His eyes were a turbulent sea of emotions, his gestures abrupt, muscles taut. "Yet the instant Barnaby appeared you poured your troubles into his ear—"

With a growl, he flung away, one hand rising to run through his hair, disrupting the elegant cut. Fascinated, Sarah saw that fist clench, tug, then abruptly release; violently he swung and paced back, halting before her, eyes burning with naked emotion.

"You deliberately hid all of this from me—all that threatened you." His voice hadn't gained in volume but in raw, tortured strength. "You refused to tell me what I had every right to know. What I *needed* to know."

He choked. His eyes blazed. *"Why?"*

A furious demand, a tortured plea.

Looking into his eyes, Sarah saw, understood, a great deal more than she had. Pain roiled in the blue, put there by all he couldn't help but feel. It was real, stark; she couldn't mistake it.

But she wasn't about to accept any more than the tiniest portion of the blame.

"Why?" With an effort, she kept her tone even, her eyes locked on the raging fury in his. "Because you made it plain that the orphanage was solely my concern, no responsibility of yours, that matters pertaining to it held no interest whatever for you. You made it very clear that the orphanage was a part of my personal life, and not in any way a part of yours."

She hesitated, then went on, "Isn't that what you've been telling me for weeks—ever since we married? Isn't *this*—not knowing, not being bothered, not being included in my life—what you *wanted*?"

Seeing blankness creep across his eyes, sensing his sudden loss of anchor, she paused, then, still holding his gaze, more quietly stated, "I didn't tell you because I believed you didn't want to know."

He didn't look away, didn't turn to conceal what she would see in his eyes, even though his muscles tensed and she knew the impulse rode him.

Instead, he stood there, looking down at her, and she saw the first crack appear in his wall, saw it widen, saw the whole edifice sway, buckle, then fall, tumbling down until there was nothing left, no barrier between them.

For a moment, silence reigned, absolute and compelling, then he drew a long, painfully tight breath, blindly moved to the armchair opposite and sank down, his eyes never leaving hers.

Unshuttered, no more shields.

"I've changed my mind."

The words were low, riding on a wave of emotion. She knew he wasn't referring only to the orphanage.

Slowly he sat back, his jaw tensing, his eyes still on hers. "About everything. About us. But . . . the orphanage. We have to deal with that now. For the rest . . . we can talk about that later."

It was a question; he waited for her answer—her agreement. Recognizing that the sudden about-face had left him emotionally giddy, that he wasn't as sure, as confident in dealing with the emotions between them as she, knowing it was midafternoon and Barnaby was somewhere in the house, no doubt impatient to join them, she inclined her head.

He drew a fractionally easier breath. "Tell me about the accidents. And the offers."

She did, quickly and concisely; he was more familiar with the situation than Barnaby, so it didn't take as long.

When she finished, he studied her for a moment, then said, "What you don't know . . ."

Succinctly, Charlie told her of Barnaby's mission. He didn't need to explain the connection; from the arrested look in her eyes, she saw that immediately. He described the various avenues they'd each been pursuing—he extracting a detailed understanding of railway finances from Malcolm while Barnaby and Gabriel concentrated on identifying parcels of land the villain might target on the likely route of the Bristol-Taunton line.

Grimly he concluded, "It seems we weren't thinking far enough ahead, and so looked in the wrong direction." He glanced at the door. "We should get Barnaby—I left him studying the map in the library." He looked back at Sarah.

The news of their villain and his past had alarmed her; she'd seen the need to focus on the orphanage, on how to protect it. She nodded. "It's time for tea. We can have some while we talk."

Rising, he tugged the bellpull; when Crisp appeared, she ordered tea while Charlie sent a footman to summon Barnaby. "Tell him to bring the map."

Ten minutes later, the three of them were seated around a low table set between the chaise and the armchair, with the map spread out upon it.

After confirming that Quilley Farm would indeed be vital for any rail link between Taunton and Watchet, and that therefore their villain was all but guaranteed to be behind the offers and accidents, Barnaby reported on his investigations to date. "Nothing yet from Montague, but he liked your suggestion of searching for the source of funds—he thinks he knows how to get some answers. And Gabriel and I identified a few properties that might interest our man between Bristol and Taunton, but we found no evidence he's been active around there."

He grimaced. "Now it seems we weren't focusing sufficiently far into the future, but with the London-Bristol line only just in the earliest stages of syndication, with the Bristol-Taunton line to come after that, who would have dreamed our man would already be working on a third-generation line?"

"You said it yourself." Charlie lowered his cup. "He's cautious. Unless you were a local involved in goods transport and so aware of the growth in the region and the growth to come, there'd be little reason to imagine a line from Taunton to Watchet would be built. Certainly the commercial imperatives wouldn't be obvious."

Barnaby humphed. "He's cautious *and* clever. And devilishly in the know."

Sitting back, they sipped, and discussed what they knew of the man, and how to learn more. Sarah set down her cup. "I really don't think those solicitors are going to tell us who he is."

"Leave that to me." Balancing a small notebook on his knee, Barnaby jotted down the names of the three firms. "They're all in Taunton. Interesting that he made each offer through a separate solicitor."

"Less risk the solicitors—they're all legitimate local concerns—would find his continuing interest in the property unusual." Charlie grimaced. "Even if you do get a name, what are the odds every name will be different, and will be companies rather than a person?"

"True." Barnaby looked up. "But the solicitors had to have been contacted by someone, whether by letter or in person, and they must have reported back, presumably to that same person. We might get some clue there."

"Perhaps. Meanwhile"—Charlie met Sarah's eyes—"we'll do what we can to make the orphanage safe. Then we'll have to wait for our villain's next ploy."

A far from satisfactory situation, but by the time he followed Sarah into their bedchamber that night, Charlie was resigned to that being all they could sensibly do. Sarah's latest refusal had lobbed the ball back to the villain; the initiative was now his.

Together with Barnaby, they'd spent the evening, through dinner and later, considering ways and means to protect the orphanage and its occupants. Not a simple task. When Sarah had suggested guards, Barnaby had grown grave and pointed out that this might well prove their one real chance to catch this villain, who had already killed several times and whose scheme was putting so much at risk. With the stakes so high, they shouldn't do anything to alert him to their interest; if he got the slightest hint they were watching, waiting for him to show his hand, he'd draw back and disappear.

When all was said and done, there was a whole country and a plethora of railways in the offing; if he slipped away from them here, their chances of catching up with him elsewhere weren't good.

Sarah had been concerned for the children and staff, but had, very reluctantly, agreed. For himself, Charlie was torn. Allowing those he viewed as under his protection to remain at any risk whatever did not sit well.

Closing the door, shutting them in, alone, he paused, watching as Sarah walked slowly, still absorbed with her worries, to stand before one window. All the other curtains were drawn, but that window remained unscreened, the view over the lake and the gardens at night illuminated by the rising moon. A single candle on her dressing table and the fire burning steadily in the grate were the only sources of light in the room.

Through the flickering shadows, he studied her, her slim, slender back, the regal set of her head, the soft curls of gilded brown tumbling over her nape. Felt again the reality that she was his.

And remembered, vividly, all he'd felt earlier—all he'd had to shove behind a mental door so he could function and deal rationally with Barnaby and her, with searching for the villain and protecting the orphanage. He'd managed, but . . .

The self-horror still remained. He hadn't understood, not until that moment in the library when Barnaby's revelations had ripped the veils from his eyes, just how deeply he'd been fooling himself. He'd convinced himself that his duty to the earldom had to come first; in reality, he had no duty more sacred, more fundamental to his life, than the one he owed her.

He'd stormed into her sitting room driven by so many emotions he hadn't known which was dominant—fury, fear, rejection, hurt—sheer panic that he'd created a situation where she'd been in danger and he hadn't even known. Those emotions had left him shredded inside. Then her question—wasn't that what he'd wanted?—had brought him up short, left him facing the outcome of his emotional cowardice. His emotional withholding.

For it had been that, consciously as well as subconsciously. But he couldn't any longer pretend.

She was the center of his life—from her all else he wanted, all he *needed,* flowed. Family, heirs, the family-centered life he'd known all his life and had blithely assumed would continue to be his—for all that and more, she was the hearthstone.

She stood at the heart of his heart. He'd put her there, then tried to deny it.

Now, at last, he understood; in his mind he could see Alathea smiling. Could almost feel her patronizingly patting his cheek.

Sarah was still standing before the window, staring out. Worrying about the orphanage and, perhaps, wondering about them. About him. He'd needed the moment she'd given him that afternoon, the time to find his feet again, the time to let his whirling, compulsive emotions settle and clear. For that, he owed her . . . this.

He stirred, then slowly crossed the room. He halted beside her, shoulder to shoulder; sliding his hands into his pockets, he looked out as she did. "About us—all the rest."

She glanced at him, then waited.

He didn't meet her eyes but focused on the glass, spoke to her shadowed face reflected there. "I made a mistake and I hurt you, and for that I'm more sorry than I can say. But what's done is done, and nothing I can do can rewrite the past. However, if you agree, if you'll accept it, I'd like to start again." He paused, jaw tensing, then clarified, "To try again."

She shifted her gaze from his face to the glass, meeting his eyes as if in a mirror. She waited.

He studied her face, drew in a breath. "I . . . have trouble, difficulty, handling . . . accommodating what's between us. I don't like and actively resist anything likely to control me. All that's grown between us . . . what happens every night only confirms just how powerful what I feel for you is. That's why I fought it."

He paused, searching for words, for what he needed to say. Through their reflection, her eyes held his. *No more pretending.* His lungs tightened; his jaw did the same, but he went on, "Ignoring my instincts—turning my back on my fears—and accepting all that I feel for you will . . . not be easy. Adjusting will be worse, but openly acknowledging it and responding . . ." He drew in another tight breath, searched her eyes. "That's going to be . . . a challenge. In this room, I can manage, but outside that door . . ."

Holding her gaze, he forced himself to say, "I know what you want, but I can't promise I'll instantly reform. All I can promise is that I'll try. And keep trying . . . as long as that's what you want."

Sarah blinked, several times, to clear her eyes. Never had she expected to hear such words—such an admission—from him. Had he changed, or had she? Or had they both?

He was watching her, waiting; unheralded, the gypsy's words replayed in her mind. *Is complicated.* Indeed.

Your decision, not his.

She'd thought the big decision she'd had to make was to accept his offer, but perhaps this was the real acceptance—now she knew what he was like, and he knew her, once they'd stripped all the veils away and both knew what the other wanted, and were honest about what they offered in return . . .

She drew breath, and nodded at his reflection. "Yes, that's what I want—what I can't imagine not wanting, not ever. But . . ." He'd been honest—so much more so than she'd expected; she had to be the same. "I'll probably be watchful. Don't read that as expecting the worst . . . read it as not being sure."

His eyes narrowed on hers. After a moment he said, "You don't trust me."

She raised her brows. "With my life, yes. With my heart . . ."

He held her gaze for a long moment, then his lips twisted and he looked down.

"Perhaps . . ." She waited until he looked up again, met her eyes again in the glass. "Maybe that's what's the true cornerstone of marriages like ours. Trust. Me trusting that you won't, despite any occasional lapses to the contrary, backslide and shut me out again. Bruise my heart again. That when this threat is past, you won't revert to how you've been. And you trusting me that I won't—*ever*—use what's between us to try to control you, to force you into doing this or that. Perhaps that's what we need—that trust."

He held her gaze for a long, long moment, then he turned and faced her.

She turned to him.

He raised his hands, gently framed her face. Tipping it up, he looked into her eyes, his own unshuttered. "Perhaps."

His gaze dropped to her lips and they throbbed. The time for talking was past. He bent his head and she reached for him.

The kiss was like ambrosia and they were hungry, both needy, greedy for confirmation after the emotional upheaval. Both needing each other and nothing more.

Clothes shed like petals, sliding to the floor, discarded veils. Hands whispered over naked skin; lips touched, brushed, caressed. Lingered. Soft sighs drifted, gentle moans, hitching breaths.

The candle guttered; pale moonlight washed over them as he lifted her, as she wrapped her legs about his waist and he lowered her and filled her.

As they moved together, lips fused, bodies merging, that power rose inexorably between them—completely, openly, without reserve, they surrendered to it.

And let it rage.

Over them, through them, within them.

He lifted her and brought her slowly down; she clung, and released, and clung again, more tightly. Savored every instant, and knew he did the same; she tasted his delight through their kiss, and had no thought to hide her own.

Long fraught moments passed as they communed in the shadowed dark, he, she, and the power that held them. That linked them, joined them.

Until delight became soul-deep pleasure, and pleasure became passion; until desire caught them and fused them. Until the conflagration within them cindered every last thought they possessed.

Until the power rose and captured them, harried them and whipped them, spurred them on, then wracked them, shattered them, fractured them, leaving them broken and open so the glory could pour through their veins.

To fill their hearts.

Eventually the tide receded. Somehow they staggered to their bed and fell in. Sarah curled into Charlie's side, her head pillowed on his chest. She felt him flick the covers over their cooling bodies, then his arms closed around her.

He lay slumped, relaxed, the only muscles with any tension the ones holding her to him.

She smiled, kissed the hot muscle on which she lay; she was about to let go, let her mind drift into sleep, when he shifted and pressed a kiss to her hair.

"You misunderstood one thing I said. It's not what *you* might do that worries me—it's what *I* might do under the influence of a power I will never be able to control."

17

The villain's next ploy arrived two days later in the guise of Dean Ferris, envoy from the Bishop of Wells.

Recognizing the bishop's crest on the carriage door, Crisp dispatched a footman to inform Charlie. Sarah was with him in her sitting room; she came hurrying to the door, Charlie striding beside her, as the dean climbed slowly up the front steps.

"Dean Ferris." Sarah walked out onto the porch. "It's a pleasure to welcome you to Morwellan Park, sir."

The dean had known her for years; he smiled and took her hand between his. "My dear, I don't need to ask if you're well—God's sun shines in your eyes." Then he sobered. "Unfortunately, I'm here on a grave matter, one I fear you'll find disturbing."

"Oh?" Eyes widening, Sarah turned to Charlie, who had come to stand by her shoulder. "I'm unsure if you've met my husband, Lord Meredith." To Charlie she said, "As you know, the orphanage operates under the auspices of the Bishop of Wells. Dean Ferris is the bishop's chief advisor."

Dean Ferris hadn't encountered Charlie before; he shook his hand, shrewd blue eyes taking note of his hovering presence and the quick glance he threw her.

"Please join us inside, sir, and you can tell us of this disturbing matter." Stepping back, Charlie waved the dean and Sarah before him.

Noting his clearly enunciated "us," she steered the dean to the drawing room, then summoned Crisp and ordered tea. While they waited for it to arrive, the dean revealed that he was on a routine visit to the churches in the district, but "in light of the unexpected information the bishop had received," had decided to stop by to consult her.

Once the tea arrived and was dispensed, and Crisp had retreated, the dean turned to her. "My dear, as you've guessed, my visit concerns the orphanage. A letter was sent to the bishop, anonymous as such letters often are, but in light of the seriousness of the allegations, he determined that we should—indeed, are conscience-bound to—alert you of the matter with all haste."

She set down her cup. "What matter? What allegations?"

The dean looked uncomfortable. He glanced at Charlie. "The letter claimed that the female staff indulge in certain practices with some of the lads . . . in short, the allegations were of the most grievous moral turpitude."

Sarah stared at the dean. "That's nonsense. You know it is. You've met all the staff, and so has the bishop—you know such things couldn't possibly be true."

"Indeed." Dean Ferris nodded, both word and action decisive. "Which is why the bishop and I felt we needed to act." Leaning forward he took her hand. "My dear, these allegations, given we know them to be untrue, are . . . well, quite ghastly. The bishop and I believe this to be the work of someone wishful of inflicting serious damage on the orphanage—or on you." He glanced at Charlie. "That's why we felt it imperative we bring the matter to your attention without delay."

Sarah met Charlie's eyes, knew that he was thinking, as she was, that this was clearly their villain's next move.

Charlie looked at the dean. "Did you by chance bring this letter with you, sir?"

"Ye-es." The dean looked sheepish as he reached into his robe. "My dear, I hope you won't take it amiss if I insist Lord Meredith read this rather than your fair self. I don't think my conscience will allow me to sully your mind with such things."

She hesitated, but the dean was clearly in earnest; no sense in upsetting him. She inclined her head and watched as Charlie took the missive, unfolded it and read.

His features hardened as his eyes traveled down the page. By the time he flicked to the second page, his jaw was clenched. Reaching the end of it, he raised his brows. "Good Lord!" An expression of distaste clear on his face, he refolded the sheets. "Do you mind if I retain this, sir? Once we've told you what's behind it, and what in a more general sense is going on, you'll see why it might prove useful."

The dean wiped his hands. "Truth to tell, I'm only too happy to see the last of it. Dreadful mind, whoever wrote it."

"A dreadful mind, indeed." Settling back, Charlie explained why some unknown man was fixed on buying the orphanage—on forcing Sarah to sell Quilley Farm by fair means or foul—and how that related to a wider, long-running series of crimes, and the nature of those crimes.

The dean was appalled. "Dear Heaven."

Charlie nodded. "Luckily, this time, we're aware of what's going on, courtesy of Mr. Adair and his links with the new Metropolitan police force. However, while we know why these incidents are occurring, we've yet to identify who is behind them—who our villain is."

"And he's the same man—or men," the dean amended, "behind all the other incidents?"

"We believe so. There seems little chance that two independent groups, or men, would both think of, let alone be able to run, such an outwardly complex yet at the heart of it simple scheme." Charlie met the dean's gaze. "Whoever they are, they're careful and clever."

"And conscienceless." The dean nodded to the letter Charlie had laid aside. "To malign innocent women who devote their lives to caring for orphans is the act of a blackguard."

"A blackguard we have a unique opportunity to catch," Charlie said. "Which is why I hope you'll consent to help us."

The dean eyed him shrewdly. "I'll do whatever's in my power to assist."

"Excellent." Charlie looked at Sarah, and smiled faintly. "We spent yesterday at the orphanage assessing every possible avenue to improve its defenses without allowing our increased vigilance to show. I think it very likely our man is watching the place—he'll expect some reaction to that letter. If you, Sarah, and I visit again today, he'll guess it's in response to the allegations."

He looked at the dean. "We need to put on a charade so he believes his letter has achieved his desired result—to create trouble for the orphanage, and for Sarah. If he believes that it has, then he'll approach us with another offer. That's what we want—we need to lure him out."

The dean smiled and set aside his cup. "I haven't played charades in years."

T he rest of the day passed in a carefully scripted endeavor to pull the wool over their villain's eyes. They were sober and serious, grave and righteous when they needed to be—when they arrived at the orphange in the bishop's carriage and went inside, and when they emerged, hours later, after a pleasant and at times hilarious luncheon with the orphans, and a serious but highly motivating talk with the staff.

When they'd left, the female staff had filed out of the orphanage behind them, and lined up outside the door. Katy Carter had looked frightened and had wrung her hands in her apron, Quince had sniffed and hung her head, Jeannie had looked flushed—in truth with indignaton—and somewhat stunned, while Lily had achieved a quite astonishing sulk, sullen and dour. The dean, struggling to keep his expression condemnatory in the face of such excellent histrionic abilities, had paced back and forth, gesticulating and lecturing. In actual fact the words he'd uttered had been a benediction.

Charlie had stood back and, expression impassive, watched the performance. On his arm, Sarah had hung somewhat limply, her expression as blank as she could make it, as if the entire episode had proved simply too much and she couldn't wait to get away.

Unobtrusively Charlie had scanned their surroundings, but with the Quantocks opposite and the Brendons behind, there were vantage points aplenty from which a man with a spyglass could keep a close watch on the place. Other than ensuring the carriage had been drawn up out of the way, leaving their scene enacted before the front door in unrestricted view, there was nothing more that could be done.

Eventually, leaving the orphanage staff apparently chastened, they'd climbed into the carriage and rattled back to the Park.

They arrived in time for afternoon tea, and to receive Gabriel, Alathea, and Barnaby, who'd ridden up from Casleigh. Gabriel and Alathea knew the dean; they all settled in the drawing room and Charlie explained the latest development and how they'd dealt with it.

"Dealing with villains should always involve an element of entertainment." Alathea accepted a cup from Sarah. "It's the only way to cope with such horrors."

Smiling, the dean commended her on her wisdom.

Their shared pasts in mind, Gabriel and Charlie surreptitiously rolled their eyes.

Barnaby had headed south yesterday morning to call on the three solicitors in Taunton and see what information he could wring from them. He'd stopped at Casleigh on the way, intending to recruit Gabriel, and had found himself with both Gabriel's and Alathea's support.

"I was stunned," Barnaby reported. "All three consented to talk."

"Of course they did." Alathea selected a biscuit from the tray. "They practice locally. Losing the goodwill of both the Cynsters *and* the Morwellans would be akin to cutting their throats." Alathea looked at Charlie. "I used the title quite shamelessly." She grinned. "You were quite effective even in absentia."

Gabriel and Charlie exchanged another glance.

Barnaby, however, remained impressed. "Although we told them nothing of the details, all three volunteered what information they had on the client on whose behalf they'd tried to buy the orphanage." Glancing at Charlie, he grimaced. "As you predicted, the 'clients' were all land companies, all with addresses in London."

"All three addresses look suspiciously like solicitors," Gabriel put in. "All close to the Inns of Court."

Charlie sighed. "Given the way our villain has things organized, I suggest we resist the temptation to chase after those addresses."

Gabriel seconded that. "Either they'll be fictitious, companies that aren't real, or we'll run into solicitors who aren't amenable to persuasion."

Barnaby nodded. "Especially as communications between the solicitors and the companies did *not* go via those addresses."

When Charlie frowned at him, Barnaby grinned. "Believe it or not, our villain uses an *agent*. A flesh-and-blood man—to wit a man of average height, with brown hair, thinning on top, round face, regular features, plain and unremarkable, very neatly and correctly dressed in business-agent style, somewhere in his thirties, careful with words and manners yet definitely not a gentleman born."

Barnaby paused, savoring the minor triumph. "All three solicitors gave the same description. In each case, our man presented his credentials as the appointed agent of the relevant land company. He discussed the details of the offer, and the solicitor agreed to make said offer and was given a part payment as retainer. Subsequently, after the offer had been refused, the solicitors had expected to inform the land company via the address given, but in all three instances, the agent had dropped in—or in one case fallen in with the solicitor as he was riding back to Taunton subsequent to making the offer—and so the solicitors passed their sad tidings directly back to the agent."

"An interesting aside," Gabriel said. "Our three solicitors half expected not to receive the rest of their agreed fee, but were surprised when the agent, on being informed of their failure, promptly paid over the remainder of the sum."

Gabriel caught Charlie's eyes. "Whoever's behind this isn't the usual run of blackguard. He doesn't try to steal wherever he can—he concentrates on his aim, and otherwise behaves with complete integrity."

Charlie remembered other blackguards they'd met. He nodded. "He's not going to be easy to identify. Nothing else will give him away."

"Which leaves us much where we were before," Barnaby said. "The only path that might lead us to this man goes via the Quilley Farm orphanage."

Fifteen minutes later, Charlie, Sarah, and Barnaby stood on the front steps and waved Gabriel and Alathea off. They were riding home; as Charlie turned to follow Sarah inside, he inwardly smiled at the look he'd seen flash between Alathea and Gabriel, and the laugh that had followed it in the instant before they'd given their horses their heads and raced off.

He glanced at Sarah, then turned as Barnaby made his excuses and retired to repair the depredations two days' riding had made on his normally immaculate person.

"And now I must take my leave." Waiting for them in the foyer, the dean smiled; taking Sarah's hand, he patted it. "I'm relieved, my dear, to be able to leave you and the orphanage with such solid supporters gathered around. I'll inform the bishop of the true nature of events here. Our prayers will be with you." He inclined his head to Charlie. "And you, Lord Meredith. This blackguard must be found and stopped."

Charlie nodded. "We'll do our very best to catch him."

The rattle of carriage wheels in the drive heralded the arrival of the bishop's carriage. With Sarah, Charlie walked the dean out, saw him settled, then retreated to the porch and waved as the carriage rolled away.

A horseman was trotting up the drive; he drew to the side and, noting the carriage's insignia, bowed respectfully as it rolled past. Then with a twitch of his reins, he came on.

Charlie glanced at Sarah, hesitating beside him. "It's Sinclair." He grimaced. "No doubt he's safe enough, but the fewer who know of our plan the better. Do you feel up to more acting? You'll need to appear as if the dean put the orphanage staff through the wringer and made dire threats to close the orphanage."

Her shoulders slumped. "Exhausted, upset, and not wanting to talk about the subject at all." Leaning on his arm, she looked up at him. "I'll stay long enough to greet Mr. Sinclair—it would look odd if I didn't—then I'll retire to nurse a headache."

His gaze on her face, Charlie hesitated, then murmured, "I'm going to act irritated and annoyed—I'll say we'll speak about it later. Once you're gone I'll explain about the dean's visit and the orphanage. If we believed those allegations, I'd be insisting you sell the place—it's what our villain will expect to hear. Malcolm's starting to become known in the neighborhood. While I don't like to deceive and use him, he could be a good conduit to get our reaction to this latest gambit into the local gossip mill. If any hear an observation from him, they won't imagine he's made it up."

Sarah nodded, facing the forecourt as Malcolm trotted up. "Yes. Let's do that."

They did, and even though she said it herself, they gave an excellent performance.

When Sinclair approached she plastered a patently false smile on her lips—one that neither reached her eyes nor erased the vertical line between her brows—and gave him her hand. "Mr. Sinclair."

"Countess." He bowed, concern in his eyes. "I trust I find you well?"

Sarah pressed her lips tight, then acknowledged, "I'm afraid I've had some . . . rather distressing news." She shot a sideways glance at the rigid male looming beside her; his face wore its usual impassive mask, yet disapproval and irritation radiated from him. "I . . . ah." Raising a hand, she rubbed at that line between her brows. "If you'll excuse me, I believe I'll lie down for a while. I'm sure his lordship"—another swift glance at the censorious presence beside her—"will appreciate your company."

"Indeed, my dear." Steel flashed beneath Charlie's clipped tone. "I know how much the recent news has upset you. We'll discuss the matter later."

An ominous promise infused his last sentence. Sarah nodded to Sinclair, then, lips tight, her head rising, her body tense, walked to the stairs.

Watching her go, Charlie quashed an impulse to applaud; she'd conveyed "fragile overset female" perfectly. One glance at the frown in Sinclair's hazel eyes confirmed he'd been convinced. Charlie waved toward the library.

Sinclair paced beside him. "An ecclesiastical visit . . . surely the bishop isn't the cause of the countess's malaise?"

Charlie recognized the question as not quite correct—not a question a gentleman should ask in the circumstances. Yet although mildly irritated that Malcolm harbored sufficient interest in Sarah to inquire into what was clearly a private matter, he pounced on the opening the question afforded. Reaching for the library door, allowing a definite frown to show, he glanced along the corridor as if confirming there was no one about to eavesdrop, then waved Malcolm in, followed, and shut the door.

He led the way to his desk. "I'm afraid the countess has unwittingly become involved in a rather"—compressing his lips, he dropped into his chair—"unsavory situation at the orphanage. By involved I mean through her association with the place, not that she personally is implicated in any wrongdoing."

"Of course not." Malcolm sank into the chair before the desk.

His accents harsh, Charlie continued, "The bishop's advisor came to inform us of the problem, which had come to the bishop's ear. Steps have been taken to deal with the staff involved." Picking up a pen, he tapped it on the blotter. "It will, of course, be necessary for the countess to distance herself from the place—a point she will no doubt appreciate once she has rested and regained her equilibrium."

Malcolm frowned. He hesitated, then diffidently said, "I understood her association with the orphanage is both long-standing and in the nature of a legacy."

Charlie nodded curtly. "However, under the circumstances she'll no doubt find some other charity to fill her time, and her godmother is dead, after all." Pointedly he fixed his gaze on the folded sheet Malcolm had drawn from his pocket. "Is that the report on the Newcastle-Carlisle syndicate?"

Malcolm blinked at the sheet as if he'd forgotten he held it. "Ah—yes. You said you'd like to see it." Reaching over the desk, he handed the sheet to Charlie.

Charlie took it, opened it, and kept his attention and comments focused on matters financial for the rest of Malcolm's visit.

When Malcolm eventually rose and took his leave, Charlie saw him out, then inwardly sighed. He scrubbed a hand over his features, trying to obliterate the last traces of the contemptuous—contemptible—role he'd been playing. Rigid, controlling, unforgiving, ruthless in his protection of the earldom and its reputation, and prepared to ride roughshod over his wife's feelings in pursuit of that goal—he'd led Malcolm to believe he was that sort of man . . . even though it was all pretense, he felt besmirched.

Almost guilty by association.

Shaking off the feeling, he set out to find Sarah—to reassure himself, and her, that he wasn't that sort of husband at all.

Two days passed before their efforts bore fruit in the form of a solicitor's clerk, dispatched from his employer's offices in Wellington to lay what the solicitor had plainly believed was a straightforward offer to buy Quilley Farm for a mildly staggering amount before the Earl of Meredith and his countess.

Charlie sat in an armchair in Sarah's sitting room, battling to hide a grin as he watched her, seated on the chaise, give the hapless clerk a pointed lesson on the proper way to approach a countess over a piece of property said countess owned.

Once the clerk was reduced to babbling, all but groveling at her dainty feet, she deigned to haughtily accept the written offer he held out to her.

Sarah glanced over the papers, noting the sum and the absence of any client's name. She looked up, and waved the clerk away. "Wait in the front hall—I wish to discuss this matter with my husband."

She waited until Crisp, who had lingered by the door, escorted the obsequiously bobbing clerk away, then handed the papers to Charlie. "No name, but the amount is larger than last time."

Barnaby had been standing before the French doors, ostensibly looking out; now he joined them, going to the armchair to look over Charlie's shoulder, scanning the pages as Charlie turned. "Wellington—that's west of Taunton, isn't it?"

Charlie nodded. "About ten miles." Finishing with the last sheet, he flipped the others back. "Other than the lack of name, this is a simple enough offer." He glanced up at Barnaby. "What do you think—should we run with your plan?"

Nodding, Barnaby reached for the papers. They'd spent hours discussing their options—or rather their lack of them. "I'll take your answer back to this solicitor. Doubtless he has no more real information than the others, but if the villain follows his usual pattern the agent will appear to learn your answer. When he does, I'll be there. I'll follow the clerk back—we'll let him ride ahead alone in case the agent approaches him along the way."

Charlie studied Barnaby's face. "Be careful."

Barnaby smiled sweetly. "I will be." He glanced at Sarah. "You'll need to be careful, too, and keep up the pretense of being exercised over the orphanage. With a villain like this—one who may well appear perfectly respectable—you can never tell when he, or someone he knows, will be watching."

Sarah grimaced, but nodded. "If you're going to ride to Wellington, you won't be able to return tonight."

Barnaby's grin grew intent. "No matter—I'll stay in Wellington until I meet this agent."

. . .

Later that night Charlie lay beside Sarah in the downy comfort of their bed, and prayed that Barnaby had met with success. The sooner he could dispense with the role of domineering, disapproving husband the better.

With Sarah all warm feminine limbs, boneless in the aftermath of the pleasure they'd shared, snuggled against him, her head nestled in the hollow of his shoulder as if it were made just for her, his arms loosely yet definitely holding her to him, satisfaction was a rich drug sliding through his veins.

The taste of innocence transformed, rich, passionate, and even more addictive. He wanted to secure it forever, to know that it would always be his.

He would do anything, literally anything, to ensure it was.

That impulse—that commitment—clashed badly with the role the current situation forced on him.

The sensation of her resting so trustfully against him only strengthened his welling resistance to the pretense they'd enacted over recent days, whenever any outsider was present. Sarah had summoned Mrs. Duncliffe and Skeggs to inform them of the dean's visit and ensure that the staff's good names remained unblemished, just in case the villain thought to start a whispering campaign to further pressure her into selling. But mindful of the need for secrecy, they hadn't been able to tell either the vicar's wife or Skeggs the full truth; instead, they'd had to convey, not by word but by suggestion, that Charlie was privately insisting that Sarah turn her back on the orphanage.

Nothing could be further from the truth. Worse, his assumed role demanded he behave in a manner that ran directly counter to his needs. To how he wanted, now and forever, to behave with her.

To how he knew and accepted he *needed* to behave if he wanted their marriage to be all that it could be.

They'd laughed after Mrs. Duncliffe and Skeggs had gone; as if sensing his discomfort, Sarah had smiled and teased, easing the emotional cuts and scrapes the interlude had inflicted, both on her and him. Yet he couldn't help but feel—irrationally perhaps—that in even acting as he was he was betraying her and their love.

He still inwardly flinched at thinking of that word in relation to himself.

Which illustrated why he needed to end the charade, to be free of the villain's unexpected influence so he could concentrate on overcoming his ingrained reaction to admitting to love. To letting it show, to letting it weave through his interactions with Sarah regardless of the where and when. Fighting free of the mental conditioning of decades wasn't a simple matter; he was still too frequently conscious of the prodding of the latent belief that love was too dangerous an emotion to let loose in his life.

Yet he was determined to succeed, to overcome and eradicate that entrenched resistance and so give Sarah and their marriage what both needed from him to not just survive but thrive.

Perhaps if he could say the words aloud? He hadn't—he knew he hadn't. That was a milestone he could aim for and achieve.

A small milestone, perhaps, but didn't the philosophers argue that if one could articulate a commitment, one stood a better chance of meeting it? That certainly held true for investing; why not for marriage?

So he needed a declaration, something that rang true, that she would know came from his heart.

Words, the right words.

He was reasonably certain they weren't "Are you pregnant?" even though he suspected she might be. She hadn't said a word, and he wasn't sure he had the right to ask, at least not yet . . . and it might be better if he waited until she told him; he had a suspicion that was one of those feminine declarations at which wise men feigned complete surprise.

Back to the right words. His mind circled, examined, wondered . . . until he fell asleep.

Two days later, with the afternoon light softening over the hills, Sarah set out from the orphanage on Blacktail's back to ride home to Morwellan Park. She smiled at how quickly she'd adjusted to thinking of the Park, Charlie's home, as hers. From her first day as his countess, it had felt right—like a comfortable glove sliding about her, fitting perfectly.

Eager to get back, she let Blacktail's reins ease. Behind her, Hills, the groom Charlie had insisted she take, kept pace.

She'd ridden to the orphanage purely to check, to reassure herself that everyone was safe and that there'd been no further accidents. There hadn't been, and everyone was coping with the increased level of vigilance they'd all deemed the best way to guard against further attacks.

Charlie had intended to come with her, but Malcolm Sinclair had called to discuss some reports on investment banking that Charlie had promised to share with him. Although they'd preserved their charade before Sinclair, Charlie had been torn; he'd patently wanted to send Sinclair packing and ride north with her instead.

She grinned, holding the moment close, clutching to her heart all that it meant. The wind whipped her hair back; she laughed and leaned forward to pat Blacktail's sleek neck.

A faint whiz was all she heard before fire lanced across her back.

She gasped, and pain sliced through her. She stiffened, trying to breathe, to ignore the spreading agony.

From behind she heard a cry—Hills. Blacktail's reins slid from her weakening grasp; the gelding thundered on. Something had hit her on the back; through the fiery pain she could feel something there, stuck to her, bouncing with Blacktail's gait. Anchoring one hand in his flying mane, she clung; with her other hand, she groped behind her, trying to feel what had struck her—she felt a shaft, and feathers. Just touching it made her gasp, made her head swim.

When she opened her eyes again, she saw blood, wet and red, on her glove. An arrow?

Her mind could barely take it in.

Flailing to catch up with her, Hills drew alongside. "My lady!" His face ashen, he reached for Blacktail's reins.

"No!" Sarah gasped. "Don't stop. Whoever shot it—they're still there."

If she hadn't leaned forward . . .

She let herself slump onto Blacktail's neck. "The manor." Her voice was weak, but Hills heard. "Let him run and he'll take me there."

Keeping her eyes open was too hard. She let them close, but forced her mind to follow their progress—she'd ridden this route countless times; she knew every inch of the way.

She knew when Blacktail swerved to take the path to the back of the manor. Sensed the change as he moved off the grittier bridle path onto the beaten earth running between her father's fields.

Then came the wooden bridge over the stream; each step jolted her. She cried out, nearly swooned, but managed to cling to the last remnants of consciousness . . . until cobbles rang under Blacktail's hooves and he halted.

Snorting, tossing his head, in the manor's stable yard.

She heard shouts, calls, a confusion of voices, then hard but gentle hands were lifting her down . . .

Sighing, she let them have her, and slipped into shrouding darkness.

S prawled in an armchair before the fire in his library, Charlie studied Malcolm, who was seated in the other armchair across the hearth reading one of Charlie's investment banking reports from London—and willed him to read faster. Still, it no longer truly mattered. He glanced at the windows, saw the afternoon closing in. Sarah would soon be back. Indeed—he inwardly frowned—he would have expected her back by now.

Had there been some problem at the orphanage?

He shifted, surreptitiously glancing at the clock. Nearly four o'clock. She *should* be back by now. Perhaps she'd returned but hadn't thought to look in . . .

His inner frown deepened; she'd know he'd want to know—he couldn't believe she wouldn't at least look in to tell him all was well.

The impulse to rise and go and find out—if she was home, and if she wasn't, to ride out to meet her and find out what had delayed her—welled, *but* . . . Malcolm was still a valuable source of information, and he had promised to go over the intricacies of investment banking in return for Malcolm's insights into railway financing.

Another two minutes ticked by in silence. Charlie was assembling the words to excuse himself to at least go and learn if Sarah had come home when heavy running footsteps echoed in the corridor outside the library.

Startled, both he and Malcolm turned to the door as it burst open.

Crisp rushed in. The man had actually run down the corridor; Charlie was on his feet even before Crisp said, "My lord, it's Lady Sarah. Hills has just ridden in saying she was shot while riding home from the orphanage."

A desolate chill clutched Charlie's heart. "Shot?" He was already moving to the door.

Crisp turned with him. "Hills says with an arrow, my lord. He's quite sure of that. She was struck in the back. It happened before the manor—she's there. Hills says she swooned, my lord, but her father said to tell you the wound isn't life threatening."

Charlie was striding rapidly down the corridor. Then he remembered, halted and turned back. And saw Malcolm following some paces behind, his face pale, his expression as drawn—as grimly horrified—as Charlie felt.

Malcolm brusquely waved him on. "Go! Don't worry about me."

Charlie didn't wait for more; he turned and ran for the stable.

On Storm's back, Charlie thundered north across his fields, taking the fastest route to Conningham Manor and Sarah.

Five minutes later, Malcolm Sinclair left Morwellan Park by the drive; on his black gelding he also turned north, keeping to the road.

Sarah woke to the gentle, soothing touch of her mother's hand smoothing her hair back from her forehead. The fiery pain in her back had eased, faded; the sensation now felt like a large raw scrape.

Opening her eyes, she blinked. She was lying on her side, her head in her mother's lap. Gingerly she raised her head and slowly pushed herself up, registering the slide of her blouse over a bandage across her back.

"Gently, now." Her mother helped her up; when Sarah sat straight and steady, she released her. "There now." She looked across the room. "Miss Twitterton, perhaps you could ask Cook to send up that chicken broth now."

Consulting her head and discovering it steady, feeling stable enough on the familiar window seat in the back parlor, Sarah looked around, saw Twitters's skirts disappearing around the door, and Clary and Gloria, both with eyes wide, regarding her avidly from across the room. They looked as if they had questions ready to burst from their lips. Before they could decide which to ask first, she looked at her mother. "Was I really shot with an arrow?"

Lips thinning, her mother nodded. "A quarrel from a crossbow. Your father's ropeable—there's simply no reason anyone should have had such a weapon out, not in this season."

Sarah tried to reach behind her; she winced as skin and muscle protested.

"No need to touch it." Her mother caught her hand and drew it away. "As luck would have it, Doctor Caliburn was here talking to your father. He cleaned the wound and said it was little more than a deep scratch." She patted Sarah's hand, then released it, drew in a breath and let it out with, "He said you were very lucky."

Hearing the quaver in her mother's voice, ruthlessly suppressed though it was, Sarah summoned a smile and squeezed her hand. "I'm all right—truly."

Other than the painful scrape on her back, she was. Shifting around, she looked out the window at the gathering dusk. "What time is it?"

"A little after four. We sent your groom to inform Charlie, of course." Her mother shook out the short jacket Sarah had been wearing, and the remnants of the blouse that had been beneath it. "The jacket can be washed and mended, but the blouse isn't worth the effort. That's Clary's you have on."

Sarah glanced down at the fine linen decorously covering her, then flashed a smile at Clary. "Thank you."

Clary waved dismissively. "Never mind that—what did it feel like? The arrow going in, I mean."

"Clary!" Lady Conningham bent a severe frown on her bloodthirsty daughter.

But Sarah grinned and thought back. "Like a burn, actually."

"That's enough, girls." Lady Conningham quelled Gloria with an even more dire frown as Twitters reappeared bearing a tray with a bowl of Cook's famous restorative chicken broth.

"You need to build up your strength," the diminutive governess sternly advised as she laid the tray on a small table before Sarah. "No doubt the earl will be here shortly and you won't want to swoon again."

Hiding a smile at Twitters's ability to always know just what argument to employ to get her charges to do anything, Sarah dutifully picked up the spoon and sipped.

She'd never swooned before; somewhat to her surprise, she did feel in need of sustenance.

Just as she laid the spoon in the empty bowl, the crunch of hooves on gravel drew all eyes to the forecourt—to Charlie as he flung himself out of the saddle and strode to the front door.

Her mother regarded her, a worried frown in her eyes. "Are you well enough to stand?"

Carefully Sarah got to her feet; Twitters hurriedly removed the table and tray. Other than a twinge across her back, she felt no lasting ill effects. Her head remained steady; reinforced with chicken broth, she felt tolerably normal. "I'm perfectly all right."

And she wanted to go home. With her mother and Twitters hovering, ready to fuss, let alone Clary and Gloria straining at her mother's leash, wanting to demand every gory detail, while the manor was comfortable it was no longer her place.

The realization crystallized in her mind—then the door was flung open with such force it nearly hit Clary, who yelped and caught it.

Charlie didn't seem to hear. Framed in the doorway, his eyes, darkened and burning, raked her—cataloguing every tiny detail from her head to her toes. Reaching those, his gaze flashed up to her eyes. With the same painful intensity he scanned her face, her eyes, her expression. "Are you all right?"

Surprised—faintly stunned—to see him so shaken, to be *able* to so openly see his emotions, raw and naked in his face, displayed without thought before her mother, Clary, Gloria, and Twitters, she mentally shook herself and hurried to find a smile and hold out her hands. "Other than a wound on my back—and I have it on excellent authority that that's little more than a deep scrape."

He muttered something—she thought it was "Thank God!"—then he crossed the room in two strides, took her hands only to draw her nearer, then gently folded her in his arms, careful not to touch her wound, the fingers of one hand tracing oh-so-lightly over the bandage across her back.

"Hills said you were hit below your shoulder blade." He murmured the words against her hair.

She couldn't believe how comforting his warmth was, how soothing it felt to have his strength surround her.

The sound of a throat being cleared had him lifting his head and turning, but he didn't let her go.

"Perhaps," her mother said, "we should adjourn to the drawing room."

Sarah knew the instant Charlie realized that he was not just wearing his heart on his sleeve, but waving it for everyone to see. He stiffened; the muscles in the arms around her tensed, but they didn't ease—he didn't release her or set her back from him.

She caught his sleeve, tugged. When he glanced down at her, she spoke to him rather than her mother. "Actually, I'd prefer to start back to the Park before full dark."

Her mother said, "I really don't think—"

"Of course." Charlie cut across her mother without compunction. "I'll borrow your father's carriage."

Holding his gaze, she grimaced lightly. "I rather suspect I'll do better on Blacktail. The carriage will jar the wound more than Blacktail's stride, and the way home is all across fields, no hard roads."

He frowned. From the corner of her eye, Sarah saw her mother open her lips to protest, but she paused, then reluctantly closed them.

"If you're sure you're well enough to sit a horse." Charlie was still frowning, but his gaze had grown distant; she sensed he was planning, then he refocused on her and nodded. "Very well. But if we're going to ride home, we'll need to leave now."

He turned to her mother and with his usual charm smoothed her ruffled feathers, reassuring her that her chick would be in safe hands.

Sarah hid a grin; he wouldn't be thrilled to know that it was his earlier blindness to all but her that her mother found most reassuring, that it was that that had her unbending enough to accompany them to her father, and thence to the stable yard.

Charlie lifted Sarah to her saddle. He stood by her stirrup, holding it and watching as she settled her skirts and picked up the reins. She seemed strong enough, but she was moving carefully—and he knew she wanted to go home.

And with that he had no argument.

He turned away, shook hands with Lord Conningham, then swung up to Storm's back. He steered the big hunter to come up alongside

Blacktail, then with brief nods to her family, they slowly walked out under the stable arch, past Clary and Gloria, who were smiling brightly and encouragingly, then they turned both horses' heads south.

At first they just walked, then Sarah pushed Blacktail into an easy canter. Charlie kept pace—until they were over the first rise and out of sight of those watching from the manor.

"Rein in." He watched as Sarah—rather more tight-lipped than she'd been in the stable yard—obeyed.

When Blacktail halted, she turned her head and looked at him, brows rising.

He halted Storm beside her, then edged the big gray close to Blacktail's side. Transferring his reins to one hand, he reached for her. "Come here."

That she allowed him to grasp her waist and lift her over to sit across his saddle with no protest told him he'd been right; her wound wasn't as unpainful, as unaffected by riding, as she'd hoped.

"I'll be all right," she murmured as he settled her legs and skirts, her undamaged side to his chest.

"True, but this way will be less painful. Lean against me."

He took Blacktail's reins and tied them to a ring on his saddle, then he curled one arm around her, supporting her and holding her to him, picked up Storm's reins, and rode on.

Cradled as she was, his body, his spine, cushioned her against any jolts, any sharp movements. Gradually, she realized and relaxed; with a sigh, she rested her head against his shoulder.

His jaw, which had clenched, eased. Inside him, something unlocked, released. He touched his lips to her hair. "Your father sent word that the wound wasn't life threatening, but he didn't say how bad it was—and Hills didn't know."

She looked up, met his eyes, then she raised a hand and touched his cheek. "I really am all right."

He nodded, then exhaled and felt the last of the black fear that had gripped him seep away. "Tell me what happened."

She was silent for a moment; he sensed she was frowning when she replied, "I don't know. I was riding along. Hills was only a length behind. I'd jumped the stream—it was a little way beyond that. I leaned forward and patted Blacktail's neck—and that's when the arrow struck."

"Hills said he didn't see anyone, but that you were well past the point where it happened when he got a chance to look back."

She nodded. "I was galloping and dropped the reins, so Blacktail took off."

Charlie asked no more questions. He didn't like the direction of his thoughts; he wanted to mull over them before he shared them. Storm and Blacktail knew the way to their stable; he kept them to a slow canter and let them find their way, while he held Sarah close and let his mind and all his senses absorb the reality that she was safe, whole, still with him. Still his.

Malcolm Sinclair didn't draw rein at his rented house in Crowcombe but rode on, northward toward the coast.

Lips compressed, features grimly set, he urged his black up the rise toward Williton. "Exercise *patience*." He muttered the words through clenched teeth. "Be *discreet*. So the fool tries to kill her! What the devil does he think he's doing?"

There was no one around to hear, much less give him an answer. Cloaked in suppressed fury, he pushed his horse on.

18

The head stableman, Croker, was waiting when they reached the stables at the Park. Hills was there, too, anxious and concerned. Sarah noticed others hanging back, could almost feel their relief when they saw her able to sit and smile, albeit weakly.

Both Croker and Hills grinned back. They held the horses; Charlie dismounted, steadying her as he did, then he lifted her down. He let her toes touch the ground only long enough to change his hold, then swung her up in his arms, careful not to press on her wound.

She continued to smile. Charlie carried her out of the stable yard and across the lawn. She waited until they were halfway to the house and no one else was near before, eyes on his face, she ventured, "I can walk, you know."

He glanced briefly at her, then looked ahead. His jaw set. "Just humor me."

A small enough boon, one she could easily grant.

He would have set her on her feet to open the side door, but as they neared, it opened; Barnaby stood back, holding it wide.

Charlie grunted his thanks, angled her through the doorway,

then resettled her in his arms. He looked down at her. "Where to?"

"My sitting room. There's still more than an hour to dinner."

Charlie started down the corridor. Barnaby ranged alongside. "If you're up to it, you might tell me what happened."

Like Charlie, his face was pale, his expression deadly serious. Sarah's smile took on a tempered edge. "Indeed—you'll need to hear."

There was no doubt in her mind—or Charlie's or, once he'd heard the details, Barnaby's—that her "accident" could be laid at their villain's door.

Comfortable and at ease in the cozy warmth of her sitting room, she related her tale, then Charlie added Hills's observations.

Barnaby let his head fall back against the armchair in which he'd sprawled. "I hadn't imagined he'd pursue the land from that angle."

Standing before the hearth, Charlie frowned at him. "What angle?"

Turning his head, Barnaby met Charlie's eyes. "If Sarah dies without issue, the property reverts to you, and given that we've been projecting the fiction that you disapprove of the orphanage . . . it's reasonable to assume that if Sarah died, especially in some way connected with the place, then after emerging from mourning, you'd be entirely willing to wash your hands of Quilley Farm. It doesn't connect with the Morwellan lands—it's a small, unproductive, unattractive property for a landowner like you."

Charlie sighed and closed his eyes. "You're right. And as there's clearly no rush to secure the property our villain can happily play a long game . . ." Opening his eyes, he glanced at Sarah, then met Barnaby's blue gaze. "When this is over and we lay our hands on him, I intend to extract payment for each and every injury he's caused."

Barnaby's lips lifted in a feral grin. "I'll hold your coat."

Sarah inwardly shook her head at them. She studied Barnaby; he'd been absent since riding south in the wake of the solicitor's clerk. "Did you learn anything about the agent?"

Barnaby's expression darkened. "No—other than that he's a very sharp cove." He glanced at Charlie. "I hung back and followed the clerk all the way to Wellington, but the roads in and out of Taunton lack cover—the agent might have seen me and decided to play safe, I don't know. Regardless, I followed the clerk to his lodgings, then as it was late, I left to find rooms for the night.

"The next morning I spoke with the solicitor and persuaded him to assist us. His description of the agent was the same as all the others, so it seems it's always the same man, and in this case the solicitor—Riggs—was quite sure the man wasn't local. Which"—Barnaby raised a finger—"means that we might be able to find him if we search. People in the country notice those who are not locals."

Barnaby's lips tightened. "Unfortunately, when the clerk arrived, I learned that the agent had just happened to run into him in the tavern in which he habitually takes refuge in the evenings, avoiding his landlady. If I'd known, I would have remained on watch, but . . ." Barnaby grimaced. "Suitably encouraged, the clerk told the agent that a friend of the family—to wit, me—would be in Wellington the following day to discuss the offer for Quilley Farm with the agent. Apparently the agent looked grave and said the offer was final, a take-it-or-leave-it proposition, and he wasn't interested in any discussion. He said his client would take the lack of immediate acceptance as a refusal and gave the clerk an envelope with the remainder of the solicitor's fee."

Charlie softly swore.

"Indeed." Barnaby looked grim. "I'm growing devilish tired of tripping over this agent. I'm going to turn my sights on him and scour the area—someone will have seen him and noted him as a nonlocal. He's been around for weeks now—he can't have remained totally hidden for all that time." His eyes narrowed; his voice grew harder. "And when I find him, I'm going to persuade him to lead us to his master."

Looking down at him, Charlie faintly raised his brows. "I'm so glad you said 'us.'"

Deciding that the civilizing influence of a good dinner wouldn't go amiss, Sarah rose and shook out her woefully crushed skirts. "I'm going to change for dinner. Half an hour, gentlemen."

Charlie watched her like a hawk as she walked to the door; aware of it, she turned and flashed him a reassuring smile before opening the door and heading for their apartments.

Charlie lay on his back in their bed and watched a shaft of moonlight creep across the room. Sarah lay beside him, sated and sleeping. Over dinner they'd gone over every aspect of their villain's game that they knew or felt confident enough to guess—only to conclude that they were still a long way from identifying him.

Instead of remaining in the dining room to pass the port, he and Barnaby had adjourned with Sarah to her sitting room; he was starting to feel as comfortable in that room, with her, as he was in his library. They'd discussed the best places for Barnaby to start his search, then revisited their safeguards for the orphanage, reluctantly accepting that they didn't dare set watchers in the surrounding hills; there was simply too great a risk the villain would sight them and pull back.

Speaking with Barnaby had reminded Charlie of the wider implications of the villain's scheme, yet to his mind, to his instincts, the imperative to capture and unmask the man was now sharply personal.

The events of the afternoon replayed in his mind, together with the revelations they'd brought. The cold dread that had gripped him when he'd heard that Sarah had been injured wasn't a feeling he would ever forget, yet against it, balancing it, was the relief—sheer, abject, and revitalizing—that had washed through him in the instant he'd seen her, standing beside her mother, hurt, perhaps, but still very much alive.

While the highly sane, logical, rational, and arrogant side of him was only too ready to point out that that dread, and the despair and desolation that had lurked behind it, ready to sweep in and claim him if she'd been taken from him, was the price he paid—and would have to pay for the rest of his life—for allowing love to claim him, another part of him, a part he was only now coming to recognize and know, simply smiled and held to the glory of his relief, to the warmth and joy he derived from caring for her, from fussing over her as he'd never liked being fussed over himself . . . he was starting to understand the bone-deep satisfaction, the intangible gratifications, of loving her.

Despite the dread, he still wanted that, with every fiber of his being wanted to seize and secure that, even if it meant embracing love to do it. Fear of the dread, of the despair and desolation, wasn't enough to turn him from his path, to keep him from seeking the joys of love.

Sarah murmured in her sleep and snuggled closer; his arms instinctively tightened, then he remembered her wound and forced his muscles to relax. She was there, with him; that was all that mattered.

She'd been there, with him, from the instant the door had closed behind him after he'd followed her here from her sitting room. She'd bathed earlier; he'd looked in and made sure her maid was in attendance—that being so, he'd retreated. But when they'd returned, they'd been alone, and she'd turned to him without hesitation. More, with intent.

He'd been concerned for her wound, worried that too vigorous movement would cause her pain; she'd made it plain that wasn't her concern—taking him into her body and loving him, explicitly and implicitly, had been her goal, her sole and consuming focus.

Lying back he'd surrendered and let her have her way, let her ride him to sweet oblivion. What he'd seen in her face, her eyes, what he was sure she'd seen in his, had gilded the moment, rendering it precious, investing it with glory revisited and reclaimed.

Somehow stronger.

He sensed she was strangely pleased with him, with how he'd behaved at the manor, but he couldn't imagine how he could have behaved in any other way. He'd felt warily uncomfortable when he'd realized how openly possessive and protective he'd been, but she hadn't seemed to mind.

Which was just as well. Acting less so would have been beyond him.

At the moment, between them, all seemed to be progressing, if not quickly, then at least in the right direction. He might not always know what it was he did that she approved of, but instinct seemed to be guiding him in that.

Reassured, his mind drifted toward sleep, then out of the veils a memory rose. Of him at their wedding breakfast making a vow—another he'd subsequently let fall from his conscious mind. Then, farsightedly, with unerring instinct, he'd vowed to do all he could to make her happy.

He was back on track to fulfill that vow—and part of that would be telling her that he loved her. Admitting, aloud, for the universe to hear, what he felt for her.

He had a library full of books; somewhere he'd find the words.

If there was one truth he'd finally recognized, it was that receiving love simply wasn't possible without giving love in return—and, ultimately, owning to it.

Quite why his sex found that last so daunting . . . sleep tugged and his hold on reality slipped. He let go, leaving that everlasting mystery of the universe unbroached.

Sunday afternoon found Malcolm Sinclair striding along the wharves of Watchet. His cold hazel gaze scanned incessantly, noting this man, then that. His quarry unsighted, he turned into the town's streets and systematically quartered them, looking in at every tavern he passed, every shop.

Eventually, temper quivering in every line of his large frame, he halted at the upper end of the High Street. He had no idea where Jennings was; he'd been hunting for him for most of the past night, and all of the day. He'd even risked riding through the hills north of Quilley Farm, but had seen no one.

Looking down the sloping High Street, he scanned all those in sight—all those who could see him. He'd been in Watchet frequently over the past weeks; the locals either knew who he was, or had grown accustomed to seeing him about their town. Deciding that speaking with his henchman was presently more important than the risk that someone might see them together, he swung on his heel and stalked farther up the High Street, then turned along the last lane on the right.

Jennings had rented the tiny fisherman's cottage at the far end of the lane. Malcolm walked straight past it and onto the narrow, rocky path that climbed toward the hills. Halting a little way on, he turned and looked out to sea, as if studying the fall of the land and the layout of the town.

The cottage and the small lean-to stable at its rear were also in his line of sight. There was no horse tied up in the stable.

Malcolm swore. He debated, but given Jennings's last action, laying his hands on the man's reins was imperative.

After another glance around, he walked farther along the path, then circled down, eventually entering the cleared patch at the rear of the cottage. The back door was unlocked.

It went against the grain, but there was nothing he could do other than leave a note. Tearing a leaf from the tablet he always carried, he wrote in block capitals, the better to disguise his hand.

His message was simple: COME AND SEE ME TONIGHT.

He left the note open on the table, weighed down with a glass.

There was nothing anyone else could deduce from those words, but Jennings would know precisely what they meant.

Quietly leaving the cottage, Malcolm strode away.

H e reached Finley House as the last of the light was fading from the sky. Using his latchkey, he entered and made his way through the silent, empty house to the library at the rear, the only room other than his bedchamber abovestairs that he used.

Slumping into the armchair before the hearth, he mentally shook his head, still trying to grapple with the tangle of events that had so unexpectedly trapped him in its coils. Glancing up at the clock on the mantelpiece, he saw the card he'd left propped against it—an invitation from Lady Conningham to dine with her family and other guests that evening.

The sight was a vivid reminder of all that had somehow, entirely unintentionally on his part, come to be put at risk by his scheme. Charlie, Sarah, and their life together, here in the peace of a gently rolling countryside.

He hadn't appreciated how precious such a reality was, not until he'd seen it, then experienced it—in large part vicariously through Charlie's and Sarah's eyes. Until then he hadn't known that lurking deep in his psyche was a longing for just that sort of life. He realized that now, knew how much on one level he envied Charlie, yet he in no way begrudged Charlie his good fortune. Perhaps because Charlie was so very like him, not just in looks but in mental ability, in their shared acuity, their liking for finance and the simple joys of making money.

Admittedly, Charlie walked unswervingly on the straight and narrow while he found excitement along murkier paths, yet that was a reflection of the influences and guidance each had received in his formative years, rather than any intrinsic difference. Charlie had had his family and the Cynsters; he had had . . . no one, unless one counted his late and unlamented guardian, Lowther, who'd been forced to put a pistol to his head rather than face the scandal of his involvement with the white slave trade.

In business Charlie might walk in the light while he spent half his time in the shadows, yet at base they were remarkably alike.

Malcolm's lips twisted in self-deprecation. Lowering his gaze, he stared at the flames licking over the logs his housekeeper had left burning in the grate. No matter how much he might fantasize, he knew he could never have what Charlie now had within his grasp. What truly irritated, however, what got under his skin and irked, was Charlie's refusal to appreciate what was offered him, what life had laid on his plate, to grasp it and be suitably thankful.

Perhaps it was the five years between them, the maturity, and the encroaching loneliness of which day by day—every day he saw and appreciated what Charlie had—he became more sharply aware, the sense of opportunities missed, of a life with so little beyond money to show for it, so bleakly devoid of all personal human achievement, that made the chance Charlie had before him so obvious—and so fired Malcolm's determination that Charlie should seize it.

He couldn't have it, but Charlie could.

Vicarious living, indeed, yet that was all he had open to him. And with Charlie so like him . . . strangely, it mattered.

Which meant he had to tell Jennings to forget about the orphanage. His inability to contact his henchman and settle the matter stung—he hated any sense of not being in control—yet presumably Jennings would find his note and, as always, obey; he would come to the house late tonight, sliding through the dark so no one would see him.

Malcolm glanced at Lady Conningham's invitation. Unable to attend church due to his search for Jennings, he'd sent a note to Morwellan Park that morning; the lad he'd sent had returned with a few lines from Charlie assuring him Sarah's injury was minor and that she was already back on her feet.

That being so she'd almost certainly be at her mother's dinner, and he wanted—felt compelled—to see for himself, to reassure himself that she'd suffered no lasting ill from Jennings's overenthusiasm. That impulse was strange to him, fueled by an emotion he didn't understand; he knew he didn't feel about Sarah as Charlie did, yet seeing her through Charlie's eyes, he'd come to admire and respect her in a way he'd never done with any other female. But he didn't just wish her well; he wanted her and Charlie to be happy.

He couldn't have that life, but Charlie could—and if he had any say in the matter Charlie would.

Malcolm rose. Jennings wouldn't arrive until midnight; there was no reason he couldn't spend the evening at the manor, in excellent company, assuring himself that Sarah was well and, if the opportunity offered, steering Charlie, oh-so-subtly, to accept and embrace all his wife offered him, all that he could have.

Ironically amazed at finding himself championing such an act, he headed upstairs to change.

Charlie looked across the Conningham Manor dining table and counted his blessings. Sarah sat opposite, transparently recovered from her ordeal, with only the occasional twinge tweaking her lips when she stretched too far or inadvertently brushed her sore back against something.

He'd spent all day on emotional tenterhooks, wanting to wrap her in protective layers, yet he knew how irritating she would find that, and while she'd smiled at his careful questions, she'd made it clear she considered herself all but fully restored.

The light in her eyes, the soft, natural blush in her cheeks as she laughed at something Malcolm, seated beside her, had said, reassured and comforted him as no amount of words could.

Despite her interaction with Mr. Sinclair, Sarah was intensely aware of Charlie's regard—of the focus that hadn't shifted in the least, not since yesterday when he'd walked in to find her in the manor's back parlor. His attention, his care, had been unwavering. That morning, he'd left her sleeping, allowing her maid to wake her only when it was time to dress for church. He'd guessed, correctly, that she hadn't wanted to miss the service, inevitably raising speculation as to why. But immediately they'd emerged from the church at the head of the congregation, he'd whisked her straight to their carriage and home, avoiding the usual ambling and chatting on the lawn.

She'd steeled herself for it, and had been quietly relieved not to have to exert herself mentally or physically. On reaching home, when she'd insisted she would be fit enough, he'd agreed to send a groom to her mother to confirm their intention to attend this dinner, but had countered by insisting she rest until then; bringing various reports and news sheets, he'd settled in the armchair in her sitting room and silently kept her company while she napped on the chaise.

They'd shared the light luncheon Crisp had brought in, then

she'd napped some more until it had been time to bathe and dress for dinner.

Charlie had been openly solicitous during the journey in the carriage. On reaching the manor, she'd made a point of allaying her mother's concern; the last thing she wanted at this point—when Charlie was at last growing easy with her—was for her mother and sisters to descend, with the best of intentions no doubt, but she wanted to cling to those moments alone, make them last for as long as she could. To give him as much time to practice as she could. They would be going to London soon to join Serena and Augusta at Morwellan House for the Season; that would be time enough to allow others into their joint life.

Until then she wanted to concentrate on fusing their lives, and it seemed he was one with her in that.

The knowledge made her glow. She was entirely conscious of how happy the change in him had made her, and if beneath it all she felt a trifle vulnerable, as if this were all too good to last, then that was her cross to bear—her challenge—and she had every intention of meeting it and keeping her lingering uncertainty to herself until it died.

While the dessert course was laid before them, she let her gaze travel around the table. She knew everyone and everyone knew her; it was a comfortable occasion.

Barnaby had been absent all day, combing nearby villages and hamlets for the elusive agent. He'd returned, disappointed but still determined, just in time to change and join them in the carriage. He was presently seated beside her mother, entertaining her with some London scandal; the absorbed expressions on all the nearby faces confirmed his reputation as a raconteur.

Mr. Sinclair was chatting with Mrs. Ravenswell; Sarah turned to Lord Finsbury on her other side—just as a distant pounding erupted.

Someone was hammering violently on the front door.

Sarah exchanged a startled glance with her father as the conversations around the table died; men's raised voices, tones urgent, became more audible.

Then the door was thrust open; Johnson, the butler, swept in. One look at his face had all the men rising.

"My lord . . ." Johnson looked at her father, then at Charlie. "It's the orphanage, my lord—it's on fire!"

. . .

Ten chaotic minutes later, mounted on one of Lord Conningham's hunters with Sarah beside him on a dappled mare, Charlie thundered north—toward the garish red glow that was lighting the night sky, crackling and smoking on the high ledge above Crowcombe, cast into sharp relief against the dark bulk of the Brendon Hills rising behind.

He glanced sharply at Sarah, noted her pale, set face. Barnaby was riding on her other side, with Malcolm beyond him. Various grooms and stable hands from the manor followed, as many as could find mounts; the gardeners, carting various implements, had set out in a dray via the road. All the other, older men at the dinner table had taken their carriages home as fast as they could to dispatch their households to assist.

Looking ahead, Charlie inwardly swore. From what he could make out through the haze of smoke enveloping the site, the back wings of the orphanage, at least two of them, were well alight. The main part of the house seemed unaffected as yet; squinting, he could make out its gray bulk against the glare from the flames rising behind.

He glanced again at Sarah. She'd insisted on riding with them; while he would have much preferred she traveled more safely with the dray, knowing how much faster the cross-country route was and how vital she would be in imposing order on what was sure to be pandemonium, he'd muzzled his protests and put his efforts into ensuring she was on a sound horse, one calm enough not to balk at the smell of smoke.

Looking ahead, he didn't bother swearing, but saved his breath. He was going to need it.

They jumped the stream, then flowed up the slope. They had to halt on the other side of the fence; no horse would willingly jump it, facing the inferno twenty yards away. They all slid from their saddles, appalled at what they saw; tying his reins tightly to the fence rails, Charlie took Sarah's—she was so stunned she was standing staring—and did the same for her, then he turned to her; grasping her shoulders, he drew her to face him.

He caught her eyes. "They need you." She blinked, then drew in a breath and nodded, and looked again at the conflagration. Grasping her waist, he hoisted her over the fence, then vaulted it himself. The rest of the men followed.

It was difficult to know where to start. Charlie paused for a second, taking stock, then grabbed Sarah's sleeve. "Gather the children—all of them—and get them back beyond the edge of the forecourt. Right back off the gravel."

She nodded, blinked, and coughed as a cloud of smoke swirled around her. Catching up her cloak, she covered her nose and mouth and darted into the fray.

Gathering Barnaby and the other men with a glance, Charlie headed for the rear of the building.

He'd been right. Two of the wings were wreathed in flames. The third, northernmost wing had a charred, smoldering blackened patch at one end of the thatched roof; the patch glowed and darkened as it spread, but the thatch hadn't caught fully alight.

Men were trying to heave water onto the thatch, but the roof was too high. All they could do was douse the walls and pray. Others were fighting to keep the flames roaring through the two burning wings from attacking the main house. With its stone walls and slate roof, it had yet to be affected.

The smoke was intensifying. Charlie made his way past men from Crowcombe village who'd been the first to arrive to help. Armed with charred blankets and sacks, many were trying to beat the flames into submission while others rushed back and forth with buckets and pails, throwing water as high as they could.

Chaos and confusion reigned, along with a certain raw-edged panic. The men from the manor found sacks and pails and ran to help. Charlie stopped long enough to direct the men to concentrate on the sections where the wings met the main house. "The rest of these two wings are gone—we can't save them." He stopped to cough, then pointed toward the main building. "The best we can hope for is to save the main house." He went along the southerly wing, pulling men away, shouting and pointing until they understood.

Barnaby leaned close and yelled over the hungry crackle of the flames, "I'll tell those working on the central wing." He was gone before Charlie nodded.

Tacking through the melee, Charlie made it to the well, where Kennett was heaving water up as fast as he could.

"Lucky salty water douses flames just as well as fresh." Kennett hauled up another pail and tipped it into a waiting bucket. He let the emptied pail attached to the well's rope rattle back down into the water, then started hauling it up again.

Charlie glanced around and spotted the manor's stableman. "Jessup—get a few of your strongest men to spell each other on the well."

"Aye, sir." Jessup pointed to a brawny stableman. "Miller, you take over. I'll send two of the gardeners to help when they get here."

Charlie hauled Kennett away. "You know this place best. We need to stop the flames from spreading to the main building—and to the north wing if we can manage it."

Kennett looked as Charlie pointed, then coughed and nodded. "Aye."

"I've already told those working on the south wing, and someone's doing the same for the central wing. You go and take over the north wing—it's the only one we've any chance of saving." Charlie stopped to cough, then yelled, "There are other men on the way—grab whoever comes past and keep them focused on saving the main building, and the north wing."

Kennett nodded and lumbered away; within yards he was swallowed up by the billowing smoke.

Charlie paused only to dip his kerchief in a passing pail of water, wring it out and tie it over his nose, then he plunged back into the melee.

It was a nightmarish scene with the two huge old wings fully alight, garishly painted in flaring oranges and reds, in black and swirling, choking gray. Gusts of heat billowed out, searing and scorching. The fire was like a living being, surging and swallowing, roaring and whooshing. Eating, consuming.

Charlie started at the south wing and worked through the lines of men, seeking out the children. He'd noticed them as he passed, smaller, slighter beings desperately trying to save the only place most had ever called home.

He found Maggs, but when he ordered the boy to leave his pail and go around to the forecourt and safety, Maggs's jaw set and he stubbornly shook his head. "We're more use here!" When Charlie scowled and opened his mouth to argue, Maggs wailed, "We have to help!"

Looking into Maggs's face, smeared with soot, his eyebrows singed, his hair dusty, Charlie read the desperate plea in the boy's—youth's—eyes. He hesitated, then said, "Only those over twelve. All the others have to get back to the forecourt and report to the countess." He grabbed Maggs by the shoulder, took the pail from his hand and gave it to a passing man. Leaning down, he spoke into Maggs's ear. "You're in charge—find all the other children who are helping. Twelve and above can stay and help if they want—all the others to the forecourt."

Through the dense smoke, Charlie spotted a figure with flying pigtails. He swore. "Who's the oldest girl?"

"Ginny." Maggs coughed.

"Is she out here helping?"

Maggs nodded. "Saw her by the well before."

"Find her. Tell her to go around and collect all the girls—every last one—and get them back to the forecourt. They're needed there to help the countess and the staff with the younger children."

Maggs nodded and pointed with his chin. "That's her over there. I'll tell her." Maggs twisted his shoulder from Charlie's restraining grip and started after Ginny.

"Maggs!" Charlie waited until the boy stopped and turned back to him. "Keep track of the boys who stay to help. If this gets worse"—Charlie glanced up at the flames engulfing the south wing, then looked back to catch Maggs's eyes—"if I give you the word, I want you to gather all the boys and get them to the forecourt. No arguing. If Kennett or I tell you to go, you get the others and go."

Maggs swallowed, and nimbly danced back as the flames billowed near where he stood. He glanced back at Charlie and nodded. "Yeah—all right."

He stumbled off. Charlie drew in a short breath, looked up at the south wing, then turned as more men from the estates of the landowners who'd been at the manor arrived.

Keeping a few, he sent most to report to Kennett and directed others to help with the central wing. More men arrived with buckets, pails and sacks; fresh, they fell on the flames, allowing those who'd been fighting for longest to step back and catch their breath.

Charlie broke off beating flames back from the junction between the main house and the south wing. He redipped his kerchief; retying it, he squinted down the line of men. Everyone was soot-streaked and filthy; he picked out Joseph Tiller, chest heaving, crouched, head bowed, over the pail he'd been swinging.

Taking the jute sack he'd been wielding with him, Charlie circled the south wing to check how Barnaby was faring. He yelled encouragement and directions as he went. He passed Malcolm on the way, grimy and gasping; with a group of men he was flailing at flames not so much trying to save what they'd devoured but to deaden them and reduce the chance of them spreading.

Rounding the end of the south wing, Charlie found the smoke was even thicker in the courtyards between the wings. He had to go more slowly so he didn't knock down others and they had a chance to see and avoid him.

Like the south wing, the central wing was steadily burning, but as Charlie had done, Barnaby had sacrificed the rest of the wing to the flames and concentrated on keeping them back from the junction with the main house. At first glance it seemed that they'd succeeded in that, but squinting upward as he stumbled past men and the ruined playgrounds between the wings, Charlie thought he saw the thatch close to the main house glowing.

Just pinpricks here and there; embers at least had got that far. However, the bulk of the thatch adjoining the main house had yet to flare.

After checking with a Barnaby not even his mother would have recognized, Charlie went on to find Kennett. As he rounded the north wing, he realized that the noise from the fire—the flare of flames, the constant whooshes, the cracks and crackles and the pervasive roar—had been gradually, very gradually, decreasing. They were winning, turning the tide. The fire was abating.

Kennett thought the same. "But we've a long ways to go yet. We have to keep the flames down, have to let them burn themselves out. Ain't no other way."

Charlie was squinting up at the thatch. He really didn't like that thatch. "Is there any way we can separate the wings from the main house? Create a gap that we can defend?"

Kennett grimaced. "Would that we could, but those roof beams go right on in under the main roof. The rafters are tied together, and then there are even bigger beams connecting each floor. If I thought we could hack our way through them, I'd say we should and right quickly, but those timbers are feet thick, old and weathered and as hard as iron. You'd need explosives to break them."

"Or fire," Charlie murmured.

After a minute he said, "So all we can do is dampen everything down as far and as fast as we can. Once the flames subside, we'll get ladders up against the main house and douse the thatch and rafters from that end."

He turned as a fresh wave of men came around the house—workers from farther afield. They carried hoes, picks, axes—all manner of implements, including a few long-handled rakes.

Charlie waved them on. "Go around to the central and south wings and start pulling down what's already burned. Start at the ends—leave the areas near the house that the other men are concentrating on. Work from the ends toward them."

Most of the men nodded and went. One man carrying a long-handled rake hung back. Frowning, he nodded up at the thatch under the eaves of the main house. "Thought you'd want us to pull that section away first, so's it can't catch alight and spread to the main house."

Charlie exchanged a glance with Kennett. He turned to the man, but it was Kennett who answered.

"Nay, lad—the weather's been cold and that thatch is damp. Likely it's doing us a good turn and smothering any flames trying to eat along the rafters. We'll need to leave it until last, and even then be careful how we go about removing it."

The man replied with an "Oh," but Charlie barely heard him as Kennett's words and those glowing pinpricks he'd seen—on, in, or *beneath* the thatch?—connected. Dread blossomed. He refocused on the man. "Were there any others with long-handled rakes? Other than those who came this way?"

The man blinked at his urgency, then nodded. "Aye." He coughed. "Some went around the other side." His gesture indicated the other side of the house.

Charlie swore, spun on his heel and ran.

19

Charlie flung himself around the end of the north wing. A mass of men were attacking the walls at the ends of the wings; desperate, he plowed through them—then heard the sounds he'd feared and dreaded.

A sudden gush was followed by a powerful *swhoosh,* and a fresh gout of flame spewed high into the air, immediately followed by cries and oaths as, dismayed, men fell back.

Charlie raced around the south wing. Skidding to a halt, he looked up. Squinting through the thickening smoke, he saw his worst fears confirmed. Men with long-handled rakes had come around the southern side of the house and, thinking as the other man had, had pulled down the thatch where the south wing abutted the main house—letting air play along rafters that, smothered and starved of air, had been smoldering.

The flames had gasped, then roared, ravenously feeding now that they had unrestricted air to burn.

Even though he'd known what to expect, Charlie stood and stared, beyond horrified. There was no way they would stop the flames now.

From where he stood halfway along the south wing and back from the burning walls, he could see what Kennett had meant about the rafters and roof beams tying into the frame of the main house.

The fire wasn't going to stop at the stone walls—it was going to gobble along the beams, straight into the main house.

A sudden roar and cries came from the inner courtyards. One glance was enough to see that the gush of flames in the south wing had carried over to the central wing. Its roof, too, was now fully alight, flames licking greedily up to and under the main house's eaves.

Then came a massive crack as some beam exploded—followed by a bellow, a communal cry of rage as the fire leapt across and like a ravening beast fell on the north-wing thatch.

In less than a minute, they'd gone from tentative hope to utter despair.

Charlie looked around and saw Maggs. He lurched over to the boy and grabbed his arm, pulling him close to gasp, "Go—*now*. Get the others and go!"

Maggs glanced into Charlie's face, his own soot-stained with runnels down his cheeks where smoke and despair had made him cry. He hesitated, then, face falling, he nodded and ran.

Barnaby appeared at Charlie's shoulder. "I've pulled all the men out of the courtyards—they're one minute away from becoming a death trap."

Scanning the south wing, now lit eerily from within as the fire, consuming the thatch above and so gaining even more air, ran amok, Charlie nodded. "Let's get everyone back. We can't do anything more, and lives are more important than buildings."

Grim-faced, Barnaby nodded. Turning, he grabbed the first man he saw, yelling at him to go out beyond the forecourt and take all he met with him. Charlie worked his way along the south wing. He checked that someone had moved the horses well back, picketing them out in the field, then went to join Barnaby. They worked their way around the rear of the inferno, collecting everyone, checking for stragglers as they went.

Massive booms erupted from the south wing, then a part of its roof collapsed, sending up a shower of sparks, feeding the swelling roar of the flames.

The fire was a beast that had got away from them.

Charlie and Barnaby together had to drag Kennett away from the north wing. "We *can't* save it!" Charlie had to yell the words in the man's face before he finally slumped, gave up fighting, and let them lead him away.

Pulling back, Charlie paused at the front end of the north wing and looked back, squinting through the dense smoke, but he could see no one, no movement in the shadows beyond the glare of the fire; they'd got everyone away. Consoling himself with that, he turned and jogged to catch up with Barnaby and Kennett as they crossed the forecourt to the arc of people waiting and watching.

It was a milling, shifting throng; many women from the village had come up to help with the children. They were seated in little groups here and there, trying to calm and soothe away fears.

Imagining how real those fears would feel, his heart leaden, Charlie looked around for Sarah. He couldn't immediately see her in the stunned, dispirited crowd. Moving along the edge of the forecourt, he was scanning the faces—when Sarah erupted out of the line a little way along. She stood staring, plainly horrified, at the house, then she turned and saw him. Picking up her skirts, she raced toward him. "We're missing two babies and Quince!"

Breathless, she grabbed his arm. "I saw her bring some of them out early on—she said she didn't need any help. But we only have four. She left them with women scattered about—everyone thought the others were with someone else. But they aren't, and no one's seen Quince recently—she's definitely not here."

Charlie looked at the house with the rising glow of the fire behind it.

"Oh, no!" Sarah clutched his arm. "Look!"

She pointed to the northernmost window of the attic. Behind the thick glass, a shadowy figure was struggling to open the sash.

"Her arm's broken." Katy came up beside Sarah. "She won't be able to heave that up."

Joseph came stumbling up. "The attic stairs are at the south end— up against the wall of the south wing. They'll be impassable by now."

Charlie swung to Kennett, standing staring, stunned, beside him. Grabbing Kennett's shoulder, he shook him. "The ladders, man— where are they?"

Kennett looked at him, abject horror in his eyes. "They were in the courtyards." He swallowed. "They're gone."

Barnaby appeared. "I've checked—none of the others brought ladders. Two ostlers from the inn at Crowcombe are riding back down to fetch one."

They all looked at the house—at the attics and the frantic figure struggling with the window. At the thickening smoke billowing up from behind the main roof, reaching forward to embrace the building, the hot glare of the angry flames rising behind.

"We can't wait." Pulling his arm from Sarah's grip, Charlie started striding across the forecourt, then he broke into a run.

By the time he reached the porch protecting the front door, he knew what he'd have to do. Quince had seen him coming; he'd waved her to the center window of the attic, above the front door and the porch roof.

There was a lattice attached to the side of the porch; Charlie prayed it would hold his weight. Carefully, distributing his weight as evenly as he could, he started climbing. The wooden slats started to give—he flung himself upward, caught the ridge of the narrow porch roof and scrambled up.

Barnaby watched. When Charlie heaved himself up and straddled the ridge, he called, "Don't bother trying to break those panes—they're too small and the glass will be too thick. Can you reach to push open the sash?"

Charlie looked up, then slowly got his feet under him, balancing on the ridge. The stone wall gave him something solid to lean against. Putting his chest to it, he reached up to the window that courtesy of the symmetry of the façade was directly above the porch. He got his fingers under the edge of the sash and eased it up—it was stiff, but it rose, then Quince managed to get her good hand and arm under it and heaved it up.

She gasped as fresher air rushed into the attic. "Thank God! Wait there, I'll get the babes."

"No—wait." Charlie grasped the lip of the window; scrabbling with his toes against the stone, he hauled himself up and in. He tumbled through and landed on the timber floor—and felt the heat seeping through the boards.

As he struggled back to his feet, he heard someone—Barnaby he felt sure—scramble up onto the porch roof.

Quince appeared through the murk and handed him a bundle. She frowned. "What—"

He silenced her with a gesture. "Bring the other one as quick as you can."

The fire was in the beams below the floor; how long they would hold he had no idea.

Leaning out of the window, he passed the first little bundle, well wrapped but worryingly silent and still, down into Barnaby's waiting hands.

He watched as, balancing precariously on the roof, Barnaby crouched and passed the bundle down to a multitude of hands eagerly reaching up.

Charlie turned and took the next bundle from Quince. "That's the last?"

"Yes. I'll go down—"

"*Don't*. Move." He infused the words with every ounce of command he possessed. "Just wait."

The fire was building beneath his feet; he could hear the welling roar. The floor below was a mass of flames. There was no way out for them that way.

Quince fidgeted, but remained by his side as he lowered the last baby. The instant the bundle left his hands for Barnaby's, Charlie straightened and stepped back.

"What . . . ?" Quince shrieked as he swept her up in his arms.

"Your turn," he informed her. "It's the only way out."

With her broken arm, she couldn't help herself to any great degree; Quince had to let herself be manhandled out of the small window, down into Barnaby's steadying hands, then down again, to where Kennett was waiting to grasp her hips and ease her to the ground.

The instant she was safe, Barnaby turned to Charlie, his face drawn and tense. "Get out—*now!*"

The last word was all but drowned by a huge crack—then a roar as flames raced across the ceiling above Charlie's head.

He'd been aware of the fire below, but he hadn't looked up.

The entire roof of the house exploded into flame.

Barnaby leapt off the porch roof.

Charlie grabbed the windowsill and dived out of the window head-first. He landed like a cat on the porch roof. Before it could give way under his weight, he leapt for the ground. He landed and rolled, coughing—aware everyone else was fleeing.

Gasping for breath, his lungs seared and burning, he looked up and back; smoke-stung eyes streaming, he had to blink frantically before he could focus—and see the inferno the farmhouse had become.

As he lay there watching, the roof started to fall—gathering momentum, it caved in with a roar.

"Come on!" Someone was tugging frantically at his shoulder.

He turned his head, and realized it was Sarah.

"You're too *close*!" she screamed. "Come on—get up! We have to get back!"

He felt as if he were in a dream; it was so difficult to get his limbs to move. With Sarah's help he got to his feet. They'd only staggered a few paces when a huge explosion detonated behind them. Sarah glanced back and shrieked.

Instinct took over. Charlie grabbed her and hauled her to him, sheltering her with his body.

Something struck him on the back, felling them both.

It hurt.

Sarah wouldn't stay down. She wriggled frantically; he couldn't make out what she was saying. Then she leapt to her feet; using her cloak to protect her hands she pushed and pushed—until the weight pinning him slid to one side.

He tried to breathe and coughed so hard he felt dizzy, weak. Sarah's hands wrapped in her cloak patted all over his shoulders and back, then she grabbed his arm again—just as Barnaby skidded in the gravel on his other side.

"Come on—get moving, Morwellan." Barnaby seized his other arm.

Between Sarah and Barnaby and his own feeble efforts, he managed to get his feet under him, managed to let them steer him across the gravel to where row upon row of anxious faces waited, rouged by the flames.

The row parted, clearing a space for them. Barnaby let him down. Charlie sat; drawing his knees up, he laid his forehead against them and concentrated on breathing.

Sarah sat beside him. He knew it was her without looking, felt her cool hand brush his cheek. Then she tucked her hand in one of his and leaned lightly against him as the orphanage burned.

. . .

The cool air revived him. Long before the last walls collapsed and the fire started to subside, he'd recovered enough to start formulating the necessary plans to deal with the disaster.

The flying beam that had hit him and Sarah had been flung out when the attic floor collapsed onto the floor below. The width of the gravel forecourt had protected all those watching from similar dangers, but the damage many had sustained while fighting the flames was quite real.

The children had to be his—and Sarah's—first priority.

Slowly rising, he helped her to her feet. He held her hand, looked down at her pale, soot-streaked face, and simply said, "We'll rebuild."

She smiled weakly, mistily up at him, blinked rapidly, then nodded. "We'll build better—no thatch."

His lips twisted. "Indeed. Definitely no thatch."

"I keep telling myself that we've lost nothing that really matters, nothing that can't be replaced . . . but the children. Most have lost every last little thing they ever possessed."

After a moment, he said, "We can't give them back the mementos, but perhaps we can give them new ones. New memories. Better memories." She flashed him another, rather stronger smile. He caught her eyes. "Now—how many children are there, and what groups can we break them into? How many groups, how many children in each?"

Sarah opened her mouth to answer, hesitated, then said, "Let's find Katy and the others—we should plan this all together."

Charlie nodded. They started moving through the crowd, making no secret of their intent—to deal with the immediate problem and look ahead, rather than dwell on the massive loss. Although the fire still raged strongly, they ignored it—or rather made use of its warmth and light as with the staff from the orphanage, assisted by many of those who'd come to help, they started gathering the children.

Maggs and Ginny came up and waited patiently until Sarah and Charlie looked inquiringly their way.

"Can we go and fetch our things, miss?" Ginny asked.

Sarah tried to smile but her heart wouldn't let her. "I'm so sorry, Ginny." She put one hand on the girl's shoulder, with her other waved at the ruin of the farmhouse. "I'm afraid there'll be nothing left."

Maggs elbowed Ginny. "That's not what she meant. We—all of

us—stacked everything we could out back, in the lee of the hill, before the fire got properly going." He shifted, then looking at the ground, admitted, "Staff wanted us to help, but, well, some of us've been in fires before. We didn't want to take any chances. So while we older ones helped, the younger ones ferried—their things as well as ours." He jerked his chin toward the rear of the burning ruin. "So everything's back there—we just need to fetch it. And we're sorry about not helping more, but . . ."

Guilt choked him; he kept his eyes cast down.

Charlie clapped him lightly on the shoulder. "A very wise decision." He exchanged a glance with Sarah. "I'm sure no one, least of all the orphanage staff, would begrudge you what you've saved, nor the time taken to save it. We all did the best we could, but this time . . . that wasn't good enough."

Maggs glanced up at Charlie, confirmed he meant what he said. "So can we go and fetch our things?"

"Let's see if we can't make that easier." Charlie scanned the crowd, then beckoned Barnaby over. A few quick words, a suggestion or two, and Barnaby was in charge of a group of men hauling the orphanage cart around the side of the house, well away from the still angry flames, heading for the lee of the dark hill behind the orphanage, with the older children in close attendance, many carrying lanterns so they could search for their possessions. The younger ones had ferried their goods earlier; the older ones were happy to return the favor.

"That's some small relief." Sarah turned back to Katy. Between them, Sarah and the staff had agreed on their dispositions—which children would go together and who would supervise. On hearing Sarah and Charlie's suggestions on where they would go, the staff visibly relaxed.

"So it's agreed then," Sarah said. "We'll keep the older children together—they'll be best accommodated at Casleigh. Mr. Cynster and Lady Alathea will know how to cope, and Joseph and Lily can stay there, too—we should keep their studies and daily lives as ordered as we can." She went on, sending the younger children to the manor, where her mother, sisters, and Twitters could be counted on to assist Jeannie and Jim to keep the youngsters amused and happy. "All the babies, Quince, Katy, and Kennett will come to the Park. I'll need you three close so we can make plans for the new orphanage."

The staff nodded, exhausted and relieved.

Charlie touched Sarah's sleeve. "I'll go and check what carriages Gabriel's summoned. We may need more."

Sarah nodded and briefly squeezed his hand, then released it and turned back to the staff. As Charlie moved away, he heard them organizing to split the children into their groups, ready to be ferried away.

Gabriel, Alathea, and Martin Cynster had ridden all the way from Casleigh; although they'd arrived too late to help fight the flames, they'd brought numerous grooms, all mounted, with them. While Alathea had joined forces with Doctor Caliburn, tending to the injured and dispensing salve for the numerous burns, Gabriel and Martin had moved through all those present, determining how much transport would be needed to ferry exhausted men and women home to their beds, and were steadily dispatching their grooms to ride to all the nearby houses with carts and carriages with requests for said conveyances. There were no households in the valley likely to refuse a Cynster request.

Charlie found Gabriel and detailed the children's needs.

"I've already summoned all the carriages from our three houses," Gabriel said. "The children and staff can have first call on them—it's been a dreadful night and we need to get them out of the cold. The shock will be bad enough as it is."

Charlie looked at the still burning farmhouse. "Those of us up to it will make sure the fire's contained before we leave."

Gabriel nodded. "We'll call up enough carriages and carts from the other houses for all too exhausted or injured to ride."

Charlie moved on. Barnaby returned with the orphanage cart piled high. He grinned through the soot blackening his face. "The children did well. It seems all of them got their favorite things out."

Glancing at the glowing ruin of the farmhouse, Charlie murmured, "A small mercy."

Later, with Barnaby and a handful of stalwarts, Charlie circled the farmhouse, watching the flames slowly sink and die, checking the surroundings for any smoldering fragments thrown out by the numerous explosions. The stable, barn, and outbuildings at the back of the orphanage had survived. While most of the walls of the main building still stood, they'd have to be pulled down; the wooden frames within the stone had been devoured.

"It'll take days for this to burn out completely." Barnaby halted beside him on the south side of the farmhouse.

Charlie nodded. He glanced around at the men who had helped. "Thank you all. We've done all we can for tonight."

The men shook his proffered hand, then shambled across the forecourt to where the last carriages were waiting to take them home, horses that had been ridden to the scene tied behind. The children, their goods, and the orphanage staff were long gone. Alathea and Martin had left with those destined for Casleigh; Gabriel and Sarah remained, farewelling the last stragglers.

Beside Barnaby, Charlie walked slowly across the forecourt. Images from the hellish night played across his mind. He frowned and scanned the few men still left. "Have you seen Sinclair?"

"He had to leave," Barnaby said. "He was helping from the first. Later he was standing next to me after the rescue, when the main house went up—I've never seen such naked horror on a man's face. In fact, he looked so ill I wondered if he had a weak heart. When we started to organize, he said he had to go and take care of something." Barnaby grimaced. "I'm not sure it wasn't his horror he needed to deal with—he seemed deeply affected."

Turning his head, Barnaby studied Charlie's face. "You do realize, don't you, that the back of your coat is burned through?"

Charlie raised his brows. "Is it?" He shifted his shoulders and felt the uneven pull of the fabric, felt pain, muted and distant, as skin tugged—and remembered Sarah pushing the burning log off his shoulders and patting his back . . . He shrugged. "It's not that bad. I'll survive."

They joined Sarah and Gabriel as the last of the carriages rolled away. Charlie caught Sarah's eyes. "We've done all we can here—we should head home."

She sighed and nodded. Slipping her hand in his, she turned to where their horses stood, the last four remaining. Gabriel and Barnaby fell in behind them.

"Any idea how it started?" Gabriel asked.

Charlie and Sarah glanced back in time to see Barnaby nod.

His face had set, his expression beyond grim. "Some of the children, mostly older ones, the lad Jim, and Joseph Tiller all saw it happen. Flaming arrows—some aimed at the thatch, others at bundles of what must have been oil-soaked rags tucked in crannies around the wings. He, whoever he is, wasn't taking any chances that the thatch wouldn't catch—it didn't in the north wing where it was most exposed to the weather. Even with the other two wings we might have saved them if it hadn't been for the rags tucked under the eaves."

"But"—Charlie shook his head—"when did he plant the rags? The staff have been keeping a continuous watch, even at night."

Barnaby shrugged.

They walked on, frowning, then Sarah sighed. "It would have been earlier today." She glanced at the others. "It's Sunday. All the staff and the children go down to the church at Crowcombe. They'd be away for an hour and a half, maybe more. Only Quince is left, and she's mostly with the babies in the attic. The attic windows overlook the forecourt. Quince would have kept watch, but if the man approached from the rear, she wouldn't have seen him."

"And the long ladders were kept in the courtyards between the wings." Charlie shook his head.

They reached the horses; he lifted Sarah up to her saddle, then swung up to his.

They all paused for one last look at the wreck of the orphanage, still glowing an angry red through the crisp winter night.

Gabriel, his tone harsh, spoke for them all. "Whoever this blackguard is, we have to stop him."

Malcolm intended to do just that. He'd ridden to Finley House in a wretched, tormented state, emotions he'd never experienced before battering and raking him. What he'd seen that night had literally turned his stomach—not with queasiness but with sheer, unadulterated guilt.

He felt as if his heart—more, his soul—were literally being strangled. This had to stop—he had to stop it—now. Tonight.

The knowledge that he could had allowed him to calm, to wash the soot from his hands and face, brush it from his hair, to dress in fresh clothes and sit once more behind his desk, and with a massive effort of will wrench his mind free—detach it from all he'd seen, all the implications—enough to plan.

As always, his plans were cold-blooded, calculated to a nicety. They wouldn't just work, they would work precisely as he intended.

He was waiting, sitting behind his desk in a gloom relieved only by the flickering light from the fire at the other end of the room when Jennings scratched at the French door. Malcolm rose and let his henchman in, wordlessly indicating the chair before the desk. Closing the door, he quietly locked it and slipped the key into his pocket.

He turned back to the desk.

Jennings settled comfortably in the chair. Stretching out his legs, folding his hands over his developing paunch, he grinned confidingly as Malcolm rounded the desk to resume his seat. "I got your note. But I expect you'll have seen the action up at the orphanage tonight. The countess is sure to sell now—she'll need the money if she wants to re-build."

Malcolm let himself sink into his chair, battling a surge of cold fury. Jennings wasn't made uneasy by the lack of light; Malcolm had for years been extremely careful over anyone, even by chance, seeing them together.

Tonight, the dimness served another purpose. It hid the rage in Malcolm's eyes.

He took a moment to study Jennings; he hadn't changed all that much from the young man Malcolm had found and first used in London—was it nearly seventeen?—years ago. A trifle stockier, a few lines in his round, unremarkable, eminently trustworthy face. His even temper, his open expression, his directness in speech and thought, and his above-the-norm intelligence had recommended him to Malcolm. Those attributes remained.

What Malcolm hadn't, until the last few days, properly appreciated was that Jennings had no conscience. He had caution, and a healthy vein of self-preservation, but . . .

"The orphanage . . ." Malcolm paused to ensure he had full command of his voice. Jennings was accustomed to his long pauses, but a quaver of fury would alert him before Malcolm wished. "Did it occur to you that some of the children might get caught in the blaze?"

Jennings shrugged. "Possibly, but it was a reasonable risk—they should have had time to get out." When Malcolm didn't immediately reply, Jennings added, "And it's not as if we've balked at a necessary death in the past."

Beneath the desk, Malcolm's fist clenched, yet his tone was even, his voice mild as he said, "Quite. However, I've never before thought to ask . . . just how many deaths have we been responsible for?"

Thumbs tapping, Jennings briefly consulted the ceiling, then grimaced. "I can't say I've kept score, exactly, but ten? Some number like that."

"I see." Malcolm was finding it harder and harder to rein in his cold fury, especially as it wasn't directed solely at Jennings—more than half his rage was directed at himself. Slowly he rose; slowly, considering his words, he circled the desk. "I'm not sure if you've noted it, but this is the first time I've . . . seen you in action. In all our other projects, I briefly visited the area, identified the land required, then returned to London and sent you to acquire it. I never returned to the area. However, in this case, when I came to this area to scout out the valley I fell in love with the place and stayed, and so started to get to know the local people and appreciate what they have here—the lives they lead, the community, the peace. For the first time in my life, I thought I'd found a place I'd like to call home, to buy a house, settle down, perhaps even think of marrying and having a family."

Not a hint of the feelings roiling beneath his surface showed in either his voice or his face.

Settling against the front edge of his desk, he inclined his head to Jennings. "Admittedly, when, during our first few projects, you'd return to me without the required title and stumped for ways in which to persuade the owner to sell, I outlined various ways in which people—any normal people with the usual aspirations and emotions—could be prevailed upon to part with their land—avarice, supersitition, accidents, and so on. From my point of view that advice was theoretical. Distanced, detached. I never saw you actually use any of those methods." He paused, then added, his voice still even, devoid of any emotion, "For instance, I never knew about those deaths."

Jennings blinked up at him, unsure of his direction. "That's true."

"If I'd *thought* about it, of course, I would have guessed how things were—what you were doing. I knew what methods you were employing to persuade, and if I'd *thought*, I would have realized what that meant, but . . . unless I actually *see* things with my own eyes, they remain abstract. Theoretical, not truly real. They don't touch me."

He finally looked Jennings directly in the eye, and smiled faintly. "So, you see, until now, I haven't come face-to-face with the human and emotional consequences of my—our—actions. I haven't, until now, had to acknowledge even in my own mind any responsibility for the human outcome of my schemes." He held Jennings's gaze. "I have to tell you that witnessing our methods of persuasion as applied to the orphanage has come as something of a shock."

They were now close enough for Jennings to glean some sense of the turbulent emotions Malcolm was suppressing. He shifted uneasily, a puzzled frown in his eyes. "But . . . I've just been following your orders. Doing what I thought I was supposed to."

"Oh, indeed." Malcolm acknowledged that with an upraised hand. "However, my question to you is: How could you?"

Jennings blinked.

Abruptly Malcolm dropped the shield concealing his emotions. "These were *good* people—kind and generous and *deserving* people." His fury and condemnation blazed forth. "They were helping children—children who had nothing and no one."

Like him.

He sucked in a breath as that realization stung, then went on, his voice harsh, unforgiving, his diction frighteningly precise. "Let me explain how I feel about your actions regarding the orphanage now that I've been obliged to see them firsthand. I assume you were too far away from your handiwork to notice that I was there, helping to fight the blaze."

Jennings's expression was a medley of incomprehension and dawning suspicion, and beneath that a rising fear.

Malcolm kept his eyes locked on Jennings's. "So I was there to witness not just the devotion of the orphanage staff, not just how everyone around, everyone who could, came running to help. Not just how important to the countess the orphanage was and how much sheer anguish our actions caused, but how, despite his disapproval of the place, the earl unstintingly tried to save it. I was *there,* Jennings, rooted to the spot by my own contemptible fear when Meredith and his friend risked their lives—actually put themselves in the way of death—to save two mewling pauper babes and their bitter stick of a nurse. For the first time in my life, Jennings, I understood what noblesse oblige means—finally understood what the words 'courage' and 'caring' really mean."

Resisting the urge to rise and pace, Malcolm stayed sitting on the edge of the desk and held Jennings's gaze unwaveringly. "Until I came here I didn't believe love, selfless courage, noblesse oblige, or any of man's other supposedly finer qualities truly existed. I'd never come across them, never had them paraded before my face in a manner impossible to dismiss—never been forced to acknowledge that they are real. Now, thanks to our latest project and your actions—your interpretation of my advice on methods of persuasion—my eyes have been opened."

One long-fingered hand relaxed on his thigh, the other on the desk behind him, Malcolm watched Jennings tense. "Indeed. Understanding as I now do, knowing your actions on my instructions have caused so many so much pain, so much terror, heartache, anguish, and loss, has left me stricken, Jennings, down to the depths of what I suspect is my soul. I never knew I could feel this way—never knew remorse was within my repertoire. But I feel it now—relentlessly. I feel blackened, empty, besmirched—guilty." He paused, then softly added, "And you, Jennings, are guilty, too."

Jennings gripped the chair's arms, but before his backside left the seat, Malcolm clipped him over the ear with the short brass candlestick he'd rested behind him on the desk. Jennings groaned and slumped, unconscious.

Malcolm rose, retrieved the rope he'd left waiting behind the desk, and swiftly tied Jennings's hands behind his back, then hobbled his ankles. Drawing a kerchief from his pocket, he neatly gagged the man.

After drawing the curtains over all the windows, Malcolm returned to his desk and lit the lamp. Once it was burning brightly, he sat again in his chair. He wondered if he should feel sorry for Jennings, for involving the man in his schemes, but that, it seemed, was an emotion he hadn't developed. From the first he'd recognized in Jennings the same lack of conscience, the same total absence of compassion that—until recently—had been his; if it hadn't been through his schemes, Jennings, like his late and unlamented guardian, Lowther, would have found some other route to perdition.

Setting a fresh sheet on the blotter before him, he picked up his sharpened quill and opened the ink pot. He dipped the nib; his gaze drifted to the three letters stacked to one side of the blotter and he paused.

Then, lips tightening, he looked down and wrote.

The letters had arrived the day before while he'd been out searching for Jennings. Deeming them less important, he'd let the letters lie;

he'd opened them an hour ago when he'd sat down to wait for Jennings.

From three separate, highly regarded London legal offices, each letter had informed him that one of his personal companies—those with Malcolm Sinclair listed as a director—was under investigation by the authorities; each solicitor had been obliged to hand over all documents and records dealing with said company. Three solicitors; three companies. The letters had been dated four days before.

He'd sat for a good ten minutes, staring at the letters, trying to imagine how the authorities had known to investigate those companies. They hadn't committed any illegal deed, weren't connected in any way with any of the land companies he'd used to profiteer from the railways . . . well, except for . . .

On a sudden, sickening rush he'd seen the single flaw in his magnificent creation—the one thread that connected his personal companies to the land companies. Rereading the details of the letters, he'd found confirmation; one solicitor had written that the authorities were interested in a payment made *to* a particular land company.

The one link he'd never thought to hide, and someone had thought to search for it.

He'd sat staring across the room as minutes ticked by and the realization that he was facing absolute and utter ruin solidified in his mind. The instant his name cropped up, his reputation as a major investor in the railways would be seen for the connection it was—and once they had his name . . . it wouldn't be easy but eventually they'd find evidence enough to hang him.

He'd considered the prospect for a full minute, then had shrugged and refocused on his plan to deal with the current situation. In light of that, ruination was immaterial.

He wrote steadily for some time.

Then Jennings stirred; laying aside his pen, Malcolm rose and rounded the desk. Grasping Jennings's arm, he hauled him upright. "Walk." He'd left just enough play in the ropes about Jennings's ankles for him to shuffle along.

Groggy and dazed, Jennings tried to resist, but Malcolm propelled him out of the library, along the corridor, and into the kitchen. The wooden cellar door stood open, propped wide. Seeing it, Jennings panicked and fought to resist, but with Malcolm—taller, heavier, and, as

Jennings was discovering, a good deal stronger—behind him, he couldn't gain sufficient purchase on the slate floor to even slow the approach of the yawning blackness.

Malcolm paused just before the threshold and murmured, "If you stop struggling and descend the stairs yourself, I won't have to hurl you down them."

Jennings hesitated, still tense but unable to do anything to save himself, then the fight went out of him. He nodded and carefully edged his foot forward.

Malcolm grabbed the lantern he'd left waiting, already lit, and followed, one hand wrapped about one of Jennings's arms more to steady the man as he lurched down the stairs than to restrain him.

He was already well and truly restrained.

Once in the cellar, Malcolm pointed Jennings toward a stool set against a supporting column. Jennings shuffled over and collapsed onto the stool; before he knew what was happening, Malcolm looped another rope around his chest and tied it off on the other side of the rough-hewn column.

Returning to where Jennings could see him, he considered the man, then turned for the stairs.

"*Hmm?*"

Glancing back, raising the lantern, Malcolm met Jennings's eyes. "Why?"

When Jennings nodded, he hesitated, then said, "Because unexpectedly—and extremely belatedly—I appear to have developed a conscience." He paused, then, brows rising, amended, "Or perhaps I finally realized I possessed one, and why—realized what I was supposed to do with it."

His lips twisted wryly. "You want to know what I'm going to do?" Jennings nodded. "I suppose, given we've been playing these games, you and I, for nearly seventeen years, I owe you that much."

Briefly, Malcolm outlined his plan. "While I'm perfectly prepared to bear full responsibility for all I've done, I will not accept responsibility for your actions. While the ideas were mine, all the active decisions were yours. You've not at any time over the last fifteen and more years been operating under my direct orders—I long ago left you to your own devices, your own initiative."

He paused, then said, "Do you remember Mrs. Edith Balmain?"

He waited until a spark of recognition lit Jennings's dulled eyes. "Yes, that's right—back at the very beginning, our scheme with Lowther. On Lowther's demise, Mrs. Balmain was kind enough to give me some advice—she warned me to keep my thoughts, my schemes, to myself." He studied Jennings, then murmured, "Would, for both our sakes, that I'd listened."

He lowered the lantern; in the dimness he looked at Jennings one last time. "They'll come for you tomorrow, before evening I'd imagine. I'd advise you to throw yourself on the court's mercy."

Turning, Malcolm made his way to the bottom of the cellar stairs. A series of mumbles had him glancing back. "What about me?"

Jennings nodded emphatically.

Malcolm smiled, perfectly sincerely. "By the time they come for me, I'll be gone."

20

With Sarah, Barnaby, and Gabriel, Charlie headed south at little more than an ambling walk. Gabriel was the freshest; he held his mount back beside Barnaby's and kept a careful eye on the rest of them as they let their mounts carry them home.

When they reached the Park's stable, Croker and one of his lads were waiting to take the horses and let them stumble up to the house. The startled looks on the men's faces confirmed just how filthy and bedraggled they were.

Gabriel remained mounted. He paced alongside them as they slowly made their way out of the stable yard.

Sarah looked up at him. "It's so late—dawn can't be that far off. Won't you stay the night here? It's miles to Casleigh."

Gabriel smiled and shook his head. "It may be late, but Alathea won't sleep until I return and report that all is well—or as well as can be expected."

Beside Sarah, Charlie snorted. "Meaning you promised her you would in order to get her to leave in the carriage with the children."

Gabriel chuckled. "Your understanding of the married state is clearly improving."

Charlie humphed; he, Sarah, and Barnaby halted in the drive and waved Gabriel off. Atop his huge hunter, his dark figure was quickly swallowed up by the shadows as he headed farther south. Lowering their arms, the three of them walked slowly, one foot in front of the other, across the lawn to the side door.

Crisp and Figgs were waiting to receive them—with warmth, reassurances, and glasses of spiced wine that Figgs insisted they drink. Unable to summon strength enough to argue, they meekly did as they were told while Figgs and Crisp, both plainly struggling to subdue the urge to comment and fuss over their appalling state, reported on the arrangements made in their absence.

"We've put the babes in the old schoolroom," Figgs said. "Miss Quince and Mrs. Carter are in the rooms off it, and we've accommodated Mr. Kennett in the main servants' wing. They're all settled in, poor dears—quite exhausted they were—and one of the maids is keeping watch over the babes for the rest of the night."

Draining his glass of wine, Barnaby returned it to Crisp's tray. He nodded to Charlie and Sarah. "I'll see you at breakfast tomorrow. We'll have to think what's the best way forward."

Crisp assured Barnaby that hot water would be dispatched immediately to his room and sent a hovering footman to attend to it.

"Now my lord, my lady." Crisp turned back to Sarah and Charlie. "A hot bath is being prepared in your chambers as we speak. If there's anything further you need, any assistance—"

"Thank you, Crisp, Figgs." Sarah summoned strength enough to take charge; she had a strong suspicion that if she didn't, she and Charlie would be treated as the children both Crisp and Figgs still remembered them as. "Your arrangements have been exemplary—we knew we could count on you. His lordship and I will manage admirably."

She took the empty glass from Charlie's slack fingers and replaced it with hers on Crisp's tray. "Now—is Gwen waiting for me?"

"Indeed, ma'am," Crisp replied. "She's supervising the filling of your bath."

"In that case, I believe his lordship and I have all we require." She linked her arm with Charlie's; he'd been careful to keep his back away from Crisp and Figgs throughout. "We'll see you in the morning—breakfast at ten, please."

"Indeed, ma'am." Crisp bowed. Figgs bobbed a curtsy.

"Thank you both," Charlie said, nodding in dismissal.

He yielded to Sarah's push on his arm and turned with her, moving toward the main staircase and their apartments beyond.

Horrified gasps erupted from behind them.

"My lord! Your coat—" came from Crisp

"You've been burned!" Figgs all but shrieked.

With a small resigned sigh, Sarah halted and turned back—stopping Figgs's and Crisp's instinctive rush toward them. "It's not as bad as it appears. Doctor Caliburn took a look at it and gave me some salve." She flourished a pot she'd pulled from her pocket. "He instructed me in what to do. Now if you please, we really should retire so I can tend his lordship's wounds."

Watching the performance over his shoulder, Charlie capped it with a distant nod, then faced forward again and, arm in arm with Sarah, continued on.

When they were on the stairs and out of earshot, he leaned closer and murmured, "I had wondered how on earth we would manage to get free—in terms of fussing, Crisp and Figgs have always been able to give Serena and even Alathea lessons." He glanced down at her face. "Thank you for saving me."

Sarah humphed. "As your injuries were sustained while you were saving me, it seemed only fair."

Charlie chuckled weakly. "But I had to save you because you'd already saved me, remember?"

"But you were on the ground needing to be saved only because you'd climbed into the attic to save the babies and Quince." They'd reached the doors to their apartments. Sarah paused and looked into his face; smiling softly, she raised a hand to his cheek. "Each of us did our part in saving something tonight, but you most of all." Stretching up, she touched her lips to his. "Thank you."

He looked down into her eyes and returned her gentle smile. "It was . . ." He hesitated, then said, "Both my duty and my pleasure."

He opened the door and they went in, crossed the foyer and entered their bedchamber.

Sarah went straight to the adjoining bathing chamber, checked that they had all they might require, then dismissed Gwen, sending her to her bed.

Then she returned to the bedchamber, where Charlie was twisting in front of the cheval glass, trying to see his back. "Come in here—no, don't try to take your coat off yet."

She bullied him into the bathing room and made him sit on a stool close by a sideboard with a basin atop it. A sponge lay in the warm water in the basin; she squeezed it out, then applied it to the burned areas on his back.

Pressing gently, she dampened each burned spot, then moved to the next. Charlie sat still, slumped, feeling tiredness drag at his limbs. "Did Caliburn examine my wound?"

"He looked at it when I asked him to—you wouldn't have noticed. He didn't need to examine it closely—he'd seen what had happened. Your coat's burned through and your waistcoat as well, but while the shirt got burned—it's turned brown and flaked away—the skin beneath is scorched rather than burned."

"Because you got that log off my back so quickly."

"Hmm."

He got the impression she was concentrating, that he wasn't supposed to distract her with talk; perhaps, as Gabriel had said, his understanding of the married state was improving.

His lips quirked, then lifted. His wandering mind registered that after all that had passed during the long night, to be able to smile—easily, with a gentle happiness that warmed his heart—was a singular blessing.

Another gift he owed to her.

She finished her dampening, then urged him to his feet and helped him ease coat and waistcoat off together. He took his coat and held it up to inspect the damage, then she filched it from his fingers and dropped it on the floor.

"Shirt next." She helped him with the buttons, but stopped him before he could try to shrug it off, making him wait while she dampened the burned areas again before he did.

Standing behind him, she helped, eventually drawing the shirt down his arms and away; before he could turn, she sent it to join his coat and prodded lightly on the back of his shoulders. "The bath next—that's what Doctor Caliburn ordered. Then I have to smooth the salve on."

He had no real argument with the doctor's orders, only with the manner in which she believed they should be followed. He dutifully sat and pulled off his boots, letting her help, then stood again and stripped off his breeches.

She'd flitted away to test the bathwater; he waited until she returned and seized his arm to tow him to the tub—then he seized her. Deaf to her protests, he bundled her out of her stained and bedraggled gown, dispensed with her petticoats and chemise, sending all to join the growing pile, then he scooped her up in his arms—spent half a second glorying in the sensation of her silken skin against his, her curvaceous weight held against him—then he climbed into the bath and carefully sat, settling her before him.

She humphed, then wriggled around. Grabbing the sponge from the lip where she'd left it, she plunged it into the water, then with determination in her face and a warning in her eyes, set it to his skin and proceeded to wash the soot and grime from his arms and chest.

Lips curving, he leaned back—neck on the lip to prevent his shoulders from touching the tub—and let her. He watched her face while she did; a strange, soothing calm descended and enveloped them.

Held them when he reached out and took the sponge from her, and set to work sponging her ivory limbs. They took turns, cleaning, soothing, caring, washing each other's hair, until they were both clean.

He stood and reached for the waiting pails, rinsing her off, then using the last on himself. Towels left warming before the fire soon had them dry, then, arms looped about each other's waist, they propped each other up as far as the bed.

Tiredness was dragging at them both, but Sarah poked and fussed until he sat up and let her tend his scorched skin. Drawing his knees up, he slumped over them so she could reach more easily.

Her fingers lightly brushed, then soothingly spread the cool cream over the heated spots on his shoulders and back.

He closed his eyes and savored her touch; if he'd been a cat he would have purred.

Sometime during her ministrations, he fell asleep.

He woke to find himself slumped on his stomach, with the covers propped across a bolster on one side and Sarah on the other, so the covers wouldn't weigh on his injuries.

She must have prodded and pulled to get him arranged as he was; the thought—the image it conjured—made him smile.

Eyes closed, one step away from sliding back into his earlier, deeply restful slumber—into a peace he'd never experienced before she'd lain by his side—he let his mind skate over the events of the night, and what waited for them tomorrow.

Despite the horrors of the blaze, a feeling of victory pervaded his recollections; they might have lost the orphanage building but they'd saved the orphanage—the children, the staff. And if anything the commitment to it, both from themselves and the local gentry as well as the surrounding community, had been strengthened through seeing the place threatened, and through its communal defense.

There was something very powerful about joining together to defeat a mutual foe who threatened an institution the community suddenly remembered had real value.

In the wake of the blaze, tomorrow would be filled to overflowing with organizing, coordinating, arranging, and deciding.

He imagined it, envisioned how busy he and Sarah would separately be—and while one part of his mind jibbed that they would have no time to spend together, alone, another part reminded him of the glory of togetherness they now shared. All it needed was a look, a touch, and that glory was there, whether they were in a crowded room or alone.

It was theirs, and now always would be. Embracing it—having the courage to embrace it—had made it forever his. Theirs.

There was, despite all, much to celebrate.

Including the fact that Sarah really was pregnant—he was sure of it. As he'd held her against him, her head slumped on his shoulder, and gently washed her stomach, he'd felt sure it was just a touch more rounded than it had been. He'd been tempted—so tempted—to tell her then and there how much he loved her. It had hardly seemed any great thing, not when their love, his and hers, had been wrapped all around them, an all but tangible force.

He hadn't found any fancy words—none he deemed appropriate, none he could imagine saying with sincerity, and when he spoke he wanted it clear that whatever words he said came from his heart.

But perhaps fancy words weren't necessary.

He'd been about to speak, trusting to instinct and her understanding, but she'd raised a hand and delicately smothered a yawn—and he'd realized just how exhausted she, and indeed he, had been. The impulse to speak had faded; when he finally uttered the words, he wanted her to remember them, and not imagine later it was some dream.

But he would tell her soon.

She—and Alathea, Gabriel, and all the others—were right. A marriage based on love was worth fighting for.

Worth any sacrifice he might ever have to make.

While the rest of the world slept and night softly faded with the oncoming dawn, Malcolm Sinclair sat at the desk in his library, quill flying across parchment. Page after page lay stacked by his elbow; he felt no hesitation in writing—no second thoughts.

Dawn was a glimmer on the horizon when he finally sighed, and straightened. With a flourish he signed at the bottom of the last page, then carefully sanded it. Gathering the sheets, he folded them, then lighting a candle, he melted some wax and carefully afixed his seal over the ends.

Then and only then did he pause, pen poised over the front of the packet. Then, lips curving, he fluidly wrote: "To Whom It May Concern."

Done. He sat back and surveyed the packet; gradually, his gaze grew distant. A frown slowly formed on his austerely handsome face, but then he shook it aside and drew two fresh sheets to him.

The two notes took but a few minutes to pen. He signed and sealed them, then rising, propped the larger packet prominently on the desk. Turning out the lamp, he picked up the two notes, walked to the French doors, and drew aside the curtains. In the faint light he crossed to the small side table that stood beside the armchair before the fire.

Easing open the side-table drawer, he drew out Edith Balmain's diary. Nudging the drawer closed with one knee, he stood contemplating the book in its silver-plated covers for a silent minute, then turned and, taking the book with him, left the room.

Sarah woke to find herself alone in their bed. Warm and relaxed, she felt curiously content; she stretched, then remembered the events of the night. And realized why.

Out of the bad, something good often came. Her aunt Edith had frequently said so, and she'd been a very wise woman.

Rising, she rang for Gwen, then washed and dressed. Leaving Gwen exclaiming over their discarded clothes, she headed for the breakfast room.

Her orphanage had just burned to the ground, yet she'd never felt more confident and at peace with her lot.

Charlie was seated at the head of the breakfast table, Barnaby on his right. He looked up as she entered and met her eyes; she beamed a glorious smile at him, knowing with just that look that he felt it, too—that he felt as she did.

This morning was the beginning of the rest of their life. Their joint life. If the events of the night had demonstrated anything, they'd demonstrated that.

The future lay before them to make of it what they would, but the successful merging of their lives was already under way.

As Charlie had stated, they'd rebuild—and build better.

Filling her plate, surprised at just how hungry she was, she dispensed with formality and went to sit on Charlie's left. He was waiting to draw back her chair.

As soon as she was settled, Barnaby spoke. "I'll be leaving within minutes—I've already asked for my horse to be brought around." He glanced at Charlie, then explained, "We've decided that we need to inform the authorities about what's been happening here. I'll ride to London and tell Stokes, then come back and continue my search for the agent. He'll still be here—they'll expect you to sell, but he'll likely wait for a few days at least before making his next offer. But with the fire at the orphanage, we have an immediate, investigatable crime, and Stokes and the rest need to know that—that the game truly is afoot, and the dice are being rolled in earnest."

He mopped up the last of his ham. "It'll also give me a chance to check with Devil and see if Montague has unearthed any clue."

Sarah nodded. "We'll have a great deal to do here, organizing the children and the staff, let alone dealing with the farm."

Charlie nodded. Reaching for her hand, he closed his around it. "I'll go to the farm with Kennett. We'll sort out what has to be done to make the ruin safe. It'll take days to get it damped down and secure, but we'll make a start."

"There's the animals, too," Sarah said. "Jim turned them out into the north field. Perhaps Squire Mack would take them for the moment?"

Charlie nodded. "I'll ask him."

"Meanwhile . . ." Sarah wrinkled her nose. "I'm going to have to write to the bishop. 'I greatly fear, your lordship, that the orphanage burned down.' Goodness only knows how I'm going to phrase that."

"Never mind the bishop—and I'm sure he'd agree," Charlie said. "Make lists of what the children and staff need—aside from all else, you're sure to sustain visits from your mother, Mrs. Duncliffe, Alathea and Celia, let alone the other local ladies, all wanting to know what they can do to help. They'll probably give you a day's grace, but for your sanity's sake, you'll need to have a list of requirements by tomorrow."

Sarah laughed. He was right. "I'll manage."

A chair scraped; smiling, Barnaby set down his napkin and rose. "I'll leave you two to your endeavors, and get on with mine." He waved them both back as they started to rise. "I know my way out, and you both need to eat. And I'll be back before you know it, as soon as I can." His easy expression faded, hardness replacing it, a predatory glint gleaming in his eyes. "This is one villain whose downfall I don't want to miss."

With a nod and a salute, he left them, striding out to the front hall.

As the sounds of his departure faded, Sarah gave her attention to her plate and Charlie did the same. They ate in companionable silence, then, replete, she sighed and sat back.

Charlie was sipping his coffee, his gaze on her face.

She smiled, just for him, letting her happiness show. "It'll be better, won't it?"

He held her gaze, then set aside his cup, reached for her hand, and lifted it to his lips. He kissed, his eyes steady on hers, and confirmed, "Much better." After a moment, he added, "We'll make it so."

An hour later, Malcolm Sinclair met his housekeeper—a woman from the village who came in to clean and cook for him—at the front door.

He smiled charmingly. "Mrs. Perkins, I apologize for not mentioning it yesterday but I won't need you for the next week or so—I've been called away and will be leaving later today. If you'll accept this . . ." He handed over a plump purse. "Your wages to date plus a retainer. I'll let you know when I return."

Mrs. Perkins quickly checked the coins, discovered his "retainer" would cover a full week of her services, and smiled happily. "Of course, sir. It's been a pleasure doing for you, and I'll be happy to come again once you get back."

She bobbed a curtsy and turned back down the path, no doubt already planning what to do with her unexpected free time.

Malcolm remained in the doorway until she'd passed out of the gate and disappeared down the street. Stepping back, he closed the door, then shrugged off his morning coat.

Donning a rough workman's jacket, then pulling a wide-brimmed felt hat low over his head, covering his distinctive wheat-blond hair, he drew on heavy leather gardener's gloves before picking up the sack of tools he'd left waiting behind the door. Hefting it, he strode down the corridor, old boots thudding on the polished boards. Going through the library, he let himself out by the French doors to where his horse stood saddled and waiting.

Charlie surveyed the blackened ruins of Quilley Farm. The wings had been reduced to smoldering heaps of charred wood and soot-streaked rubble, but in the main building flames still flickered and flared, working their greedy way through the skeleton of wooden beams buried within the stone walls.

In some places, the stone walls had bulged, then crumbled, heavy blocks tumbling haphazardly to the ground. Sections of wall still stood—liable to crumble without warning.

He pointed. "We'll need to get grapples and haul them down—we can't risk them falling on anyone wandering by."

"Aye." Beside him, Kennett nodded, grim and set. "We'll do what we can today, but most likely we'll have to do it bit by bit, as the fire finishes with each section."

Charlie considered the unstable walls and the piles of rubble behind the main house. "Let's leave the stone until later today. We need to spread the debris at the back and make sure what's left is fully doused."

He glanced back at the steady stream of men toiling up the slope. Many carried tools on their shoulders. The first had appeared as he and Kennett rode through Crowcombe.

Greeting the men who'd reached them, he led the way around the main house. After pointing out what had to be done, he picked up a rake and set to.

Throughout the morning, he worked alongside the men. Engaged in the relatively mindless chore, they chatted and talked. At first they watched their words around him, but gradually they relaxed, eventually directing queries his way, wondering about his views on the local hunt, on the plan to resurface the road through the valley, and countless other local matters on which he did indeed have both views and influence.

By the time they broke off for a late-morning ale supplied by the Crowcombe innkeeper, he'd learned more about the problems facing the local people, the whys and wherefores, than he had from hours of listening to their masters.

Leaning on the rake, his coat tossed over the nearby fence, he quaffed the ale, then blotted his brow with his sleeve. The day was cool but fine, with the scent of spring dancing on the wind.

He glanced around at the men; all had accepted his authority without question—more, they'd looked for it. To them it was right and proper that he, a Morwellan, an earl of Meredith, should be there, giving them orders, taking responsibility. That was how local communities worked.

Yet he hadn't been there, not for years, and if it hadn't been for Sarah, he wouldn't be there now. Without his connection through her, dealing with the ruin would have been her father's responsibility, and at his age he would have sent one of his senior workers; definitely not the same thing.

The Cynsters lay far to the south; the area around here looked to Meredith for their lead, and he was not only the earl but significantly younger and more bodily able than most of his neighbors.

His place was here, among these people. Being available to them, keeping an ear to the soil so he knew what troubled them.

His responsibility lay here, not in London.

What truly surprised him was how well that glove fitted, how comfortable he felt in the role.

Duty had always featured highly in his life, but he hadn't before thought much of this facet. Yet he'd embraced one new aspect in his life, and was actively changing said life to accommodate it. Perhaps this was another aspect that—in light of that other—would now fit better. Better than the life he'd thought he and his perfect wife would live, mostly in London, cut off from what he now realized was an essential part of him, of who he really was, of the man he now wanted to be.

"M'lord?"

He turned to see one of the older men beckoning.

"We've found a section of the fence that's burned through—looks like burning thatch landed on it. Can you come and say what you want us to do?"

Charlie straightened, laid aside the rake, and followed the man around the building.

A little after noon, Malcolm Sinclair, garbed in an elegant morning coat, tight buckskin breeches, and spotless linen, every inch the sophisticated London gentleman, strolled the short distance from his front gate into Crowcombe village proper.

Halting on the stone stoop of the local solicitor's office, he paused. He rarely used local people as his tools, but in this instance, using Skeggs seemed both appropriate and wise.

Deliberately turning, he looked up at the broad shelf of land above the village—at the black, still smoking ruin of Quilley Farm. He considered the sight, debating whether some might think it a fitting symbol for the end of his ambitions.

After a moment, he turned and, opening Skeggs's door, calmly went inside.

Sarah didn't get a chance to write to the bishop until early afternoon, when they finally got all six babies fed and settled for their nap. She found the small, tiny, perfect people utterly fascinating—far more than she had a mere few weeks ago.

That, presumably, was another sign of her likely condition. She wasn't sure . . . yet she hoped. Prayed. That, she felt, would be the crowning glory, the final perfect piece in her newly constructed life. But she wanted to be sure before she told anyone. Even Charlie.

Especially Charlie.

At their wedding she'd seen the look in his eyes when Dillon and Gerrard had spoken of their sons; she didn't need to wonder what his reaction to her carrying his child would be. But because she knew how much it would mean to him, she had to be sure. Absolutely sure.

Her sitting room having been temporarily commandeered as a sorting room for linens, she took refuge in Charlie's library; pulling up the large chair to the desk, she selected a pen from the set he kept nicely sharpened.

She found paper and ink, then settled to her task. As she'd prophesied, finding acceptable phrases with which to break her news was not a simple matter, but when the clock next chimed the hour, she'd achieved what she considered a satisfactory result. Sealing the missive with Charlie's seal, she laid it on the blotter for him to frank.

A tap fell on the door; she looked up as it opened and Crisp glanced in.

"Ah—there you are, ma'am. A note from Mr. Sinclair, brought by one of the lads from Crowcombe."

"Thank you, Crisp." Sarah lifted the sealed note from his salver.

"The boy said no reply was expected, ma'am." Crisp bowed and withdrew.

Hunting out Charlie's letter knife, Sarah broke the seal and unfolded the single sheet.

"Oh! How wonderful!" Sinclair had written that he'd found her aunt's diary—in "the most surprising place." Sarah wondered where it had been, then quickly read on.

Unfortunately, Sinclair wrote, he had to leave on urgent business, and given the press of errands he had to complete before he left, he couldn't allow himself the luxury of calling on her to place it in her hands. However, he wondered if she would have time to ride out and meet with him—he had promised himself that he wouldn't leave the area before he'd taken in the famous view from the bridge across Will's Neck falls. He would be passing that way at three o'clock—if she could meet him there at that time, he would hand over the diary and explain where he'd found it.

Alternatively, if she was unable to meet him, he would return the diary when he came back to the area, although he couldn't say when that would be. Given its intrinsic value as well as its nostalgic value to her, he was reluctant to entrust its delivery to other hands.

Sarah glanced at the clock. It was fifteen minutes past two o'clock—plenty of time for her to change and ride up to the falls.

She wanted the diary, wanted to hear where he had found it, and with the taint of smoke still lingering in her lungs, the fresh air and exercise would do her good.

One of the easier decisions she'd had to make that day. Rising, she headed for the door to give orders for Blacktail to be saddled while she changed into her riding habit.

T wenty minutes later, Charlie was organizing a group of men with grapples and lines, testing the stability of the walls still standing, when a lad from Crowcombe village approached.

"Message, m'lord." The boy tugged at his cap and proffered a folded and sealed sheet. "From Mr. Sinclair. Him as is staying at Finley House."

Charlie accepted the letter. Hunting in his pocket, he found a coin for the lad and dismissed him.

He glanced at the men, but they knew what they were doing. Stepping back, he leaned against the fence, broke Malcolm's seal, spread open the sheet, and read.

All animation leached from his face.

Devoid of salutation, Malcolm's message was blunt.

I will shortly have your wife. As you read these words, she's riding up the track to the bridge over Will's Neck falls. If you wish to see her again you will do precisely as I ask. Don't hesitate, don't think—most important don't imagine that you understand what I have planned. Don't try to organize anything, don't attempt to raise any alarm. Do remember that there is a direct line of sight between the bridge and Quilley Farm—I am presently watching you through a spyglass.

Leave the farm and ride to the bridge. Do as I say, and fair Sarah will still be yours, entirely unharmed, by the end of the day.

Act, and act now—or you will lose her.
We'll be waiting for you on the bridge over the falls.

Charlie stared, unseeing, the black lines dancing before his eyes.

Icy dread welled within him; it coalesced, closing like a fist about his heart. He'd never felt so cold in his life. So chilled.

But he knew what he had to do. Precisely as Malcolm asked.

Drawing in a huge breath, straining against the iron vise locked about his lungs, he remained still, outwardly calm, and forced himself to consider . . .

But there were no alternatives. No one he could contact, no one near he could call on for help with this.

Especially as he knew Malcolm Sinclair didn't bluff.

Stuffing the note in his pocket, he walked off, heading for where Storm was tied. As if pressed for time, he swung back and from a distance called to Kennett, "I've been called away—I have to go. I'll try to get back later—until I do, you're in charge."

Kennett's unconcerned, laconic wave would make it clear to any watcher that whatever he'd said hadn't been any warning or alert.

Pulling Storm's reins free, Charlie swung up to the gray's back and set off as fast as the gelding could go down the lane to Crowcombe—to the track leading to the bridge over Will's Neck falls.

21

Sarah walked Blacktail up the last steep stretch of track leading to the bridge over Will's Neck falls. She didn't hurry; she was sure she'd be in time. Swaying with Blacktail's gait, she drank in the solitude of the upper reaches of the hills, punctuated by occasional glimpses of lush green valleys and the sparkle of the distant sea caught through breaks in the trees bordering the track.

The morning's clouds had dispersed, letting sunshine wash the land. With each breath of cool, clean air came the promise of spring, and more, of new beginnings.

Sarah's lips lifted; determination and confidence thrummed steadily through her. The orphanage building might be gone, but they'd all survived and would only grow stronger and better for the trial.

She and Charlie had found their way through the initial difficulties in their marriage—and they, too, were stronger for it, growing more so with each passing day because of the testing times.

A sense of peace and future purpose had sunk deep into her bones by the time she reached the clearing where horses were usually tethered while people went to see the views from the bridge.

A tall black horse bearing a gentleman's saddle stood patiently waiting; Sarah tied Blacktail to a branch farther along the clearing, then, sweeping up the trailing skirts of her riding habit, walked on along the narrowing track.

The bridge, spanning the sharp, knife-slash of gorge down which the falls tumbled, lay around the next bend. It was possible to ride across it and on along the track coming up from the other side, but the track led nowhere other than to the bridge; most people came to see the view, then rode back the same way they'd come up.

She rounded the bend and there was the bridge—four yards of wooden planks lashed together and supported by stout ropes slung between massive wooden piers sunk into the rocky banks on either side—with Malcolm waiting, hands lightly braced on the rope hand-rail, looking down the gorge to the valley far below.

He heard her footsteps and turned; smiling, he raised one hand. The silver cover of Edith's diary flashed. Delighted, Sarah smiled back, then gave her attention to the short slope leading down to the bridge.

Because it was slung, the surface of the bridge was lower than the banks. Horses could manage the steep connecting slope with ease, but when, as it almost always was, the area was damp, the descent was more tricky for humans. Luckily, someone had placed rough-cut stones to form a set of deep steps along one side of the slope; the train of her habit looped over one arm, Sarah carefully made her way down them.

The bridge was four paces long, but barely one wide; Malcolm was standing just beyond the center where the views were best. Stepping down onto the planks, Sarah felt them give a little, felt the bridge sway more than she'd expected, but it steadied immediately; perhaps it was her balance. Did pregnancy make one giddy?

Or perhaps it was the almost disorienting effect of the incredible roar surging up from the water raging and tumbling beneath the bridge. Swollen by the recent thaw, the falls were in full spate; the water was a living raging beast, gushing, crashing, leaping, savagely hurtling down the steep chasm of the rock-strewn cleft the bridge spanned.

Every now and then, a cloud of fine spume gusted high enough to envelop the bridge.

Malcolm was waiting, watching her with one of his nicer smiles on his lips—one she recognized as genuine. He was very like Charlie with his ability to charm, but she'd learned some time ago to tell truth from fiction. Smiling equally genuinely in reply, she joined him.

"Thank you for coming." He had to bend his head and lean close for her to hear over the thunder of the falls. He handed her Edith's diary.

Sarah took it, turning it in her hands, then quickly flipping through the pages. It appeared completely undamaged. "Where did you find it?"

She looked up at Malcolm's face.

He met her eyes. His smile had faded, leaving a sincere but serious expression in its wake. "It was in the drawer of the side table in the library at Finley House."

"How . . ." She broke off, frowning. "Finley House—isn't that where you're staying?"

"Yes. I put it there."

He made the statement so baldly, she still wasn't sure she understood. "*You* took it from the Park . . ." She suddenly remembered he'd called on the day she'd discovered the diary missing. He'd left her in the rose garden, having earlier left Charlie in the library, and had walked back to the stables via the terrace—past the open French doors of her sitting room.

His eyes locked with hers. "I see you've recalled—it was the work of a minute to take it from your escritoire."

Astonished, she frowned more definitely. "But *why*?"

He glanced at the diary. "Because your aunt and I had met before. When you reached the entries for May, you would have read that your aunt believed that I was if not responsible for, then certainly the architect of a scheme involving white slave traders that the authorities had just shut down." His lips twisted. "She was correct."

His gaze grew unfocused. "She was a remarkable woman—already old, tending toward feeble, yet with needle-sharp wits and so astute. She'd known my parents, apparently quite well. She called me in, told me to my face that she knew my mind was the one behind the scheme, that although I wasn't the villain who had set it in motion, that didn't absolve me of all blame, then she warned me against allowing my schemes, as she called them, to be used by others in the future." He grimaced and refocused on the diary. "Then she wrote it all down and left it to haunt me."

Sarah continued to frown. "But if Aunt Edith said you *weren't* the one at fault, and the authorities saw no reason to charge you, then surely what she wrote, while perhaps pithy and true, related to you as a young man—as you must have been then, in 1816. An indiscretion of youth. I might have noted what she wrote, but I wouldn't have *said* anything."

Malcolm met her eyes, and smiled. "No, you wouldn't have—not publicly. But, you see, I'd decided to remain in the area, to buy a property and make my home here, and I've come to value both Charlie's and your good opinion. More, given Charlie's interest in investing in the railways, I couldn't take the risk you might mention what Edith had written, or worse, show him."

"Why?" Suspicion was rising, instinctive and compulsive, but of what Sarah couldn't yet fathom. "What would Charlie have seen in my aunt's writings that I wouldn't have?"

Malcolm held her gaze for a long moment, then said, "With what Charlie already knows of me and my reputation, combined with Edith's insight into the way my mind works, together with the information that I had once before strayed from the straight and narrow—with all that before him, Charlie would have wondered if I wasn't still indulging in such schemes.

"And as I am"—his voice hardened—"that didn't seem wise. From merely wondering, it's a very short step for a financial mind as brilliant as Charlie's to see the possibilities. To imagine what schemes I might have devised. Once he had, he would have felt compelled to check . . . and once he did, he might well have stumbled across enough information to suggest that at least one such scheme was indeed in operation. And while he couldn't have connected it with me, simply having him with that suspicion in his mind wouldn't have been at all comfortable for me."

Sarah licked her suddenly dry lips. "You just admitted you're operating some scheme—what?"

His hazel eyes held hers; when his lips curved again, she felt very much as if he could read her mind.

"Charlie really doesn't deserve you—you're much quicker of mind than he realizes. But yes, you've guessed correctly—as Charlie eventually would have if he'd ever read your aunt Edith's words. The investor set on buying Quilley Farm is me."

Sarah stared at him. Despite his words, she couldn't really believe . . . "*You* are the villain behind . . . behind all the accidents at the farm?"

Her temper sparked—ignited. She swung her arm out, dramatically pointing across the valley to the ledge where the blackened ruin still smoked. "*You* are the one who burned the orphanage to the ground?" Abruptly she realized, blinked and let her hand fall. "No—you couldn't have been." Confusion swamped her. She refocused on his face. "You were with us—sitting beside me at my parents' dinner table—while someone was firing flaming arrows at the orphanage."

He looked at her as if irritated she'd quieted—that she hadn't kept railing at him. As if he wanted her to rail at him.

When she didn't but just frowned at him, waiting for an explanation, he frowned back. "No, I didn't." His tone had turned precise. His lips tightened. "But that's not the point. If you read that"—with one long finger he tapped Edith's diary—"you'll understand. I have never, not at any time, done anything illegal. I've never harmed anyone or caused any accidents, let alone arranged anyone's death. I have committed no crime. Not personally, not directly. *However*—just as Edith states—that doesn't absolve me of the blame."

His voice hadn't risen, but had gained in intensity, as had the glare with which he pinned her, as if from being quick-witted she'd suddenly become obtuse. "So no, it *wasn't* me who burned down the orphanage—and no, I didn't know it would happen, not then or ever—I hadn't given any specific orders about the orphanage at all. I was horrified when you were shot and injured—I spent the next two days hunting my agent to try to call him off. All I'd told him was that I wanted the title to Quilley Farm, and that there was no rush, as long as it eventually became mine."

Caught in his gaze, Sarah saw the anguish—entirely real and unfeigned—that flowed into his eyes.

"Then last night . . . I was with you, Charlie, and the rest when we heard that the orphanage was alight. I rode with you, worked with Charlie and the others to try—totally futilely—to beat back the flames." He focused on her eyes. "No one there had a better reason than I to fight that fire. But I was helpless to stop it—I had to stand there with you and watch the place burn, see and hear the terror and upset of the children—see and know how much pain and heartache I'd caused with my scheme." He held her gaze unwaveringly, his expression unshielded, his emotions entirely unscreened. "On top of it all, I had to watch Charlie and Barnaby risk their lives to save babies *I'd* put at risk—and know, beyond question, that I lacked both their courage and their compassion."

He paused, then went on, his voice lower but still clear, "I had to stand there knowing that the anguish visited on you and everyone else was *my* fault—*my* responsibility. That as Edith had warned all those years ago, it should be laid at my door."

Again his gaze grew distant; Sarah watched, too caught in the moment, in his revelations, to think or move. Despite his confessions, she felt not an iota of threat from him.

"I'd always thought I was so clever—thought I was so successful." His voice had dropped to a murmur she had to strain to hear over the thundering crash of the falls. "Instead, the truth is, I've been an abject failure."

He refocused on her, then drew in a breath and seemed to come out of his trance—to return to the here and now. His lips twisted, wry and self-deprecating; he raised his voice so she could more easily hear. "And now everything's falling apart. The authorities are finally on my trail, and crime or no, this time they won't let me escape."

She stared at him. "Why are you telling me this?"

"Because I want you to understand. I want *someone* to understand before I go." He searched her eyes, clearly wondering if she did. "I can't tell you how much I regret not listening to your aunt. If I had . . . but I can't change the past. I arrogantly did precisely what she'd warned me never to do, and now I'm reaping my just reward."

Sarah looked into his eyes and knew he was sincere. She wasn't quite so sure he was sane. He seemed determined to embrace his guilt, to own to it—to make a clean breast of it. Even though he intended to escape.

But while his confession had made her wary, she could still sense no threat from him; no matter his words, she found it hard to fear him. She sincerely hoped that wasn't because he looked so much like an older Charlie that her instincts had become confused.

"So." She moistened her lips. "What now?"

"Now . . ." His gaze went past her; he looked back along the track toward the clearing. As if he'd heard something.

She glanced back.

And heard him murmur, voice once again low, "Now I intend to put one thing right before I leave—do one thing of which Edith Balmain would approve, and how fitting that it should be for her niece."

Turning back, Sarah looked at his face. There was something there, becoming clearer in his expression—a sense of refined strength and purpose—that had her edging back.

Quick as a flash, he shackled her wrist. She twisted it, tried to tug free, but although his grip wasn't tight enough to hurt, it was unbreakable.

"Don't fight me." He glanced briefly at her before again looking over her head toward the track. "I have absolutely no intention of harming you, or Charlie, not in any way." Unbelievably, his lips quirked up at the ends. "That would be counterproductive, to say the least."

She stared at him, then glared. "You're talking in riddles." *Like one demented.*

He glanced at her; his face had resumed its usual impassive mien. "I've said all I want to—need to—say to you." Lifting his head, he looked at the track. "But I haven't yet finished with Charlie."

She finally heard the hoofbeats he'd been listening to nearing the clearing, their thunder a more regular tattoo above the rumbling roar of the falls.

Suddenly not at all sure of her safety—of his sanity—she looked up at him. "What is this all about?"

For a moment, she didn't think he would reply, then he stated, coolly, collectedly, "As I said, my life is unraveling before me, entirely out of my control—what remains in my control is how I deal with that."

The hoofbeats drew nearer. She looked up as Charlie reined in before the lip of the steep slope. His face stony and set, he looked at her, then at Malcolm. From where he was he'd be able to see the hold Malcolm had on her wrist, and Edith's diary in her other hand.

Without a word, Charlie dismounted. He looped Storm's reins over the saddle, then pushed the big hunter back toward the clearing; the gelding ambled off toward the other horses.

Charlie started down the track, nimbly switching to the rough-hewn steps as he descended. The roar from the falls made it futile to speak until he was closer.

"*Stop!*"

Charlie looked up at Malcolm's sharp command. Stepping down to the second last step before the bridge, Charlie studied Sarah; she appeared as shocked as he felt and if anything even more confused, yet although uncertain, she was still calm.

Halting, he raised his gaze to Malcolm's face. Despite what he now knew, and what he'd guessed, in meeting Malcolm's hazel eyes he still saw . . . the same man he'd until half an hour ago admired. "It was you all along, wasn't it? The investor wanting to buy the orphanage? *You* are the one behind the land companies profiteering from the development of the railways."

Despite the lack of evidence, the connection had clicked into place in his mind—and fitted. It might even explain why they were there—Malcolm had realized he could lure Sarah with her aunt's diary, and through Sarah lure him . . . although what Malcolm hoped to gain by having them there was presently beyond him.

Malcolm's brows rose, but his expression remained impassive. "I wondered how long it would be before you worked that out. I didn't think it would be so soon." His tone suggested he was pleasantly impressed, then his lids flickered and that sense of pleasure faded. A second ticked by, then he said, "Ah . . . of course. It was you, wasn't it, who thought of directing someone to search in retrograde—to seek the *source* of the funds rather than try to follow where the profits went?"

Charlie held his gaze, and didn't reply.

Malcolm's lips quirked. "Indeed—who else?"

There was one big problem with the scenario forming in Charlie's mind. He'd seen Malcolm's horror when he'd heard Sarah had been shot, had seen him fighting as desperately as any of them to beat back the flames that had engulfed the orphanage. Eyes narrowed on Malcolm's, he tilted his head. "What happened? Did your henchman run amok?"

When Malcolm stilled, but didn't respond, Charlie asked, "Who is he?"

Malcolm dismissed the question with a flick of his free hand; his other hand still gripped Sarah's wrist, resting on the rope handrail between them. "Don't worry about him—you'll learn his name soon enough. At present he doesn't concern me." Malcolm's voice hardened. "You, however, do."

Charlie hesitated, then held his arms out to either side, palms displayed. "You told me to come—here I am."

He shifted to step down to the next rock.

"*No!*" Malcolm's tone made him freeze. Catching his eye, Malcolm nodded to the piers anchoring the bridge. "Look at the ropes."

Charlie did, and felt his lungs seize. The stout, reliable ropes that had anchored the bridge for years had been cut, and spliced with thinner ones. The ropes now anchoring the bridge on which Sarah and Malcolm stood were significantly less able to support weight.

"Both ends," Malcolm said. As Charlie's gaze swept past him to check, he continued, "I've calculated the forces, the strain—you know how it's done. The ropes as they now are will support the weight of two people, but not three." Malcolm paused, then went on, "So if you attempt to join us, the bridge will collapse and you will be responsible for sending us all, Sarah included, to our deaths."

With his head he indicated the raging water breaking over jagged rocks below. "And it is, indubitably, death waiting down there."

"He's telling the truth." Sarah spoke for the first time since Charlie had arrived. Pale, she met his eyes, her expression quietly horrified. "The bridge swayed when I stepped on it." Her gaze dropped to the spliced ropes. "I didn't realize why."

Malcolm let a moment pass while they assimilated their position, then spoke to Charlie. "As you've no doubt by now realized, there is no way of resolving this impasse other than for me to let Sarah walk off the bridge."

Slamming a mental door on the devastating panic that threatened to swamp him, and the bleak berserk fury it inspired, Charlie met Malcolm's gaze. He, too, let a moment pass, remarshaling his wits, ruthlessly focusing his mind, then asked, "What do I need to do to get you to free Sarah?"

Malcolm smiled. "I would say nothing too onerous but . . . you only have to do two things. The first is to listen."

Charlie caught Sarah's eyes, searched them. She was frightened, yes, but not panicking. From her confusion, it seemed she was as much at sea over what Malcolm intended as he. Keeping Malcolm talking while they decided what to do seemed wise.

Raising his gaze to Malcolm's face, he arched his brows. "To what?"

"To a tale of love . . . and loss." Malcolm raised his brows back, faintly challenging. "A familiar tale in some ways, but rather twisted in others."

Charlie saw the glance Sarah threw Malcolm, and started to wonder if her uncertainty wasn't due to being unsure of Malcolm's sanity—something he, too, was starting to question. The scenario seemed increasingly bizarre, but if Malcolm wanted to talk, and wanted him to listen, he was happy enough to oblige. While Malcolm was talking, he wasn't focused on Sarah, and clearly had no immediate plans to do anything to her. Well and good. Charlie was perfectly capable of listening attentively while simultaneously planning.

With a nod to indicate he was listening, that Malcolm should proceed with whatever tale he wished to tell, Charlie settled on his rock step, feet apart, weight balanced. During negotiations, hands often revealed more than one might think; he slid his into his breeches pockets.

Malcolm smiled, but the gesture didn't warm his eyes. "Throughout these last weeks, I've come to respect your intelligence, your acumen—you are every bit as brilliant as I. But in one area you're an abject fool. But example always teaches better than exhortations, and as we're in so many ways alike, let me describe for you how your life might have been. You might, like me, have been born to parents who simply never had time for you. Born into a family with no siblings, no connections to any wider family, you might, as I did, have grown up entirely alone.

"You might, as I did, have polished your mind by immersing it in purely theoretical problems—the sort that one learns to wrestle with at school. Without anyone around you who cared in any way—parents dead, guardian uninterested—you might, as I did, have grown to adulthood knowing only the challenges and triumphs conjured by a brilliant mind, and nothing of the joys so many take for granted—the simple pleasures of human interactions.

"However . . ." Malcolm paused.

Charlie blinked, thrown entirely off his mental stride by the unexpected direction.

Malcolm's lips curved, and he went on, "Your life was never like that. You were born into a family who cared—you spent all your formative years surrounded by people who loved and cared about you. And whom you loved and cared about, too. More, as the heir to an earldom, you were conditioned from your earliest years to receive the accolades that brings. The position has responsibilities, yes, but it also has intangibles by way of reward. Not just status, but the knowledge that you're needed, that you, yourself, make a real difference in people's lives—a difference they appreciate. You have at your command the power, and the ability to wield it if and as you choose, to influence the lives of many for good. You can bring relief and happiness to others, while I . . . I've only been able to bring darkness and despair."

Malcolm held Charlie's eyes, his gaze incisive. "Yet until recently you've been reluctant to commit your time and energies to such acts. For your sake, I do hope that's one thing the affair of the orphanage has permanently changed."

Charlie's face felt like stone. "Your legacy?"

Malcolm's lips lifted; he inclined his head. "If you will. But that—the potential of your position as earl—is the more minor point I wished to address.

"Before I depart, I wanted to tell you—for no one else ever would, and no one else *could* with quite the same understanding—that you will be a fool beyond reclamation if you don't reach for and embrace love and all it offers you. If you don't embrace all that Sarah has from the first offered you."

Charlie stared at him, nonplussed, frankly stunned.

"Indeed." Again Malcolm's lips quirked in self-deprecatory amusement. "Not the usual topic gentlemen discuss. Nevertheless, I will speak, and you will listen." He caught Charlie's eyes, his gaze level and unwavering. "*Love* is what life is about—what gives a man's life its meaning. Without love, in all its many forms, life is meaningless, no matter how much I and those like me might wish it otherwise. I understand that now. My life has been an empty shell, a husk that once I leave will blow away on the lightest breath of time's wind."

His voice remained even, his tone level, but passion and sincerity ran beneath. "I never searched for love, never craved it, because I had no idea what it was, much less what it could mean to me. Watching you—and Sarah—opened my eyes and taught me that truth. That would only have happened with you, because I can't pretend you're not like me—that but for fate's fickle chance, I could be you, and vice versa."

This time when he paused, Charlie sensed he was looking inward, critically surveying the self he'd confessed to being, then he seemed to shake aside the vision, draw a deeper breath and refocus on Charlie's eyes.

"The time for me has passed—it's too late for me to learn a new credo. But for you . . . you have before you the chance I would, now that I know enough to value it, kill for." An expression of impatience flitted briefly across Malcolm's features. "Have you any idea how frustrating it's been watching you equivocate over accepting love? Your indifference, your rejection of a gift I would kill to have, was . . . an outright insult. All you've had to do is reach out and take it, but no. You've hesitated, again and again, over seizing what I would do anything to have someone offer me."

Eyes narrowed, he seemed to read Charlie's mind, his reaction; slowly, he shook his head. "Yes, I envy you—all of it—but I know it's not for me. Sarah and all she offers is not for me, nor any of the rest of it. I'll willingly hand it all back to you—your life and all its potential— in the hope that now I've spoken, you'll value each and every gift as it deserves."

In some indefinable way Malcolm seemed to draw himself up, as if mentally stepping back. He hesitated, then continued, "And perhaps, when this is all over, when you remember me, you'll also remember that Malcolm Sinclair would have been an entirely different man had he been offered half of what life, fate—and so many other people— have lavished on you."

He held Charlie's gaze. "Be grateful for your life, accept it, embrace it—and all it holds for you."

Charlie had every intention of doing exactly that. While he hadn't needed Malcolm to point out the benefits to him, he couldn't deny that, except for his already mended relationship with Sarah and they'd concealed that while in Malcolm's presence, Malcolm had read his earlier equivocal attitude—to love, to the embrace of family and position— faultlessly.

Malcolm had fallen silent. Consulting his own turbulent feelings and gaining some inkling of how exposed Malcolm must feel, how distracted and unsteady on his mental feet, Charlie nodded once to show that he'd understood, then asked, "The second thing I have to do to induce you to let Sarah go—what is it?"

The smile that slowly curved Malcolm's lips was both eerie and mesmerizing.

"It's very simple." His voice was only just strong enough to carry over the crashing of the raging water. "Tell her why I should."

Charlie looked into Malcolm's steady hazel eyes, and understood perfectly. But . . . the peace, almost content he sensed in Malcolm's gaze made him seriously question—again—the man's sanity. He licked suddenly dry lips. "Why are you doing this?"

Sarah was still on the bridge, close beside Malcolm—shackled there. She'd listened without a word, carefully following their discussion. On a few occasions she'd been tempted to speak; her lips had parted—to defend him, Charlie had not a doubt—but each time she'd stopped on the brink of speech, and fallen silent. For which he gave abject thanks.

But now her eyes, too, were filled with wariness; no more than he did she know what to make of Malcolm's direction.

No more than he did she trust it.

Malcolm sighed. "Because you haven't yet said the words, have you? She needs to hear them—and so do I. My one last request, my price if you will. If you utter the words, I'll know you've come that far at least, however reluctantly."

He'd already traveled a great deal farther than Malcolm knew along the road to accepting and embracing love, and the full potential of his life. But although he fully intended to say the words, it galled him to think that the first time Sarah heard them, he would be speaking them under duress.

He didn't want that; he doubted she did, either.

Yet if that would release her, he'd speak them and any other words Malcolm required . . . if he could be certain that Malcolm was sane. Now that he'd heard Malcolm's comparison of their lives . . . he'd admitted to envy, but did resentment fester beneath? If so, how deeply did the poison reach?

How much of his intellect had it affected? How much of his will? His integrity had, by his own admission, never been particularly strong.

Those thoughts and speculations whizzed through Charlie's mind, alongside the estimations of load and bearing, of impact and reaction, he'd been calculating while dutifully listening to Malcolm's discourse.

Ultimately everything—Sarah's life and his—depended on one act, and one reaction. If he admitted his love for Sarah, aloud in words for both Malcolm and Sarah to hear, what would Malcolm do?

Would he adhere to his strange bargain and let Sarah walk off the bridge to safety? And then what?

Alternatively, would he, cold-bloodedly as he'd proved he usually was, let envy rule and strike back at Charlie—by removing the love he'd finally laid claim to in the cruelest possible way?

If Malcolm grabbed Sarah around the waist, he could hoist her and fling her over the rope railing before Charlie could prevent it.

As Malcolm had made a point of noting, certain death waited below.

Regardless of everything, all possibilities and considerations, did Charlie trust in Malcolm's sanity enough to stake Sarah's life on it?

Drawing in a deep breath, he met her eyes—and knew *she* didn't trust Malcolm that far. Given that . . .

His hesitation had irritated Malcolm. "Just say the words." Impatience colored his tone. "This will be my last act before I leave—for once a purely altruistic gesture. But"—his gaze sharpened—"don't, pray, try to stretch that uncharacteristic emotion too far." He paused, then said, "It's time to start talking."

Charlie drew in another breath, looked at Sarah and saw his own question—what was best?—mirrored in her eyes. There was only one answer he could give. "Trust me."

He drew his hands from his pockets and jumped down to the bridge.

The shock on Malcolm's face was entirely unfeigned.

Charlie seized Sarah, wrenched her from Malcolm's hold, turned, swinging her, and tossed her up onto the slope beside the steps.

The bridge lurched. Charlie grabbed the rope handrail—then realized it was unraveling and about to come free. Feeling the planks beneath him tilting, he flung himself forward, diving for the nearest anchor post.

He got one hand to it—but not far enough around to give him sufficient grip to haul himself to safety.

Behind him he heard Malcolm swear. *"You bloody fool!"*

The lashed planks tipped and swung—two of the anchoring ropes had pulled free, one at either end. The other two were now under impossible strain. Any second they would give.

Charlie gathered himself, then heaved himself upward, trying to get a better grip on the smoothly rounded pole slick with moisture thrown up from below—and sensed Malcolm close behind him.

Felt strong hands grasp one booted foot, cup it, and hoist him.

He slung an arm around the anchoring post. Sarah, leaning down from above, grabbed his shoulder and sleeve—then her eyes went past him and she screamed.

Charlie glanced back.

And saw a sight he didn't immediately understand.

With his weight no longer on the twisted, tilting bridge, the last two ropes were under strain, but still holding . . .

Except that Malcolm had a knife in his hand and was hacking at the one remaining anchor to their bank.

As Charlie stared, the rope parted.

Malcolm's head flashed up—their eyes met for one instant.

Then the bridge fell, crashing against the opposite rock bank, and Malcolm was gone.

For one instant, Charlie and Sarah both simply stared at the empty space. Straining his ears, Charlie heard not a splash but a hitch in the rhythmic thunder of the water—then the roar continued and the water rushed on.

Above him, Sarah gulped, then latched more firmly onto his coat and tugged. "Come up!"

Before he fell, too.

She'd screamed when she'd seen Malcolm, behind Charlie, pull the knife from his boot—but he hadn't even glanced at Charlie.

Now she understood; that hadn't been his purpose. That had never been his aim. He'd told her he'd never harm her or Charlie—that it would be counterproductive . . . she recalled the strange smile on his lips when he'd said that, and gulped again.

She tugged and heaved as Charlie inched upward. The bank was naturally faced with rock in large smooth sections; there were very few cracks or ledges he could use. She hauled in another breath, tightened her grip and backed as, with her help, he slowly eased his weight higher, up around the post, until he was on the upper side of it and could get one boot across to the steps.

Scrabbling backward, unheeding of the damage to her velvet skirts, she kept the fingers of one hand locked in his coat, until he scrambled high enough to collapse on his back beside her just beyond the top of the slope. A slope that now led straight into a yawning crevasse. She checked that they were both sufficiently on the flat that they stood in no danger of an injudicious movement sending them sliding down— then she collapsed on her back beside Charlie.

They lay side by side and simply breathed. They gazed up at the sky, blue with just a few wisps of clouds racing and chasing across the expanse.

For long moments they remained silent and still—for herself, she didn't know where to begin—then Charlie lifted one hand, found hers, and closed his around it.

"He was right about a lot of things, but wrong about one. A declaration of love given under duress is worthless." He paused, then went on, his grip on her hand tightening, "I love you. You know I do. I've been searching for the right words, but these are the only ones I know. You are *everything* to me. My sun, my moon, my stars—my life. Without you, I could no longer be me—the me I need to, and want to be. I would give my life for yours, at any time of any day, without hesitation. But I'd much rather live my life alongside you—and care for you and love you for as long as fate allows. That's the only reality I now know. And if I haven't had the courage to say the words before, then I intend to say them to you every day for the rest of our lives. I love you." He lifted her hand to his lips, and kissed their linked fingers. "Never doubt it."

Sarah had turned her head to watch his profile as he spoke; now she smiled mistily. "I love you, too, and always will—as you know." Coming up on her elbow, she leaned in and kissed his cheek. Studied his face for an instant, then added, "As you've always known . . . haven't you?"

He hesitated, then shifted his gaze to meet hers. "Not consciously. But on some level . . ." Lifting one hand, he smoothed back her hair. "I think that's one of the reasons my eye fixed on you."

She shifted and rested her head on his shoulder. They both again looked up at the sky. "I still can't believe it—what he did."

A moment passed, then Charlie said, "I'm still not sure I understand it."

She hesitated, then said, "Before you arrived he said he wanted to put one thing right—an act my aunt would have approved of—before he left. I think he saw ensuring our marriage worked as being that one thing."

"I can't fault him in that choice—our marriage is important. And the connection between him and me—our friendship—obviously had bearing on that, too." Raising one hand, Charlie touched her head, let his fingers gently smooth her hair. "Regardless of his intent, regardless that it was his doing that put us all at risk on the bridge, I don't think I would have made it if he hadn't boosted me up."

Sarah found his other hand, twined her fingers in his. "I thought, when he demanded that you listen, and then speak, that he must be insane. I started to get frightened. I couldn't imagine what he would do once you did."

"I know. I couldn't, either. That's why I jumped down instead."

Their hearts had slowed. Sarah sighed. "He meant to *go,* didn't he? All along he meant to die."

They were both locals; they knew the falls. Knew there was no chance that Malcolm had survived.

"Yes." Charlie drew in a deep breath, then exhaled. "This was another of his clever schemes designed to accomplish a number of things. To return your aunt's diary to you, to force me to listen to his lecture on love, to force me to tell you I love you, and . . . to give him a way to depart this life. If he'd wanted to save himself he could easily have done so. When I jumped on the bridge and swung you free, all he had to do was dive for the other side. He would have made it to safety without a doubt—he had plenty of time. And there's no way he didn't know that. Instead, he came to me, to make sure I was safe."

"And then he hacked through the rope."

Charlie thought about that. "He'd come prepared with the knife because he assumed I would speak, then you would walk off the bridge to me—and then he'd cut the ropes while I was helping you up the steps. Neither of us would have been able to stop him."

Another long moment passed, then Sarah sighed and sat up. Charlie did, too. His arm about her, shoulder to shoulder they looked across the yawning crevasse.

"He was a strange man," she said.

Charlie nodded. As if uttering an epitaph, he added, "A man who'd never known love."

They got to their feet, brushed the dirt and damp leaves from each other as best they could, then Sarah retrieved Edith's diary from where she'd tossed it to safety farther along the track. Together they walked slowly to the clearing and the waiting horses.

22

Beside Sarah, Charlie clattered into the stable yard at the Park. He still felt faintly disoriented, still grappling with all that had occurred at the bridge, still assimilating the facts and emotions involved.

Croker came to take the horses. He exclaimed at Charlie's and Sarah's state, but accepted Sarah's gentle but firm assurance that despite appearances they were both perfectly well.

"Bedraggled once again," Charlie murmured as he and she started across the lawn to the house. "Crisp and Figgs won't approve."

Sarah looked down at the silver-plated diary she held in both hands. Her faint smile faded. "What should we tell people?"

He understood what she was asking. During the slow journey down from the falls, she'd told him what Malcolm had said before he'd arrived at the bridge. But now that Malcolm was dead and gone, how much did they need to make public? "I—"

He broke off as the thump of approaching hoofbeats reached them. They turned to watch as three horsemen, riding hard, thundered up across the fields, then swung onto the drive leading to the stable yard.

Gabriel, in the lead, saw them; checking his hunter, he trotted over.

Barnaby followed, along with a greatcoated individual Charlie recognized. "Inspector Stokes," he murmured to Sarah. He'd met Stokes on a number of occasions.

Taking in their state, Gabriel narrowed his eyes. "What's happened?"

"In a moment." Charlie looked from Stokes to Barnaby. "You couldn't have reached London. What's brought you back hotfoot?"

His expression like granite, Barnaby met his eyes. "You may not believe it, but our villain is Sinclair."

Charlie nodded. "We've just learned the same thing." He glanced at Sarah, then looked up at the three men. "Why don't you leave your horses with Croker, then wait in the library. Give us a few minutes to change, then you can tell us what you've learned, and we can tell you our news."

Barnaby frowned, but Gabriel nodded. "Good idea."

He wheeled away; Stokes followed. With an impatiently curious look, Barnaby was forced to fall in with that plan.

Twenty minutes later, Charlie opened the library door, held it for Sarah, then followed her in. The other three had gathered in armchairs before the fire; as Sarah approached they all rose.

Charlie introduced Stokes to Sarah.

A tall, dark-featured man, neatly and soberly dressed, the inspector bowed. "A pleasure, countess."

Sarah smiled. "I've ordered tea and crumpets." She looked around at the faces. "I daresay we could all use the sustenance."

She sat on the chaise; Charlie sat beside her as the others resumed their seats. He caught Barnaby's eye. "You first."

Barnaby hesitated, then acquiesced. "I never made it to London. I ran into Stokes near Salisbury. He was riding this way with news of Montague's discovery."

Barnaby glanced at Stokes, who took up the tale.

"Montague did as I believe you suggested"—Stokes inclined his head to Charlie—"and searched for the source of the funds used to buy land for subsequent profiteering. He concentrated on one property, one amount. The instant he traced it to an account owned by Malcolm Sinclair, he realized the implication. Montague took his suspicions to His Grace of St. Ives."

"Devil checked further," Barnaby said. "He spoke with Wolverstone, who put him on to Dearne and Paignton." He looked at Sarah. "As it happens, Paignton's wife, Phoebe, is a connection of yours."

"Cousin Phoebe?" Sarah frowned, then her eyes widened. "At one time she lived with my aunt Edith. Did Phoebe know Malcolm Sinclair?"

Puzzled, Barnaby shook his head. "No, she didn't. But her husband, Paignton, did. As a minor, Malcolm Sinclair had been involved with his guardian in some scheme connected with white slave trading. Back in '16. Paignton, Dearne, and some others exposed it."

"But Malcolm Sinclair wasn't charged," Sarah said, "even though the scheme was suspected to be his creation."

Barnaby stared at her. "How did you know?"

Sarah held up the silver-plated diary she'd brought with her. "My aunt Edith suspected that, and told him so—and advised him to re-form his ways. She wrote it all down in here. And I inherited this volume of her diaries."

"As you can see, the diary is distinctive. Sinclair recognized it and stole it so Sarah wouldn't learn the truth about his past," Charlie said, "and perhaps tell me, who might then suspect that his interest in railways could have a reason beyond simple investing."

"Indeed." Stokes started to say more, but paused when the door opened; he waited while Crisp and a footman brought in trays of tea, toast, and crumpets. The lure of honey, jam, and fresh butter caused a temporary hiatus, then, having wolfed down a crumpet, Stokes washed it down with a draught of tea and set down his cup.

He glanced at Charlie. "We've grounds enough to reel in Mr. Sinclair, and plenty of questions for him. I was on my way here, to take him into custody and back to London, when I ran into Mr. Adair. His news about the orphanage fire only gives us yet more reason to take Sinclair up immediately."

"They stopped by Casleigh to let me know what was afoot." Gabriel's smile was predatory. "Naturally, I invited myself along."

"And of course we stopped here, so you could come, too." Barnaby frowned as he searched Charlie's impassive—unenthusiastic—face. "After all, you know him best . . . what is it?"

Charlie sighed. "Sinclair's dead."

The announcement was greeted with exclamations and disbelief; when those faded, Charlie explained what had happened—that Sinclair had used the diary to lure Sarah to the bridge over the falls, and then used Sarah to draw Charlie there as well.

"He made a clean breast of it all," Sarah said. "He was truly regretful, repentent—he didn't try to deny his part in it at all. They were his schemes, and he accepted that the blame rested with him."

"But he had an accomplice who, if I understood correctly, was overenthusiastic in interpreting Sinclair's orders." Charlie narrowed his eyes, recalling. "Sinclair implied we'd soon learn the accomplice's identity, but he didn't say more about that."

"How did he die?" Barnaby asked. He and Stokes were leaning forward, caught up in the tale.

Charlie looked at Gabriel. "He'd weakened the ropes anchoring the bridge so that they'd only support the weight of two people. When I arrived, he and Sarah were on the bridge. After he'd made his confession and said all he wanted to say, he let Sarah walk off the bridge. The instant she left it, he hacked through the ropes. He fell."

It was the story he and Sarah had agreed to tell; the rest of Malcolm Sinclair's revelations had been for the three of them alone.

Gabriel paled. "Good God."

Stokes looked from Gabriel to Charlie. "Are you sure he's dead?"

Gabriel caught Stokes's eyes. "We'll take you to the bridge—the place where it used to be, Inspector, and you'll see. No one could possibly survive such a fall." Gabriel glanced at Charlie. "In effect, Sinclair took his own life."

Barnaby and Stokes decided they should nevertheless check Malcolm's house in Crowcombe. While they rode north, Charlie and Gabriel organized a search for Sinclair's body.

An hour later, after dispatching various groups to search the rushing stream below the falls, Charlie, Gabriel, and Sarah were standing around Charlie's desk poring over a detailed map of the area when striding footsteps in the corridor heralded Barnaby and Stokes's return.

They entered, looking even more stunned than when they'd left.

"What?" Charlie asked.

Barnaby fell into a chair. "Incredible." He shook his head. "He'd left a confession covering more than a decade of schemes, with enough detail to keep any judge happy, all neatly signed and sealed, propped on his desk with a note telling us we'd find his accomplice tied up in the cellar, and that we should check with the local solicitor for further information."

Stokes had come to look at the map. He glanced at the others. "When he decided to right his wrongs, Sinclair didn't hold back. His confession will save us, the authorities in general, and the public untold time and expense, and when we went down to the cellar, his accomplice—the agent Mr. Adair's been searching for—was all trussed up waiting."

"*He's* not going to confess, but with what Sinclair's given us, that won't be a problem." Barnaby's gaze grew hard. "We didn't read the whole of Sinclair's confession—there's pages and pages of it—but we read enough to be certain that Jennings—the agent—will hang."

"But that wasn't the end of it." Stokes took up the tale. "We went to the solicitor's, a few doors down the High Street. Seems Sinclair made a new will yesterday." Stokes looked at Sarah and Charlie. "In it, he asks that restitution be made to those families and individuals who've been harmed by his schemes in the past, although he says the railway companies themselves shouldn't be compensated as it was their own inefficiencies and greed that enabled him to get so much money from them. After all restitution has been paid, he's stipulated that the residue of his estate should go to Quilley Farm orphanage, for the rebuilding of it, but not in the same place, with the rest of the funds to be used to run the orphanage, and establish others like it as needed." Stokes paused. "He's named you two"—he nodded at Charlie and Sarah—"as executors of his will and trustees of the orphanage fund."

It was Charlie's and Sarah's turn to look stunned.

Gabriel spoke, sounding a trifle awed. "You said there were twenty-three earlier cases of suspected profiteering. Even after paying generous reparation for those, from what I've heard from sound sources of Sinclair's fortune, there's going to be a massive amount left for the fund."

"Assuming the courts allow the will to be exercised," Barnaby put in, "but even without a body, his assets would be confiscated as the majority must have derived from what were originally ill-gotten gains."

Stokes nodded. "He even thought of that, and left a letter begging the courts to let the will stand. And in the circumstances, with all he's done with his confession, and handing over his accomplice, and now that he's dead by his own hand, saving us the bother of his trial and execution, I imagine their lordships might well look favorably on the money being used for orphaned children." Stokes shrugged. "Who knows—even in that, he might be saving them the bother of having to decide what to do with such an amount."

Gabriel grinned. "We can leave that to Devil and Chillingworth. I can't imagine there'll be many peers keen to see such largesse disappear into the Crown's coffers."

Feeling a trifle giddy, Sarah sank slowly into the chair behind the desk. "He wanted to do something right, something good—he said so." She glanced at Charlie.

He met her eyes. "It seems an eminently good use for those funds he amassed through *legally* investing his ill-gotten gains."

Barnaby slowly shook his head. "I still can't get over it—the complete confession, the accomplice trussed and waiting, the will, his death. It's as if he suddenly woke up and was shocked with himself."

"It happens," Stokes said. "Something will trigger it and they'll realize what they've done, what they've become, and suddenly they can't stand it anymore."

"Self-disgust." Charlie looked at Sarah, then met Barnaby's eyes. "That was definitely there when we spoke with him."

"But"—Barnaby leaned forward—"what triggered it?"

Charlie glanced at Sarah, and didn't reply. That it had been through Malcolm's remaining in the area and seeing things, relating to things, from Charlie's perspective, and through Charlie's link with Sarah understanding so much more, was too private a revelation. Too much something that they alone knew, had shared and now understood.

Malcolm Sinclair had gone, and left them to live. More, he'd adjured them to live life to its fullest.

Sarah smiled softly at Charlie, and said nothing, either.

"So." Stokes peered at the map. "This is the bridge?" He pointed.

Gabriel nodded, then traced the path of the stream below the falls. "The falls themselves face west, but later, here, the stream strikes a ledge and turns north, and then eventually east until it runs into this lake." He tapped the map. "It's small, but deep. From there the water exits via the river to the east and eventually runs into Bridgwater Bay."

"So we're likely to find the body between the bottom of the falls and the lake." Barnaby had come to stand beside Stokes.

Charlie exchanged a glance with Gabriel. "We've sent searchers to cover that stretch. The streambed through that section is extremely rocky, and with the recent thaw, the water is running high. If we don't find the body before the lake, or around its shores, the chances are we won't find it at all."

Stokes straightened. "I'll go and have a look at these falls, then check with the searchers."

Barnaby nodded. "I'll come, too." He glanced at Charlie. "We'd better see this through to the end."

Neither Charlie nor Gabriel saw any need to join the search. Sinclair's body would either be found or it wouldn't.

Together with Sarah, Charlie walked to the stables to see the others off. Gabriel departed for Casleigh, to report to Alathea, Martin, and Celia, all of whom had met Malcolm Sinclair.

Barnaby rode out with Stokes, leaving Charlie and Sarah walking slowly hand in hand back to the house.

Later, standing at the base of the falls looking up at the rock steps that used to lead to the bridge, Stokes shook his head. "Must have been a huge shock, walking off that bridge, then seeing it and Sinclair fall."

"Look at this." Barnaby dislodged a splintered plank from between two rocks. They were standing a good fifty yards from the jagged rocks onto which the falls constantly thundered; between lay nothing but more broken rocks over which the water churned and surged.

Turning from the stream rushing by in full spate, Barnaby showed

Stokes the plank. "It's a piece of the bridge. The wood's weathered and hard as nails, yet the edges have been frayed like flax." He glanced back at the falls. "If it'll do that to hardened wood, imagine what it will have done to a body."

Stokes grimaced. He, too, looked up at the falls. "They were right—only divine intervention could get a man through that, and I doubt any such grace was extended to Sinclair."

Nevertheless, in a mutual quest for thoroughness and completeness, Stokes and Barnaby continued following the stream, checking in vain with the searchers they came upon and sending them back to the Park.

Dusk was falling by the time they reached the lake. There were three men there. Harris, the head gardener from the Park, came forward. "We've been right around, sir—twice. No body in the weeds by the edges, and none we've spotted anywhere in the lake. However, as you can see"—he nodded to where a visible current was rippling the lake's surface—"the water's running high and the current's that strong he might well be out in the middle of the channel by now."

They glanced in the direction Harris indicated, to the leaden expanse of the Bristol Channel not all that far away.

Stokes grimaced. "We've done all we can." He nodded to Harris. "We'd best all get back before night sets in."

"Aye, sir." Harris touched his cap and gathered his lads with a look, and they trudged off to where they'd left their horses.

Barnaby and Stokes had left their mounts at the point where the stream from the falls entered the lake. They started walking back.

"I have to admit," Stokes said, "I never thought to see the end of this—not so soon, nor yet so neatly." He glanced at Barnaby. "Your father's going to be pleased, and the other governors, too." Stokes grinned and looked ahead. "And you'll be back in London in time for the start of the Season, with all those balls and parties."

Barnaby groaned. "That's the one flaw I can see in Sinclair's otherwise exceptional planning. As long as I was chasing some crime of that magnitude the pater would have kept my mother from descending on me—at least in person. Now . . . I'll just have to invent some other investigation to excuse my disinterest until a real one comes along."

Stokes regarded him affectionately through the gathering gloom.

"But I thought that's what all you toffs do—look over the young ladies presented and choose your wife from among them. Isn't that how it's supposed to go?"

"Theoretically, *assuming* one intends to wed. But I'm a third son. No real reason I have to get leg-shackled, no matter what m'mother and her cronies believe. Not that I've anything against marriage—not for others. Well, there's Gerrard and Jacqueline, Dillon and Pris, and now Charlie and Sarah, and I can see and appreciate what they have, *but . . .*"

"Not for you?"

Barnaby wondered why he was speaking of such things, yet he and Stokes had grown considerably closer over the years they'd worked together; if there was one man who would understand his stance, it was Stokes. "It's not so much 'not for me' as . . . can you honestly imagine a lady, Stokes—and do remember that my mother would gasp her last if I married anyone but a lady, and moreover one of suitable degree—can you truly imagine a lady of that ilk being content for me to devote so much of my time to something as unmentionable in polite circles as criminal investigations? To being perfectly happy when I drop everything and hie off into the country, or don some disguise and disappear into London's underworld, in pursuit of some villain who needs to be exposed?"

"Hmm." Stokes had attended enough tonnish gatherings in his official capacity to have some comprehension of what Barnaby meant.

"And that's aside from the potential stigma involved, and the constant courting of tonnish excommunication if somehow I get things wrong." Barnaby snorted. "It would never work. She'd be in hysterics in less than a week."

After a moment he went on, "*This*—investigating and the associated endeavors—is what I enjoy doing most. I'm good at it, and you and the pater and the other governors need me. You have no one else who can take on this sort of work within the ton." He hesitated, then continued, more to himself than Stokes, "This is my career. I've carved it out for myself, and I intend to pursue it, and there's no lady on earth capable of making me turn away from it."

Stokes made no response; Barnaby expected none. They reached their horses, swung up to the saddles, then looked at each other.

"What now?" Barnaby asked.

Stokes considered, then said, "I see no point in looking a gift horse in the mouth. With his fit of conscience, Sinclair's made this easy for us, and I'm going to accept that boon. I'll ride back tomorrow and report the presumed death of Malcolm Sinclair." Stokes looked back along the rock-strewn stream. "I can't imagine we'll find any trace of him now."

Barnaby nodded. Wheeling their horses, they headed for the Park.

Later that night, in the earl's bedchamber, in the earl's bed, Sarah lay slumped in her earl's arms, warm, sated, and content, happier than she'd ever thought she'd be. Beneath her cheek, Charlie's heart thumped, steady and strong. Although every muscle in her body felt unraveled, she tightened her arms about him.

"I had one bad moment above the falls—one dreadful instant when I thought I might lose you." Lifting her head, she looked into his face, into his shadowed eyes. "You'd just managed to get your arm about the anchor post and I was trying to haul you up—and Malcolm drew the knife from his boot."

Charlie held her gaze; raising one hand, he brushed back her hair and cradled her face. "You thought he was going to stab me?"

She nodded. "For one fleeting instant." She shuddered, then laid her head back down, clinging to his warmth, and even more to him, to the solid reality of his body beneath hers. "But it was enough." She tightened her grip on him even more. "I never want to lose you. I never even want to *think* of losing you again."

His chest shook, a small, wry chuckle, then his lips brushed the top of her forehead. "Now you know how I feel. Just the thought of losing you is enough to . . . eradicate my ability to think."

His fingers played in her hair, then smoothed, stroked. "I had no idea what he was about. All those things he said of me, most if not all were true, but I'd already realized for myself, or you'd made me see them, made me face the reality and see the need to change. All I could think about was what he might do with you once he realized I wasn't going to argue, once he realized that I'd already accepted, was already embracing, all he wanted me to. Instead of listening to his lecture, I was thinking about how to get you to safety."

Her lips curved. She dropped a kiss on his chest. "I couldn't fathom his direction, either, but I never felt he was a threat to me. To you, I wasn't so sure."

"And now, amazingly, it's over. Like some trial, we've won through to the other side, and the future lies before us, ours to make of it what we will." He paused, then said, "I know what I want." His hand found hers where it lay on his chest; his fingers closed around hers. "If you agree, we'll live here primarily, spending only the usual few weeks in London—in spring for the Season, as much of it as you wish, and in autumn when Parliament sits. But for the rest, we'll stay here, where there's so much for us both to do. Here where we're surrounded by family, estate, and the local community. They need us here, at home, and it's where we should be."

Her head on his chest, Sarah drew in a breath, held it, then said, "And this is where we should bring up our own family . . . don't you think? Here, where we were children, where we know every inch of the land, and where everyone knows us and will know them, and they'll be safe?"

He didn't say anything for a long moment, then prompted, "They?"

She stared at their hands, linked on his chest. "I *might* be expecting, but . . . I'm not absolutely definitely sure."

Lifting her head, she looked into his eyes, saw . . . and narrowed her own. "You know, don't you?"

From the wild look in his eyes, he wasn't sure what to say. "I . . . ah, *wondered*."

She drank in the sight of him in a near-panic over how she might react, then she smiled, a cat with a whole jug of cream, stretched up and kissed him. "In that case, we can *wonder* for a little longer together. I don't want to tell anyone until we're sure."

He nodded. "Yes. All right."

She frowned in warning as she settled back. "Not even Dillon and Gerrard."

"Hadn't crossed my mind." He blinked at her, then said, "I was thinking . . . if you're not feeling up to it, we could skip going to London for the Season—Mama would understand."

Sarah laughed, feeling even more joyous and carefree. "Not a chance." She snuggled back down into the warmth of his arms. "There's dozens of ladies expecting to meet us in the capital and a mere pregnancy is no good excuse. And"—she poked his chest—"if you think to use my condition as an excuse to confine me, I suggest you think again."

After a moment, his arms firmed around her. "If I can't confine, can I coddle?"

She tilted her head, considering; her smile felt glorious. "Coddling I might permit."

Then she chuckled. "Charlie—that is *so* unlike you. Asking permission."

Smiling, Charlie settled her more comfortably over him, his arms closing about her more securely. "I've changed." He had; he was amazed by how much. He dropped a light kiss on her hair. "I love you, and this is where I want to be, here, at the Park, with you, and our children when they arrive."

He finally understood why Gerrard, Gabriel, and all the others had so readily abandoned their London-based lives after they'd wed; London's delights held little allure compared to what waited for him here, his to embrace. He glanced down at her. "This is where I belong."

It was, completely and utterly and forever more.

All was right, more than right between them, yet there was one truth he owed her. Eyes on her face, what he could see of it as she lay relaxed and so trusting in his arms, he said, "This—our love—still scares me. I know that it can, and will, control me. It has more than once already, and doubtless will over the years to come. And that ... worries me."

She lifted her head and looked at him, then she folded her hands on his chest and settled her chin on them so she could see his face, meet his eyes. "Why?"

Despite all, his first impulse was to draw back, but he forced himself to tell her. "Because I fear it will ... make me do things I shouldn't, make me take risks that ultimately might place you, or our children, or the earldom and everyone who relies on it, at risk." He paused, then, his eyes on hers, added, "Like my father."

Her expression conveyed her puzzlement, her question.

He drew in a tight breath. "My father ... loved us all. Very much. Perhaps too much. He became obsessed with making life better for us—and through that obsession he took risks, financial risks." He paused, then told her, "He very nearly brought the earldom to ruin. If Alathea hadn't stepped in, he would have."

Her eyes lit with understanding, and a compassion he hadn't expected. "Was that why you . . . didn't want to love, and then fought against allowing love beyond this room?"

He nodded. "I thought if I could keep it in here . . . I never make financial decisions here."

It sounded ridiculous now he knew what love was, yet she didn't laugh. Instead, she studied him, then she reached up and framed his face, and looked deep into his eyes. "You are not your father."

When he opened his mouth, she cut him off. "I knew him, remember? You are nothing like him—not inside. You're like Serena—capable, practical, and clear-eyed. You would never make the mistakes your father did—just look at your reputation as an investor, at how Gabriel regards you, how Malcolm described you. But regardless of all else, you're so much stronger than your father ever was. Love might rule you, but it will never cloud your mind to the one duty you hold highest of all. You'll never put me, or anyone you feel responsible for, let alone love, at risk—you won't even allow us to be in danger."

She smiled mistily at him. "Maybe you can't see that as clearly as I—or anyone else who knows you—can, but you are *you*, Charlie, always and only you—and what you are, and have always been, is a man devoted to protecting people, not harming them, not putting them at risk. Not even love, with all its power, can change what's at the heart of you—and in reality, love wouldn't. Love, with you, will always work with you, not against you. It will strengthen you, not weaken you."

Pausing, she held his gaze, then quietly said, "There's no danger for you in love, in loving me. No danger for me in having you love me."

She searched his eyes; what he saw in hers made his heart contract. Then she smiled, leaned close and brushed his lips with hers. "And that's why our marriage will work—because of our love."

He waited until she drew back so he could meet her eyes. "And strength. Your strength. My sort doesn't count."

She grinned. "And protectiveness—yours, and mine."

His lips twisted wryly. "And understanding. Yours, almost entirely." He held her gaze, felt himself drowning in the blue, in the love that shone so brightly he could barely breathe. "And one other thing. Trust. I trust you to be right in all things to do with love."

She smiled. "And I trust you to be all that you are—which is all that I wish for. And because of that, I always will be right when it comes to us and our love."

Sarah drew his lips to hers and kissed him—then let him kiss her, let love bloom unfettered, let passion rise and desire burn, and once again sweep them away.

To the paradise they now shared, to the glories of the oneness that together they'd embraced. That together they created.

Later, Charlie settled them again in the billows of their bed. The moon shone brightly, its shimmering light streaming through the window to fall across the covers. Feeling blessed beyond measure, grateful and honored to the depths of his soul, he held out a hand, cupping his palm in the stream of light—half expecting, given the magic enfolding them, to be able to sense its weight.

Instead, as he twisted his hand in the pure, silvery light, he recalled an earlier fascination. One that had lured him to this, to the here and now, to the love and the life he now wholeheartedly embraced. To his future and all it would rightly be.

His earlier fascination with Sarah, and with the elusive, addictive taste of innocence.

T he same moonlight that lay in benediction over Charlie and Sarah in their bed also shone down, pale and cold, over the Bristol Channel and the Severn Estuary. Slanting over the dark ripples of the waves, it silvered the edges of a black shape washed up by the tide on the shingle of a deserted beach along the shore of Bridgwater Bay.

Sodden, tattered, and torn, the wreck of a man lay cast up on the rough sands, left there by the retreating waves.

But there was no one to see. No one to wonder who he was, where he'd come from, or why he was there.

No one to care.

So it remained while the moon sank and finally set.

But eventually, inevitably, the sun rose. And the world came alive.

Also available from Piatkus by Stephanie Laurens:

ON A WILD NIGHT

'Where are all the exciting men in London?'

After spending years in the glittering ballrooms of the ton,
Amanda Cynster is utterly bored by the current crop of bland
suitors. Determined to take matters into her own hands, one
night she shockingly goes where no respectable lady ever should,
but where many an intriguing gentleman might be found.

But titillating excitement quickly turns to panic when Amanda
discovers she's quite out of her depth. She looks around for
help – and is unexpectedly rescued by the Earl of Dexter.
Lean, sensuous and mysterious, he has delayed re-entering
society, preferring instead a more interesting
existence on its fringes.

He's the epitome of the boldly passionate gentleman Amanda
has been searching for, but although his very touch makes it
clear he's willing to educate her in the art of love, Amanda has
to wonder if such a masterful rake can be sufficiently tamed
into the ways of marriage.

Praise for Stephanie Laurens:

'Stephanie Laurens' novels take my breath away. With her vivid,
exuberant style and lush sensuality, she weaves a story that
satisfies with every page'
Lisa Kleypas

978-0-7499-3723-2

THE TASTE OF INNOCENCE

Charles Morwellan has no intention of following in the footsteps of his family – marrying for love – and therefore wants to find a bride before fate finds him. He is convinced that it was total devotion to love that caused his father to shirk the responsibilities of the earldom and is determined not to make the same mistakes. What Charlie doesn't realise is the woman he chooses, Sarah Conningham, wants nothing less than a love match and she has no intention of letting Charlie get away with pushing her out of his life. Now, it's up to Sarah to convince Charlie that you really can have it all.

Praise for Stephanie Laurens:
'All I need is her name on the cover to make me pick up the book'
Linda Howard

978-0-7499-3863-5

WHAT PRICE LOVE?

Despite his dangerous air, Dillon Caxton is now a man of sterling reputation, but it wasn't always so. Years ago, an illicit scheme turned into a nefarious swindle, and only the help of his cousin, Felicity, and her husband, Demon, saved Dillon from ruin. Now impeccably honest, his hard-won reputation zealously guarded, he's the Keeper of the Register of all racing horses in England, the very register Lady Priscilla Dalloway is desperate to see. She has come to Newmarket, determined to come to the rescue of her horse-mad brother who has fallen into bad company

Together, Dillon and Pris uncover a massive betting swindle. Assisted by Demon, Felicity, and Barnaby Adair, they embark on a journey riddled with danger and undeniable passion as they seek to expose the deadly perpetrators. And along the way they discover the answer to that age old question: what price love?

Praise for Stephanie Laurens:
'I love it! Really enjoyed . . .'
Cathy Kelly

978-0-7499-3712-6

SCANDAL'S BRIDE

'He will father your children . . .'

When Catriona Hennessy, honourable Scottish Lady of the
Vale, receives this prediction, she is exceedingly vexed. How can
she unite with a rake like Richard Cynster – a masterful man
with a scandalous reputation? More shocking still is her
guardian's will that decrees that she and Richard be wed within
a week! Though charmed by his commanding presence, and
wooed by his heated kisses, she will not – can not –
give up her independence.

So she forms a plan to get the heir she needs without taking
wedding vows. Richard is just as stunned by the will's command. Marriage had not previously been on his agenda, but
lately he's been feeling rather . . . restless. Perhaps taming the
lady is just the challenge he needs. But can he have the rights of
the marriage bed without making any revealing
promises of love?

Praise for Stephanie Laurens:

'Stephanie Laurens' heroines are marvellous tributes
to Georgette Heyer'
Cathy Kelly

978-0-7499-3718-8

THE TRUTH
ABOUT LOVE

Gerrard Debbington is one of the most eligible gentlemen in the ton, Gerrard is besieged by offers from London's most sought-after beauties, but as the ton's foremost artistic lion, there's only one offer he wants to accept – the chance to paint the fantastical but seldom-seen gardens of reclusive Lord Tregonning's Hellebore Hall.

That chance is dangled before Gerrard, but to grasp it he must fulfill Lord Tregonning's demand that he also create an open and honest portrait of the man's daughter. Gerrard loathes the idea of wasting his time and talents on some simpering miss, but with no alternative, he agrees . . .

Only Gerrard is stunned by the deep emotions Jacqueline Tregonning stirs in him. He is soon convinced that Jacqueline is the soulmate he needs as his wife.

978-0-7499-3727-0

THE PERFECT LOVER

Simon Frederick Cynster is determined to find a wife. However, nothing could be more tiresome than having every blushing miss on the marriage mart thrust upon him. So he discreetly begins his search at a house party at Glossup Hall . . . and is astonished that the lady who immediately captures his interest is Portia Ashford.

Simon has never considered Portia as a potential bride. He's known the raven-haired beauty since childhood; she's wilfully independent and has always claimed to be uninterested in marriage. But an unexpectedly heated kiss abruptly alters the rules of their decade-long interaction. Soon they begin to long for the moments they can spend in each other's arms.

But all is not as it seems at Glossup Hall. As Simon and Portia begin to explore the depths of their mutual passion, a shocking murder is committed . . .

978-0-7499-3725-6

THE PROMISE
IN A KISS

When a handsome man literally falls at her feet while she's walking though a moonlit convent courtyard, Helena knows he must be there for a scandalous liaison. Yet she keeps his presence a secret from the questioning nuns – and for her silence the stranger rewards her with an enticing, unforgettable kiss. What Helena doesn't know was that her wild Englishman is Sebastian Cynster, Duke of St. Ives.

Seven years later, Sebastian spies Helena from across a crowded ballroom. This heiress is dazzling London society with her wit and beauty, tantalising all the eligible men with the prospect of taking her hand in marriage. But Helena is not looking for just any husband. She wants an equal, a challenge – someone who can live up to the promise of that delicious, never-forgotten kiss.

978-0-7499-3724-9

Do you love historical fiction?

Want the chance to hear news about your favourite
authors (and the chance to win free books)?

Mary Balogh
Charlotte Betts
Jessica Blair
Frances Brody
Gaelen Foley
Elizabeth Hoyt
Eloisa James
Lisa Kleypas
Stephanie Laurens
Claire Lorrimer
Amanda Quick
Julia Quinn

Then visit the Piatkus website and blog
www.piatkus.co.uk | www.piatkusbooks.net

And follow us on Facebook and Twitter
www.facebook.com/piatkusfiction | www.twitter.com/piatkusbooks

piatkus